I0633569

COUNTING COUP

THE MAKING OF AN ABBOT

THE BENEDICTION OF PAUL

PATRICIA MCCLURE

WAYZGOOSE PRESS

Copyright © 2025 by Patricia McClure

All rights reserved.

No part of this book may be reproduced in any form or by any electronic or mechanical means, including information storage and retrieval systems, without written permission from the author and publisher, except for the use of brief quotations in a book review.

Print ISBN: 978-1-961953-18-5

Cover Design by Get Covers

To those who have touched our lives with their love and left us wanting more.
My brother James Lindenfelser. (1963- 2022)

CONTENTS

CHAPTER 1

NO PLACE FOR A CROW

I know not if the voice of man can reach to the sky.
I know not if the mighty one will hear as I pray.
I know not if the gifts I ask will all granted be.
I know not the word of old we truly can hear.
I know not what will come to pass in our future days.
I hope that only good will come, my children, to you.

Woman's song from the Hako Pawnee. This ceremony celebrates the union of Earth and Heaven, and the genesis of life. It is performed with prayers, invocations, and eagle dances in order that the participants may have long lives.

Tn southeastern Montana on the Apsáalooke reservation on October 31, 1948, the Feast of All Souls, Judith Knows the Song took a beating. Three children sat in the yard next to the burning pit. Endow marched past them in search of alcohol. Four-year-old Marie paused and looked between her father and the single-wide trailer. The door to the trailer opened, and Judith stepped out, clutching her swollen belly. Marie ran to her. Rebecca noted her other arm hung at an awkward angle.

"Rebecca, get Marie inside," Judith said, her voice sharp.

Ten-year-old Jimmy nodded and stepped forward to help his mother down the three steps to the ground. She winced as she moved. Six-year-old Rebecca snatched Marie from following Judith.

"Where are you going?" Rebecca asked as her mother headed to the yard.

"Out."

Rebecca looked at Jimmy, and he shook his head, scooped up Marie, and entered the trailer.

At one in the morning, on November 1, the Feast of Saints, Judith Knows the Song entered the bar on Squirrel Drive. She sat, her arm in a cast, and joined her husband, Endow. They drank until dawn, then zigzagged the road and stumbled into the house.

Rebecca rose from the bed she shared with her siblings and poked her head into the hallway. She hadn't slept well after her mother had left them.

"Go to bed," her father said, pushing her back into the door-less room.

Rebecca's body entered the hall as soon as his boots clunked on the floor. She stood, blocking Judith's passage. Rebecca knew about birthing babies, for she helped Grandma Tiama with herbs during deliveries. She could tell that Judith's belly was flat.

"Well?" Rebecca asked, crossing her arms.

2

Judith swayed in front of her. The plastered arm spoke of the hospital, not a medicine woman. There was only one hospital in Indian country: Mary, Mother of Perpetual Help. It was a white-staffed institution. Only the desperate chose it—the dying sought home.

"Nothing, it's gone. The ancestors took it."

A broken arm and no baby. Rebecca stepped aside and felt a weight trying to pin her to the floor. She had dreamed of when she would hold a warm, squirming sibling in her arms.

Rebecca spoke to the ancestors in her heart. *It is ours. I'll bring it home.*

She moved to the pile of clothing to find something to wear. She needed a layer of shirts to cover her skinny body as she shook her brother. She slipped a pair of socks on her hands to wear as gloves.

"Jimmy, where in the hospital do they keep the dead?"

Ten-year-old Jimmy opened a dark eye. "What?"

"Where are the dead at the hospital?"

"Morgue. Basement. Go to bed, Rebecca."

"No. I need to get one of ours. We don't leave our own alone."

Jimmy pulled himself up onto his elbow. "What are you talking about?"

"The baby."

"Too early. Babies take nine months. It has only been seven."

"Seven months and twenty-eight days. The baby came."

"The midwife hasn't been here," Jimmy said, yawning.

"They set her arm. She went to the hospital. She said the baby is with our ancestors. Why would she leave the body there?" Rebecca asked, her voice cracking. It was miles away.

"Not my problem," Jimmy mumbled as he curled up in the blankets, pulling them over his head.

Rebecca fought the urge to kick him. She took three deep

breaths and headed to the kitchen, where she packed saltines, Oreos, and elk jerky into her drawstring bag. Then she tiptoed the hall to her parents' room. In the dim light of dawn, she grabbed a pair of jeans. Swift fingers weaseled through pockets, searching for cash. The heavy breathing and rhythmic snores muffled her movement. So intent was her hunt that she didn't notice the sounds had stopped. She froze.

Marie stood looking at her. She whimpered, and Rebecca pointed to the sleeping parents. Judith sat up, confused, until she saw Marie. Rebecca pushed her sister toward the bed. Marie climbed in between the smoky bodies. Rebecca waited, stiff and scared but not guilty. She was just doing what she had seen so many times before: her mother scrounging money from her father's pockets.

The sounds of sleep resumed, and Rebecca crawled out of the room. She stepped outside, and the sky greeted her in flames of red and orange. A shiver shook her body as she ran to the shed. The ground crunched with frozen moisture. A bat swooped and dived as she pulled open the door.

"Sorry, *dakáakdeepe*—family. I will close the door. *Aho*, for letting me disturb you. I know you're tired and just want to rest."

She stood on her tiptoes and grabbed a woven basket. It was her great-grandmother's basket, soft and misshapen. She checked to make sure she had the things needed to bless the body. Her eyes stung as she fingered the pouch she had made for the baby. The pattern was zigzag, and she could see the mistakes, the bumps where she hadn't quite gotten the porcupine quills to lie flat, and her colors were not as clear as she had hoped. She spent hours quilling the soft tanned leather as Grandma sorted herbs. In the dim light, she could see the empty jars, and they reminded her that she needed to return them to Grandma Tiama for medicine.

The salves were for her mother to soothe a black eye or large bruise. Rebecca was learning the process for all the herbal remedies.

She tossed her head and started the long walk to the hospital. The bats were not a good sign. They came around at death, her father told her. It was true, for the bat appeared when the mongrel collie had died.

Six dogs followed Rebecca as she trudged on, but since she didn't feed them, they left her on the side of the road. Soon, a rumbling engine passed by her. A truck with a missing taillight stopped three feet ahead. The door opened with a screech. Rebecca climbed into the cab. The vehicle reeked of smoke; the floor was littered with cigarette butts. She recognized the man. He worked the ranches, but she'd have gotten in even if she hadn't known the driver. A ride was a ride, and the Rez was large.

"Where you headed, Cousin Daughter?"

"Hospital," Rebecca said.

"You sick?" the man asked, eyeing her.

"No, just gonna visit."

"Well, now you will have more time."

They drove in silence as the sun sparkled on the frozen landscape. Her thoughts banged together. *Rescue the baby. Was her basket big enough? What if they stopped her?*

You are a warrior. Act like one. She wished she had brought Marie. Everyone bends at Marie's sad face. They often got food when Marie stood observing tourists eat.

The bats drifted back to her mind. Normally, she liked bats. She and Jimmy sometimes watched them leave the shed at dusk to hunt and guard the night. The bats stirred her senses at this moment, and everything felt heightened. The engine pinged, and the spring in the seat poked her thigh.

Rebecca nodded her thanks as she climbed out of the truck and stood in front of Mary, Mother of Perpetual Help's doors. She had heard that nobody stayed, and doctors came and went like the seasons.

It was a small, busy hospital, but it seemed large to Rebecca as she strode in. The smell of shampoo and flowers made her nauseous. She watched the rug cleaner whir at the end of the hall-way. There were people milling about. A few sat slumped in chairs.

Marching to the directory, she studied the sign. There was no listing for the morgue. Jimmy had said the basement.

Grandma had taught her to read when she was Marie's age, and she had done the same for her sister. Marie was not that inter-ested. Rebecca watched her draw animals on the letters rather than learning the sound and meanings. This frustrated her. She abandoned the role of sister teacher.

She noticed people standing near the elevator. She followed them in. They pushed buttons and rode up. They exited, and she peeked out. The people here were very much alive. Where were the dead? There was no D floor, only a B button.

That must be for the basement—at the bottom.

She pressed the lowest button on the panel. The elevator rumbled and her stomach flipped. The doors opened, cool air rushed in, and she stepped out as the heavy aroma of chemicals caused her to gag.

No place for a Crow.

She straightened her backbone at the sounds of jovial voices. She approached them--two white men and one Apsáalooke man.

"Where's the baby?"

The men looked at each other.

The white man yawned. "No babies here."

"Died this morning. Are you sure? Check."

"This is a prank. Who sent you here? Was it Nurse Marilyn?"

The Apsáalooke man motioned for her to follow him.

"Little Sister, who are you looking for?"

"My baby."

He flipped through the papers on the clipboard. He shook his head. "No babies passed this way."

Rebecca fought back tears. Had her mother dumped the baby on the road before getting to the hospital?

"Follow me. Do you have a name?"

"Knows the Song," Rebecca squeaked. She had come so far.

"Thought I recognized you. I am—"

"Edgar C. Running Bear," Rebecca said. She was familiar with his family.

"Yes."

"I saw a *dakáakdeepei*."

"Dreamed or saw? White ones?"

"No, saw, in the shed." She shifted her basket to her other arm.

"White bats symbolize death. Bats ask you to be open and ready for something new. Be brave, Little Sister. Things are not always as they appear."

They rode the elevator to the third floor. Maternity. Rebecca saw Elanna Running Bear, Edgar's sister. She and Edgar had won the push dance competition in August. Elanna's braid was pinned to the top of her head. Rebecca touched her own braids, realizing that she had forgotten to redo them before she left.

"Knows the Song?" he asked Elanna when she came to him.

Her face darkened. Elanna's voice fell to a whisper. Rebecca strained to hear.

"It's a preemie."

Rebecca tried to recall that word "preemie."

"She didn't want it. We could not make her stay. Often the moms leave or they don't want to see the baby die."

The word "die" caused Rebecca to smile. The baby was alive. Things were not as they appeared. The elevator dinged and a family with children and balloons poured out. Rebecca darted behind the nurses' station and then to the windowed wall. She stood on her tiptoes and peered into the glass bassinets of pink and blue blankets. Knows the Song was not there.

She held her frustration in check.

Brother Bat, show me where to look. *Aho.*

She headed down the hall where a nurse sat reading behind a small desk. An alarm made her jump. The nurse frowned, entering a small space. Rebecca dashed in before the door closed. She pasted herself against a wall and slid out of sight. The area was dim, with abandoned equipment standing sentry. The heat caused Rebecca to sweat. The beeping pounded in her ears.

The nurse pushed a button, and the noise stopped. This was not a place for babies. It was damp, dark, and the hissing sound that filled the room made Rebecca wish she had peed earlier. The woman scrubbed before checking the infants in the boxes. The square shape reminded Rebecca of what white men used when they buried their dead.

Another alarm echoed in the hall. The nurse headed out of the room.

Rebecca walked to the sink and washed, repeating the ritual the nurse had performed. There were three glass boxes which, to Rebecca, looked like ovens. She peered into the first box. White and bluish. Then the second. White. Finally, the third box. Brown and tiny. The name tag read, 'Male-Knows the Song.' She reached inside through the circle opening. Her hand trembled as she touched the boy.

"There you are," she said in her native tongue. "I have been looking for you. I've something for you." She reached inside her basket for the pouch. The size of it dwarfed the infant.

With the quick hands of a raccoon, she tucked the bundle

under him. He was beautiful, just like the dolls she had seen in the windows of toy stores.

"Oh, my God. What are you doing in here?" a nurse with brassy orange hair asked.

Rebecca jumped, banging into the equipment. She calmed herself and narrowed her eyes, attempting to look fierce.

"You can't be in here," the nurse with the orange hair said loudly. Her shouts brought Elanna to the room.

"He's mine," Rebecca said to Elanna.

Nurse Orange reached for Rebecca, who stepped away.

"She can't be in here. They don't expect that one to make it," Orange explained as Elanna stepped between the two in the crowded space.

"Then no harm will come if she stays," Elanna said, pulling Rebecca behind her.

"The mother might object."

"The mother has gone home. She assumes the child is dead," Elanna said. Sadness edged her voice.

Rebecca rolled her eyes. Yes, that is what Judith wants.

Orange glared at Rebecca, who glowered back at her.

"I'll take care of this," Elanna said to her co-worker.

"It's on your head," Orange said as she tucked a clump of wild hair behind her ear before turning to march out of the room.

Elanna crossed her arms and turned to Rebecca.

"What's wrong with him?" Rebecca asked.

"He was born too early. I can count months."

"Why is he in a box?"

Elanna explained the need for constant warmth and regulated oxygen. Rebecca studied the device with keen interest.

A beeping alarm made Rebecca jump. Nurse Elanna moved to the washing station as another woman entered. Rebecca stood unnoticed amidst the flurry of attention being given to the bluish infant in box one.

She moved to her brother and whispered, "Do not make those alarms beep."

CHAPTER 2

WISDOM, SECRETS, AND SILENCE

If we wonder often, the gift of knowledge will come.

Arapaho Proverb. Arapaho are Native Americans historically living on the plains of Colorado and Wyoming.

As Rebecca slept on a bench in a waiting room, a hand shook her.

"Becca," Marie exclaimed, her joyful face was two inches from Rebecca's nose.

Rebecca smiled and then frowned. Marie had a bruise on her cheek. Rebecca placed her hands on her hips and shot a sour look at her older brother, Jimmy.

Why hadn't he... no he was only ten. He could not stop Endow.

She touched her sister's cheek.

"Jimmy said I have to be a better quacker."

She hadn't ducked when their father, Endow, took to beating Judith. Guilt shadowed Rebecca's mind. If only she had been home. Had her mother tried to use Marie as a shield? So many times, after a beating, Judith would rock and cuddle Marie. The child wore Judith's blood like war paint.

"We have a brother," Rebecca said as Marie climbed into her lap. She hugged her little sister.

"No. The baby is gone. *Basahke* told me so," Marie said. "I'm the baby."

Jimmy crossed his arms.

"I'm still the baby." Marie pouted as she squirmed to the floor.

"We have a new..."

Jimmy punched Rebecca's arm.

Four-year-old Marie crossed her arms and stomped her foot.

"Yes, you are the baby," Rebecca said, rubbing her arm.

Marie hopped about, pleased that her place was secure.

"You can't continue doing this, you're just a little girl. Come home."

"Not until our brother comes home."

"He doesn't need you. Marie needs you."

Rebecca flinched and pushed her tears back. This was her fault. They all knew to keep quiet and hidden when Endow's fist flew.

"How are you eating? Sleeping?"

"There are food trays in the hallway. I go for a walk and collect. It's enough."

Jimmy grunted. They always took care of each other. Money was a luxury and Endow drank most of it away. The little clan had survived.

The sun struggled to rise, making the sky a peachy gray. Jimmy looked out the window.

"Come home. You know nothing about babies."

Jimmy hadn't seen her helping their brother survive. He was growing strong.

"He needs me."

Marie skipped around the room, touching the chairs as she went. Jimmy handed Rebecca a backpack.

"We need you. He will die. It will make you sad."

She was already sad. Nobody wants him, not Momma, not Marie, not even Jimmy.

"No. You're wrong."

"I've seen signs. They're dark. Come home." Jimmy tossed his head as his braid whipped the air.

Rebecca's stomach twisted. Jimmy's signs. Sometimes he was right, but often he missed the message. She thought his guide would be a turkey, not a hawk, as he often boasted.

"What signs? He's a baby, we can help him." Did he know? Had the ancestors sent him a message? She studied him as his foot rubbed the carpet. No. He was telling tall tales. This baby was special. She couldn't tell him that their brother had blue eyes. He would make her leave. There was time for the truth later.

"Come home."

His repeated words filled her with guilt and made her chest hurt.

"Stop saying that."

Marie pushed her way between them, holding the casing of a snake.

"Jimmy found a snake skin. See."

Rebecca shivered in the warm sun of the room. Snakes should be asleep. It was too cold for snakes. Rebecca didn't like snakes but admitted that brother snake had once sprung at her as she walked a path, forcing her to take a different route. That led her to a lost little girl. Maybe a snake in winter meant survival, a sign of hope.

"Come home."

"Is there mud in your ears? No, I will stay to the end." Someone had to be there. We take care of our own.

Jimmy shrugged and then hugged her.

Marie squeezed into the embrace. Rebecca hugged them harder, wishing they wouldn't leave, knowing they would.

Jimmy lifted Marie up to carry her back to the trailer at the end of the dirt road next to the open field five miles away from Mary, Mother of Perpetual Help Hospital.

REBECCA WAS as silent as an owl as she studied the nurses' routines around the preemies.

One evening, as she snatched a roll from a tray, she overheard a couple talking about names. She watched them filling out papers. The tribe would give him a name if he stayed.

He needs a name. A name was important. Her babies were Girl Lane and Boy Knows the Song and Boy Johnson. Those were not names. She went to Elanna and asked her for help.

"What name should he have?" Rebecca asked, even though it might be unwise to name the child so early. She hoped that having a name would make him stay longer.

"Knows the Song. That is your family name."

Rebecca took a deep breath and flexed her hands. Elanna was not getting it.

"No. A name for the papers. I read the tag, Baby Boy, but that is not a name."

"You mean a birth certificate? Your parents will give him his name."

Rebecca gave her an incredulous stare.

"You're right. They will not. But your grandmother, and the gifts…" Elanna paused.

"Grandma can give him his Apsáalooke name. I'll give him his white name. A strong one, for the papers, for the outside world. Everyone needs a name and so they belong. You get more than one name. Grandma told me. So, he'll have more than most."

Elanna nodded. "We have a book of names that moms look at. It's all European names." She brought a worn book of names, and Rebecca combed through A to Z, settling on Karl, because it meant a strong, free man. She also looked up her name and was satisfied with its meaning; the one that binds. She named the other two infants. The boy was Boney and the little girl, Blue.

Rebecca sat for hours, watching her brother. When the nurses were not around, she took him out of the box, tucked him under her shirt, and held him close to her chest. She watched the other mothers cry at the door, fearful. They rarely came in to see their babies. Why should they? Rebecca had overheard the nurses say these infants were disposable. She didn't see that. She saw life. Her only worry was Karl's blue eyes. He should have dark ones. He had a head full of black hair, his skin was the right color. But his eyes startled her every time he looked at her. Blue eyes. How can he be ours? There were no blue-eyed Crows. She remembered stories of Howls in the Winter. She was not sure. Was there a blue-eyed Apsáalooke woman? Or was it a tall tale to keep children from wandering into the hills alone?

The doorway was crowded with curious aides and nurses. Rebecca was glad they had stopped trying to tell her to go home. She was also happy they hadn't found the bundle she had placed under her brother.

"Why are you letting her stay?" an aide asked. "She's a kid. Where are her parents?"

Orange rolled her eyes. Rebecca held her breath.

"She's here because that's her brother. Besides, it's not like she can do any harm. Since she has been here, the alarms are less frequent," Elanna said.

"I take care of myself," Rebecca muttered.

"What about germs and stuff?" a young girl in a striped uniform asked.

"They are disposable babies. The mothers no longer visit, they've been told to go home. They're just waiting for the day."

"The doctors will have our heads."

Nurse Orange shook her head. "They only come to sign the death certificate."

"They're in a utility closet, for Christ's sake. It's where we store the leftover equipment and supplies."

"That's kind of funny, babies in the supply room."

That explained the lack of light and space, thought Rebecca. This wasn't a room for healing. It was a room for dying.

"It just costs too much. We're lucky to have these old incubators and Doctor Whitmire who let us use them."

"Yeah, Whitmire has a heart. Pity. Other doctors send them to the morgue, hoping they die before they get there."

"You can't blame them. These kids are underdeveloped. They'll never be like the ones born on time."

Rebecca put her hands to her ears. She didn't want to hear this. She hummed loudly to drown out their bad spirit talk and rubbed her hands with the smelly oil and then rubbed Karl's body slowly.

"What's she doing now?"

"It smells like lavender," Orange said.

"He'll be slippery."

Rebecca's hands were still oily, so she moved to box two and rubbed Boney, too.

All three needed frequent feedings. Blue always seemed to gurgle and struggle, which triggered the alarm and upset Boney. One day, Rebecca took the eye dropper she fed Karl with and propped Blue up like a dish towel. She glided from baby to baby, like a mother bird, dropping thick milk into each one's mouth.

"What are you doing?" Elanna asked when she came in to feed the infants.

"I was just trying to help. That girl doesn't swallow good, it comes back out."

"Good observation and clever solution." Elanna left and returned with droppers for all the infants. "Where are you sleeping?"

"Around. I don't want to leave him alone for too long. He needs me."

"Edgar and I work different shifts. You could come home with us. Eat and then come back. You need sleep too."

Rebecca yearned for a long nap. Sleeping in the waiting room on different floors made her cranky.

"*Aho*, I will consider this."

Elanna chuckled. "Little sister, you'll do this. It'll help."

Rebecca sighed. It was nice to have an older sister. The babies kept her busy all day, yet she missed Jimmy and Marie. She worried and wondered if they were well. Life at home was an impending thunderstorm. A pattern and one could heed the warning signs. Duck and cover. She recalled too many nights huddled under a mountain of blankets as still as a fox in a field. The noise was always deafening, and sleep evaded her for days afterward. This was their life, her life, and she had survived.

REBECCA SAT OUTSIDE THE PREEMIES' room. She caught the sound of tinkling bells. She held her breath. A tickle of panic rose inside her. What should she tell them?

Grandma Tiama and Grandma Doli appeared in the hall, huffing and puffing. They had climbed the stairs. Orange looked up from her desk, her eyes wide with surprise. There they stood, one tall and one short, both garbed in the old way, a thick leather belt with a big coin purse. Rebecca loved that purse because it always held something special. The hem of their cotton dresses met the top of their leggings as they shuffled to her in their worn moccasins. Each wore a different colored shawl and scarf. She loved the dark blue and pumpkin yellow which Tiama wore and the red and white of Doli. Rebecca rushed to them, and they hugged her as she relished the aroma of wood smoke and cedar.

She felt closest to her maternal grandmother, Tiama. They did so much together. The tribe called her grandmother's daughter. That is how it was. Marie had become Judith's favorite; a new baby would not change that. A twinge of sadness touched Rebecca, a longing for that motherly bond.

"We have come," Doli said as they stood in the hallway.

"I need fresh air," Rebecca announced. The grandmothers exchanged looks.

"Take the elevator. I'll meet you outside, in front," Rebecca said. The old women shook their heads.

"I'm hungry. Why didn't you come sooner?"

"*Balakbia* did not tell us," Tiama said. "But the night he was born, I heard singing."

"Those were howls from the timber wolves," Doli said.

"He had arrived. The song said so."

How did they know?

"Did Jimmy tell you?"

"No Jimmy, no Judith," Tiama said and glanced at Doli. "No Endow. Just wolves howling in winter. Wolves singing of a birth."

Jimmy should have told them.

What if they reject him? Blue eyes belonged to white. But he is mine. She would make them understand.

"I'm hungry," Rebecca said as she moved to a little room. There was a table and some chairs. Rebecca had seen the doctors and nurses meet there.

Tiama reached into her satchel and handed the girl fry bread and pemmican and a package for later. Her mouth watered from the heavy taste of the jerky. She could smell the pungent grease oil she had often carried home for Judith to use on bruises.

"We are here to see. Why can we not look? What are you hiding? What is the secret?" Tiama asked.

Rebecca stopped crunching the dried elk meat, wiping the crumbles from the table. She was no longer hungry.

But what if they don't want him, either?

"Come," Rebecca said, taking each grandmother's hand and leading them to the closet.

Shoulder to shoulder, they stood over Karl.

"So small," Doli said. "Too small."

"Alive," Tiama said. "He breathes."

Rebecca unplugged the alarm and lifted the lid to the box and oxygen hissed as it escaped. She didn't want to upset the white shoes. With an icy finger, she touched his twig-like leg. The infant shivered, opened his eyes, and protested with a cry.

Rebecca closed the lid.

Grandma Doli drew in a sharp breath, leaving a nose print on the glass.

"See." Rebecca's head fell to her chest. "Something's wrong with him. I fear he belongs to someone else. I want him to be mine."

Grandma Tiama chuckled. "Oh, child, he is ours."

Rebecca looked at Tiama. Had she moved into the land of the ancestors, where the lights dimmed, and voices haunted you? Great-grandma Odina lived in that land. Not recognizing her children and talking to the ancestors.

"Put your glasses on," Rebecca said.

"I don't need my glasses to tell he is ours," Grandma Tiama snapped as Doli snickered.

"*Basahkaale*, his eyes are blue," Rebecca said with a stomp of her foot.

"You are right," the old woman said. "He has the eyes of Cold Feet. The singing was Sings in the Night."

"Or *cheete* howling," Doli muttered.

Grandma knew the difference between timber wolves and singing.

Cold Feet, the name sounded familiar. Then Rebecca remembered the story about a fur trapper who had lost his furs in a winter storm in the 1700s. A woman named Sings in the Night had found him, nursed him to health, and married him. He was a white man.

"I don't understand. This can't be Sings in the Night's son," Rebecca said. "That was too long ago."

Doli snorted and smirked. Karl's cries were muted under the glass as he turned red.

"My daughter is loyal," Tiama quipped, giving Doli a sharp glance. "Your line must be tainted. More white than red. My daughter is Endow-bound. Has she not remained even though he has the white man's disease?"

Rebecca understood the white man's disease. Many of her clan had caught it. A disease in a brown bottle.

"Our granddaughter is wise," Doli spoke, biting her words. "She is wise."

Rebecca noticed Tiama hadn't argued the last point. She had listened to the murmuring that white blood tainted everyone. She had seen breeding for the color of horses and the eggs of chickens. Did it work that way with people?

"They said a baby's eye color will change," Rebecca said over her brother's mewing cries.

The two Elders stared at the blue-eyed infant, who had stopped crying to stare back at them.

"It will not," they said together. "No, it will not change."

"What are we going to do?" Rebecca asked.

"What we always do," the two replied. "We always move forward."

They opened the box. Tiama ran a thin crooked finger down Karl's arm. Doli pushed the bundle back, tucked the thin hospital blanket around the boy,_and—smiled. Karl's face puckered.

Tiama swayed. The two women bumped shoulders and then sang. The room filled with their voices. Karl's thin arms flapped and he grabbed his grandmother's finger.

"He's strong for one so tiny," Tiama said. "Strength in smallness."

"I'm afraid," Rebecca said sadly. "Blue eyes are mean." The only blue-eyed people she met were white and unkind.

"He will make his way. Everyone does. Howls in Winter had blue eyes. She was a powerful healer. Blue eyes are gifted. You will see. What happens, happens," Tiama said.

Rebecca crossed her arms. "How did this happen? I don't know what to do." Tears dripped down Rebecca's cheeks.

"You know. You're doing it," Doli said as she leaned in and placed her wrinkled lips on Karl's forehead.

"I'm only a little girl."

"You're a healer. The grizzly is with you."

Rebecca frowned as she ran her finger over the lid of the box. These old women talked in riddles.

Wisdom, secrets, silence. She was too young to vision quest. She didn't have blue eyes.

"I don't want a grizzly. Everyone avoids them and they sleep half the year."

Doli clicked her tongue. "And that is bad? Their evidence surrounds you."

"Are you saying I am stinky?" Rebecca crossed her arms. "They are grumpy and lumpy."

"The animal picks you, little girl. You don't pick the animal," Tiama said. As she extracted her crooked finger from his tight grasp, closing the lid to the box.

"Why aren't you staying?" Rebecca asked.

"Not our time. He is yours," Doli said, turning to Tiama. "Teach her. She needs to understand. Show her."

"She will learn soon enough. Tomorrow comes, and she will learn. All she needs to do is ask."

"What? What will I learn? Ask what? I'm asking."

They squeezed her between them. Their scent of burning wood and spice lingered as they left. One took the elevator and one to the stairs.

Tomorrow, it was always tomorrow with the old ones.

CHAPTER 3
RECESSIVE GENE

When you know who you are; when your mission is clear and you burn with the inner fire of unbreakable will; no cold can touch your heart; no deluge can dampen your purpose. You know that you are alive.

Chief Si'ahl (Chief Seattle). 1786-1866. Duwamish and Suquamish leader, ecological protector, visionary, and orator.

Two weeks after the grandmothers' visit, Judith, Rebecca's mother, showed up sporting a black eye and swollen lip. She marched into the room and peered into the box. Karl stared back at her. Judith gasped and covered her face with her hands.

"It's okay, he'll fatten up," Rebecca said. "I named him Karl. It means the strong one."

Judith straightened, throwing back her shoulders.

"Come with me," Judith said.

"Ihkaa, I cannot."

"Come with me. It's time to go home, your Basahkaale said."

Rebecca shook her head. "She would not say that."

If Grandmother said anything, it was, "Take all of your children home." Grandma stood by the family, helping where and when she could. Rebecca grabbed her satchel. There was a homemade balm for her mother in the package that Grandmother left.

Her mother's frightened face confused her. She had expected her to say, "Good job."

"Ihkaa, what's wrong?" Rebecca asked, handing over the jar of salve.

Judith took the jar and tucked it into her pocket. "We need to leave."

"But the baby," Rebecca protested as her mother grabbed her shoulder.

"He's not ours. Look at your siblings. He's not ours."

"Basahkaale said he is. She said there is a story." Rebecca held onto her mother's arm. "Tell me the story of Cold Feet or Howls in Winter."

"Those stories are false. There was no French fur trader. Our clan would never..." Judith shook her daughter off. "Stop spinning tall tales."

"Basahkaale does not lie." Rebecca stomped her foot.

Rebecca had listened when the nurses talked. Most of their words she could not understand.

"Ihkaa, who is Recessive Gene?"

Judith's face scrunched.

"They say Recessive Gene must have visited to give Karl blue eyes, I kind of..."

Rebecca did not see the hand coming until it smacked her cheek. Her eyes watered. What had she said wrong?

Judith yanked, pulling her out of the room. Rebecca tugged to free herself. Judith's nails dug into her arm. Rebecca tried to pry the fingers off.

"We're going home."

"Not without him."

"He's not ours."

Their voices brought Orange from the nurse's station. Rebecca saw Marie running toward them, dodging the people in the hall.

"Becca," Marie shouted as she hugged Rebecca.

"We're going home," Judith said, shaking her daughter. "You cannot bring him."

"I will. I must."

"Enough. Stop this at once," Orange said, glancing around nervously.

"Ihkaa, which one is ours?" Marie pulled on her mother's shirt and pointed to the window wall at the end of the hall. Judith shook Marie off. She landed on her butt and whimpered.

"You will not," Judith said.

Rebecca waved Marie to her; the puckered face girl scampered into her embrace.

"He is ours," Rebecca said.

"He's not."

"Mrs. Knows the Song, he's your baby," Orange said. "If you don't want him, we have social workers who can arrange that."

Rebecca gasped. Nobody was going to give Karl away. He was Apsáalooke. She had claimed him.

"Which one?" Marie raced to the window of babies as mothers pulled their heads back into their rooms. "Which one?"

Judith's face turned dangerous, and she pushed Rebecca, who

landed with a thump on the floor. Rebecca grunted as a foot connected with her shoulder.

"Why are you letting her stay here?" Judith asked, her voice venomous.

Orange stepped backward. "I'm not. I mean, she has been helpful. The infant lives."

"When it shouldn't. This is just like your kind, always interfering in things you don't understand. Rebecca let's go."

Rebecca had seen Tiama use her voice to overpower Judith. She stood, squared her body, stiffened her legs, and knotted her arms, hugging herself tight. "No."

Orange stepped between mother and daughter.

"Mrs. Knows the Song, stop this."

"Go home, Judith," Rebecca said with the authority of her grandmother. "I am staying with my brother. Take Marie and go home." Judith stepped back as if struck. Then she glared, turned, picked up the whimpering Marie, and marched to the elevator.

"It'll be fine," Rebecca said to Orange, who stared after the pair.

Rebecca rubbed her cheek and sniffled. Saddened and confused, she walked to her brother.

"You're a lot of trouble," she said to Karl, who cooed and wiggled. "That was your momma, but it'll be fine."

Not long after her mother visited, Rebecca said goodbye to Boney. He had flourished and gained enough weight that he left for home with his elated parents. His leaving made life easier— there were only two babies to hold. Still, they had to wait their turn. Rebecca sat with Blue tucked into her shirt and a shawl wrapped around her like a front sling. She sang and rocked. The mother of Blue lingered at the window. Rebecca waved her in. The woman was young and thin.

"Momma, do you want to cuddle your baby? She would like that," Rebecca said.

The woman, with coaxing from Rebecca, tucked the infant next to her skin. Rebecca did the same with Karl. They sat quietly, rocking, and talking to the babies when the door opened.

A man in a white coat stood staring at them. "Who are you? What is going on here? Isn't this a supply closet?"

"Close the door. You are letting the warm air out," Rebecca scolded. The nurses crowded around. The man turned to them. His cheeks puffed.

"Whose babies are you holding?"

"Doctor Whitmire, those are the preemies," Orange said.

"That can't be. I have their death certificates here." He flipped through the papers on this clipboard.

Elanna spoke. "Please just step out and watch. We can explain."

The door closed and through the window, Rebecca watched the white coat's arms flap and point, his face reddening as if he were about to cry.

"Oh dear," Blue's mother said.

"Do not worry, Orange is fiery. I think your Blue will go home soon. I call her that, but you can name her some pretty name. She has grown strong. You should come and visit. She really likes to hear your heart."

The mother smiled. "She is Daisy."

"I like that name."

Doctor Whitmire stood outside with a clipboard for many days. He was young, with long hair and an intense stare. Rebecca wished she could see what he was drawing and writing. One afternoon, he entered the space. Rebecca tried to ignore him.

"Can you read and write? English?"

Rebecca rolled her eyes. This man was stupider than most.

"Yes."

"Good. I want you to fill out these charts about them." He nodded to the infants.

"They have names, Karl and Daisy."

Doctor Whitmire glanced at the babies. "Can I do some tests? Get their weight?"

"Karl weighs a gallon, and Daisy is about a sack of apples."

The doctor smiled but did not question her more. But upon returning to the closet, she found it cleaned out and two chairs replaced the broken equipment.

Two weeks after the grandmothers' visit, Judith, Rebecca's mother, showed up sporting a black eye and swollen lip. She marched into the room and peered into the box. Karl stared back at her. Judith gasped and covered her face with her hands.

"It's okay, he'll fatten up," Rebecca said. "I named him Karl. It means the strong one."

Judith straightened, throwing back her shoulders.

"Come with me," Judith said.

"*Ihkaa*, I cannot."

"Come with me. It's time to go home, your *Basahkaale* said."

Rebecca shook her head. "She would not say that."

If Grandmother said anything, it was, "Take all of your children home." Grandma stood by the family, helping where and when she could. Rebecca grabbed her satchel. There was a homemade balm for her mother in the package that Grandmother left.

Her mother's frightened face confused her. She had expected her to say, "Good job."

"*Ihkaa*, what's wrong?" Rebecca asked, handing over the jar of salve.

Judith took the jar and tucked it into her pocket. "We need to leave."

"But the baby," Rebecca protested as her mother grabbed her shoulder.

"He's not ours. Look at your siblings. He's not ours."

"*Basahkaale* said he is. She said there is a story." Rebecca held on to her mother's arm. "Tell me the story of Cold Feet or Howls in Winter."

"Those stories are false. There was no French fur trader. Our clan would never..." Judith shook her daughter off. "Stop spinning tall tales."

"*Basahkaale* does not lie." Rebecca stomped her foot.

Rebecca had listened when the nurses talked. Most of their words she could not understand.

"*Ihkaa*, who is Recessive Gene?"

Judith's face scrunched.

"They say Recessive Gene must have visited to give Karl blue eyes, I kind of—"

Rebecca did not see the hand coming until it smacked her cheek. Her eyes watered. What had she said wrong?

Judith yanked, pulling her out of the room. Rebecca tugged to free herself. Judith's nails dug into her arm. Rebecca tried to pry the fingers off.

"We're going home."

"Not without him."

"He's not ours."

Their voices brought Orange from the nurses' station. Rebecca saw Marie running toward them, dodging the people in the hall.

"Becca," Marie shouted as she hugged Rebecca.

"We're going home," Judith said, shaking her daughter. "You cannot bring him."

"I will. I must."

"Enough. Stop this at once," Orange said, glancing around nervously.

"*Ihkaa*, which one is ours?" Marie pulled on her mother's shirt and pointed to the window wall at the end of the hall. Judith shook Marie off. She landed on her butt and whimpered.

"You will not," Judith said.

Rebecca waved Marie to her; the puckered-faced girl scampered into her embrace.

"He is ours," Rebecca said.

"He's not."

"Mrs. Knows the Song, he's your baby," Orange said. "If you don't want him, we have social workers who can arrange that."

Rebecca gasped. Nobody was going to give Karl away. He was Apsáalooke. She had claimed him.

"Which one?" Marie raced to the window of babies as mothers pulled their heads back into their rooms. "Which one?"

Judith's face turned dangerous, and she pushed Rebecca, who landed with a thump on the floor. Rebecca grunted as a foot connected with her shoulder.

"Why are you letting her stay here?" Judith asked, her voice venomous.

Orange stepped backward. "I'm not. I mean, she has been helpful. The infant lives."

"When it shouldn't. This is just like your kind, always interfering in things you don't understand. Rebecca, let's go."

Rebecca had seen Tiama use her voice to overpower Judith. She stood, squared her body, stiffened her legs, and knotted her arms, hugging herself tight. "No."

Orange stepped between mother and daughter.

"Mrs. Knows the Song, stop this."

"Go home, Judith," Rebecca said with the authority of her grandmother. "I am staying with my brother. Take Marie and go home." Judith stepped back as if struck. Then she glared, turned, picked up the whimpering Marie, and marched to the elevator.

"It'll be fine," Rebecca said to Orange, who stared after the pair.

Rebecca rubbed her cheek and sniffled. Saddened and confused, she walked to her brother.

"You're a lot of trouble," she said to Karl, who cooed and wiggled. "That was your momma, but it'll be fine."

Not long after her mother visited, Rebecca said goodbye to Boney. He had flourished and gained enough weight that he left for home with his elated parents. His leaving made life easier—there were only two babies to hold. Still, they had to wait their turn. Rebecca sat with Blue tucked into her shirt and a shawl wrapped around her like a front sling. She sang and rocked. The mother of Blue lingered at the window. Rebecca waved her in. The woman was young and thin.

"Momma, do you want to cuddle your baby? She would like that," Rebecca said.

The woman, with coaxing from Rebecca, tucked the infant next to her skin. Rebecca did the same with Karl. They sat quietly, rocking, and talking to the babies when the door opened.

A man in a white coat stood staring at them. "Who are you? What is going on here? Isn't this a supply closet?"

"Close the door. You are letting the warm air out," Rebecca scolded. The nurses crowded around. The man turned to them. His cheeks puffed.

"Whose babies are you holding?"

"Doctor Whitmire, those are the preemies," Orange said.

"That can't be. I have their death certificates here." He flipped through the papers on this clipboard.

Elanna spoke. "Please just step out and watch. We can explain."

The door closed and through the window, Rebecca watched the white coat's arms flap and point, his face reddening as if he were about to cry.

"Oh dear," Blue's mother said.

"Do not worry, Orange is fiery. I think your Blue will go home soon. I call her that, but you can name her some pretty name. She has grown strong. You should come and visit. She really likes to hear your heart."

The mother smiled. "She is Daisy."

"I like that name."

Doctor Whitmire stood outside with a clipboard for many days. He was young, with long hair and an intense stare. Rebecca wished she could see what he was drawing and writing. One afternoon, he entered the space. Rebecca tried to ignore him.

"Can you read and write? English?"

Rebecca rolled her eyes. This man was stupider than most.

"Yes."

"Good. I want you to fill out these charts about them." He nodded to the infants.

"They have names, Karl and Daisy."

Doctor Whitmire glanced at the babies. "Can I do some tests? Get their weight?"

"Karl weighs a gallon, and Daisy is about a sack of apples."

The doctor smiled but did not question her more. But upon returning to the closet, she found it cleaned out and two chairs replaced the broken equipment.

ONE MORNING A FEW WEEKS LATER, Nurse Elanna Running Bear was waiting in the room and not dressed in her uniform.

"Come," Elanna said, placing Karl in a picnic-like basket.

"What's wrong?" Rebecca asked.

"Nothing, all is good. You get to take Karl home."

Energy, like a jolt of coffee, surged through Rebecca. Home.

"We need to hurry." Elanna peeked out the door and grabbed Rebecca's hand. As they rounded the nurses' station, the elevator dinged. A police officer and a man in a suit, followed by Joseph Long Horn, stepped into the hall. Orange drew their attention as Elanna and Rebecca slipped into the elevator, hitting the button several times.

"What's Joseph Long Horn doing here?"

Elanna swung the basket back and forth as Karl fussed.

"Don't ask questions," Elanna said as she rushed them out of the hospital.

Rebecca realized the tribal police were there for her and Karl. "But we are Apsáalooke. Karl is Apsáalooke. They can't take him."

"Sometimes being Apsáalooke isn't enough. I'll take you home now."

Rebecca climbed into the car. "Is it okay for Karl to come home?"

"He weighs a gallon, doesn't he?" Elanna asked with a laugh.

"Yes, he does. Don't I have to pay?"

"They have to find you first."

Rebecca thought long and hard. We pay our own way. Take nothing that isn't ours. She would come back and pay for his stay.

Elanna drove Rebecca to the single-wide trailer at the end of the dirt road and left her with formula and diapers. Rebecca stood in the yard, looking at the sagging porch and falling gutter. She noticed the sand cherry bush had a hint of life on its bare branches. The dogs came up to her, hoping for a treat.

"Shoo, I got no food for you."

Rebecca entered the house and saw that nothing had changed. The brick still held up the sofa, dishes towered in the sink, and Endow snored loudly in the bedroom. She was sure her mother did not tell her father about the baby. To Judith, Karl didn't exist.

So, this is it. No welcome home, no crib.

Rebecca unpacked the baby from the basket and carried the infant on a tour of the single-wide. "That noise is your daddy. He works hard and harder, so you won't see much of him. He drinks the same and tells lots of stories. Some are snake tales. You'll learn to tell the difference. He isn't so bad. You just need to stay low when he has no drink. It is a weekly thing. Friday's mostly because the money runs out by Wednesday."

She pointed to the mattress on the floor. "This is our room, our gathering space." She nodded to the room at the end of the narrow hall. "Their room." She nodded to the right. "For cooking. Not much, but home. Don't you worry. I'll take care of you."

When Endow woke up and saw the blue-eyed infant, his fists pounded his wife, and the children huddled in their bedroom.

"You should have given him away," Jimmy hissed. "This is your fault."

"No. It's Recessive Gene's doing."

Jimmy laughed until hiccups stopped him. He mopped his face with a clean diaper cloth.

"There is no one named Recessive Gene. Endow thinks he is a white man's baby. He has blue eyes."

"Grandma Tiama said he's ours. Grandma told me about white blood."

The shouting increased. A thump shook the wall.

"Doesn't matter what Grandma says. Endow can barely feed us. That makes him mad. Don't be blind. Do you not see us? We are living in a shabby trailer. Our cupboards are empty," Jimmy said, picking the threads of a hole in his jeans.

"We live like everyone else. We are not special," Rebecca said as she jiggled Karl. She wanted answers. "Have you been told the story of the blue-eyed one?"

Jimmy slumped back against the wall. "Howls in Winter is a story to keep us from wandering into the mountains."

"A story that teaches. A story has answers. Grandma always tells us to listen."

Jimmy scooted farther into the room as a plate shattered outside the doorway.

"Not all stories are lessons. Some are tales to frighten little kids," Jimmy said, poking Marie with a finger.

A lamp crashed to the floor. Karl's lips pursed and quivered as Rebecca held him.

"I am a-feared," Marie said as Jimmy patted her head. "I no like Howls in Winter. She was a witch. I heard her singing in the Pryor Mountains."

Rebecca had listened to many stories about the ancient ones. Each person had a story. She remembered the tale of the blue-eyed woman. She imagined Howls in Winter as pretty and the people jealous. She was a medicine woman with power. She lived alone, not like other Crows.

Judith's voice was pleading in tone as she tried to reason with Endow.

"I've been to the mountains. They're just that," Jimmy said as Marie covered herself in a hill of blankets.

"What about Cold Feet? Do you know that story?" Rebecca asked, recognizing the pattern of fight, beg, plead, promise, normal.

Jimmy shrugged his shoulders. "Stories belong to families. You need permission to tell them."

Grandma's words came back to her, "All she needs to do is ask."

"I think it is our story," Rebecca said.

The wall thumped and thumped. Karl wailed in Rebecca's arms.

Rebecca's stomach churned.

"Shut him up. He's only making it worse," Jimmy said.

Rebecca stuck her finger in Karl's mouth. "Hush, this is how it is. Let it bounce around you."

Marie sniffled and crawled deeper into the covers.

It seemed like hours, but eventually, the yelling stopped. Then there were quiet sobs and murmured apologies and promises of change.

Marie slept. Jimmy read his comic book. Rebecca folded and counted diapers. Karl sucked his fist.

Her parents stumbled down the hall to make love with the same angry rage.

On a frigid evening in February, Rebecca trudged through the snow. The howls of the wind mixed with Karl's wails, creating a sound of misery that filled Rebecca with despair.

"I don't know who is noisier, you or Karl," she shouted into the storm.

Her movement was slow, and her feet ached. Every house, shack, trailer, and teepee looked like white lumps. Weekly she had walked door to door like a Girl Scout selling cookies, asking for milk from the new mothers.

"Cold Feet, guide me to Grandma. I cannot see the path."

Do not give up.

Her eyelashes clinked together, but she could not stop. The infant in the cradleboard howled.

If he screams, he is alive.

A bright light shone in a window, the only light she could see.

She pushed her way through the drifts of snow. Finally, three more steps to the door. A blast of warm air caused her heavy eyelashes to drop and tears to drip down her cheeks.

"Granddaughter, it's two in the morning. I could hear you from miles away."

"This baby won't stop crying." Rebecca wiggled out from under her burden, clunking her brother to the floor. Snow plopped and formed into puddles.

Tiama helped Rebecca pull off her stiff clothing. She dug deep inside, under the furs of the cradleboard for the red-faced infant. She unwrapped the squalling baby and held her breath.

"I just changed him," Rebecca said as she covered her mouth and nose.

Tiama filled the basin with warm water and bathed the infant.

"Do you have a name?" she asked the balled-up baby.

"He doesn't talk. His name is Karl, it means strong one."

The baby stopped crying in the warm water, but still his hands were in fists and his legs hugged his belly.

"That is not his name. That is the name you gave him. Get me the buffalo fur."

Rebecca brought the soft skin to her grandmother and snatched a piece of fresh bread. It was as if Grandmother planned her arrival, the house ablaze, warm, and smell of venison stew on the stove.

Tiama frowned and rubbed the baby's belly. Rebecca watched intently. Grandma did not appear to be bothered by Karl's eyes. She had noted that Karl's blue eyes caused a reaction. Some held their breath, and others wanted to touch him. There was a power in those eyes.

"What's wrong with him?"

"Gas. You need to give the baby fresh milk," Grandma

explained as she rolled the baby side to side. Then, placing a hand under his belly, she tilted him like a teeter-totter. Karl farted, and Rebecca giggled hysterically.

Karl relaxed and stretched his long skinny limbs out and stuck his fist into his mouth. Rebecca ladled stew into a bowl.

"This baby needs food. He's hungry for food."

Rebecca crossed her arms. She had fed him.

"Julia Morning Star gave me frozen milk. It's for tomorrow. I fed him milk from Tilly Stones in the River. Then he started screaming."

Tiama shook her head. She took out a jar of mush from the icebox and set it on the stove.

"What's that?"

"Rice and powdered milk."

"I get breast milk and freeze it and then run it under hot water," Rebecca said as she stuffed a glob of bread and stew into her mouth. She savored the flavors of sage and pepper.

"No, you heat it up. It must be warm like one's belly."

"He doesn't like warm bottles," Rebecca said, getting a bottle from the cupboard trying to be helpful. She had never warmed the milk, just thawed it.

"Did he tell you this? Because that's not the song I heard him singing. He sang his misfortune all the way here."

"He can't be hungry, and the milk didn't stink."

"He's telling you he's hungry. Do you have frozen mud in your ears? Listen. Do not use Tilly's milk. She eats wrong. She's round and her baby is a stick."

There was truth in that statement. Tilly's baby was thinner than Karl.

"He'll get fat if I feed him so much," Rebecca said as she wiggled her fingers in front of his face. "He would drink all day. I only get leftovers from the nursing mothers. I cannot ask for more than our fair share."

"Impossible for this one to get fat. Feeding often will not make him fat."

Tiama removed warm milk from the stove, and tested it with her tongue before she filled a bottle.

"I get powdered and use it for cereal. It tastes yucky. *Basahke* said it must last until they give us more. I mix it with syrup, corn syrup. He likes it."

Grandmother's face darkened. "No. Feed him as much as he wants and often and never watered down. No more syrup."

"It tastes better," Rebecca muttered.

"If you need, come here. I will feed anyone who needs it. A story for food that is the only price I ask."

Rebecca nodded solemnly.

"He doesn't cry much," Rebecca said, removing her finger from the baby's tight fist. "That's how I knew he was sick. He cried too hard."

"You are a wonderful mother. School is starting. Bright Penny will want you there. What will you do with him? Marie is too little to take him."

A surge of joy ran through her. She liked school, but Grandma was being silly. "He goes with me. He is mine," Rebecca explained. "I take care of him."

After four ounces and a loud burp, Karl smiled.

"Now, it's dream time for little girls, baby boys, and grand-mothers. Daylight comes early."

Rebecca dressed for the long walk home.

"You are here, so you may as well stay. My bed is big enough, and I get lonely. You'll stay."

Grandmother led both children to her bed by the fireplace.

Rebecca curled her body around Karl, who cooed and wiggled beside her. Blue eyes took in the surroundings, the drying herbs that hung from the ceiling, antlers, and tanned hides. The fire crackled as the wind cried outside, alone. A smile filled Karl's toothless mouth when he focused on Rebecca. Grandma cuddled next to Rebecca and sang.

All is fine now, she thought as her eyes grew heavy.

CHAPTER 4
ELK EGRESS

It does not require many words to speak the truth.

Hin-mah-too-yah-lat-kekt (Chief Joseph). 1840-1904. A passionate, principled Nez Perce resistor to his tribe's forced removal, and a renowned humanitarian and peacemaker.

Rebecca sat on the porch of her grandmother's house, listening through the open window to the Elders discussing education. The government outside the Rez insisted the children go to a school off tribal land.

School attendance depended on the day, and Rebecca knew their teacher, Bright Penny, kept a close watch on who was there. Rebecca admired Bright Penny. She was there every day, teaching one or sixteen. Rebecca had almost stopped schooling because Bright Penny said "no" the day she showed up with Karl. Rebecca insisted Karl would not disrupt the class. Bright Penny allowed it as an experiment. That was two years ago. She was the envy of all the girls, for she had a live baby. Karl's presence seemed to bring more girls to school.

"This is 1950, not 1850. Haven't they figured out we are not leaving the land?"

There was a snort.

"They did this before. It did not work then."

"Oh, but it did," Bright Penny said. "They took the children, took our hair, our names, and they tried to take our language."

"We have not assimilated."

"Our children don't attend school now because of the trauma," Bright Penny said. "They abused or worse, killed many of our children. That has not been written into the history books, but we remember."

Rebecca picked at the peeling paint. She had missed several days because Karl had a fever. Being a parent at age eight was challenging work. She missed being carefree and alone.

"I don't like school. Grandma went to a government school. She said she learned to distrust the white world. She received cruelty and fear," Tilly Stones in the River said. "Children died there."

Growls of assent followed her remarks. Rebecca had heard the tales of the boarding school roundups. The thought of dying away from the Rez sent chills up her spine.

"What if we don't send them?"

The aroma of tobacco floated through the window as the children and dogs ran in the yard.

After a long silence, Gwen Short Legs spoke. "We have our lawyers looking into that."

"What do they want?"

"They want us to stop pushing for what is ours. If we stay

uneducated, they can break us. School off the Rez worked. Tilly, you and your children carry the burden of your grandparents. That is three generations of Stones in the River without education," Bright Penny said.

"I fear it's an attempt to separate us. If they keep children away from us, then they can claim we abandoned them," Mark Knows the Song said. "We cannot let them do this."

Rebecca agreed. She did not want to leave the Rez, Karl, or her family. The kids had to come to school. She would talk to the grandmothers. They would make it happen.

"You will always live here," she said to two-year-old Karl, who was wrapping her beads around his arm.

"He's a baby," Marie said. "A stinky one."

Rebecca prepared to change Karl's diaper. He was not interested and ran around the table. Rebecca's temper flared and after several attempts to grab the moving toddler, she stuck out her foot. With a loud thump, the child hit the floor and whimpered. Rebecca made haste to change his diaper. As she reached for a dry cloth, Karl sunk his teeth into her forearm. Rebecca let out a shout and poised her safety pin above the boy.

Grandma Tiama stepped outside.

"Rebecca," Tiama said. "What has happened? Why the howling?"

"He bit me," she said, pin still in hand.

Tiama took the pin from her as Karl crawled away. She looked at the purplish indentation on the girl's arm. From the shelf, she took down a jar of oily herbs.

"Put this on it," Tiama instructed as she snatched the half-naked child. Karl wiggled and squirmed.

"Don't bite your sister," Tiama scolded. "She's not edible."

Marie giggled.

"You're a wicked brother," Rebecca rebuked.

Karl continued to squirm. Rebecca slapped his thigh and ordered him to stay still. Karl wailed as a red mark appeared.

Tiama finished diapering Karl and snatched the ointment from Rebecca. She smeared the red mark.

"He bit me," Rebecca said again, angered at Grandma's reproach.

Grandma didn't look at her. When you break the heart of an Apsáalooke, they will not look at you.

Rebecca's breath grew ragged.

"This violence needs to stop. What you do returns to you. We are all connected. We don't need more Endows. Don't make another."

"He bit me," she said more insistently.

"You're his teacher. Teach him a kinder life."

Rebecca hung her head. She shouldn't have hit him.

"He knows red marks and purplish green," Marie said. "He's bad. *Basahke* will not see him. He broke her. But I like him."

Tears ran down Rebecca's cheeks. Poor motherless child.

Karl scooted toward her, touched his wet cheek, and then touched hers.

"I sorry," he said.

"Me too," Rebecca said as she pulled Marie and Karl into a hug.

Grandma Tiama kissed the top of Rebecca's head.

IN MID-SEPTEMBER, a big bus came and took the children. The tears fell on both sides. As the bus rumbled on, a dark silence hung in the air. The dirt road and dust turned into hard pavement. Rebecca leaned over the sleeping Marie. Her heart was aching. She could no longer see Karl, who had run after the bus shouting her name. The echo of his voice stabbed in her chest. The Rez dogs stopped following.

"Jimmy, have you ever been this far?"

He looked out at the rolling landscape and shook his head. Gone were teepees and trailers replaced with fences and large sprinklers. Then open plains with the blue-gray hills in the distance and dried grass blowing in the wind.

"I don't think we will be home tonight," Rebecca said, wondering who would take care of Karl. In the past when they came, they took the babies. She didn't understand why they took the little ones.

"How do you figure that?" Jimmy asked.

"She's right. They're taking us to a strange place, and we'll die like the buffalo," Nation said. She was Jimmy's age, twelve, and she was the daughter of a council member.

Rebecca squirmed. "This doesn't feel right."

"You always say that. This is a day for school. We go home tonight. You're talking crazy."

The pit of her stomach hurt. Jimmy was wrong. The other children on the bus were eerily quiet and the younger ones continued to sob into the laps of their siblings.

"We're prisoners now," she whispered as Nation nodded.

"We need help," Nation said as she closed her eyes, and reached for Rebecca's arm. "Help me call the ancestors. Make the bus stop."

Jimmy snorted but stopped when Rebecca shot him an arrow-filled glare.

"I need to get home."

Jimmy nodded again. "If they stop the bus, I could run."

"What if we all run?" Nation asked.

A deep fear gripped Rebecca as Marie drooled on her pant leg. "The little ones would not make it."

"They would slow us down," Jimmy said.

Nation scooted closer to Rebecca. "No, don't run. What if they shoot us? They could shoot us. I saw a rifle next to the driver."

She needed to get home. Her heart was fading. She now understood those words. Grandma Tiama used them whenever a Crow member flew away to the white world, even if it were for a good reason, Grandma would say, "My heart is fading."

"Talk to the boys. We have to get home."

Jimmy darted to the group of older boys to make a plan. Rebecca and Nation touched foreheads, breathed together, and chanted to the ancestors, begging them for help.

"Do not let fear overtake you," the Warrior whispered in Rebecca's heart.

The bus came to a sudden halt, jostling the children who cried out. Marie sat up and reached for Rebecca. Worry creased her round face.

"*Iichiilikaashe*," Nation shouted as she stood on the seat, looking out the window.

Rebecca and Marie glanced out. A herd of sixty elk meandered down the road in front of the bus. The driver honked his horn. The animals were unimpressed and moved slowly, encompassing the long yellow bus.

Rebecca turned and gave Jimmy an *I told you* gaze.

"See, see," Nation said. "The *iichiilikaashe* are a sign. They'll not separate us from our families. Our ties are strong. They cannot cut them even in this faraway place." Her words stirred the children, and they became restless.

Rebecca had never seen so many elk in one spot. She had heard that, like the buffalo, they were disappearing.

Windows opened and the musky smell of hide and dirt drifted in. Snorts from the bulls and the cracking of ankle joints reminded Rebecca of drums at a powwow. Children cried and called out to their families, asking the large animals to send messages and help.

"Sit down," the woman with almost-white hair shouted.

Several children reached out to touch the wild beasts. Antlers bumped against the steel exterior of the bus.

"Stop that, this instant," the short lady said as she wobbled down the aisle. The bus driver picked up his rifle and leaned out of his window.

"Do not kill them. You have not smoked your gun," Rebecca said over the chaos. "You need to respect them. Don't make them angry. If you do, your family will starve. Let the boys shoo them away."

"Yes," Nation echoed. "The boys will scatter them."

Rebecca knew they did not understand her words. They were white and had forgotten that every animal needed to be asked permission before you killed it. All weapons had to be purified through smoking to assure the animal's sacrifice was honorable.

The short woman moved to consult with the driver. Jimmy and several boys pushed themselves to the back, near the emergency hatch. Rebecca moved among the children, telling them that the strangers were taking them to the Pryor Mountains. The children's eyes grew large with fear. One needed a purpose to approach the mountain of the Little People. The dwarfs that lived there were ferocious. Howls in Winter dwelled there. Panicked children crowded the aisle. The adults shouted and cursed as the boys crawled out the back. Rebecca's heart thundered wildly as she watched them go.

The man stuck his rifle out the window and fired. Elk scattered. Children screamed and Little Bird Morning Star took a deep breath and fell to the floor.

"He shot her spirit," Nation whispered to Rebecca. Although

most had not found their spirit guides, Little Bird's collapse was a sure sign that she and the elk were connected.

"He didn't kill one. She'll be alright. She's frightened," Rebecca said as she placed the pale and limp Little Bird with her brother. The two girls helped the children take their seats, while the adults shouted at each other. Nation and Rebecca clasped hands.

"*Aho*, for giving your life to protect us. Please forgive them. Do not let us starve. *Aho*," Rebecca prayed.

"Do you have medicine for Little Bird?" Nation asked. "Will she die?"

Rebecca shrugged her shoulders. She didn't know this world and she, like Nation, just wanted to go home. Rebecca watched the elk running at a distance alongside the bus. They would tell the Elders

REBECCA SLIPPED OUT OF BED. Her feet protested the icy floor of the brick warehouse. The children slept on the floor, curled up under thin blankets. Whimpers filled the hall as she passed by them to the window. She stared at the barren landscape, at the fence that surrounded them. This was not a school; it was a prison. At least there were windows. They could see the sky and mountains. But where were the curtains? They needed curtains to protect the children from the night spirits. Maybe it was too late for them and the spirits.

"What have we done?" she asked. The white man gave, and it was bad for the Indian.

"The older boys got away, thanks to the Elk tribe," Nation said as she sat next to Rebecca.

Nation slipped her hand into Rebecca's. "They want the names of the boys who ran. Nobody is talking. Mostly they cry."

"Someone will betray us. We'll have to forgive the one who tells."

They had sent the children to bed without food. Rebecca knew it was a punishment for their misbehavior on the bus. She also knew hunger, having gone without meals at home. Hunger made people do things they wouldn't otherwise do.

"I'm scared," Nation said.

Rebecca squeezed her hand. "Jimmy got away. He'll tell the Elders. Help will come. We need to be strong for the younger ones."

CHAPTER 5

THE WISDOM OF KARL

Children learn from what they see. We need to set an example of truth and action.

Howard Rainer, Taos Pueblo-Creek. Author, teacher, poet, and photographer. Program Administrator of Native American Educational Outreach Programs at Brigham Young University.

T he chill of the morning bent to the rising sun, heralding warmth. Karl walked on the dirt road. Flies buzzed around him, and his wet diaper was heavy.

"Icky," he said to the dogs, who followed him. "Off."

Karl pulled his soggy diaper off and watched the dogs race after a rabbit. Naked, with only his green rubber boots and sweaty feet, he clunked his way in the direction the bus had taken Rebecca. Every day since she had left, he rose and walked. She had been gone too many days. Every night, someone would return him to the trailer. It had rained last night, and puddles filled the potholes. He stomped in one, laughing at the cold water spray. The rope around his waist was soaked, and he sucked the moisture out as his wet unbraided hair stuck to his back.

He had gotten a late start because his mother, Judith, had tied him to the porch, and it had taken time to chew his way through the rope. A truck rumbled by as his boots sloshed.

Someone tossed a bottle out of the window, and it clunked on the dirt road. Karl stopped to examine the brown glass with its foamy liquid.

He sniffed the rim.

"Beer," he announced. He didn't like beer. The brown glass was pretty. He poured the rest of the liquid on the ground. Then, picking up a few pebbles, he placed them in the bottle and shook it, listening to the sharp clink.

Karl stopped at a tall bush of buffaloberries.

"I hungry. *Aho*, Momma bush." He helped himself to the red globes.

"Sour," he said to the rocks, hoping he would find Rebecca soon. She would feed him. She always did. Karl marched on.

When he saw Jane Two Feathers in her rocker on her porch, he smiled.

"For the love of God, not again." Jane cursed as she got up. This was the third day she had found Karl alone.

"Fry bread?"

"What is wrong with those two?"

Karl looked around. Nobody was with him, only rocks.

"I hungry," he said, just in case she had mud in her ears. Adults seemed to have that kind of ear trouble.

"Child, where is your cover-up?"

"Wet."

Jane pursed her lips. Her pipe wobbled up and down. Karl liked Jane. Her fragrance was a mixture of cinnamon and tobacco. She looked at the knotted rope, took out her pocketknife, and cut it off, then she took his hand and led him inside.

Two glasses of milk and half a loaf of bread later, Karl rubbed his full belly. Jane combed and braided his hair.

"I pee," he said.

"Oh God, no. Outside—off the porch." Jane lifted the child and ran him to the little landing, pointing him away from her rocking chair.

A trail of wet followed them from the door to the edge.

"Becca, be happy. Not wet anymore. I go now."

"Karl baby, don't you think you need clothing?" Jane asked.

The day was warm, clothing seemed unnecessary. He stepped to the ground to continue his journey.

"Wait up," Jane called as she grabbed her tobacco pouch and pipe. Together, they walked. Karl babbled about the ants, the eagles, and the rocks, interspersing his thoughts with his need to find Rebecca. The afternoon gave way to painted clouds as another day ended.

As they walked, a bedraggled figure came toward them.

"Jimmy," Karl shouted and ran to his brother, clinging to him like a woodruff burr. "Becca?"

"She's not here," Jimmy said, pulling the child from him. "Where are your clothes?"

"Need Becca," Karl chirped.

"Where are the others?" Jane Two Feathers asked.

The long trek home took its toll on Jimmy, and tears fell from his eyes.

"Jimmy sad," Karl said as Jimmy patted his head.

"They're not bringing them back. I don't know where they took them. But they're not bringing them back. The elk came and tried to make them stop, but they shot at them. I fear they will starve."

Jane took both boys by their hands and led them to the End of the Road Tavern owned by Dan Green Tree on the Plain.

Dan shook his head when he saw Jane, Jimmy, and Karl.

"I hungry," Karl said, climbing the barstool.

"Endow, can't you keep that little one at home?" Dan asked.

Karl's father looked up. "Tied him to the porch just this morning."

"Like a stray dog," Jane muttered under her breath as she set both boys at a table. "Dan, we need food and water."

Dan nodded and returned with water. Jimmy gulped his first glass.

"Slow down, son," Jane said.

"Jimmy sad. I go pee," Karl said as he climbed from the chair and ran to the tavern door, pushing it open and making a puddle for patrons to wade through.

Dan turned his attention back to Jimmy.

"They went east, but I escaped. We didn't know what to do. Ziggy and Jerry are out there. They couldn't keep up."

"I'll get the truck. We'll find them," Dan said.

They turned and looked at Endow. His head rested on his arm. He was smiling, glassy-eyed, with his hand wrapped around a coffee mug.

"Becca, I go too," Karl said.

Jimmy wolfed down the sandwich handed to him, and followed Dan out of the tavern.

"Jimmy," Karl wailed as the older boy left.

"Come, baby, we have council business," Jane Two Feathers said as she tied a towel around the boy's waist.

"Was that Jimmy?" Endow asked.

Jane narrowed her eyes. "Do you not even recognize your own children?"

"That one is not mine," the unshaven man grumbled.

Jane laughed. Except for the blue eyes, Karl had the features of his father. Jane chose to not argue with a drunk.

Chief Long Neck stood. "Enough," he said. "We've been arguing too long."

"Becca home," Karl said for the thirtieth time as he sat on Grandma Tiama's lap.

"We need to bring our children home," Jane Two Feathers said to the murmurs of others.

"How?" Two Beak asked.

"Nothing is stopping us from going and getting them," Gwen Short Legs said.

"No laws?"

"What they did was kidnap our children. We are within our rights," Gwen Short Legs said.

Karl slipped off Grandmother's lap and toddled to the chief. Too much talk. Karl tugged on the old man's shirttail and the chief bent down to the child. Karl took the man's braid like reins on a horse.

"Come, we go. Get Becca, now."

"Yes," Chief Long Neck said. "Now. We have heard. We will act."

REBECCA WIGGLED HER TOES. In the cramped space, it was all she could wiggle. She watched the light creep under the door. She had heard about punishment. She never dreamed they would lock her in a closet. She listened to the voice in the hall as she breathed through her mouth. The smell of her own urine made her queasy.

Panic rattled inside her.

This was not a school. This was a dying place. Where was Jimmy? The tribe didn't come. Visions of Jimmy running free through the fields caused her to clench her teeth.

"You've always been selfish," she said.

Was he free? Was he taking care of Karl? Karl needed her. In her heart, she sensed he was alive. He had to be. She regretted singing to comfort the younger children. If only she had sung in English. The younger children were sad, and their tears caused Rebecca to remember Karl. She sang the old songs to calm him, and it worked on them, too. Little Bird had stopped speaking any language since the elk egress. The adults didn't like her, and they didn't like Rebecca. She could not please the matrons and speaking Apsáalooke wasn't her only offense.

"I want out," she called. There was no answer. There were sounds earlier, but now it was silent.

"I'll die in a closet because I dared to challenge them. Remember me as she who stood strong." Tears rolled down her cheeks. The six adults at the school were going to win. She had her six coups within a week. She spoke out against the lack of food, books, and fresh air. They believed her to be the one who encouraged the children to ask when they would go home.

Marie's sweet voice came to her. They bribed the younger ones with candy, and Marie always had a large stash that she shared with anyone who was being punished by the teachers. She overheard they would be placed with white folks. That meant they would never see their families. Marie would be one of the adoptable ones. She was ever-smiling and polite. The adults let her follow them around. She was like a lost puppy.

Marie's voice came again. "She is in there."

I'm dying, thought Rebecca.

"They locked it," came a voice.

"I have keys," Marie said. "Here under the floorboard. I've been collecting them."

Rebecca stirred. Sweet, complacent Marie, whom the adults doted on, was not oblivious to the world, just watchful. She would never again think of her sister as stupid.

The keys rattled, and the door to the closet opened. Light and fresh air cascaded in. Rebecca squinted.

"Becca, we're going home," Marie said, tugging her arm.

The other child coughed and gagged. Rebecca opened her eyes. Nation's hand pulled her crumpled from the space.

"We have to go. You stink like a white man."

Shame rose to Rebecca's cheeks as she willed her legs to move and push herself to a standing position. Nation was right. She reeked.

With the help of Nation, she stumbled onto the bus. She folded herself up, biting her lower lip, trying not to cry. Within minutes, a group of girls surrounded her, standing on the seats making a human screen. The bus driver said nothing. Rebecca changed from odorous clothes to ill-fitting, mismatched ones. The girls opened the window, and the stinky clothing flew out like a flag of freedom. Rebecca ran her fingers through her matted hair, trying to unsnarl the knots.

Were they going home? There was only one adult with them, the driver. Together Nation and Rebecca counted the children. They were all there--some with bruises and sores, others with coughs and runny noses. At least they had not lost a child. If they were going home, the medicine woman would fix the sick ones.

"We're going home," Marie said with conviction.

"I saw Gwen Short Legs, early this morning before they started piling us into the bus," Nation said. Rebecca hoped but kept her joy locked away until she saw the familiar landscape of teepees. At the border of the Rez stood the tribe. The children whooped and shouted at the familiar faces of their parents. They came to a stop on tribal land and the driver dashed out, abandoning the keys and bus.

Parents and children rushed for each other. Rebecca exited the bus with Marie.

"Baby," Judith called as she pushed through the crowd and scooped up Marie.

"Where are Karl and Jimmy?" Rebecca asked, scanning the people.

Judith's dark eyes stared hotly at Rebecca. Then she wrinkled her nose. "You endangered Jimmy's life, sending him into the unknown with your selfish plan. My brave Jimmy is well, no thanks to you. We are a tribe."

Rebecca clenched her fists. What did her mother know about the tribe? She was always abandoning them, leaving them to fend for themselves, putting Endow's needs before theirs.

"This is your fault. You brought him home when I told you not to. His eyes spy on us and bring the white man's ways. They should have taken him."

The woman was crazy. Karl's eyes were not windows. He was a baby. She had her precious Marie and warrior Jimmy. Nothing else mattered.

Marie shrugged her shoulders while her mother pulled her away from Rebecca. Sympathy filled her eyes.

"I'll remember," Marie said, easing the sting of their mother's words.

Where was Karl? He was only two, and alone. Tears clouded her eyes. She was no better than her mother abandoning him.

The crowd thinned out as she wiped the water from her eyes. A sudden push practically knocked her over. Karl squeezed her leg.

"Becca, I hungry," Karl said.

Rebecca hugged him and looked him over. He looked fine. She hugged him again.

"I hungry," Karl said, pushing her fussing hands away from him.

She turned to see Jane Two Feathers and Dan Green Tree on the Plain.

"Me too. Where's Jimmy?"

"Jimmy sad," Karl said.

"Jimmy's fine. Come, we'll feed you and tell you the tale of a two-year-old's wisdom," Jane Two Feathers said.

CHAPTER 6
COLD FEET

Everything on the earth has a purpose, every disease an herb to cure it. And every person a mission. This is the Indian theory of existence.

Hun-Ishu-Ma (Christine Quintasket; Mourning Dove). 1884-1936. Arrow Lakes and Okanagan leader and author.

Five-year-old Karl elbowed his way between Tiny Stones in the River and Little Bird Morning Star to sit at Grandma Tiama's yellowed Formica table. Grandma fixed dinner for anyone that needed a meal. The price? A story. Grandma knew everyone's story.

"Me first," Tiny Stones in the River shouted. "My story is about the stones in the river. They told me how they travel from Canada down the Yellowstone to Otter Creek."

"More likely they got lost at Crazy Mountain," Rebecca said.

Nation opened the oven, and the smell of fresh bread filled the air. She wiggled her way around the kitchen to the counter to slice the hot loaf and then handed slices over the tops of heads. Grandma Tiama pulled out a wooden bowl of butter. Karl scooped out a dollop, placing it on the steaming bread. Rebecca squeezed behind chairs and bodies to dish up stew into waiting bowls.

"This is my story," Tiny said. "They didn't get lost."

"Well, unless they had wings, they couldn't get to Otter Creek. That's in Cheyenne country. We are Apsáalooke. Your rocks got lost. Our river is the Little Big Horn. At least pick what flows on the Rez," Rebecca said with her twelve years of authority. They lived in Montana, not North Dakota. Yellowstone was below them on the map.

"An eagle took them," Tiny said, crossing his arms and attempting to appear big. Tiny remained tiny, the same age as Karl, but half the size. Grandmother Tiama had been right all those years ago when she had told Rebecca not to feed Karl Tilly Stones in the River's milk to him.

Little Bird spoke up, "Perhaps they came down Plum Creek."

"You mean *Buluhpa'ashe*," Rebecca corrected.

Karl's head popped up from his bowl. He knew that name. It was Apsáalooke for what the whites called Judith's Creek. Momma's creek. Rebecca had been teaching him the real names for the places where they lived. He wondered if everything had two names.

"Are you an atlas?" nine-year-old Marie asked, stabbing the butter.

"I didn't make the land and the rivers. They have to meet for one to travel on them," Rebecca said.

Karl knew you couldn't fly over the mountains unless you had wings. The Apsáalooke people had lost their physical wings a long time ago, but in their hearts and minds, they could soar with eagles. He wished he had real wings. He would slip away from bullies.

"Otherwise, you have to pull out your canoe like in the *Adventures of Happy Weatherman*," Little Bird added.

Karl scrunched his face. He hadn't read that book. Little Bird sometimes spoke of strange events and when questioned where she learned them, she would say, "A little bird told me."

I wish she said nicer things, thought Karl. Her mean remark about him not being a real Crow last week had hurt.

"It's in that history book," Little Bird said. "But the Elders remember."

Did she mean Meriwether Lewis? Rebecca had told him Lewis named the *Buluhpa'ashe* River after his wife Judith. Endow told him they named it for his mother. Karl thought it might be a snake's tale, but he liked the story. He wished he could tell the truth from the lie.

Did the Little Bighorn flow into Lodge Grass Creek? Many rivers snaked the map of Montana. Karl remembered his father had camped by a river when they had taken him and Jimmy hunting. The memories warmed him.

"They don't all connect," Rebecca said as she handed Tiny fresh bread.

"All rivers lead to the ocean," Nation said.

"Or into a lake or Mother Earth," Marie said.

"Can I finish my story?" Tiny shouted over the wagging tongues. "Anyway, stones have a story to tell, and I collected them and brought one for each of you. If you look and listen, you will learn their wisdom." He reached into his bulging pockets and handed out stones. Not pebbles, but medium-sized heavy rocks.

Rebecca received a sharp-edged one. Karl thought that fit, because she could be rough sometimes. His stone was flat, plain, and ugly compared to the others. But maybe it held a secret yet to be discovered. He slipped it into his pocket, and it pulled his jeans down on his slender waist.

"My story," Marie said. "Is about—"

"Pansies, daisies, and butternut squash," Rebecca said, patting the top of her sister's head. "A love story."

"It's better than your stories about Braves, animal spirits, and wise women," Marie retorted, refolding her napkin.

"Mine aren't fantasies. They're the truth," Rebecca said, tilting her head slightly down.

Karl squirmed. Her stories creeped him out, and sometimes the events she told came to pass.

"Girls, the world is filled with tales," Grandma Tiama said. "We all have one. I want to hear them all."

"My turn," Karl said. The others groaned.

"You always tell the same one," Tiny whined.

"It's my story," Karl said, proud of knowing his clan's story. "Ask me to tell it." One needed permission to tell a family story.

"Let Grandma tell it. She tells it better," Marie said as she smiled sweetly at him, not noticing his glare. His blue-eyed power was wasted on her.

"*Basahkaale*, tell me my story," Karl begged.

Grandma made a horrible face, puckered and sour, as if that narrative were distasteful. "I hear so many stories, I might need help."

"I will help you," Karl said as Grandma turned to the other children.

"We'll all help."

"Good. Rivers come from the same source. We are all connected."

The children sat in silence, pondering her words as she settled herself on the sofa. They abandoned their meals and encircled her. Rebecca cleared the table and tended to the dishes.

"Long time ago, after the dreams. Do you remember the dreamers?"

"Yes, *Basahkaale*, the dreams the warriors had. The same dream, two different men. Dreams of the pale people coming," Marie said.

The dishes clanked in the sink and the aroma of stew lingered.

"Good, just checking. It's important to acknowledge your dreams. These scruffy, smelly men left a stink wherever they went. They came to trap for fur. Pale men, sickly looking, and short, like the Pryor Mountain men. Our people watched and often let them into camp. Why not? These strangers filled us with curiosity."

"How smelly?" Tiny giggled.

"Like a *daxpitchee* in the summer?" Karl asked, visualizing a blubbery summer bear.

"Like a male *iishbiixisshe* when a female is ready?" Nation asked.

Wrong. A bobcat was too small. One hardly saw a bobcat.

"Yes. You could hardly stand to have them in your teepee."

Rebecca snorted as she dried her hands on a towel and sat with them. She carried a basket of peas and beans.

"But one was different, not so stinky," Marie said.

"No, his odor lingered like a *xuahchee*," Rebecca said, wrinkling her nose. "Sings in the Night showed him how to not reek."

Karl covered his nose and mouth. Skunk spray stunk.

"Why did they smell?" Tiny asked.

"They were afraid of the water," Karl said, scooting closer to his sister Rebecca. Everyone wanted the river. It gave life, quenched thirst, made things clear and clean.

"That's silly," Little Bird said, bouncing in her space.

"But true. They feared it would make them ill. Give them the chills and freeze their lungs. They refused to bathe in the river. They did get wet. The rain drenched them, repeatedly trying to wash the stink off," Grandma explained.

"And..." Karl encouraged.

"Question. Was this when the animals were human?" Little Bird asked.

Karl turned to Rebecca. This was her question to answer. He had seen her talking to the creatures. He had tried, but they ran away. They came to Rebecca. That wasn't fair. She didn't have blue eyes.

Grandma took an empty bowl and put it in front of her. She reached into Rebecca's basket, taking out a handful of green beans.

Rebecca cracked open a pea pod. "No. That was a long time back. This story happened in recent times. But we remember and retell all our stories."

Grandma smiled as she continued. "One winter, close to when the night steals the light of day, Sings in the Night went out to check her traps. Her husband had been a great warrior and provider. When he died in battle, she had learned the manly ways and could live alone. As she checked for what Mother Earth had given her, she heard a noise." *Crack.* Grandma snapped a green bean and the younger children jumped.

"Was it *itbuuisee*?"

"Was it a *cheete*?"

"No, Brother Bear would have been snoring in winter," Little Bird said, wagging his head like an elder. "Brother Wolf is not that loud."

That was true, thought Karl. On one hunting trip, Jimmy had taken him to where a grizzly bear slept. It was stinky and noisy, but mostly thrilling.

"Was she scared?" Marie asked, leaning closer to Grandma.

"Not Sings in the Night," Nation said, sitting up taller. "She might have been young, but she had warrior blood. And she had her amulet to protect her."

"She hummed a little tune and followed the sound. She saw him under a tree."

"Was he dead?" Tiny asked, his eyes big with wonder.

"No, silly, he made a sound," Nation said, patting his knee.

"Well, maybe he died after he made a noise."

Grandma Tiama chuckled as Rebecca dropped the peas into a metal bowl with a series of four plunks.

Tiny glowered at Nation. "*Baashchiilisdaake* make noises after you lop off their heads."

Marie and Karl trembled. Karl wondered what the chickens had said.

"He was a wooly man with a black beard and translucent skin. He was injured and shivering. Sings in the Night figured he wouldn't survive under that tree. She fashioned a travois and rolled him onto it. Through the winter night, she headed to camp, and her voice rang out in the silence, warning beast and men of her approach."

"Was she scared?" Marie asked again.

Grandma reached over and held her granddaughter's hand. "Would you be afraid?"

Tiny, Little Bird, and Marie nodded while the other three slowly shook their heads.

"Sometimes we are fearful. Sometimes we need to be," Grandma said. "Heed your fear."

"But she did it anyway," Rebecca said, dropping more peas into the bowl.

"Yes, she took him into her teepee, and nursed him through the fever."

"Why would she do it?" Nation asked. "He was white."

"It was necessary," the three youngest children said in unison.

Yet Karl wondered why it was needed. Sometimes kids threw rocks at him and pushed him, calling him an apple. He looked at his arm. He was the color of earth, not red, and he wasn't white inside. His hair was black, his cheekbones high, but his eyes were blue. Sadness tried to push away his pride.

"She fell in love with him. He became her husband," Marie said, sticking her tongue out at Rebecca. Karl laughed. Rebecca thumped the back of his head.

"And they lived happily ever after," Grandma said as heads swiveled her way, disbelief written on their faces.

"No. Not the end," Tiny said.

Grandma grinned as the creases defining her pride.

"What was his name?" Little Bird asked.

"The best part—you left out the best part," Karl said, crossing his arms.

Grandma snapped more beans and pursed her lips, shaking her head. "What was his name? Oh, it was so long ago. I think I've forgotten."

"They called him Cold Feet," the children chorused.

"Because his toes never warmed," Marie said with a giggle.

"His baptized name was Pierre Durand," Rebecca said.

"What's baptized?" Little Bird asked.

"White man's bath time," Nation snorted, sending Rebecca into giggles.

Karl sat up on his knees. This was his story, and the best part was coming.

"Sings in the Night let him out of her teepee, and they shocked the entire tribe because in her arms was a baby."

"I can't believe she hid him," Nation said. "Nine months is a long time to keep a secret."

"Yeah. Why didn't she say I love this guy?" Tiny asked.

"Perhaps she feared what they would say. I think presenting the baby was the best way," Marie said, her brown eyes soft.

Rebecca's chin dropped to her chest, and then she looked up and rolled her eyes.

Marie crossed her arms. "She wasn't ashamed."

Nation placed a hand on Marie's shoulder. "We all have tainted blood."

"Not me, I'm all Indian," Tiny said, sitting up tall.

"Me too," Karl chimed in.

"But your white leaks out," Little Bird said. "Mine doesn't."

The room grew quiet. The ticking clock on the wall sounded like thunder.

Karl swallowed hard. She was wrong. They were all wrong. He was Apsáalooke.

"My skin is as brown as yours."

Little Bird placed her arm next to his. They were both the same rich hue of mahogany.

"You can't judge that way, skin, eyes, size," Tiny said.

Tiny was the smallest boy on the Rez for his age. They sometimes would put him in a baby stroller and fool tourists into giving them treats. Everyone loved babies.

"We all belong to Mother Earth, all of us. Not every leaf is green," Grandma said. "It's not what you look like, it is what you do. Sings in the Night's actions honored the tribe. She cared even if his feet were cold."

"Is this a true story?" Little Bird asked, grabbing a pea from the bowl.

"Yes," Rebecca, Marie, and Karl said in unison.

"All stories have truth and fiction in them. All tales reveal something to us and about us and the storyteller. Our stories have a secret piece that makes us wonder and hope," Grandma said.

"Yeah," Little Bird said. "Sometimes you can't tell the proper version, so you tell half a story."

Nation and Rebecca exchanged a glance and moved closer to Little Bird. Karl wondered what part of her story she had left out.

Grandma sighed loudly and continued, "Many children were blest to them. Three girls and two boys."

"Hey, you're forgetting something," Karl said. The story was taking too long. Too many questions.

Tiny giggled.

"What?"

"The blue eyes," Karl said, pointing to his own. It was okay that his white leaked out. He was still Apsáalooke.

"Oh, is that what happened?" Grandma asked. "I thought you made a coup and stole them from the white men."

"I did not steal. They gave me the gift," Karl said. He could take and touch. He was brave.

Rebecca and Marie jostled each other.

"He had blue eyes. That is why she loved him," Karl said. "He did, she did."

Rebecca wagged her finger in the air. She didn't like to love talk.

"Yes, she did," Marie said, but it didn't sound sincere.

"Blue eyes don't happen very often," Grandma said. "You are the third blue-eyed Apsáalooke in our clan."

"Mama says those are spy eyes," Little Bird said.

Rebecca crossed her arms. "White men don't need spies. Their mouths are open all the time and the mud is in their ears."

"My dad says blue eyes will save us," Nation said.

"From what?" Tiny asked as he turned to Rebecca, as if waiting for confirmation.

"I don't know. He's nothing special."

Rebecca tugged on Karl's braid.

But Karl didn't believe her. Blue-eyed Apsáalooke were connected to the spirit world and unique knowledge of the white man. He shivered with excitement. He would be powerful someday.

CHAPTER 7
INCOMPLETE CIRCLE

What is life? It is the flash of a firefly in the night.
It is the breath of a buffalo in the wintertime.
It is the little shadow which runs across the grass and
loses itself in the sunset.

Isapo-Muxika (Crowfoot). 1830-1890. Blackfoot peacemaker, orator, Chief of the Siksika First Nation, and warrior.

On a sweltering day in August, six-year-old Karl, Tiny, and Juniper romped through the field. The grass cracked under their feet. They had been swimming and their thick braids dripped moisture down their backs. They paused. Someone was whistling.

"It is daylight," Karl said as Tiny trembled next to him.

Everyone knew whistling was dangerous at night. It invited evil spirits. The sun was high. No chance of that.

Juniper nodded his agreement.

Ahead of them was a group of older boys standing near a grove of trees. They paused and looked in the shade's direction. It would have been nice to stop and rest from the relentless sun.

"Hey, guys," Crooked Nose called.

Karl took a step away. Crooked Nose never called to them. He was usually chasing them.

"What you want?" Tiny asked as Karl shook his head. Tiny was always inviting trouble.

"Come here and see what we found."

The breeze shifted, and a stench came with it. The odor of decay. A bear would not leave his dinner. Karl looked for scavengers. He only saw the three older boys.

Juniper covered his nose, but the curiosity of what had died made him brave.

"No, Crooked Nose," Randy Gray Horse said. "Get lost, cousins."

The two older boys squared off as Tiny continued to approach. Juniper moved toward Randy, Crooked Nose, and Simon Little Owl.

"Tiny, stop. Don't you smell it?" Karl asked. But Tiny continued to move forward.

Randy pushed Crooked Nose. They never fought each other. Something wasn't right. Were they going to cover Tiny in deer guts? They needed to leave before the evil touched them. The spirits of the dead sometimes lingered, especially if not properly thanked. There was danger lurking.

Crooked Nose stumbled back and then righted himself, smiling at Tiny.

"Tiny, come on, we got grape soda at the trailer," Karl said. He liked grape soda, and Tiny did, too.

Too late.

Tiny let out a squeak. Simon snorted. Crooked Nose's front teeth shone under his tight lips.

Karl ran past Juniper to be beside Tiny. The air was rancid, and he suddenly felt a chill.

Together they stood looking at a man who lay propped up against a Sugar Maple tree, his chin resting on his slightly bloated chest, black hair hanging.

"Is he dead?" Tiny asked. "Or is he sleeping it off?"

Karl felt Juniper pressing against him. Flies covered the body like a tarp.

"Too many flies. Nobody alive could stand that," Juniper said.

"Maybe the flies are drunk," Tiny said, stepping back.

The gentle breeze shifted.

"Who is he?" Karl asked, covering his nose and mouth.

Crooked Nose laughed. "Your *Biilapxe,* your father."

Karl clenched his fist. He now realized why Crooked Nose had that name.

"It's not his real *Biilapxe*. The wrong color of eyes," Simon Little Owl said.

"Stop," Randy Gray Horse growled.

Karl leaned closer. Crooked Nose gave him a shove.

"Give *Biilapxe* a hug," Crooked Nose said as Simon laughed.

Karl stumbled, scrambling back from the man. A cloud of flies rose and descended.

"Knock it off," Randy Gary Horse hissed. "Don't be so cold."

Karl sat at the feet of the man, recognizing the agate belt buckle, and the peacock design on the boots. His stomach turned. The vacant brown eyes stared at him. He moved to get away, tripping over the dead man's leg. He landed face down in the dirt. The flies buzzed.

"Is it Endow?" Tiny asked.

"No," Karl shouted, jumping up and facing Tiny and spitting dirt from his mouth.

"It is, isn't it?" Karl shoved Tiny, and the smaller boy fell to the ground.

"Oh, Karl," Juniper said as Karl turned and ran from them.

It was.

Karl ran until his lungs hurt, and then he dropped to the ground, his breath ragged and deep, his head barely visible above the tall golden grass. He sniffed his hand. Did he smell like death?

He needed to find Rebecca. She would tell him how to keep the negative spirits away.

Tears streaked his dirty face. He was only six, but he had seen dead animals. Dead meant not coming back, ever. His *ashishkawauuhawate* would not be complete. His family would be broken. That was not good. Broken caused problems. What if the second soul was waiting? He had touched his dead father; would death come for him? Damn that brown bottle, the white man's disease.

Rebecca would tell him what to do.

Karl stood and then sat down. He wasn't sure what her reaction would be. Would she be mad? She never liked Endow. Did he like Endow? He wasn't sure. The man was his *Biilapxe*. They had spent time together fishing, hunting, and at the tavern. Now that was over.

Eagles cried overhead, circling in their leisurely pattern. Karl knew the eagles would carry his prayers to the Great Spirit.

He didn't know what to say. The eagles rode the winds and called. Karl watched them.

"Good luck, *Axee*. I miss you," Karl whispered, wiping his tears.

He rose and ran home. His body ached. He paused a moment and then raced through the vegetable patch, narrowly missing the gourds and zucchini. Barely hearing Marie's scolding about squashing the squash. He stopped when he saw the tribal police car. Then he noticed Rebecca sitting under an umbrella drinking a coke, her feet pushing on the side of the trailer. She raised her free hand to her lips to silence him. And then pointed upward to the window. She was listening.

"How long has he been gone?" came the male voice.

"I was with him at the tavern last week."

"He must have gotten lost. Sorry, Judith. Is there anything I can do?"

"It's fine. We'll be fine."

Tribal Officer Jack stepped out onto the porch and down the steps.

"Hey, blue eyes, where did you go swimming, a mud hole?" he said, patting Karl's head.

Karl looked down at his dirt-streaked body. The words stung like wasps.

"Sorry about your dad. If you need anything, call me," Jack said.

"*Aho*, we'll be fine," Rebecca said.

Karl stared at Rebecca and together they watched Officer Jack leave.

"*Biilapxe*, Endow is dead," Karl said.

The chair clunked to the ground, and Rebecca pursed her lips. "Yeah, I know."

He stared at her. Questions swirled. "How do you know? Was it the eagles?"

She pointed to the three catfish that hung from a hook dripping water onto the porch. Vacant eyes stared at him, and he looked away.

"It was all I could catch today. The catfish told me to make the best of it. It's time to embrace something new."

Rebecca recognized all the reasons animals crossed your path. They had been human once and still communicated if one stopped to listen. Rebecca always listened.

"Dad is under the Sugar Maple tree. I will never eat syrup from the tree."

Marie appeared with two large zucchinis.

"*Biilapxe* is dead," Karl said.

"I told you the catfish was a bad sign," Marie said. "I don't like change."

The door to the trailer opened, and Judith stepped out. She wore a tank top and blue jeans. Her tan purse hung over her shoulder. Karl and Marie rushed to her. She pushed Karl away and hugged Marie. Karl balled his fists.

"Sorry, *Ihkaa*," Marie said. Judith pushed Marie away from her as she tugged her tank top straight.

"Stop calling me that. Use Momma." Judith grabbed her heels and righted her purse.

"Where are you going?" Rebecca asked.

Judith turned and scowled as she put on her heels. "Out."

"Now?"

"I don't answer to you," Judith said.

The odor of the fish wafted under his nose, and the flies buzzed. Karl darted to the tall grass and heaved.

Judith glanced between fish and daughters. She pointed her chin at Rebecca.

"You best place them in the sun on the drying rack."

"Yes, *Ihkaa*, I mean Momma," Marie said, pressing herself closer to Rebecca.

Judith marched past Karl and down the dirt path and headed into town.

Rebecca walked over to where Karl was and placed a hand on his forehead.

"I am not sick. He had flies and stunk."

"You saw him, dead. That's not good," Rebecca said. "Did you touch him?"

Karl nodded. "Am I going to die?"

"I'll get the sage. We'll smudge the negative away."

"I don't like change," Marie said with a sigh.

Together, they went to the fire pit. A small sandy spot with brick. Marie set up the smoking poles for the fish. Karl rubbed his hands together, worrying and hoping everything would be alright. He didn't want to die.

That evening, the house was quiet. They sipped grape soda. Someone had left a cold case on the porch. With the absence of Endow, an eerie silence resonated in the trailer. The children sat in the living room on the three-legged sofa. The duct-taped poodle lamp glowed, its nicotine-yellowed shade contrasted with the black fringe that hung at the bottom.

There would be a burial gathering, with food, talk, and more food. Karl's mouth watered at the thought.

"Where's *Basahke*?" Marie asked, breaking the silence.

"Tavern," Jimmy and Rebecca said in unison.

Karl wondered why. Endow was not there. He was under a tree. The grape soda cooled his hand.

"What'll become of us with *Basahke* gone?" Marie asked.

"We'll take care of ourselves," Rebecca said, picking at a hole in the sofa.

"Was it the brown bottle?" Marie asked. "Will it happen to us?"

Rebecca nodded.

"Only if you give in to the white ways. Endow was weak," Jimmy said, picking up his basketball.

"No," Karl said. "He was not weak. He was a warrior. I miss him."

Jimmy thumped the orange ball against the wall. "We are better off without him and his disease."

"Are you happy he's gone?" Marie asked.

"I am not," Karl said, grape soda dripping in his hand.

"We're not happy," Jimmy said.

"Is *Basahke* happy?" continued Marie.

"Probably. He can't hurt her anymore," Jimmy said.

"Maybe she'll be nicer," Karl said. The tension of the bottle was gone. Momma would be happier.

"I want Momma," Marie said, tears forming in her eyes.

Karl watched Rebecca's face turn dark. She was not loyal or fond of *Basahke*.

"Who will lead us?" Karl asked.

"I'm the man now." Jimmy rolled his basketball across the floor, knocking over the empty bottles of soda. They clunked and spun. Jimmy was sixteen and spent most of his time playing basketball.

"You gonna get a job?" Rebecca pushed the stuffing deeper into the hole she had made. "He brought in money when he didn't drink it all."

Did they need money? Rebecca was concerned, so it must be important. Karl could feel her worry. The hole in the sofa was now two fingers wide.

Marie sniffled. "I want two parents."

"We have each other. Stop whining," Rebecca said.

Marie wiped her nose on her sleeve.

"Don't be a bitch," Jimmy said, putting his arm around Marie.

"It's not my fault he drank himself to death. He wasn't a great guy."

"Yes, he was," Karl and Marie said together.

"It's not my fault he left us."

Rebecca stood up quickly, knocking over the taped lamp. It fell to the floor. The light flickered but refused to die. The pink head of the dog rolled. They all looked at the split pieces, three legs, and a cracked body. A vision of Endow under the tree flashed in Karl's mind, causing him to shiver even though he wasn't cold. Rebecca stomped out of the room. The screen door smacked, causing Karl to jump.

Jimmy unplugged and picked up the lamp, taking it outside.

"Don't be so mean. They are just kids. Don't worry. I can work."

"Do you think she will come home?"

Karl hadn't thought about that. What reason did Judith have to return? Endow was the money. They were a money pit. Drunk Endow called them that. Tears filled his eyes as he reached for Marie. Together, they hugged and cried.

"Come," Rebecca said, standing in the doorway, lamp cord dangling from the broken shaft. "Stop your crying. It was only a broken lamp held together by tape. It's time to put it away. Jimmy, get a shovel."

Marie and Karl looked at each other.

"Can we keep the shade?" Marie asked.

"The light bulb is still good," Karl added. "We should keep that."

Together they buried the shattered pieces of the lamp in the backyard, thanking it for its warm light in the darkness.

AT THE BURIAL CEREMONY, very few words were spoken of the man —only tales of a boy named Endow. Karl wondered how a good boy could become a disliked man. The stories did not match. The children ate and stayed with their grandmas and uncles. Grandma Doli wept, which brought tears to Karl's eyes. Judith and the children stood silently. After days of feasting, Rebecca and Karl walked home, stomachs full and arms laden with leftovers.

"Grandma Doli is very sad," Karl said as he sat on the mattress with Rebecca eating yet another chicken leg.

"Yes, her son has died."

"Was he a good man?"

Thirteen-year-old Rebecca shook her head. "I don't know. I think not."

"Where are Jimmy and Marie?"

"Jimmy's shooting hoop. Marie's with *Basahke* at the tavern."

"Dan Green Tree on the Plain doesn't like kids in the bar. He told me so."

Rebecca nodded. "Things are going to change."

"That is what Marie said. Is the change that Marie is gone?"

Rebecca shifted on the mattress. "No, I'll get her tonight. She doesn't like to be around Judith when she's drinking. She will come home."

"Does *Basahke* have the brown bottle disease? Will *Basahke* come home?"

Rebecca snorted and refolded the blanket next to her.

She doesn't want Judith home.

"It's the white man's disease. She will come to be around Marie."

That made sense. Marie always had the key to Judith's heart. Marie could shorten a beating from Endow, but not without occasional injury to herself.

The brown bottle held danger. The brown bottle hid the truth. The liquid was pale as piss and ruined many tribal members. Karl frowned. Poor Marie, the bottle followed her. Karl slipped his hand into Rebecca's.

"You will not miss him," Karl said, having reexamined the truth. "Our circle is broken."

"He was never part of the circle," Rebecca said as she squeezed his hand.

Karl nodded, not sure he understood what she meant. Endow was their father, and the brown bottle loomed dangerously close, like nettles on the trail.

In the night, Karl heard Rebecca leave. He listened to the gentle snores of Jimmy. When she returned, she had Marie with her.

"Welcome home," Karl said, as Marie snuggled close to him. She reeked of cigarettes and alcohol. He shut his eyes to sleep, his circle complete.

CHAPTER 8
MOMMA BASAHKE

In Tewa, there is no word for family, but there is a word for all of us."

Dr. Tessie Naranjo, Santa Clara Pueblo. Author, teacher, and independent scholar.

K arl remembered the words of Marie and Rebecca. Things would change, and they did.

Peace settled around the little trailer at the end of the dirt road.

Karl arrived home from a twilight adventure with Marie to shouting. They hadn't heard shouting for months.

"You stole our money. You're drunk. Get out."

Karl and Marie stood frozen near the front door of the trailer, the evening fun dissolving at their feet.

The brown bottle had visited.

The door to the trailer banged open. Jimmy stumbled backward as Rebecca pushed him again.

"You're a cunt," Jimmy shouted. "Where did you get that money? If it's our money, why are you hoarding it?"

Rebecca rushed at him, both hands raised. Jimmy fell on his ass. Karl knew where the money came from. He had watched her get the money that people left on tables at the bar, slipping it into her pocket. Debbie Greenhopper tried to stop her, but Dan Green Tree on the Plains shook his head no. Karl got the impression Rebecca's actions were wrong. But he didn't ask her because he didn't want her mad.

"Stop it, stop it," Marie yelled. "He's our *basaale*."

"He stole from us," Rebecca said, spittle flying from her mouth.

"Oh, Jimmy," Marie said as she placed her hands on her hips. "He's still our brother. He'll die outside. I don't want a dead *basaale*."

Rebecca crossed her arms. "I don't want to live with drunks or thieves."

"He's sorry, aren't you, Jimmy?" Marie bent to help him up.

Jimmy stood up and teetered.

Karl watched. Yep, he's drunk. He recognized the swaying like a branch on a windy day walk.

"Please, Becca, let him come in," Karl said, remembering the dead body of Endow. He had figured out the night and the drink killed his father.

"Fine, but he sleeps in the drunkard's room."

Rebecca stomped into the trailer.

"I am hungry," Karl said as he followed her inside and the stench of cooked rhubarb greeted him. His stomach clenched at the thought of the sour sauce. Rebecca continued down the hall to their bedroom. Marie helped Jimmy to their parents' room. Karl opened the freezer and dumped ice cubes into a bowl. At least they were not sour.

REBECCA WAS off fishing and checking traps. He had wanted to go with her, but she insisted he was too noisy. The days were turning bitter and the smell of snow hung in the air. Karl piled blankets on top of himself, snuggling into the smells of his siblings. He pretended he was a bear hibernating.

Marie sat reading and nibbling on a stale piece of bread. Karl's stomach growled. He would wait for Rebecca's meat. In the quiet, a car's tires crackled on the gravel. Karl wondered who had arrived.

"Hi, Momma. I've missed you," Marie said.

The heavy odor of perfume slithered under the blankets.

"Are we alone? I have been thinking. Maybe it's time for you to come with me."

Karl froze. He didn't want Marie to leave. He listened to the old chair creak. Marie must have sat up straight.

"Where are we going?"

Judith's heels clacked on the floor like a cat's tail, back and forth, waiting at a mouse hole.

"Away from here. I need a fresh start. I can't live like this anymore."

"Rebecca will smudge. The evil spirits will leave." Marie's book closed with a thud.

"Not that. There's an entire world out there. It's time to live. We need money. Just look at this place."

"It's alright. Do you have any money?"

Rebecca was always complaining about money. Momma gave Marie money. Marie gave it to Rebecca. Karl smiled. Well, almost all of it. She squirreled some and when she and Karl were out, she would buy him penny candy. Karl heard the click of the purse.

Marie got money. Maybe tonight they could have soft bread with their meat.

"I have a job and I want you to live with me."

"But what about the others?" Marie asked.

"They'll be all right."

"I don't want to leave them."

"Don't be silly. You'll have new clothes that are not Rebecca's hand-me-downs."

"But we're *ashishkawuuhawate*, family."

"When Endow died, he took that with him. Things have changed."

Karl scratched his arm. The blankets were getting hot. This was not the change he wanted. Rebecca was taking care of them. All was calm, even with hunger in his belly.

"I don't wanna leave," Marie said, her voice taking on a plaintiff plea. He was familiar with the hiccupping sound. Marie was crying. She cried a lot when she thought everyone was asleep. Momma needed to listen.

"Stop being difficult," Judith said. Karl recognized the tone in her voice. It was the rattle before the snake struck.

"Don't make her go," Karl said, pushing the blanket off.

Judith's eyes narrowed. "You little sneak." She grabbed his arm and shook him. The golden bands on her wrists jangled. "You keep your mouth shut."

Karl's teeth rattled in his head. She raised her arm.

"Momma, he won't talk," Marie said. "I'll go."

Judith released Karl with a shove and he crash-landed in the spot where the poodle lamp had once sat. He licked the blood from his lip, looking at the woman before him. She had short hair and war paint on her eyes.

"You better keep quiet." She turned to Marie. "You pack your things, be ready, we'll leave soon. I'll buy you new clothes. No more leftovers for you."

"*Aho*, Momma," Marie said, her voice shaky but sincere.

After Judith left the trailer, Marie gave Karl ice cubes to suck on.

When Rebecca arrived, she took one look at Karl's fat lip and frowned.

"What happened to you?" Rebecca asked.

Karl sucked on the ice cube. He would not talk.

"*Basahke* is planning on taking me," Marie said. "I don't want to go. I want to be with you."

Rebecca set the dead rabbit on the table next to Karl.

"I figured she was planning something. All of her clothing has disappeared."

Karl never noticed that her closet was empty. He had seen the kitchen shelves go bare.

"I don't want to leave. She wants me to go with her into the world."

A shocked face appeared on Rebecca. "That's not good. I hoped she'd found another guy and moved in with him. I should have known she was off the Rez."

Karl ran his fingers over the rabbit. It was still warm and soft. Outside, the birds were speaking loudly, but he did not understand what their message was.

"I don't want to leave, Becca," Marie said, pacing the room, her eyes wild.

Rebecca grabbed a knife and went to the porch to sharpen it.

"I need to think."

Jimmy came up whistling and spinning his basketball.

"*Basahke* is trying to take Marie away from us," Rebecca announced.

They were *ashishkawuuhawate*. Momma couldn't take her own

daughter away, but he knew she only wanted Marie. They should leave now.

"We should go away, camping," Karl said, rubbing the rabbit's limp paw on his cheek. He enjoyed camping.

"In winter, that's a dumb idea," Jimmy said, bouncing the basketball on the porch.

The blade on the razor strap hissed in a steady rhythm as Rebecca sharpened her knife. The ball thumped like a drum on the porch boards.

"When's this happening?" Jimmy asked.

"I don't know. She said to be ready," Marie said, pacing the porch in a circle.

Rebecca handed Jimmy the sharpened knife. Jimmy skinned and gutted the rabbit. Rebecca heated a pan on the stove.

"Becca, what are we going to do?" Marie asked, wringing her hands.

"Nothing. Go with her when she asks."

Marie cried. Karl felt his throat tighten. He didn't want to lose Marie.

Jimmy dropped the sliced rabbit into the pan, and it sizzled, giving off a sweet gamey odor that made Karl's mouth water and his stomach talk.

"I've got a plan. You'll have to be sick, real sick. Then she comes and gets me because *Basahke* doesn't deal with sick." Rebecca gave Jimmy a stern look. "It will work and we will be ready, all of us. We will be together."

Karl nodded. Rebecca was right. Momma always handed them to Rebecca when they were with fever.

Marie disappeared a day later.

. . .

AFTER A WEEK, Karl doubted Rebecca's words. The packed bags stood by the door. They were not going anywhere. He knew Marie sometimes did as she pleased. Had she decided life was better without them? Regret filled him. He should not have begged her for candy.

"Becca, Marie is not coming back. It has been too long," Karl stated one day after they finished their meal of pemmican and carrots.

"I think he's right," Jimmy said, stuffing wood into the stove. They were sleeping in the living room next to the only source of heat.

"The weather's keeping her from coming," Rebecca said.

Karl looked outside at the hard, frozen snow. How far away was she? How sick was Marie?

"How will she get here if she is sick and cannot walk?"

"Crap, you didn't think of that. What if Marie took too much of your herbal stuff?" Jimmy said. "She doesn't follow instructions well."

Rebecca pulled a blanket around her as she moved away from them. "*Basahke* has a car."

"Marie's animal guide is a coyote," Karl said. "She told me."

"That's right, she's cunning and loyal," Rebecca said.

"Yeah, and she has no qualms about deceiving outsiders to protect herself or the ones she loves. Who does she love more, Judith or us?" Jimmy asked.

Karl felt his chest get heavy and his eyes blurred. Every morning, Rebecca stood on the porch. The larks were bringing messages to Rebecca. Karl watched her, leaving food for them. What message were they bringing?

"I told her what to do. We have to wait."

"She is going to come, right, Becca?" Karl asked, scooting closer to her.

He watched Rebecca exchange a glance with Jimmy.

"Yeah, everything's going to be fine," Jimmy said as he poked the fire.

THREE WEEKS LATER, Karl sat on the sofa as the wood stove glowed, listening to Rebecca tell a story. The sound of a car motor filled the night. A bright light flashed into the trailer. Rebecca grabbed Karl and made him stand next to the back-packs. The door to the trailer opened. Judith stood framed by headlights.

"Come on, let's go, Rebecca," Judith said, her voice full of impatience. "Well, are you coming or not?"

"*Ihkaa*, what's wrong?" Rebecca asked.

"Marie's sick. I need you to make her well."

Rebeca nodded and plodded to the kitchen and appeared to be searching for something.

Jimmy cocked his head, and Karl knew to dart out of the trailer. Karl ran out into the snow-covered yard in stocking feet, diving into the back seat of the large green Ford Falcon.

Marie was in the back seat. Karl touched her hot, sweaty hand.

"We are here," Karl said, scrunching down on the floor behind the passenger seat. Rebecca cautioned him to be invisible. He pulled his wet sock off and placed it on Marie's forehead.

Jimmy hoisted the suitcase into the trunk and slid into the front seat. Rebecca tossed the backpacks into the back and climbed in. She lifted her sister's fevered head onto her lap, wrapping a blanket around her.

Judith got into the driver's seat and fired up the car.

Rebecca handed Karl his moccasins.

"You had best behave if I take you to town. I don't want any trouble and stop calling me *Ihkaa*."

"We won't be trouble," Jimmy said, pushing Karl down, so he stayed hidden. Karl laid still, toes cold and shoes in hand.

From the floor of the Ford Falcon, the heater blasted Karl's toes warm. Rebecca gave Marie a stick to chew on. They were together.

Karl woke up, disoriented. Nothing smelled right. Gone were the odors of burning wood. He slipped off the oversized chair and went in search of his siblings. The apartment was small and clean. Three doors were in front of him. As he stood pondering, a door opened, and Jimmy stepped out of the bathroom.

"Where is Rebecca?" Karl asked.

"In there, performing her magic. I guess this place will work. At least there's food."

Karl was torn. Should he eat or see Marie? His stomach won, and he followed Jimmy to the kitchen.

Rebecca exited the door on the right.

"She'll survive."

Karl waved his spoon in the air. Marie had chosen them. He shoveled cereal into his mouth.

"Judith works at night, so we must be silent during the day. She is sleeping now," Rebecca said, looking at Karl. "Marie is in school. We'll do the same tomorrow."

"Not me," Jimmy said, mashing the flakes into his milk.

"Me either," Karl echoed.

"We are off the Rez. We'll do as the whites do. You're going to school. You don't have to learn anything."

"Not me," Jimmy restated through a mouthful of cereal. "I'm not going."

"What are you going to do?" Karl asked, shoving a large spoonful into his mouth.

"I'll be an Indian," Jimmy said. "Play basketball. I'm taller than most and good."

"Out here? They hate us out here. No, you'll get a job," Rebecca said. "She won't support us. I've seen her closet of new clothes. She has never sent us money."

Jimmy snorted. "Perhaps I'll go back to the Rez. They want me there and I can play basketball."

Rebecca put her nose next to Jimmy's. "You're with us or against us. You can't have it both ways."

Karl held his breath.

"I want you to stay," Rebecca said, pulling back.

"Me too," Karl said.

"Fine, I'll stay."

The door opened as Marie teetered out. She slumped her way to the table, eyes puffy, rimmed in red like she had been crying for weeks. She looked parched. Karl rushed to her and hugged her. Their circle was complete again.

CHAPTER 9
STUPID WHITE PEOPLE

Brother... I would tell you in a most soft, loving, and friendly manner to go back over the mountain and stay there...

Tamaqua (Chief King Beaver). 1710 - 1770. Diplomat, leader, great peacemaker, and Chief of the Delaware Nation. Words spoken at the treaty conference in Kukuski, Pennsylvania.

The afternoon was sunny as thirteen-year-old Rebecca walked into the business office of Mary, Mother of Perpetual Help Hospital. It was the last day of October, and she needed to pay Karl's hospital bill. Once a month, she made this trip to pay their debts. Three dollars. She had worked hard to gather the money, scrounging pennies, loose change, and an occasional dip into Judith's purse. She pushed the button to the second floor and strolled to the business office, where a few people sat waiting. A blonde woman called "next," and Rebecca stepped up to the counter.

"Can I help you?"

"Yes, I have a bill to pay. Here's three dollars. I'd like a receipt. The account number is 46890, and the name on the bill is Knows the Song."

The woman's over-painted eyelids blinked at her.

Rebecca repeated herself.

"This bill is too old. It's seven years old. That account is closed. I'm sure they have sent it to collections. You have only paid half of what is due."

"The account is not closed. You're mistaken. I bring money every month. The money is real."

"It isn't enough. That bill is over $400."

"No. I've paid three dollars every month for six years. I have paid $216. I have proof. You have always accepted my money. I pay my debts."

Rebecca placed the money on the counter. The woman pushed it back. Rebecca moved it toward the woman, giving her a warrior look.

"Where's Mrs. Brandenhoff?"

"She retired."

What did that mean, *retired*? She didn't recognize that word. Rebecca had assumed it was for a vacation. On the Rez, you had a job until you died, or were given something else by the tribal council.

"She always accepted my payment. You need to do this."

The woman shook her head and crossed her arms, refusing to pick up the bills.

Rebecca sighed, took the money, turned, and marched to the low table next to the seats. She pushed the magazines to one side, climbed on top of the table, and sat cross-legged, glaring at the woman.

"Get off the table," Blondie shrilled.

The other patrons in the room snickered.

What was wrong with this woman?

Rebecca continued to eye the woman, who tried to ignore her.

The clock on the wall counted the minutes. Rebecca fumed. This was a waste of her day. She had dinner to fix and a bus to catch. They now lived closer to the hospital, but if she missed the bus, she would have a long walk home.

The woman marched out of her office. She stood in front of Rebecca and tried to pull her off the table. When that didn't work, she struggled to tip the table. Rebecca slid off and darted through the office door, locking it.

The phone rang. Rebecca watched the woman's face turn red.

"Do you want me to answer that?"

"No!" the woman screeched. "Open this door immediately or I'll call security."

Rebecca smiled. "I can do that for you."

The woman growled and stomped out.

Rebecca looked over at the desk. She saw her account. Blondie was right. It said closed, but Rebecca was certain she owed more. She should have asked more questions.

Security arrived. He was a member of her clan. Even though he wore his hair short, his tanned skin gave him away. The patrons sat glued to their seats. One woman took out her knitting and smiled.

The man asked about the problem.

"They won't take my money," Rebecca said. "I have a bill to pay. She won't take my money."

The security officer laughed and then stopped when he saw Blondie's face.

"Call the administrator, Dr. Whitmire," he said, crossing his arms and taking a seat with the patrons.

Blondie smirked. Rebecca discerned that Doctor Whitmire had clout. Blondie exited. The security man grinned. Rebecca noticed the keys on his belt. He could open the door, but he just smiled. *What is wrong with him? He has the means and authority. Why doesn't he unlock the door?*

A man wearing a suit and name badge entered. He looked at the security guard and then at Rebecca. He turned to Blondie, who was smirking at Rebecca.

"Miss Jones, what's the problem?"

"That girl wants to pay a past-due bill."

The man in the suit blinked hard. "So, what's the problem?"

"It's a seven-year-old bill. It's past due several times over."

"I pay my debts," Rebecca said in a loud voice.

"What name is this debt under?" Doctor Whitmire asked.

"Knows the Song," Rebecca said. "I'm Rebecca Knows the Song. Mrs. Brandenhoff always took my money. I'm not tricking you. I have cash. Not trinkets and beads."

Silence filled the room. *Had her harsh words reminded them of their past broken treaties?* Rebecca swallowed hard. Doctor Whitmire's face held a bemused smile. The man before her had an intense stare and short-cropped hair. He looked vaguely familiar. *Where had she seen him?* The memory remained hidden.

"Miss Jones, please give this young lady a receipt and credit the account."

"What?" the blonde woman's face turned a blotchy pink.

Rebecca moved to the outside of the counter, paid, and took the receipt. She turned and held out her hand to the administrator. He shook it, and the people who had lingered in the waiting room clapped.

"Thank you, Doctor Whitmire. I will return in a month."

The man grinned. "I'm convinced that you will."

Rebecca marched out of the office and raced to catch the last bus. Once seated, she wondered if all white people were so stupid.

"NOT *AWAASE* AGAIN," Karl wailed. He liked beans, but today worry nibbled his hunger. The smell sickened him. He knew if Jimmy was cooking, it was because Rebecca was not home. Neither Marie nor Jimmy seemed worried. He feared she had left for the Rez. He missed the Rez, and his friends. The teachers and kids at the white school treated him as if he were stupid, speaking slowly to him as if he didn't understand English. He wished he could work like Jimmy. Work meant money, and money got Jimmy new things. Of course, Jimmy had to donate to Rebecca's household fund.

"Eat or be hungry. Your choice," Jimmy said, as Marie set the table.

The door to the apartment opened, and Rebecca entered. Karl rushed across the room, giving her a hug that almost knocked her over.

"Where have you been?" Karl asked.

"I was paying the bill, and dealing with a stupid white woman," Rebecca said as she got the bowls down for dinner.

"What bill?" Karl asked.

"The hospital bill for your birth. They wouldn't take my money. Can you believe it? That's why it took so long."

"If you were smart, you wouldn't pay," Jimmy said, setting the pot of beans on the table. "It's not like they can take him back."

Karl worried he was in danger of being taken away. Was he the reason money was tight? Jimmy worked at an auto shop, but they never seemed to have money.

"I miss Momma," Marie said as they sat at the table.

They ate in silence, each wrapped up in their own feelings

about Judith. Karl didn't miss Judith. She rarely spoke to him, and when she did, it was not pleasant. He had learned to stay out of her way.

They had been living in the apartment for a year. If they kept things clean and were quiet, Judith tolerated them. Karl noted Judith depended on Jimmy to fix things, and she was teaching him how to drive. Even though Karl had seen Jimmy use a car. Life was peaceful enough. Judith no longer drank and only yelled at Karl when she was tired. On weekends they traveled to the Rez. Those were the best days. Grandma Tiama didn't serve beans.

Judith worked evenings and slept during the day. She didn't stay home on her days off. Karl liked that because when she was around, Rebecca sent him to their shared bedroom. It wasn't fair. Marie got to go into Momma's bedroom, but they had never invited him. He had explored the room once. It was pretty with the lace and flowers. He guessed that was why Marie liked it. In their room, everyone had a corner. If you wanted to be alone, you hid in the closet.

With the dishes done, Karl and Marie sat and worked on homework as Jimmy plopped himself on the sofa with a cola.

Rebecca stepped out of Judith's bedroom, surprising Karl. He hoped she hadn't misplaced anything because if she did, then he would be blamed.

"Damn it all to hell. She always ruins everything."

"What are you moaning about?" Jimmy asked.

"Judith has gone and knocked herself up," Rebecca said, holding up a pair of Judith's jeans. Karl looked at the jeans, confused. He could see nothing that said these jeans were special. They were blue and denim, like all the jeans he had seen.

Jimmy reached for an ashtray as the TV chattered.

"How do you know?"

"These are pregnant pants," Rebecca said, stretching the front of the jeans.

Jimmy shook his head and took out a cigarette from his tee shirt pocket. "Oh, that explains why she had me drive her to the Rez."

Karl studied his math paper. He hadn't seen Judith enough to notice if she was rounder. Pregnant women were round in the belly. Why did she go to the Rez? Did she need a cradle board? Rebecca and Marie could make one. He was sure of that.

"Is this a terrible thing?" Karl whispered to Marie.

"Momma's having a baby. It's not bad."

"I like babies," Karl said, remembering his cousins. They were noisy and bossy, but fun.

"Me too," Marie said.

"Becca, we like babies," Karl announced. The idea of having a sibling to boss around sounded good.

Rebecca spun around, tossing the jeans at them.

"Momma is better. She'll take care of this one," Marie said. "I'll help her."

"You traitor, you knew."

"Momma told me. It's a good thing," Marie said, folding the pants.

"Don't you think it was important to mention to me? Are you stupid?"

Karl snorted. "Marie is not stupid. She knows how ang— worried you can get."

"It's not a good thing. She barely has enough to feed us. This is a disaster. She wanted to get rid of Karl. Why not this one?"

"Becca, that's mean, I did not ask to be here. They should take me back," Karl said, crossing his arms.

Jimmy laughed as he struck a match, and the smell of sulfur filled the air. "You're all stupid. We're getting a *Bakuupe*."

Rebecca's distress made Karl wonder if he wanted another sibling. Rebecca loved him. Surely, she would a new baby. Why was she so upset? What if it had blue eyes? That infant might take his place. He was the one with blue eyes.

"I changed my mind. No baby," Karl said. "Why does she want one? She tells me all the time how awful having me was. I don't know why she would do it again?"

"She wants this one. You were just bad timing," Marie said, rubbing Karl's head. "Perhaps the father is nice."

Sunshine and daisies. *She likes a happy ending,* thought Karl. Not everything ends happy. What if Momma didn't like this one like she didn't like him? He didn't want a baby to feel unwanted. He would like him or her.

Rebecca's eyes narrowed and focused on Marie. "Have you met him?"

Marie lowered her head and nodded. Rebecca sprung at her sister. Papers and pencils flew off the table. Karl felt a paralyzing fear as Marie cried from the smacks delivered by Rebecca.

"Too late now, Becca, unless you want to consider selling it on the open market," Jimmy said, stubbing out his cigarette and pulling his sisters apart. Rebecca flopped onto the sofa.

Karl let out a breath. Rebecca's sweetness sometimes turned sour, and she could sting you. She was nettles and vinegar to Marie's sunshine and daisies.

"Sorry, Marie."

Karl scooted closer to Marie and patted her arm as he picked up the scattered homework.

"He doesn't seem like an evil man," Marie said, wiping her nose on her sleeve. "But he is white."

"That's one point against him," Jimmy said, relighting his cigarette. "Does he know about us?"

"No. Only about me."

"Does he know Judith's pregnant?"

Marie shook her head. "Momma hasn't told him."

"Good, let's get rid of him," Jimmy said with a puff of smoke.

"Yeah, maybe he's just another stupid white man," Karl said.

Rebecca took a cigarette from Jimmy's pocket, lit it, and inhaled.

"White men are stupid," Rebecca said as she exhaled.

THE HEAVY ODOR of garlic filled the apartment. The children gathered at the table.

"Spaghetti, spaghetti," Karl chanted, banging his fork on his plate.

The door to the apartment opened. Judith entered. The children froze. Rebecca looked at the clock. It was only eight. Had they fired her?

"Momma," Marie said as she ran over to hug her. A shadow loomed behind their mother. Rebecca held her breath. Jimmy stood, ready for movement. Judith moved inside. Behind her entered a man with sandy-brown hair.

Rebecca's appetite fled as Jimmy snorted and sat.

The man was not big. His soft hands showed he wasn't a farmer. He was wiry and lean.

"Not much of a white man," Jimmy said in Apsáalooke.

"Kids, I have a surprise for you. I have someone I want to meet," Judith said. "This is Terence Mackenzie."

"We weren't expecting you, but there's enough for everyone," Rebecca said, thinking she wasn't hungry now.

"We ate," Judith said, getting two cups from the cupboard and pouring coffee for herself and Terence. Judith picked at her nails. Rebecca nibbled on a slice of garlic bread.

Jimmy gave a nod, barely acknowledging the man's presence.

He pushed his long hair over his shoulder and pulled his bandana down before crossing his arms. Rebecca knew he did not want to be someone's son. She knew she should say hello, but she crossed her arms, too.

What does she expect from us? She's not Sings in the Night, he's not Cold Feet. The family story took on a different meaning. She could see Sings in the Night bringing her lover, Cold Feet, and baby out of the teepee. The ancestor had a lot of arrogance. Did she say, "Here he is my white lover, accept him?"

"I am Karl," Karl announced.

Terence glanced at the young boy, and his eyes grew wide. "What happened to this one?" he asked.

"I got the white man's eyes. I can see into their hearts." Karl was repeating what his grandmother had told him.

"Hush, Karl," Rebecca scolded, smiling to herself, hoping that Karl's arrogance would be insulting. Karl didn't get it, but she knew white men took offense to Karl's eyes. They were chased out of stores and not allowed on buses.

"Seems there was a white man in the woodpile," Terence said with a chuckle.

"Probably was rape," Jimmy mumbled in Crow as his mother gave him a look of disdain.

Rebecca shifted in her chair.

"Children, Terence is staying with us for a while. He has business in town," Judith said.

"He has stayed before. What's the big deal this time?" Jimmy muttered as they ate.

Arms and hands darted for bread and cheese. Karl snatched bread from Rebecca's and Jimmy's plates when they weren't looking.

Judith sipped her coffee.

"*Ihkaa*, when my *Basachiite* is born, will she have brown eyes?" Karl asked through a mouthful of noodles.

Everyone but Marie froze. She continued to eat as if she had not heard Karl. Terence reached for Judith's hand.

"Who told you I was having a baby?" Judith asked.

"You look pregnant," Karl said. "Auntie Doris was pregnant, and Juniper's mom had a baby. She got so big, Juniper said she could hardly walk. Will she have brown eyes?"

"He will have blue eyes," Judith said, setting her mug down with a clunk.

Karl frowned. "I do not want her to."

"You don't get to decide," Judith said.

"Judith, are you pregnant?" Terence asked, interrupting the argument. Surprise and then delight filled his face. "When are you due? Why haven't you told me?"

Rebecca smirked. Why hadn't he noticed? Judith's roundness was showing.

"I'm having a baby. It's due at the end of the year," Judith said, her voice squeaking with annoyance.

"Who's the father?" Jimmy asked with a wave of his fork.

Rebecca smiled into her bread.

"James, please," Judith said. A sharpness couched her words.

"The child is mine," Terence said, recovering from the announcement.

Rebecca wanted to laugh. Her mother had many men overnight. She had run into them in the early morning as they left the apartment.

"Momma, that's so vile. How could you?" Jimmy sneered. "You'll not marry him."

The veins on Terence's neck constricted and bulged. The chaos was intoxicating. Rebecca felt empowered.

"Jimmy, this doesn't concern you," Judith said in Crow.

"Like hell it does. You're ruining everything. Why did you do it?" Jimmy wadded up his paper napkin, tossing it on to the table.

"James, stop this instant," Judith snapped. "It's my life too, and I deserve happiness."

"At our expense. What kind of mother are you?"

Judith stood up and crashed her fist on the table as she glared at James. "Don't talk to me like that. I feed you and clothe you. I'll hear no more. And talk in English."

Karl ducked his head into Rebecca's lap and Marie sat hunched over her plate as if in prayer. Jimmy banged his silverware. Terence reached over and caressed Judith's arm.

"Judith, calm down. We can work this out."

Was this man stupid? The evening should have sent him running. He wanted an instant family. Not one, but five? We need to work harder. Perhaps if she filled Karl up with sugar, he would start jumping around and singing.

The meal ended and Jimmy headed outside with his basketball. Terence and Judith went to her bedroom and closed the door.

Rebecca wanted to hear the conversation that Judith and Terence were having.

In the bathroom, she pressed her ear to the wall. The pungent stink of cleaner filled her nose. Marie had used too much again.

"Judith, I want you to marry me. I can provide a home for you."

"What about Marie?"

"She's welcome. They are all welcome."

"They don't like men. I told you their father was a drunk."

Rebecca clenched her fists. *Tell the truth, you don't want us.*

"I wish you had let me meet them sooner. It'll be hard, but I'm sure we can become a family."

"What about your chil..."

The knob to the bathroom door rattled, then came an insistent knocking.

102

"Becca, open up. I gotta go," Karl said.

Damn it, Karl.

She reached over and unlocked the door.

"What are you doing?"

"Shush," Rebecca hissed as she resumed her position wedged between the tub and sink.

"We'll all adjust. Two families blended into one. Trust me, it'll be fine. I'll talk to Father Lucian and arrange a date. Father Lucian is an understanding man. He'll see that the children are all baptized, and I'll adopt them."

Damn it. She had missed a critical part of the conversation. How many children did this man have? And what happened to his first wife?

"I think we should wait. Give the children time to adjust."

"Judith, we need to be a family."

"Rebecca can take care of the baby."

"She's a child. And she has too much responsibility. She's not the mother."

Judith's voice took on a hard pitch.

"Are you saying I'm not a good mother?"

You aren't a good Basahke, thought Rebecca. She was the only one they had. She looked at Karl, and her heart ached.

Karl went to flush, and Rebecca tried to stop him, but he was quicker. The crescendo ended the spying session.

Marie entered the bathroom, giving Rebecca a face of confusion.

"What are you doing?"

"She's going to marry him," Rebecca said.

"Well, duh. He loves her. She's having his baby. We can be a complete family again."

"And?" Rebecca said, grabbing a towel and wetting it.

"And what?" Marie asked. Her forehead creased and her arms

flapped.

"Never mind," Rebecca said, knowing she would never hear the words. She loves him.

The door to the bathroom opened. Rebecca shoved a toothbrush into Karl's hand.

"What are you all doing in here?" Judith asked.

"Brushing our teeth," Rebecca said, squeezing paste onto Karl's brush.

CHAPTER 10
THE MEASURE OF A MAN

Humankind has not woven the web of life.
We are but one thread within it.
Whatever we do to the web, we do to ourselves,
all things are bound together,
all things are connected.

Chief Si'ahl, (Chief Seattle). 1786-1866. Suquamish and
Duwamish, leader, ecological protector, visionary, and orator.

R ebecca hurried Karl and Marie off of the city bus. The
frigid air greeted them as they stepped out onto the highway. It was the end of Route 6. Slush splattered as the
bus headed back to town. Rebecca scanned the horizon. Pristine
snow drifts lay in front of them as they stood on the edge of the
open field on Rez land. Nothing moved.

"Where is he?" Marie asked, dropping her school bag onto the dirty snow road.

"Let's go," Rebecca said. She marched toward Grandma Tiama's. She would linger for no man.

"I want to wait for Jimmy," Karl said.

"He'll meet us on the way. Come on. *Basakaale* will have food waiting for us."

The children walked. Jimmy usually met them on Friday when they came to visit. Today he had not. With each step Rebecca took, the angrier she became. They were his *ashishkawuuhawate*, his original family. The circle was falling apart.

Too many changes. Mr. Mackenzie wanted to marry Judith. Jimmy went to the Rez three weeks ago. He had walked out saying, "I don't need a daddy." Judith hadn't even noticed; she still left him notes to do things. What sort of parent doesn't know her children are missing?

Marie hummed a tune as they walked. Billows of white floated behind her. Marie hadn't informed Judith of Jimmy's departure. That was a surprise.

There is something strange about her, too. Sometimes she blabbered on about nothing, and other times she was silent as a waiting fawn.

Jimmy's refusal to return home with them had broken the circle. He had no desire to live with the white man. Rebecca wished she could do the same. She figured Marie would not leave Judith, and if she and Karl left, the circle would not exist. As the sun lowered itself to the earth, they approached Grandma's house.

Karl took off his jacket and dragged it behind him. Rebecca tried to put his arms back in the sleeves, but he pushed her away. She stuffed her stiff fingers inside her coat pocket. Marie's nose was red from the crisp air, and Karl's face was flushed. Perhaps she had over-bundled him.

Grandma's house was in sight. The glow from the windows and smoke from the chimney made them hurry. They entered, and the rich aroma of a venison roast greeted them. Grandma Tiama hugged them as they sat at the kitchen table. The fireplace crackled and shadows danced.

"Have you seen Jimmy?" Rebecca asked.

"He's living in the trailer," Grandma said.

"Jimmy didn't pick us up. He forgot and Rebecca is mad at him," Marie said, nibbling on a slice of dripping meat.

"He's becoming a man," Grandma said.

So, he forgets? That's what a man does?

"A brother doesn't abandon his family," Rebecca said. "We're one sibling short."

"Not for long. *Basahke* is replacing him," Karl said, stuffing large slices of venison into his mouth.

"There are no replacements," Marie said, poking him.

Tiama's eyes grew wide as she turned to Rebecca.

"Is Judith pregnant?"

"Yes, Momma's having a baby," Marie said.

Rebecca pushed her plate away and wiped her eyes. This was not good news.

Grandma Tiama patted Rebecca's arm and then embraced her.

"It's all changing," Rebecca sobbed into Grandma's shoulder. "He's a white man. What if he stops us from visiting? We might forget who we are."

Judith's hair shortened as she got rounder. Then she permed it. Rebecca had never seen anyone on the Rez with curly hair. Judith was forgetting who she was.

"Don't worry." Tiama reassured her. "You'll not forget."

On Sunday, the children walked to their old home, the trailer. It didn't appear any different. The porch sagged, the shed looked weathered, and the fence around the vegetable garden bent with snow and ice. Rebecca envied Jimmy. He had a choice. Marie and Karl ran to the enclosure to break off icicles to use as spears.

Rebecca entered the house and tripped over a pair of new high-tops. The sofa still sat on one brick. She found Jimmy passed out in the bedroom. Brown bottles lay scattered around him. Next to him on the bed was a pretty girl. Her ruby-red lips were parted, and drool slid down her chin.

She headed to the kitchen. There was food. They didn't have enough food. Anger replaced envy. Worry gnawed at her. Would Jimmy find his way out of the brown bottle? Rebecca held little hope. She took the car keys that lay on the table next to Jimmy's wallet. A glance at the high-tops caused her to open the billfold and take the remaining cash.

She thought about writing him a note, then picked up the red lipstick case and headed to the bedroom. There she wrote on Jimmy's outstretched arm. "Don't abandon us again."

She filled a bag with some groceries and listened to Karl coughing outside. He had better have his coat on, she thought.

Sadness filled her as she stood on the porch. She missed the sighs of the pines, the hoot of the owl, and the coyote's song.

"Get in the car. We're going to the bus stop," Rebecca said. The two younger children whooped and ran to the Chevy with the cracked windshield.

"What about Jimmy?" Marie asked.

"He's not well," Rebecca said.

Karl bounced in the back seat. "You can drive?"

"No, but how hard can it be?" she said with a wicked smile as his blue eyes grew large.

Yet, she drove the car to the edge of the Rez. They waited for the bus in warmth. Once aboard the bus, Rebecca turned and watched snow falling, patting the keys in her jeans pocket.

. . .

REBECCA ATE HER SANDWICH—A piece of cheese between two doughy slices of white bread—as she rode the city bus home. She had written a note so she could leave school early. When they had returned from their weekend on the Rez, Karl had become feverish. He coughed, burning all night, falling asleep in the early morning.

She hoped she had enough herbs to make a poultice for the fever. She raced up the stairs to the apartment and stood frozen in the doorway. Terence was with Karl.

"See, I told you she was coming," Karl said and coughed.

"What are you doing here?" Rebecca asked.

"I had business in town. I thought I could have lunch with your mother. Aren't you supposed to be in school?" Terence asked.

"Did you get me *huppiia*? The kind with the big flat peas?" Karl asked.

He must be feeling better if he was asking for soup.

Rebecca shook her head. They only had the money she had taken from Jimmy, and she had planned to use it for medicine.

"I can't be in two places at once," Rebecca said, her tone clipped and sharp.

"Where's your mother?"

"Working. Karl is sick. I need to take care of him," Rebecca said. What was wrong with this man? Couldn't he see and hear how ill Karl was?

"I am hungry, but there is no food," Karl said as he coughed again. "I might be starving."

Rebecca filled a glass of water and mixed ginger powder into it. Karl pushed the glass jar away. Rebecca turned her back to him. Karl took the jar and sipped the liquid, making a sour face.

"I am still hungry," Karl said.

Terence opened the cupboard to find two cans and empty shelves.

What did he think he was doing?

Rebecca pursed her lips. Anger filled her. He had no business looking.

"It looks like we need to go to the store."

"I want to go," Karl said. He ran to the bedroom to put on his shoes.

Terence took the children to Martin's Grocery Store, which was several blocks from the Crescent Apartments where they lived. Karl and Rebecca stood hesitantly in the parking lot. This store had over three aisles and magical doors that opened without you touching them.

"What's wrong?"

"Nothing," Rebecca said, knowing she could not explain. This was not the store they normally shopped in. Rebecca frequented the mini-mart at the gas station. Karl ran from door to door, causing them to open and close before Rebecca stopped him. A gray-haired woman glared at them. Rebecca took Karl's feverish hand and led him inside.

"What do you children like to eat?" Terence asked.

"Beans," Rebecca said, sniffing the air that didn't reek of rotting produce.

"I hate beans."

Karl coughed, wet and raspy, and Rebecca covered his mouth.

A thin woman with two loud toddlers finally complained, "That child is sick. He shouldn't be in here."

Karl stuck his tongue out at her, and her children did the same. Rebecca hurried Karl away from them.

Terence stood in front of the medicine reading labels. Rebecca checked the day-old bread. A man in a jelly-stained apron approached her.

"What are you doing in here?"

Rebecca stood tall.

"Shopping. What are you doing in here?"

She glanced around for Terence.

"You're out of here. Come on, you little Rez rat. Go home to your teepee," the man said, reaching for Karl, who dodged away.

The man grabbed Rebecca's elbow and tried to pull her along.

"Let go of me, you big cow."

When he didn't release her, Karl latched onto the man's arm and prepared to bite him.

"Karl," Terence barked. The sound of his name said with such force caused Karl to pause. The store man lunged and knocked Karl down. Rebecca freed herself from the man's grip and ran over to Karl.

"Thanks for your help," the man said as he moved toward the children. Terence stepped in front of him, blocking his way. Confusion filled the man's face.

"Is there a problem?" Terence asked.

"We don't allow their kind in here," the man said.

"Their kind? Do you mean children?"

Terence pulled the loaded cart to him. Rebecca wondered if they should run or wait to see what would happen.

"I can take my business elsewhere. These children are with me."

The man crossed his arms. "Perhaps you should."

The cart was full, and Rebecca's heart sank. That much food would feed them for weeks. The store manager hustled toward them. Two skinny clerks followed in his wake.

"What seems to be the problem here?"

"No, problem. We were just leaving," Terence said, reaching for Karl's hand.

The store manager shoved his glasses up his nose and cleared his throat. "Terence? Terence Mackenzie, is that you?"

The other man spoke. "Those children were bothering him."

"No, you're mistaken. These are my children."

Rebecca was about to open her mouth to correct Terence but stopped. The manager and the employees looked at her and Karl.

"I didn't know you had gone and married one of them," the store manager said.

"Is that a problem?" Terence asked, pulling both children closer to him.

The manager stared at Karl, and then at Terence, obviously convinced that he was telling the truth. The blue eyes of Karl and Terence speaking over the color of skin.

"No, you do an excellent job with my books. It's just I didn't know," the manager said.

"If it's an issue, I can take my business elsewhere."

"No, no worries. See you at the end of the month," the manager said, waving his arms to scatter his employees.

"We do not live in teepees," Karl shouted. Rebecca poked him.

"We don't shop here. They're mean to us," Rebecca said, glancing back at the men. "You have power over them."

"Power? I'm an accountant, not the federal government," Terence said with a laugh.

They continued through the store. Rebecca wondered about taxes and what influence it had over people. She also worried about what Terence wanted. Nobody was that kind to Indians. She needed the food, and he was buying a lot. She would let this play out. Be like the eagle. Watching and waiting.

"I like that," Karl said as he pointed to the row of cookies. "Can we have that?"

Karl's boldness shocked Rebecca. Terence would see how hard it was to take care of Karl. She had stopped bringing Karl to the store because he wanted too much.

"Karl, people can't afford that."

Karl coughed, and beads of sweat appeared on his forehead. "Then why is it in the store?"

The cookies went into the cart.

"What are those?" Karl asked, running to the towering fruit display.

"*Buluhpashiile*, oranges," Rebecca answered.

"You do not buy these. Why?" Karl asked, as he coughed again, bending over to catch his breath.

Rebecca sighed. Karl did not understand money, food or anything having to do with keeping them fed and together.

"Look at the price. It's too expensive, and you would probably eat them all before the week was out."

"Do I like *buluhpashiile*?" Karl asked.

She pulled him away from the pyramid of balls.

"You need to buy this stuff, Becca. I think I would like it."

"How does a boy of eight not know if he likes oranges?" Terence asked.

"Our food comes out of boxes, with pretty pictures that do not look like the food Becca makes," Karl said, stacking the cans in the cart.

Rebecca sneered at Karl as her cheeks burned. She was doing the best she could.

"Maybe you should just cook for yourself," she said.

"I would rather shop," Karl said, sniffing the lemons.

"Then we would starve," Rebecca said, crossing her arms in frustration. The smell of fresh peaches filled her nose, and her stomach answered with a loud growl.

"Fresh food is cheaper than boxed and canned," Terence said. "I think we should have homemade vegetable soup."

Karl sat on the floor.

"Get up, Karl," Rebecca snapped.

"No, I want *huppiia*."

People gave them a side glance before moving along.

Rebecca yanked a startled Karl up. He pulled away from her.

"I do not want your soup. I want canned," Karl said.

Rebecca pinched him. His skin was on fire.

"Hey, that was mean," Karl whined.

"Homemade tastes better than canned soup, and you can help me make it."

Rebecca glared at Karl and smiled secretly to herself. This will surely change his mind about living with us.

Karl hung his head. "No, thank you. I do not want soup."

"What does canned soup have that homemade doesn't?" Terence asked.

Dang, thought Rebecca, he apparently knew how to deal with stubborn boys.

"Flat peas," Karl said as he moved far from Rebecca's reach.

"Lima beans. He likes the lima beans." Rebecca sighed. She couldn't decide if she should let Karl carry on or try to harness the power of Terence.

Terence laughed. "A kid who liked lima beans. We can put lima beans in the soup, son."

Several other items Karl requested ended up in the cart.

The price rang up, and Rebecca held her breath. Terence paid for the groceries, and they headed to the car.

"Becca, I do not feel good."

He laid his head on her lap.

"How long has Karl been ill? Has your mother taken him to the doctor?"

Terence asked.

Rebecca pondered whether she should mention their mother's neglect.

"No. We can take care of ourselves."

When Marie came home from school, Terence had the soup

already cooking. They had an early dinner. Karl, for all his complaints about starving, ate little.

He's sick, thought Rebecca.

Rebecca cooled Karl's fevered forehead with a damp cloth. Terence came over with a spoonful of red liquid and ordered Karl to drink it. Rebecca looked at the bottle and read the ingredients. She didn't recognize them; there was no marshmallow root, ginger, or honey.

"He has blue eyes. Did you notice? He called me son," Karl said, grinning, his head in her lap.

That's the fever talking. She didn't want him in their circle.

Rebecca listened to the heavy breathing of her brother as she did her homework. An eerie silence filled the room. The cough had stopped. She eased him from her lap. Karl continued to sleep.

"Why isn't he waking up?" Rebecca asked after four hours. A panic rose inside her. She knew remedies but not this medicine.

"He's fine. He'll wake up when he has rested more," Terence explained. "The medicine I gave him makes children sleepy. I'll stay until your mother gets home."

"How do you know?" Rebecca asked, worried that Terence had done something evil.

"I have a son. He's eight years old, like Karl. I've treated him when he has been ill."

"Why you? Where's his mother?"

Marie paused from doing her homework, pencil frozen above the page. This was the time to be bold. Rebecca needed answers.

"His mom died when he was four," Terence said. A shadow of sadness clouded his features. Marie continued to stare.

"Where is he? Who takes care of him when you're gone?"

"He's with his aunt, and I'll pick him up when I go home. Sometimes I take him with me on my longer trips. If I'm only out for the day, he stays home alone."

Alone. She looked at Karl. No way would she leave him alone.

At bedtime, Terence carried Karl to the bedroom and gently laid him on the mattress, tucking blankets around him.

The girls snuggled next to their brother.

"I think he poisoned Karl," Rebecca whispered after Terence had closed the door.

"Don't be silly. He seems nice. He wants to take care of Momma. This is better than what we had."

Sunshine and butterflies. That didn't help. Could it be sunshine and butterflies? Rebecca shook her head. Life was more like rattlesnakes and flies.

CHAPTER 11
NEW WORLD

This day you have given to me to walk on the face of this earth.
Guide me through it and protect me as I go along.

Alma Hogan Snell. 1923-2008. Crow historian, educator, and herbalist.

K arl burst into the apartment. He was ready to spend two weeks on the Rez with Grandma Tiama. It was winter break, but the kids at school called it Christmas—a holiday that honored getting rather than giving. Karl had learned about their odd celebrations.

He ran to the kitchen cupboard that normally held his snack. Empty. He had eaten cereal this morning, but now the box was missing. In the fridge, he saw only a lone bottle of milk. Strange. A familiar dread smacked him in the gut. He turned around in the room. The furniture was naked, gone were the pillow and blankets. Marie's watercolor, which hung on the wall, was gone. Fear gripped him like a magnet as he rushed to the door and opened it —14B. He was in the right apartment.

He dashed to the bedroom to find his clothes, but the closet was empty. The wind whistled through the cracked window, making the candy wrappers dance on the floor.

They had left him behind. He would go home to the Rez but he needed bus money. He felt his pockets for loose change. Two dimes. Emergency call money. Rebecca would understand if he spent it on a bus ride.

He stepped back into the living room and picked up the phone. He needed to call someone, but Jimmy didn't have a phone.

Marie entered, paused, and slammed the door closed.

"Something has happened," Karl said, pointing to the missing table and the blank wall. "Are we homeless?"

"We are never homeless. We have the Rez," Marie said.

Karl thought for a moment. That was true. His home was bigger than this square.

Marie dropped her book bag and headed to Judith's bedroom. Karl followed her. The room was empty. Gone were the matching nightstands and the lavender curtains. Marie sniffled and Karl put his arm around her.

The door to the apartment opened. Marie and Karl froze.

"Karl?"

The two breathed a sigh of relief. Rebecca was here.

"Momma's gone, again. Nothing is here."

"Are we on our own?" Karl asked, thinking it wouldn't be much different. They had slept on floors before, although he preferred the earth to a laminate. Rebecca would have to get a job. She was not yet fifteen. Karl knew she would lie about her age to be hired. Everything would be fine. They stood in the emptiness. Rebecca pulled her siblings close to her.

"You're squishing me," Karl said, wiggling from her embrace.

The front door opened, and they all jumped.

"Let's go," Judith said.

"Where are we going?" Marie asked, hurrying to keep up with their mother.

"Home," Judith said, marching through the parking lot to her car.

Karl wondered where exactly that was.Why was she allowing him to come along?

They piled into the car and headed out of town. Rebecca kept writing the street names as they turned. The city broke into open fields. Why is Rebecca writing? Surely, she didn't want to return to the apartment. Marie's braids flapped in the wind as she hung her head out the window. Worry niggled him. His stomach growled. They turned down a dirt road that led to a large farmhouse, with a huge porch that gleamed white against the gray winter sky.

Marie squealed with delight.

Judith parked the car as Marie raced up the front steps.

"This is a castle," Marie said, touching the swing and caressing the planted pots.

"It's a farmhouse," the boy in the rocking chair said.

They turned to see a broad-shouldered boy. He rocked in the chair, and it creaked on the boards.

"I think it's a palace," Marie said, undaunted by the boy's attitude. Castle or farmhouse, it was grand.

"Are you the only one?" Rebecca asked, approaching the red farm door.

"What?"

"Do you have any brothers or sisters?" she said.

Karl remembered she had worried about a big family.

"I don't have or want any."

Karl approached the boy and looked down at him. He had learned from school that his height could give him an advantage over other boys.

"Who are you?

"TK Mackenzie."

The son—Karl remembered he was eight. Terence had said they would be brothers.

No, we are different. He was short and had light-colored hair and brown eyes. They looked nothing like siblings.

"You do not look like his son."

"I do, too," TK said. "You're an Indian."

"True. You are not. I am sorry."

Karl liked the confusion on his new brother's face, and he grinned.

"This is your brother, Terence Kenneth, but he goes by TK," Judith said as she reached over and caressed his sandy-colored hair as if it were strands of gold. Karl instinctively pulled back. She had never touched him like that. He watched TK's posture change as if he were softening. Judith ushered Marie through the front door, pulling her to the stairway.

They stepped into the foyer. A large room to the right caught Karl's attention as a TV flashed pictures. Jimmy had taken the TV when he took off. Next was a room with a large wooden table. Karl stepped forward and peered to the left. A hallway with doors. This place was enormous.

Marie shouted from above. "Come see our room."

He grabbed Rebecca's hand, and they headed to the second floor.

The lavender-colored room had two windows. Karl recognized Judith's bedroom set and curtains. There was a second bed with pink-colored accents. This was not a warrior's room.

"Mother, I love it," Marie said as she rushed over and hugged Judith.

"Well, Rebecca?" Judith asked, a look of hopefulness in her eyes.

Rebecca chewed her lower lip. Karl held his breath. Would she be like the fox and wait to pounce? She did that a lot, seeing Judith and picking her moment to place requests.

"It's lovely," Rebecca said.

Fox it is. He wondered when she would attack. He could tell she wasn't happy with this change, and he wondered when the scalding words would surface.

"This is big," Karl said. "We'll fit in here just fine."

"This is for the girls," Judith said. She had spoken to him. He would be a fox, too.

He had never had a room that he didn't share with his siblings. A glance across the hall told him that TK would not be sharing either, for he stood in the doorway with his arms crossed. Karl's clothing was piled in the hallway outside of the room.

"This is my room, and I don't want to share it with you."

"That's okay. I do not want to share it with you either. I will find my spot," Karl said.

Karl opened a door above three little steps. It was an attic space, with a slanted ceiling and a window. A steamer trunk and a cedar chest held abandoned boxes layered in dust. An armoire scraped the ceiling. Karl moved to the window and rubbed the dirt off. He could see the distant hills.

"I claim this," Karl said. A place of his own.

Rebecca frowned. He could read her distaste for the space.

"I know. It's not as grand as your room." Karl gathered his belongings. "Do not be sad. It is my choice."

The next day, TK, Marie, Rebecca, Karl, and Terence tromped through the woods, looking at trees.

"What is wrong with that one?" Karl asked after Marie rejected yet another tree.

"It was too small. It needs to fill that space in the living room," Marie said.

Karl shook his head. Why were they stacking the firewood inside the house?

Rebecca grumbled to herself until Karl threw snowballs at her. She won that battle because she could cast a snowball and never miss her mark. Finally, a tree met Marie's specification, and they all helped to drag the tree back to the house.

"Why not cut it up outside?" Karl asked.

"We haven't had Christmas yet," TK said.

None of Karl's classmates had talked about a tree, only about Santa Claus and if he was real. There was also some talk about Jesus, shepherds, kings, and angels.

"Oh, this is a Christmas tree," Karl said.

TK's finger pointed to his head and made a circle around his ear.

"We should've said the prayer before we cut him down. Oh, Christmas tree, such pleasure do you bring me, thy leaves are so unchanging. Not only green when summer..." sang Karl as TK hit his own head with his hand.

"Very nice, son," Terence said as he brought in boxes.

Judith set a bowl of freshly popped corn into the living room as they argued if the tree was level. Glass ornaments, glitter, lights, and garlands came out of boxes. Rebecca sat to the side, stringing popcorn.

"This is stupid," she muttered. "We sacrificed this tree for what? Just because it's Christmas?"

"Becca, I thanked the tree with those words. I listened to the radio. Dad also said after Christmas we'll use the wood for the fires this winter. The tree has given twice."

"Stop eating the popcorn," Rebecca said, slapping Karl's hand. He realized she didn't like him calling Terence *Dad*.

"Come help dress the tree," Marie called as she hung a red ball from a branch.

"No, thanks, it's dumb."

Soon the tree shone with colored lights of red and green. The silver tinsel shimmered in the glow, a toy train chugged on the track at the base of the tree. The room smelled of pine, popcorn, and roast.

"We got to hang up the stocking for Santa," TK said.

"Now?" Marie asked, glancing at Terence. He nodded, and she rushed off, returning with three socks. "I made these for us."

Their names were embroidered on them. Theirs had geometric designs and feathers.

"Those are not Christmas stockings," TK said. Karl couldn't tell if he was jealous since theirs were new and colorful compared to his.

"The star," TK said as he carefully unwrapped the golden star. TK raced to get a step stool.

"Rebecca is tall," Karl said once he figured out what TK was doing.

"It's a tradition that the youngest in the family does this," TK said, climbing up to the top step.

"That's true. Good remembering," Terence said. "I think Karl will put that star up this year."

TK froze. "When's your birthday?"

"October 31."

"You have Halloween. You can't have Christmas," TK said.

"Enough, TK," Terence said. "Your birthday is in April, so Karl is the youngest for now. It is his to do."

"But, Dad, I've always done it."

"TK should do it," Judith said, who had been sitting and supervising the decorating.

"It's Karl's year," Terence said.

"It's Christmas Eve. Do we at least get to open a present?" TK asked as he shoved the coveted star toward Karl.

"Have you been good all year?" Terence asked.

"Dad," TK whined.

"After Midnight Mass, you know that's our tradition."

Karl placed the star on the tree. Nobody could be good for a year. He elbowed Marie.

Christmas was more than just Santa and Jesus's birthday. He also knew that at birthday parties, one gave the birthday person a gift. Worry niggled him. He didn't have a gift to bring to Mass to give to Jesus.

"I have no gift for Jesus."

"You're a dumbo. We get the gifts. It's Jesus's birthday. Not a birthday party," TK said, poking at a brightly wrapped package.

"If it's his birthday, why are we getting gifts? I thought the birthday person got gifts," Marie said.

"Jesus is dead. He doesn't need any gifts," TK said.

Karl was confused but liked the idea of getting a gift.

"Kids, clean up, and it's almost dinnertime," Judith said as she struggled to rise from the chair, drawing in a sharp breath.

As soon as Terence and Judith left the room, TK glared at them. "I hate you."

"No Santy gifts for you."

TK stepped over Karl, who was lying on the floor watching the train on its track.

Marie gasped. "Step back, step back now. Do it, do it." Marie clenched her fists as she advanced toward TK.

"You're crazy," TK said, planting himself where he stood.

"It is bad luck to do what you did," Karl said. "It'll make me sick."

TK shrugged his shoulders and crossed his arms. He wasn't moving.

"Step back over. Do it, do it, do it," Marie chanted, rocking back and forth.

"Do it," Rebecca snapped. "Or I will step over you."

Karl grabbed TK's leg, pulling him down. They rolled on the floor. The tree shook, and the train derailed.

"Get him, Karl, sit on him," Rebecca said. The cheering stopped when Terence appeared.

"Karl, TK, quit. That's not nice."

"Boys, enough," Terence boomed.

TK rolled away from Karl, who stood up with tinsel glistening on his hair.

"He doesn't believe in Jesus," TK said. "And they threatened to make me sick."

"We are a family, and you need to act like brothers," Terence said. "They will learn about Jesus and from your comment earlier about him being dead, seems like you need to learn more. Go get washed up, it's dinnertime."

Karl wanted to pounce on TK, to be the warrior, to win the fight and claim coup, but he wanted dinner more.

"What is Midnight Mass?" Karl asked as they crowded into the bathroom to wash. "What about our midnight..." Rebecca frowned at him and shook her head. Marie and TK hadn't heard him, but he intuitively knew the visits were a secret. He smiled. He enjoyed having Rebecca all to himself. Since the day they had separate rooms, she visited him after midnight.

"I don't know what it is," Rebecca said. "But it's Catholic and that Jesus guy."

"I think it'll be like a powwow with singing and dancing."

"I think you will be disappointed Catholics are not Crow. We are Apsáalooke. Don't forget what you are."

Karl wondered what was wrong with Catholics.

No matter what, Rebecca was Apsáalooke. She would never forget. Neither would he.

CHAPTER 12
NEW YEAR

Tears and pain haunt my life... But I've learned how to live, and I've learned to survive.

Chief Jim Billie. 1944- . Seminole politician, CEO of the Micco Aircraft Company, musician, songwriter, and recipient of the Outstanding Music Achievement award.

I t was New Year's Eve, and dread filled Rebecca. She missed the familiar. Too many changes—a new school, baby, house, and family. She had encountered a bat hiding in the eaves that very morning. He didn't belong there, and she feared his message. Midnight Mass and Sunday Mass were long and cheerless. They were not celebrations. She longed for her Native gatherings. Public school was hard enough with all the name-calling.

What would private school bring? She watched the priest and the nuns. They didn't dress right, all draped in black as if mourning life. She felt the spirits of the children who hadn't returned home after hearing the murmurs of the survivors of Catholic schooling.

She escaped once before. If need be, she would do it again.

Judith sat in the rocking chair. Her rhythmic movement made Rebecca jumpy. She was ready to give birth. The snow kept falling and Rebecca feared she would deliver this child. She knew she could for she had helped Grandma Tiama many times at birthings.

"I could stay home and help you with the baby," Rebecca said, watching her mother rub her belly. She hadn't moved from the rocker, and Marie was fixing dinner.

"No, your father has purchased the uniforms for school. We should not waste his money."

Her *bassaake* was dead. This man was not her father.

Marie and Karl accepted this unfamiliar man. Why couldn't she? She acknowledged his gifts, but that would not buy her. Disappointment surfaced. Life was becoming permanent with the wedding, a baby, and now a new religion. She and Karl had sat in the sweet-smelling church, whispering about the surrounding images. At least Karl stood with her, even though Marie eagerly embraced the Catholic way. They were to be baptized together with the new baby. She had dreamed of otters and fretted now that the message was for her to give in to the changes.

Karl had cringed at the fourteen pictures on the wall that depicted the Jesus walking to his death. The carvings were intricate and beautiful, but the story they told was harsh. A death march where they ended up killing the Jesus. She wished Marie would join them, but she liked the stories even when Rebecca pointed out the silliness or cruelty of the tales.

Rebecca stood in front of Judith.

"Why are you doing this?"

"It's good for me. Marie is happy. Why aren't you?"

"I want to go home."

"There's nothing on the Rez for us."

"Mother, that is who we are. You married him but you will never be white," Rebecca said, wondering why anyone would wed.

"Don't talk to me like that. You are not my mother. This baby deserves a father," Judith said, putting her arms around her belly. "If you want to go, then do so."

The cruelty of her mother's words stung. Rebecca snorted. What made this baby so special? Didn't they all deserve a mother? She would not leave Karl.

Someone shouting from the porch caught their attention.

Rebecca sighed. Karl seemed to enjoy tormenting TK. Opening the front door, she stepped out into the cold, checking to see if the lost bat had returned. He had gone.

The bright glowing Christmas lights made the snow glow like a rainbow, and icicles hung from where the heat had melted and refroze the water.

"I am Apsáalooke. Was your mom an Indian?" Karl asked.

"No," TK said, his face scrunched up as if eating sour berries.

"I was only asking cuz you got brown eyes. And Dad has blue eyes."

Rebecca winced at the reference to Terence. He would never be her father.

"So? He's my dad," TK said, crossing his arms.

Karl stood on the porch railing, balancing precariously, like an eagle on a pine branch. "And he is now my dad. I have adopted him."

"No, he's not your real dad," TK said, standing up from the bench.

"He is real. I have his eyes. The baby is my brother. It is inside my mom. You are not from my mom, but I will adopt you."

He shouldn't be adopting anyone. Adoption was not done on a whim. She knew Karl understood that. The circle of family was spinning and with each rotation, the circle got smaller.

TK huffed and white breath billowed around him. "I don't want to be your brother. The baby is our half brother. We both own him."

Karl turned on the railing with balance and grace. "There is no half or step. That is silly talk. You cannot have half a brother."

"It will be a girl and then you will have more bossy sisters. Perhaps it will have blue eyes like Dad and then you won't be the blue-eyed one."

It was a boy. Rebecca figured it out from the way her mother walked.

Karl stood straight and tense. TK had the upper hand in this word game, and it would soon become physical. Blue eyes were Karl's pride. He loved to use his oddness to overpower and disarm his enemies. He also loved to pick on TK. She had expected it earlier when Karl had crawled into Terence's lap with a book. The request—"Dad, will you read to me?"—had sent TK running from the room. The boys tussled, but she recognized that look. Karl was out for blood.

Karl jumped from the rail and knocked TK to the ground.

"Cut it out," Rebecca shouted. "Not our way," she added in Apsáalooke.

Neither boy stopped. He raised his fist. Rebecca grabbed Karl's arm. Terence appeared in the doorway.

"This fighting needs to stop. Settle this or I will," Terence said.

She knew what that meant, at least for the boys. Something physical. In the two weeks they had been together, she had seen it happen. TK and Karl seemed to shake it off, forgiving the man for his temper.

Rebecca settled the scuffle by pulling Karl to the kitchen.

"You need to stop fighting with TK," Rebecca said in Apsáalooke as they set the table for dinner.

"We're to speak in English," Marie said in Apsáalooke.

Rebecca continued in Apsáalooke. "They'll not take our language away."

"They cannot do that," Karl said. "How? Are they going to cut our tongues out?"

Marie and Rebecca exchanged a sad look. Rebecca remembered the peppery sauce they poured on the children's tongues when they spoke Apsáalooke at that school.

They gathered for dinner. Rebecca said grace.

"Great Spirit, thank you, and keep us strong and safe."

"Dad, she can't say that. We pray to God," TK said.

Why was he picking a fight with her? She glared at him under hooded eyes.

"They're the same," Karl said.

A tingle ran down Rebecca's arm. Karl shut up. She knew who to pray to. She didn't need his help.

"No. God is God," TK said, stabbing a slice of meat from the platter in front of him. He gave Rebecca a smug grin. Now she got it. He was baiting Karl, not her.

"The Great Spirit is more powerful than your God," Karl said, scooping potatoes.

"No, way. Did your Great Ghost flood the world and give you a rainbow promise?"

"Yes, there was a great flood. We already had the rainbow. Your God stole it."

"Stop it," Rebecca said in Apsáalooke. "Do not argue, God.

Terrible things could happen. I encountered bats this morning and it's winter. You know what that means. Something bad happens every time we have seen them." There were bats the night of Karl's birth, the day Endow died, and when Jimmy left. The bats meant major transitions and changes were coming. Rebecca had experienced enough deaths and change.

"No. Not bats," Marie said in English as she looked at the swollen belly of her mother.

Judith's hands encircled her unborn child. "Children speak in English. Stop talking about a bad omen. Don't invite curses upon us."

First bats, and now the new baby. She needed to talk to Marie about the upcoming birth. Was something wrong with the baby? The dream she had resurfaced—otters. Although otters symbolized ease and relaxation, they also warned that one can't continue to fight the current. Rebecca knew she was resisting the changes, but it scared her. She didn't want to lose another family member.

TK scooped more potatoes onto his plate. Marie smashed her pea with her fork. Tension filled the space between them.

"We have to leave. The otters told me to go home," Rebecca said.

"I want to stay. I like it here," Karl said in Apsáalooke, pounding a fist on the table. "He is our father. I have a room. I am not hungry."

TK shoveled potatoes into his mouth. Marie buried her peas under the mashed potatoes.

"The animals have spoken," Rebecca said.

"Do not make me leave, Rebecca. I have seen Jimmy's life. I do not want it," Karl said.

"Enough. Stop this talk. End this at once," Judith said, standing up and leaning on the table for support. "Stop talking about bats and otters. You're inviting the bad in."

But nobody listened to her.

Terence stood. His chair scraped the floor.

"I will not leave here," Karl said.

"You've been warned," Terence said, his face turning red.

Rebecca thought he was going to spank Karl.

The belt zipped through the loops and it whistled through the air. Dishes on the table banged and clattered in protest against man and child. Karl shrieked when the belt met his body.

Rebecca's heart pounded as she looked around the table. Marie stared at her plate as if it held a vision as she hummed and rocked. She would be no help. TK sat frozen. His mouth hung open, having forgotten to swallow the dinner inside. Judith sat again and rubbed her belly.

Karl begged, "Stop. I will be good."

Rebecca grabbed her mother's arm.

"Make him stop, Momma. Make him stop."

Judith looked at her, and a chill like the winter wind ran through her. "It's his own fault."

Rebecca fought the urge to slap her mother. This was not Karl's fault. Why was she enjoying this? Was she simply happy because it was no longer her getting beaten?

"Mother, this is wrong. Please." Desperation filled Rebecca as she saw Karl's face, reflecting the pain he was receiving.

She had to stop this.

Rebecca moved toward Marie and grabbed her braid, yanking hard, causing her sister's head to snap up.

Marie cried out, "Momma."

Judith stood, gripping the arms of the chair. Rebecca's hope surged. But Judith grimaced and shouted, "My water broke."

Terence released his hold on Karl. Rebecca rushed to his side.

"It's time," Judith said as a contraction gripped her.

"I'm disappointed that you were so stubborn tonight. We will finish this later," Terence said as he escorted Judith to the foyer. "Rebecca's in charge. I'll call with news."

Terence hurried Judith to the car, grabbing her suitcase as they exited the house. The snow and wind blew in the open door. The dwelling was now silent except for Karl's crying.

CHAPTER 13
GOD OF OUR ANCESTORS

They came with the Bible in one hand and the gun in the other. First, they stole gold. Then they stole the land. Then they stole our souls.

Ginger Hills, Dineh (Navajo). The Navajo Nation is an American Indian territory covering occupying portions of northeastern Arizona, southeastern Utah, and northwestern New Mexico in the United States.

R ebecca watched the taillights disappear into the night. She closed the door to the cold and fell to her knees and heaved. The little dinner she had eaten lay in front of her.

"Oh, gross," TK said.

Marie ran to the kitchen, coming back with a towel and pot.

They had to get out of here.

"You're sick. You should lie down. I'll clean up," Marie said.

"Karl," Rebecca croaked as her stomach spasmed.

Marie bit her lower lip. Karl was silent. Rebecca willed her body to obey. She rose and made her way to Karl. He appeared to be asleep. His ragged breaths rattled her heart.

"Help me," she said to Marie and TK. The two stood unmoving like poles in a teepee.

Rebecca checked Karl, running her hands over his limbs. Nothing was broken. The blood from his nose trickled onto the floor. She touched the spot on the floor with her fingers. With all five fingertips covered, she touched her face, dragging the color like war paint. Then she gathered Karl and slowly, they made their way up the stairs to his room. She helped him undress. Bruises and welts marked his body. Rebecca pinched her nose to stop the tears. He lay motionless on his bed. Judith always got up after a beating. She resumed her life as if nothing had happened. Even the time her arm was broken. She would wash, change her clothes, and fix food.

When Rebecca emerged from Karl's room to find Marie and TK waiting. It took everything within her to not clunk their heads together.

"I'm going to stay awake until midnight," TK said, breaking the silence.

"Me too. Then we go to school. I like school," Marie said.

Idiots.

School. She had forgotten that. On the third of January, they would start a new private school.

They had to get out of here.

Snow had fallen all day. Could they make it to the road? What if TK squealed? She needed an alternative plan.

"What do we do for this celebration?" Rebecca asked, hoping

they might get outside; then she would guide her siblings to safety and leave TK lost in the pines.

TK laughed. "Pots and pans. We stay up and eat brownies and at midnight welcome the new year with lots of noise."

"When do we make brownies?" Marie asked.

"Get things set up. I'll be there in a minute," Rebecca said. They raced to the kitchen. Rebecca sat on the steps in front of Karl's door.

They had to get out of here.

"Becca," came a plaintive call. She flew into his room.

"Is it school time?" Karl asked.

"No. We're not going to school. We're going to the Rez," Rebecca said.

"Not now. I am exhausted. I want to sleep. Make them save me some brownies."

She needed to make a healing tincture. A sob escaped her lips.

"I am okay, Becca," Karl murmured. "Just a little sore. I do not understand what happened."

"He hurt you and you were defending him. This will not happen again."

"I think I should have said it in English."

Would that have mattered? She had seen that crazed look in Endow's eyes, anger, fury, and then rage. The same look appeared on Terence. It was like jumping off a cliff once you step forward, you fall.

Arnica and lavender. That would heal Karl's bruises. She moved to the dresser and pried the loose floorboards up with her fingernails to find her medicine bag safely tucked in the crevice.

Karl wouldn't be ready for school. She needed a new plan. We need someone to come for us. Perhaps when we're all at school, someone might meet us there. We must be all together.

At midnight, Marie and TK screamed and banged pots outside

on the porch. Rebecca sat inside and the phone rang. She answered it. Terence informed her that all was well, and that she had a new baby brother. Another brother, one she would never meet. Sadness filled her.

Midnight came and went as the icy air kissed her cheeks when she shooed TK and Marie to bed. She parked herself in a chair in Karl's room and woke to the voices of Terence and Marie filtering up through the vents. He was home. Her heart dropped.

She glanced at Karl, who was still asleep. Rebecca smiled. She had a plan. They were all about to develop a case of the New Year's flu. Milk thistle had made Marie sick, but would that work on TK. She settled on Sweet Flag and slipped the powder into her pocket. If she couldn't leave with her siblings, nobody would leave.

When she entered the kitchen, a sleepy TK was there. *Good.*

"Your mother is fine, and so is the baby. Are you still ill?" Terence asked, reaching for her forehead as she backed away.

"I'm well now," Rebecca said. She didn't want to be touched by him.

"I'm making cocoa and pancakes. Do you want some?" Marie asked.

"Let me help," Rebecca said. She added cinnamon and Sweet Flag to the mixture and waited.

"You have a new baby brother. His name is Thomas Hayes Mackenzie. He's unbelievably cute," Terence said. "He's the first baby of the new year. His picture will be in the newspaper. Judith is getting the royal treatment."

TK filled his plate with pancakes and poured syrup over them. Rebecca sipped her milk as Terence gushed over the birth, giving details that no man should be present for. It would mar the baby. Men didn't witness a woman's sacred event. They'd boast and brag, saying my son will be a great provider, warrior, wiser than Plenty Coups but none ever said he's so cute.

That would change. A baby was work, and Judith was not a good *Basahke*. Rebecca shook her head. She still didn't understand what made Terence love Judith.

"It's a little early to name him," Marie said, sniffing her pancakes after taking a few bites.

Marie was right. Another strike on this child was to name him so early. The naming ceremony was after the child had shown something of his nature. White customs seemed rushed. Have the baby, name the baby, and send it off to school. It was better to wait.

"I don't feel well," TK said, holding his stomach.

"Me either," Marie echoed.

Terence placed a hand on their foreheads and sent the children to bed with pots.

"Good thing Momma isn't here to catch it," Rebecca said. "You should stay away from us. You don't want to bring this to the hospital. I can handle things here."

Terence agreed. As soon as he left, Rebecca placed a call to the tribal center, hoping that someone would answer. Nobody did.

She continued calling, in between making sure that TK and Marie remained ill. Midafternoon, the ringing stopped, and she got a hello then a giggle.

"This is Rebecca Knows the Song. I need you to get a message to Jimmy and Grandma Tiama. Tell them to come. We are at 1440 Cooper Road."

"Tawny, what are you doing? Silly girl."

"No, no, don't hang up."

The buzzing confirmed it. She redialed the number.

"Hello?"

Thank you, ancestors. Rebecca repeated her request.

"Hey, Rebecca. How's your mom? I heard she was pregnant."

"Yes, she had the baby, a boy."

"Wonderful, a warrior, we need strong men..."

The woman chattered on. Rebecca's knuckles turned white as she gripped the phone. This half-white baby would probably never see the inside of a teepee.

"Can you deliver my message to Grandmother?"

"Sure, honey, no problem. Tawny, get down from there. Sweetie, I gotta go. Tell your mom, hey."

Over the next few days, Terence came and went between hospital and home. Rebecca tended to her siblings, dosing them with just enough powder to keep them out of school. She tended to Karl, scared that something was wrong, for he only woke up when she brought him food.

Rebecca brought a bowl of soup to Marie's bedside and noticed that the oatmeal lay untouched.

"You can stop," Marie said. "I can fake sick. Add more lemon if you are putting it in a tea or more cinnamon. Why are you doing this?"

"We have to stay together and leave together, once Karl is well."

"I'm not leaving without Tommie," Marie said, braiding her hair as she sat up in bed.

"We cannot take a baby," Rebecca said.

"Where are we going?" Karl asked, appearing in the doorway of his sister's bedroom. The bruise on his cheek was greenish and the swelling of his eye had gone down.

Relief flooded Rebecca. "Home, to the Rez," Rebecca said. "We need to go soon."

"Why are we leaving?" Karl asked. Rebecca stared at him, and then at Marie.

"I don't know," Marie said, getting out of bed. "I like it here. I want to see my brother. I want to be with Momma. Everything is wonderful here."

Rebecca stomped her foot. "That's not true. It's not safe for Karl here. And what about Jimmy? He's our brother too."

"It is just a bruise. I am fine," Karl said. He winced as he sat on Rebecca's bed.

"You said Jimmy betrayed us with drink," Marie said as she pulled her sheets up.

Her words had come back to bite her.

"Jimmy doesn't know where we are," Rebecca said. It has been a month since they were on the Rez.

"He does not have his car. Becca still has the key. I bet he misses his car," Karl added. "He does not want us. Terence does."

Confusion poured in with the pale winter sun. What was wrong with her siblings? Didn't they see the pattern? Marie forgot about the past so quickly. Had she exaggerated the past? They had all seen what had occurred. A man who beats people. What difference did it make who was getting beaten up? The violence continued. Bile filled her throat.

"Do you need my pot?" Marie asked, fluffing up her pillow.

"No," Rebecca hissed, her eyes stinging as she bolted out of the room. Karl trailed behind her.

"What is wrong?" Karl gingerly sat on the top stair next to her. She put her arm around him. He grimaced.

"Terence's a dangerous man. He hurts you."

"I will be better. He says he loves me. Every night, he comes and tells me he loves me. Momma does not. I need his love. He is sorry."

She loved him. He didn't need Momma.

A veil of hopelessness covered them.

"You're stupid. This will happen again. I don't want to see you dead."

"I will not die. You do not kill the ones you love."

Rebecca closed her eyes, yet the tears escaped, and she let them.

KARL, TK, Marie, and Rebecca walked down the dirt road, heading home from school. They had a mile to go.

"I'm hungry," Karl said, kicking a stone.

"You're always hungry. Momma said she was baking today. I hope she made pie and cookies, and bread," TK said. "She said I get a whole pie for myself because I helped with the baby."

"You did nothing but stick your tongue out at him," Karl said, adjusting his book bag on his shoulder.

"She likes me more than you," TK said, whacking Karl with his book bag.

"We know," the three said in unison. They were all aware that Momma did not love Karl.

Rebecca understood why. TK was white, and Karl was not. She wanted a white son and sought to punish the brown one. Judith seemed to take pleasure in pinning trouble on Karl. Rebecca often ran interference for him. But sometimes it seemed like Karl wanted a beating and baited her.

"Stay away from Momma. That would help," Marie said, running red rosary beads through her fingers.

"I am not staying in my room all weekend. She's *baalaaxaache*," Karl said.

"Maybe you are *baalaaxaache*," Marie said, giving Karl a shove.

"I am not crazy," Karl said, shoving her back and grabbing the rosary from his sister's hand.

"Give me those," Marie said, as Karl draped the shiny beads around his neck. "You're going to hell." Marie grabbed his braid and yanked.

Marie was right. Judith and Karl were flint and stone. With

Terence away doing taxes, Judith's warnings of "Wait till your father gets home" triggered a palpable tension in the house.

"Give it back," Rebecca said, grabbing Karl's arm.

"Fine. Indian beads are prettier anyway. Why do you play with their beads? Did you convert to Catholicism?" Karl asked, tossing the rosary to Marie.

"We're all Catholic. We are all baptized and I pray, not play. Sister Jude said the lady appears to those who pray to her," Marie said as she started mumbling the prayers associated with the beads. "I'll see her."

TK and Karl exchanged grins.

"*Baalaaxaache*, for sure," Karl said.

"Oh, look. What's that in the cornfield?" TK pointed to a thundercloud formation in the distance.

Karl laughed and joined him in pointing. Marie pouted and ran ahead of them.

"We should call Father Lucian to confirm a sighting," Karl said.

Father Lucian. Rebecca rolled her eyes. She knew Karl liked the priest from Saint Alberic's monastery, but she didn't trust him. Grandma Tiama's words came back to her, "Let them talk, listen and consider the ones who live what they say."

"I like the Father, but the nuns are very confusing," Karl said, tossing a stone at the road sign ahead of them, making it ring with a clunk.

"Yep, they tell you to be quiet and then they ask you questions," TK said, throwing a rock, too, but missing the sign.

"The priest has magic."

"Miracles, the Jesus did miracles," Marie said, rejoining them.

"Magic, miracles. It looks the same to me. I want to do miracles. Changing things, healing, sending people to hell."

"I'll stick with the Great Spirit," Rebecca said, noticing a beater of a truck in the driveway leading to the farmhouse.

Grandma Tiama.

Rebecca dropped her book bag and ran toward the woman standing in the driveway. Grandma Tiama dressed in the old way, with moccasins and a big leather belt around her waist. Her head was covered in a scarf and a warm shawl covered her shoulders. Two men—Uncle Mark and Nate—stood beside her wearing traditional reservation hats, leather belts, and Western shirts with beaded vests.

Rebecca rushed to her warm embrace. Smoky sage filled her nostrils. Hope filled her. Grandmother came eight months later, but she was here now.

Grandma hugged each of the children, running her hands over them in blessing. TK slunk to the porch. Marie ran inside and brought Judith to the doorway, while Rebecca invited Grandma to the porch.

"Judith, I will see my grandchildren, our future." She spoke in Crow, and Rebecca held her breath when Terence appeared in the doorway behind Judith with Tommy.

"Jimmy wants his keys," Uncle Mark said, tugging Rebecca's braid. Rebecca's cheeks flushed.

"Is he still drinking?"

"We are working on that," Mark said. "It is hard when white taverns dot the edge of the reservation like barbed wire around a prison."

Rebecca understood temptation, and this one dangled like ripe berries.

Uncle Mark held out his hand, and Rebecca dug the car key from her pocket. She relinquished the key. Now she could worry less about Jimmy.

Karl hung back behind Rebecca. TK stood by the old truck.

"Daughter, you have a habit of not informing us of our legacy. I had to wait to hear from the coyotes. Did you have a ceremony?"

"Momma birthed the white way," Marie said.

Tiama clicked her tongue.

"That is dangerous, *xúuche*. I have missed my grandchildren."

"Mother, we live here, in this world." The tone of Judith's voice hit a high pitch.

"*Xúuche*, they cannot change who they are. They are Apsáalooke," Tiama said, arms crossed.

Judith sighed and stepped aside. "Welcome, Mother."

Tiama marched inside. She turned to Terence and held out her hands. He stared at her. She raised an eyebrow.

"Give her the baby," Judith said in English.

Terence handed Thomas to his grandmother. She held the infant close, breathing in his exhale. Rebecca wondered if it was too late for Tommy's spirit. Could Grandma bond him to the tribe, infuse him with Apsáalooke so late in his life?

Judith turned to Rebecca. "You should not have done this."

Rebecca tilted back on her heels. "I have done nothing. I didn't get pregnant."

Marie brought a tray of steaming mugs and cookies.

"My granddaughter knows how to treat her elders," the old woman said as she entered the living room. She laid the infant on the floor, unwrapping him as if he were a package.

Rebecca lingered in the hall while Marie chattered on about their new life. She worried since Marie was daring to speak Apsáalooke to Grandma. Maybe Terence would forgive them if he thought Grandma didn't speak English.

Terence stood next to Judith. TK edged his way into the living room, pressed against the far wall. The warriors dipped their cookies into their steamy mugs.

"Why does she not acknowledge me?" Terence asked.

Rebecca recognized the hard tone in his voice. It was the

precursor to a beating. She stepped toward her uncles. They would stop that.

"It's customary. The mother-in-law never speaks to the husband directly. She's of the old ways."

"What does she want?"

Rebecca held her breath. Had Grandma gotten her message? Was she here to take them home?

"She wants the children to visit her on the Rez," Judith said, looking at Rebecca.

Rebecca felt a pain like a wasp sting. Her hope of rescue dripped away. Rebecca kept her face blank. Judith didn't know about the call. It was so long ago. What was Judith up to?

Terence's body stiffened.

"No. Tell her no. I'll not allow it. These are our children."

"I cannot," Judith said. Rebecca gasped and then coughed to hide her shock.

The vein on Terence's forehead pulsed. Was Judith about to get it? Marie was chattering on. Karl dangled a toy above Tommy, who was naked in front of them.

Grandma looked over at Judith. "This one is healthy. This one grows fast."

Rebecca fumed. Tommy was chubby because Marie was overzealous in feeding him. Momma was still not a good mother.

"I will see my grandchildren. Bring them to me, once a moon."

Terence's hands tightened, showing his fast-growing impatience in a language he didn't know.

"What are you telling her? We'll not let the children go there," Terence said, interrupting. Uncle Mark and Nate emitted a low grunt. Rebecca heard it. They couldn't believe Terence was bold and rude enough to interfere in a woman's discussion.

"There's nothing wrong with there," Judith snapped. "Once a month. I could use the peace. Especially when you are away."

Rebecca stood frozen.

Judith was standing up to Terence. She had never stood up to Endow. A break from what? We do most of the work.

Terence reached out and stroked Judith's arm.

"I understand. Five children can be rough, the boys with their bickering and the girls with their moods, and now the baby and the..." Terence paused.

Grandma clicked her tongue. Rebecca watched Grandma's eyes move down Judith's body.

No. She couldn't be.

Grandma swaddled Tommy in a colorful blanket that she produced from the folds of her dress.

"I'll have them this summer for powwow. Don't deny an old woman her bragging rights."

"Fine, but once a month. For a weekend. Summer powwow," Judith said in English.

"Thomas?" Grandma asked. "Since there is another on the way."

"Oh, Momma, why?" Rebecca wailed.

Judith shot her an angry look. Marie ran to her mother's side, and Karl appeared next to Rebecca.

"I'll bring him to powwow," Judith said. The tone in her voice signaled trouble. "Rebecca wants to go Rez. You may take her."

All eyes turned to Rebecca. She felt the silent questions and hung her head. Her mother was like a porcupine raising its quills. So that was her plan.

"Are you leaving with *Basahkaale*? I want to go if Rebecca goes," Karl said, gripping her arm.

"Absolutely not," Judith said, her voice gentle. "I'll not lose another son."

Such lies. She didn't lose Jimmy. He left. Karl's face crinkled up in confusion. The word "son" left its mark. She had won. Rebecca knew if she left today, Karl would not go. Her words were like a tick stuck to Karl, her son. He would never receive the affection he was entitled to, not from her. Rebecca's heart sank. She couldn't leave, not now, never.

"Rebecca, is that right? Do you want to leave?" Terence asked. "Why?"

Rebecca clenched and unclenched her fist. Was Terence so blind? Didn't he see himself as an abuser? Her fourteen-year-old mind formed theory to fact. Of course, he doesn't see because when Karl has a bruise, he tells us that Karl is sick and can't go to school. He's just like Momma, dangerous. Grandma Tiama studied Rebecca's face. There was no escape.

"My daughter's daughter is always welcome home," Tiama said.

"Thank you, Grandma. I miss you all, but I'm needed here," Rebecca said, as her voice quivered.

That was the truth. She missed Little Bird and Nation, the Rez, and the familiarity of faces who knew your suffering. She knew she couldn't leave Karl, not when her mother had it out for him and could lay word traps that Karl would fall into.

"The first weekend of the month, I'll see my grandchildren. That is acceptable. Don't be white on this." Grandma nodded to her two witnesses, Mark and Nate, who had stood silent and listening.

Rebecca noticed TK circling the room like a lone wolf. Marie picked up Tommy and stood next to Karl and Rebecca.

"What about TK? Can he join us? TK is our brother. He should be with us at powwow, our biggest celebration," Rebecca said in English, looking directly at Judith.

She could play her mother's game.

TK's eyes grew large. Was he scared or happy? Judith drew in a deep breath.

"My daughter's daughter understands family. This is good. He's welcome, as is your new husband," Tiama said, waving to her two sentries. The visit was over. Hope was leaving. Tiama hugged her grandchildren goodbye and marched out with Mark and Nate at her side.

Tears filled Rebecca's eyes as Tiama left. They would not be going home.

"Why are you crying?" Karl asked. "We will see her soon."

Soon wasn't soon enough.

CHAPTER 14
FEEDING THE HUNGRY

*Indian People do not like to say that the Great Mystery is
exactly this or exactly that, but we do know there is a spirit
world that lies beyond. We are allowed to know that through
our ceremonies. We know that we will go into a much higher
plane beyond. We know nothing of hell-fire and eternal damna-
tion from some kind of unloving power that placed us here as
little children.*

Eagle Man (Ed McGaa). 1936-2017. Oglala Lakota Sioux, author,
lawyer, workshop leader, military veteran, and practitioner of
Lakota ceremonies

As faithfully as the sun rises, Judith allowed the children a weekend on the Rez.

Karl loved his weekends there since Tommy ran with the Rez dogs and the new baby, Davy, was whisked away by adoring aunties. That freed Karl to be with his friends and out of Rebecca's watchful eye.

The teepee was hot and stuffy during the arid summer months of Montana.

"Becca, please let me out," Karl called. "I will not do it again."

Today she had hauled him by the braid to the teepee. She screamed at him never to take his clothes off. That was crazy talk because everyone had to dress and undress.

"Becca, come on. It is hot in here."

He listened to the distant voices of his friends having fun. Had she gone? He stuck his head out of the flap and received a whack.

"You are mean. I hate you. I am sweating to death."

It was a lie. There was water and food in the cooler. He lay on the ground, watching the blue sky through the smoke hole. He had stripped to only his underwear to go swimming.

"Becca, what are you mad about?"

He heard her huff outside as the flap opened, and Rebecca stepped in. At sixteen, she was tall, just like Jimmy had been.

Karl backed away from her shadow. She was angry. Sitting on the furs, he hugged his legs to himself.

"I do not know what is wrong."

"You have bruises. They are visible."

"Nobody cares about that," Karl said, looking at his arm with the fading fingerprints of Terence. Everyone had bruises. He had seen a lot of kids at school with bruises. He more than most. But she hadn't caused the bruises.

"I care," Rebecca hissed.

"The Jesus had bruises."

"I wish you would stop thinking of him as a hero. He died, remember?"

He rose, so they had told him.

"It's not your fault," Karl said, knowing that was a better answer.

Rebecca threw her hands up into the air.

"They're tattoos," Karl said.

"Don't show them and don't use that word. They're not tattoos."

"Bradley and I say they are. He has more than me. Nobody cares about our tattoos. They will fade by tomorrow. I want to go swimming."

Dust rose from where Rebecca paced. She stopped, looked at him, and bit her lower lip.

"You need to stop showing those marks. If you don't, they will take you away. Forever."

"Who will come?" Did she mean the devil or the little men of the Pryor Mountains?

"Them, the foster people."

He was sure that she was telling him tall tales to scare him. He rose and went to the cooler, fishing out dried deer jerky.

"Okay, tell me where Claire is," Rebecca said, crossing her arms.

Claire McCormick was his classmate. They sat next to each other in class.

That was a dumb question. How would he know where she was? Wait, she hadn't been in school for a while.

"What happened to her?" Karl asked as beads of sweat dripped down his neck.

"They took her. Those people take kids who have bruises."

Karl had never heard of those people.

"That happens when you show people your bruises," Rebecca

said as she plopped down next to him. The musky stink of dust and sweat billowed around them.

"We are on the Rez," Karl said.

"That doesn't matter. They won't take you away from Terence and put you here. They will put you in foster. It's bad."

Karl chewed his deer stick. The peppery bite stung his tongue. He didn't want to go away. Who had he shown his tattoos?

He talked to Father Lucian, the Benedictine monk in charge of the school at Saint George's parish. His stomach churned. Had Father Lucian called those people? That wasn't what he thought would happen when he talked to the priest.

"Who told them about Claire?" Karl asked.

Rebecca shrugged her shoulders.

"Maybe the nuns. They are always checking skirt lengths, our hair, and nails."

Karl fingered his braid. Why did the nuns do that? They told him to tuck in his shirt and eat with his mouth closed.

"Becca, nobody said anything when Endow hit Momma. I do not see the problem. Everyone knows."

"That was different. They were adults. Endow had the brown bottle white man's disease."

Karl recalled the electrifying feeling of the crashes and thumps of his parents' battles. It was like the feelings he got before Terence beat him.

"It is my fault Claire is gone. I told Father Lucian about her burns. He seemed so sad. I used the words Grandma Tiama gave me. It is what it is. I did not know about the fosters."

Rebecca scooted closer and put her arm around him. She was sticky with sweat.

He shouldn't have talked. Tears formed in Karl's eyes. He would miss Claire. He had told Grandma Tiama and she didn't seem upset just sad. She loved them and he knew she would not speak of his tattoos.

He didn't have a new tattoo every day as Bradley did. It wasn't even like Claire, whose father burned her with his cigarettes. Terence only snapped when he got angry. Karl knew what would make him upset. But lately, Judith had become involved, and Rebecca was right. Judith was tricking him. Judith was pregnant again, and he was fast. He would be in control, not Momma. He would pick the beating and when.

What he couldn't get across to Rebecca was that it cleared the tension. If it happened, things felt better.

"I will try, and be better," Karl said. "She is mean. When TK bit Tommy because he was biting Davy, Momma blamed me and told Dad I started it."

"Sometimes you can't avoid her. Try. Try really hard," Rebecca said as she rose and walked to the chest of clothes. She tossed him an oversized tee shirt.

Karl put on the shirt that hung to his knees.

"It is a dress. I cannot wear this."

"Do you want to swim or not?"

"Okay. Fine. You win."

Karl ran out of the teepee to the river. Once in the water, the oversized sail floated away.

KARL GRIPPED the ruler and darted across the breezeway to the church. His heart pounded. He needed to find a place to hide this stick.

It was not fair. Fiona was innocent. Sister Mary Joseph should not have whacked her with the stick. She had enough tattoos. What did Sister Mary Joseph expect from the timid girl? She was not a warrior like Claire. Fiona was a kind girl who stuttered when she got nervous. Sister should not have scared her—all over an apple.

Karl entered the church. The smell of incense caused him to inhale deeply. He looked to the ceiling to see if the smoke lingered, taking their whispered prayers to the Great Spirit.

As he walked up the center aisle toward the Jesus, he glanced to his right and left for a hiding spot. It was in the book caddy of a pew, but which row? He would have to choose carefully because he knew that Sister Mary Joseph watched where every family sat on Sunday. She would use that ruler on the unlucky children who sat in that row. As he walked to the front of the church, he stood trying to decide which statue should safeguard the ruler, foster Joseph, or Mary Jesus. Foster Joseph was not the Jesus's real father. He could be mean or nice. Mary Jesus and Judith were the real mothers. Judith would tell on him. Marie liked Mary Jesus and prayed with those beads all the time. He approached her statue.

"Hey, Mary Jesus, I am Karl Knows the Song Mackenzie. Marie's brother. Can you hold this ruler for a bit? Sister Mary Joseph..." Karl paused and laughed. The nun held the names of the two statues. Perhaps her spirit pulled in both directions. Foster and mother. "I will tell Sister someday that I am sorry. I understand how hard it is to pick one side. But not today. *Aho*."

Karl squeezed himself behind the statue and placed the stick on the pedestal above his head. The thick dust tickled his nose. He sneezed.

"Karl Mackenzie," Sister Mary Jude called. "You come out now."

Mother Mary Jesus betrayed him. Ruler in hand, Karl slid from his hiding place and sneezed again, causing the votive candles in front of the statue of Mary to wink out. Karl glanced up at the blessed Virgin. That's what you get for telling.

The door to the church opened, and Father Lucian walked in.

"There you are, Sister. Please help Sister Mary Joseph to the convent and fix her some tea."

"She sent me to fetch Karl," Sister Mary Jude said.

"I'll take care of this," Lucian said.

The nun stood with her arms crossed. A chill caused Karl's skin to prickle as he watched. The little chickadee who lived in the church made a swoop past Sister Mary Jude. She gasped.

Karl smiled. *Aho*, little bird, thank you. The chickadee lived in the church and was the bearer of truth and knowledge. Karl realized when the bird landed on the altar that Father Lucian had a spirit guide. Karl left breadcrumbs for the bird and hoped every Sunday to see him land on the altar during Mass. The little bird confirmed the magic had occurred, the bread and wine had become the body and blood.

The nun flapped her arms, but the bird flew to the high beams. "Get rid of that bird. He's unsanitary," Sister said, smoothing her veil.

"Sister, we've tried. He doesn't want to leave. God must have a purpose for him."

She snorted, waving her hands around her head as she left.

Karl handed the ruler to the priest.

"Sit," Lucian said as he took the ruler.

Karl slipped into a pew. They sat in silence.

Rebecca's voice bounced in Karl's head. *Apologize. Say nothing more. Run away.*

"Father, will you listen?" Karl asked.

The priest nodded. Karl liked that about Lucian.

"Sister was going to hit Fiona for taking the apple off her desk. I took the apple, not Fiona. Sister lets the apples rot. Fiona has no lunch. Sister would not listen to me. I did not tell her it was me. I get hit enough. Nobody told her, so we have all been writing 'thou shall not steal,' for days."

"I have seen Fiona with a lunch pail," Father Lucian said, straightening the hymnal in the pew.

"It is empty. I give her my lunch and I collect what others do not want. We pass the food under the table, so Sister Mary Charles does not know. I got the idea from the story of the Jesus feeding the hungry. It is Apsáalooke. We take care of those who need."

"I think Sister Mary Charles would understand. What you did was very Benedictine. I will talk to her about the hungry children."

"Do not tell the foster people. I miss Claire."

A surprised look crossed the priest's face.

"Claire is doing well. She is in a better place."

Karl frowned. He recognized those lines from funerals.

"Is she dead?"

The priest gasped. "No, son, she's not dead. She's with her grandmother."

Rebecca wanted to be with Grandma Tiama, even though her words came out differently. Rebecca was pulled in two directions, too. Karl understood that tug. He enjoyed being on the Rez and he liked being on the farm. Life was full of burdens.

Karl grabbed the priest's scapular and twisted it like a rope.

"Do not report me to those people. I do not want to be fostered. I want to stay with my family."

Lucian's face scowled. "Karl, if you're getting harmed. It is my duty to protect you."

"No, a warrior takes care of himself," Karl said, sitting up taller, trying to smooth the wrinkled scapular cloth. His skin prickled a warning. Watch your words. "Things must stay as they are, Father. God let the Jesus die for the good of others. You have told us he is our example. Let me be."

Lucian gripped the ruler. "But, Karl, you are just a child."

Calm him, Tiama's voice whispered in his ear.

"It is what it is," Karl said, patting the priest's arm. Karl smiled.

"I am almost eleven. I will go on a spirit quest. I will be a real warrior soon, with the blessing and powers of my clan."

The priest's face clouded. Karl acknowledged that the man believed Catholic, not Apsáalooke. Benedictine, not secular. Time to change the subject.

"A raven like your Saint Benedict, that is a good spirit guide," Karl said, knowing he'd rather have the eagle.

Lucian pursed his lips, trying to hide a smile. "Some would argue it was a crow."

"One relies on luck and the other on his brains." Karl rubbed his fingers. They ached from all the writing. "Father, do you have anything to protect me from hell? Sister Mary Joseph said whoever took the stick would get sick, die, and go to hell. Father, I do not want to die. I do not have protection against hell. My amulet is Apsáalooke not Catholic. Do you have one that I could use?" Karl tugged on the leather string that hung around his neck and pulled out a small beaded pouch to show the priest.

Father Lucian nodded and then reached under his scapular, and Karl saw a medal pinned to his inside pocket. The priest unpinned the medal and handed it to Karl. "You are not going to hell. God doesn't work that way. Sister is mistaken. But you can have this medal of Saint Benedict." The priest turned the medal over. "*Vade retro Satana. Nunquam suade mihi vana. Sunt mala quae libas. Ipse venena bibas.* This means 'Begone Satan. Never tempt me with your vanities. What you offer me is evil. Drink the poison yourself. This will give you the protection you seek.'"

Karl held the warm medal in his hand. A wave of joy passed through him. Hell was not in his future. The Catholic medal would protect him. Opening the beaded pouch that hung around his neck, he slipped the medal in.

"Thank you for the protection. But what if God tells her who took the stick?"

Father Lucian laughed. "Sister Mary Joseph doesn't have a direct line to the voice of God, and I will not tell."

Lucian reached over, Karl instinctively took a half step away and then froze. Lucian pulled back his hand.

"Head back to class," Father Lucian said.

Karl walked back to class, scolding himself for flinching. Warriors did not flinch, and the priest did not hit him. They agreed to a treaty of silence. His pouch felt heavy. He would not mention this to Rebecca. She didn't like the mixing of Crow and Catholic. Next time he would count coup.

A SMELL DRIFTED through the church. Karl inhaled the sweetness as he lay on the pew. He recognized the odor of Father Lucian's cigars. His stomach growled loudly. He hadn't eaten in days, not since Judith had tricked him. Karl tried to sit up, for he needed to get to class, but his head spun and clunked, hitting the wooden bench.

The ache in his forehead made him open his eyes. He blinked. His head lay in Father Lucian's lap. He noted from this angle that the man's nose leaned to the left.

"Oh, thank God, you're awake," Lucian said. "How are you feeling?"

"My head hurts."

"You'll have a bump. What is going on with you? Sister Mary Charles said you were sleeping in class. Are you ill?"

"No. I am just hungry."

"Why are you hungry?"

"I am in trouble with *Akbatatdia*, the Great Spirit. I cannot eat meat, and Momma is giving me meat only. She is punishing me, but I have not figured out why."

"Are you sure you're not just being stubborn?"

"I am stubborn, but she has locked up all the other food."

Karl sat up and watched the church spin. The laughter of his mother still rang in his ears, and his throat ached from throwing up. She was like a coyote playing tricks on him. He had only asked if they had thanked the animal for its sacrifice. That was when Judith started cooking meat-filled meals. Gone were his peanut butter sandwiches. She even pointed out that the eggs were baby chicks. He didn't know if eating them was proper, so he declined.

"Sit, don't move," Lucian said as he rose and headed out of the church.

Karl wiped his nose. He could not eat meat unless he thanked the animal for its sacrifice. He coiled his braid around his arm.

Father Lucian returned with a peanut butter sandwich, chips, and an orange. With shaking hands, Karl opened the bag of chips and ate one, savoring the saltiness.

"Why are you fasting? This is not the season of Lent."

"I found out the meat we eat has not been thanked."

"Thanked? Is this a Crow thing?"

"Yes." Karl smiled. He learns.

Karl opened the peanut butter sandwich and placed the chips into the gooey brownness. "We thank your God for the food, but we have not asked permission from the animal. It is wrong to take a life. You must first ask permission. If you do not, they will stop giving you their lives, and we would starve. I do not want that. Dad does not say the words. TK told me. I cannot eat the meat. Momma has made only meat dishes. Dad said I need to listen to her when he is away. Rebecca says..." Karl hesitated. Rebecca would not like him sharing this.

Karl closed his peanut butter chip sandwich and smashed it between his hands. A soft crunch echoed in the church. Closing his eyes, he paused and then took a bite. Gooey saltiness.

"Karl, you need to eat meat."

Karl realized he needed to convince Lucian. The words, the ones said before receiving communion.

"I cannot unless I say the words. Would you take communion without the words? Lord, I am not worthy to receive you, but only say the words and I shall be healed."

Lucian tapped his long finger to his lips. "No, I suppose not."

"The action and the words are important. I need to say, 'I am hungry, brother deer. I will kill you so I can eat. Thank you for giving me this meat.'"

Lucian sat silently, his head bowed and his hands folded in his lap.

Karl wondered if he was asleep or praying. He didn't breathe hard as the nuns did when they grew silent in his presence.

"Karl, it's not a sin to eat meat, except on Fridays and days of fast. As a matter of health, you must eat meat."

"But the words."

"I understand they didn't say the words. But you didn't do the killing. I think God and the Great Spirit knew who killed the animal. The animal gave his life to you. If you don't eat of his flesh, then his sacrifice would be wasted. Which is the greater sin?"

Karl took another bite of his sandwich and chewed slowly. He hadn't done the killing. Maybe the greater sin was not eating what was given.

"Yes, you are right. I will say both prayers."

"In the future, when you have a clash of cultures, come talk to me."

Karl nodded as he peeled the orange, inhaling the citrus sweetness. He broke off a segment and handed a piece to Father Lucian.

Dinner tonight would be wonderful, and he would savor Judith's look of surprise.

CHAPTER 15
THE CIRCLE OF SILENCE

Martin Luther King said,
I have a dream,
but we Indians didn't have a dream, we had a reality.

Ben Black Elk. 1899-1973. Pine Ridge Oglala Lakota, unofficial greeter at Mount Rushmore National Memorial, nickname, "The Fifth Face on Mount Rushmore," actor, rancher, and preserver of Indian culture.

Rebecca approached the bus stop and saw them waiting. Marie, TK, and Karl with Tommy on his back.

"Where is your sweater?" she hissed at Karl, seeing that he didn't have one.

"Gone," he said, jostling his younger brother.

"When did you lose it?" Marie asked.

"I did not lose it."

Tommy reached down and patted Marie's head. From Karl's shoulders, he rode taller than TK and Marie.

"Then where is it?" Rebecca asked.

Karl shrugged his shoulders

"Then it's missing," Marie said. "You're almost thirteen. You shouldn't be losing your clothes. Our parents can't afford to keep replacing them."

Sometimes Marie sounded like a nun.

They could have enough money if they would stop making babies. There were now eight of them. Tommy was first, then a year later, Davy. The addition of the twins, Vincent and Victoria, Momma's latest mistake and Terence's new bragging point, made the house full and noisy. TK tolerated the confusion. Karl relished the energy.

"Daddy's going to be mad. You're going to get a beating," Tommy sang.

Karl lifted him off his shoulders and plopped him on the ground, walking quickly away from him. At five, Tommy knew the Mackenzie household.

If Karl returned home without his complete uniform, Rebecca was sure that Judith would say Karl did it on purpose. She always tried to trap him.

"We have to find it," Rebecca said. "TK, take Tommy home."

"Me by myself?" TK whined. He was thirteen but sometimes acted like Davy, their four-year-old brother. "But it's your turn to watch the babies. Now I'm stuck doing it. Momma won't be happy."

Rebecca drew in a sharp breath. He would betray them. He would tell, and then all hell would break loose. Then their fragile peace would be shattered.

She yearned for silence, knowing that in a house of eight children, that was impossible.

"I'll take the weekend. If you bribe Tommy with cookies, he'll be good," Rebecca said. Davy adored his older brothers, TK, and Karl. Tommy was harder. He loved to create mischief. Karl doted on the younger ones. He whispered to them in Apsáalooke. Told them stories about the times when animals talked, and all things were connected. He would make a good clan uncle.

"I want a cookie," Tommy said. "I'll behave. I want a cookie."

"Then do what TK says," Marie said, pulling Tommy up from the ground. "The twins will nap if you warm up my tea for them."

Rebecca looked at her with amazement. Marie always seemed like the innocent, scared one. Yet she could be brave. Like when she stole the keys at the boarding school.

The city bus approached.

"It's laced with chamomile. You aren't the only one who can doctor," Marie said in Apsáalooke. "I'll help you look and distract the nuns if they come by."

Rebecca nodded. Marie was the favorite Mackenzie child. The nuns never yelled at her or hit her. Rebecca worried she was getting too close to the black-clothed women. They fascinated Marie. Their classmate Sandra said she heard the "calling." The whole idea of Sandra being holy disgusted Rebecca. Sandra was a girl, just like every other girl, nothing special about her.

The bus hissed, and the doors clanged open.

"Find the sweater. I want to watch *Rawhide* tonight, not listen to screaming," TK said as he grabbed Tommy's hand and climbed aboard the bus.

Karl made to follow them, but Rebecca jerked him back.

"We're finding your sweater," she snarled.

He frowned and kicked the ground, which yielded little dust. She didn't savor having to walk the extra miles if they missed the next bus, but Karl had missed enough school with his "illness." That's what they called it when Karl stayed home after a beating.

"When did you have it?" Marie asked.

"At lunch," Karl said.

"Outside? Where? On the ground?" Rebecca asked, grabbing his arm.

"No."

He was as tall as she was. Her hallmark eye-to-eye scowl was not effective anymore. He was becoming increasing harder to reason with and often gave her half-truths.

She worried he was losing his Indian heart.

Rebecca whirled Karl to face her.

"Where?"

"On Susie. I gave it to Susie because she did not have one."

"Karl, you're stupid. You know there'll be a price to pay," Marie said.

Karl held the door to the office open for his sisters. They entered the building. The nuns were nowhere to be seen.

"But she was cold. I was not."

"Great, just great, Karl," Rebecca said. "You had two sweaters and now you have none. You will be in trouble."

The gesture was kind. Judith would not see that.

The two girls dug through the bin labeled, lost and found. Coats, hats, and scarves. Marie held up a shirt. The girls looked at each other.

How does one lose a shirt?

They both shook their heads. Rebecca stopped digging and stared at the bin. There were more than lost items here. There were shoes, sets of gloves, and pairs of socks.

"Stop giving your clothes away," Rebecca said. She saw the pain in Karl's face. She was scolding him for being Apsáalooke, for being generous and kind, but they needed peace.

Karl hung his head. She pulled out a sweater and held it up. It looked new. She took out her pen and wrote, 'K. M.' on the tag on the sweater. "Now this is your sweater, and I don't want you giving it to anyone."

She grabbed a second sweater, and stuffed it into her backpack, vowing she would leave something in return.

"Rebecca, that's stealing," Marie said, eyes wide in horror.

"I'll go to confession. Keep your mouth shut. There is more in here. This is the giveaway box. I'm only taking what we need."

"It's wrong," Marie stated as she crossed her arms.

Rebecca scowled. Did she need to remind Marie of the circle of silence?

"Fine. Let's take him home without a sweater. Then what? Momma will notice. She has been itching to pin something on him. Remember last night and the dishes? That dish has been chipped forever, and yet she said Karl did it."

"But it didn't happen. Karl didn't get a spanking for the chipped cup."

"Spanking? You call what Terence does at Judith's bidding a spanking?" Rebecca's voice squeaked.

"It is a beating," Karl said. "He cannot help it. It is like Jimmy and the brown bottle disease. Once he starts, he gets lost."

The girls looked at him. Rebecca wasn't sure if Karl's assessment of Terence was correct.

"He cannot help it. If I was not here, he might hit Momma."

They stood in reflection, remembering Endow and the ruckus of the trailer. Marie's face drooped and her lips quivered. Rebecca glared at her. She was fifteen and still blubbering. Rebecca hardened her face. Is that why Karl takes the hits from Terence? Bile burned her throat. Momma wasn't worth it.

Marie bowed her head and sighed. "Fine. I won't talk, but may God forgive you for breaking one of the ten."

They both turned to Karl in his new sweater. "You keep your mouth shut. And always keep your sweater on," they said in unison.

FEAR GRIPPED Rebecca like a snap freeze as she entered the health room at school, looking for Karl. Why don't they just leave us alone?

She had taken care of this before. Sister Mary Joseph was such a pain. She didn't understand Indian ways. Karl wasn't fighting to fight. He was standing up for the weaker kids.

"I'll take care of it, Sister. We don't need your help."

At seventeen, she had taken care of so many things. Sometimes it felt like she handled everything and everyone.

Sister Mary Joseph wasn't listening. Karl sat holding a white paper towel over his face that was quickly turning red like a fresh kill on the winter snow.

"I've had enough of this fighting. You're always fighting. This time you can stay home," the nun said, triumph smeared across her tight face.

"I was not fighting," came a muffled shout from Karl as the nun continued a rant of his imagined transgressions. "I have not done those things."

"And lying all the time. For once, I wish you would tell the truth."

"Nobody likes you," Karl said.

"What did you say?"

"Nobody likes you because you yell and you're mean."

Rebecca tried not to grin. Karl was getting bolder around these magpies. Honey words, not thistle. Would he ever learn to pick his words?

"I'm not here to be liked. You're not getting out of this one, you have been fighting. I've seen your black eyes, your bruises."

"He said he wasn't fighting. You should listen to him. My brother doesn't lie, even to you," Rebecca snapped. Sister whirled around. Her long habit took a second to catch up with her movement. She advanced toward Rebecca, her finger pointing.

"You. You are no better than him. Such disrespect for who we are and our religion."

"Yeah, I know I'm going to hell. I don't care, I'm Apsáalooke, and that is enough for me."

"If you think you will graduate with honors, you're mistaken. I'll not have the likes of you addressing our serious students."

Rebecca crossed her arms and glared. Sister Mary Joseph's face reddened, and beads of sweat formed on her exposed forehead. Her arm raised. The nun was about to strike. Rebecca braced herself. Just like Terence. Just like Endow.

Karl leaped from his chair, dropping the towel and freeing his hands. He pushed his way between them, waving his arms to deflect the nun's hand. Arms collided. The nun stepped back and lost her balance and stumbled, landing in the large linen cart.

"You insolent child!" Sister Mary Joseph screeched from somewhere deep in the cart. "How dare you?"

Rebecca and Karl stared at the nun, or rather her scuffed shoes, shuffling in midair. Karl laughed as the nun's skinny, long legs waved about furiously.

The door to the room opened and Sister Mary Thaddeus squealed. "What's going on in here?"

Sister Mary Thaddeus looked pale in her novice white veil. Rebecca thought of her as a former classmate, Sandra. She was still just Sandra to Rebecca, calling or no calling.

More like voices in her empty head. Rebecca tried to push Sandra out of the room. Sister Agnes blocked the doorway. She was a mini-buffalo of a woman, five feet tall and brick-like. There was no quick escape.

"Help our sister," Sister Agnes said to Sandra over the curses of Mary Joseph. Sister Agnes pushed her way past Rebecca to Karl. Grabbing the towel, she tilted Karl's head back and pinched his nose.

"I am okay, Sister," Karl said, his voice sounding nasally. "I was not fighting."

"Good to know," Sister Agnes said.

"I want them expelled." Sister Mary Joseph sputtered as she clamored out of the linen bin with Sandra's help.

"Good. Then we'll go now," Rebecca said, moving closer to Karl. "Don't bother calling our parents. Dad's on the road and Mom's sleeping. The twins are giving her no rest. I should be at home helping her."

Rebecca grabbed Karl's skinny arm and tried to exit the room, but Sister Mary Agnes reached for Rebecca's shoulder. Rebecca shook the woman's hand off. The nun resisted. Rebecca trembled in her grip.

"I'll take care of him. He doesn't want your help," Rebecca said, finding her anger with these women growing. "He's fine."

Agnes looked deep into Rebecca's eyes.

"He's hurt, but everything will be okay." Sister Agnes's free hand wiped the blood from Karl's face as Rebecca fumed.

"That evil boy pushed me into that bin," Sister Mary Joseph said as she tried to straighten her veil and scapular.

"Go to my office and take a rest, Sister Mary Joseph."

The buffalo nun smiled gently at her confrère, who marched away.

"Rebecca, will you find your brother a clean shirt?"

"No, send Sandra," Rebecca said. She wouldn't risk being separated from Karl.

Sister Mary Thaddeus gasped. Her gray eyes glared at the disrespect.

"Rebecca, please," Sister Agnes said. "Sister, go see that Sister Mary Joseph is all right."

Sandra bowed and turned, giving Rebecca the stink eye out of the sight of Agnes.

Sandra hadn't changed by putting on a habit.

"Keep your mouth shut and clothes on," Rebecca hissed in Apsáalooke as she left the room. Rebecca raced to the large bin of discarded clothing. Would her mother notice that Karl had a different shirt? "Clothing is clothing," the Elder inside her head said.

All would be okay. She rushed back to the room.

"Someone put Fiona's sweater in the tree. I climbed up to get it," Karl said. "I fell out because someone was throwing rocks at me."

"I'd like that 'someone's' names," Sister Agnes said.

Karl shook his head. Rebecca smiled inwardly. She wished Karl would stop being so kind. Nobody acknowledged kindness off of the Rez.

Rebecca handed Karl a clean shirt. He pulled off the blood-stained one.

She tried to stop him. They struggled.

"Stop it. I can dress myself," Karl said.

She looked at him harshly and resisted the urge to slap him as she tried to block the nun's view.

But it was too late.

"Oh my God," Sister Agnes said. "Are those bruises?"

They aren't tattoos.

Rebecca's voice rose to a sharp shrill. "He fell out of a tree. We need to go now, Karl. Come on."

Bodies filled the doorway. Father Lucian, Sister Mary Joseph, and Sandra, the snitch. They had to leave. The moment was becoming dangerous. Well-meaning adults were about to ruin everything.

"What is going on?" Father Lucian asked.

"Nothing. We were just leaving."

"Someone has been beating Karl," Sister Mary Thaddeus said.

Leave it to Sandra to state the obvious.

"No," the Mackenzie children said in unison. She would not let them break up the family. They didn't understand. If it wasn't Karl, who would Judith take her hatred out on? The little ones needed to be protected. Rebecca wasn't convinced her mother loved them. She could not live with herself if they became her new victims.

"Sister, those are harsh words," Lucian said. Sister Mary Thaddeus blanched.

I should have pounded her when I had the chance, thought Rebecca.Most of the other girls in Rebecca's class left her alone. Nobody wanted to deal with warrior Rebecca.

"That's a lot of bruises for just falling out of a tree," Sister Mary Agnes whispered.

"He's clumsy, falling and bumping into things all the time, and roughhousing with the boys. Constant boy stuff," Rebecca ranted, sounding like an angry squirrel. She wished she hadn't let Karl influence her. She should've continued the lie that Karl was sick today. No, she had let him talk her into coming to school when his bruises were still visible.

"Sister, many of our children have bruises. Not all are abused," Father Lucian said.

"Claire was," Sister Mary Thaddeus said, crossing her arms.

That was bold. A side of Sandra Rebecca hadn't suspected. Compassion for others.

"I know, but they have removed her from her home. She's safe," Sister Mary Agnes said, patting the young girl's arm.

"Sister, corporal punishment occurs, and we all see it affects our students around grade time," Lucian said with a look of regret and a glance at Sister Mary Joseph.

"I will not change grades. They get what they earn," Sister Mary Joseph said, crossing her arms. She glanced at Karl.

Rebecca could see a slight smile forming. Karl would fail her class. She had a Judith spirit.

Karl pulled on the clean shirt as he stared at Rebecca. She knew what he was thinking. He had told her that Lucian changed grades when he handed out report cards. She believed him now.

"Abuse is wrong. We should call the police," Sister Mary Thaddeus said.

Great Spirit, Sandra, drop it.

"Wrong? There's nothing wrong with discipline. God knows these children need it," Sister Mary Joseph said. "Mr. Mackenzie is a saint who took on three troubled children. If he's a little zealous in his methods, it's nobody's business but his own. It's the results that count."

"Amen," Karl said as he buttoned his shirt. Sister Mary Joseph gasped, shocked that she and Karl could agree on something.

That and his money, thought Rebecca. Terence had poured a lot of cash into the church. She grimaced every time she walked to the parish auditorium where the shiny plaque on the door read "Mackenzie Hall."

"This is wrong," Sister Mary Thaddeus said, her face turning red.

Karl moved in front of her. "Sister Sandra-Mary Thaddeus, there's nothing you can do. If you call the authorities, they will take me away. Please do not take me from my family, my brothers, and sisters. They need me. I need them. Please, do not take away from the only family I have."

"This shouldn't be happening," Sister Mary Thaddeus insisted.

"It is what it is. You could adopt me," Karl said, his blue eyes opened wide and unblinking.

Tears dampened the young nun's cheeks.

"I thought not," Karl said.

Karl's words thumped in Rebecca's heart. It is what it is. She felt like a pebble in a stream as the water washed over it.

"Father Lucian, Sister Mary Joseph." Karl turned and let his blue eyes stare at them. "I would live with either of you if you would have me."

Rebecca remained silent. She was stunned at her brother's boldness.

Lucian heaved a heavy sigh. Sister Mary Joseph's eyes narrowed. He had unified them and led them into a treaty of silence.

"What are you going to do, Father? That child pushed me," Sister Mary Joseph said.

"Why did you push Sister, son?"

"She was going to hit Rebecca. Nobody hits my sister," Karl said. Rebecca's heart surged. He was protecting her. In an instant, sadness filled her. He was protecting her.

"Sister, in the future, I'll handle problems with the Mackenzie children, all of them. Bring them to me if you have an issue." The priest gave Sister Mary Joseph a piercing gaze. The nun's face flushed as she pursed her lips and nodded.

Father Lucian turned to Karl.

Lucian cleared his throat. "Karl, is someone hurting you?"

There was no pause or hesitation in Karl's response. He was talking like a warrior, like a man with his head held high.

"Would you tell me if someone was hurting you?"

Karl leaned closer to Lucian.

"Maybe."

Father Lucian ruffled Karl's hair. "I'll see you in confession on Friday, Karl."

Karl walked past the nuns and priest with determined steps, like a warrior leading a successful war party, head held high.

Rebecca followed in stunned silence as pride shone in her eyes. He had picked his words. He had united the group. They were all about to enter the circle of silence. As wolves before the kill, forever bound in the silent watch.

CHAPTER 16
APSÁALOOKE

You must speak straight so that your words may go as sunlight to our ears.

Shi-ka-She (Chief Cochise). 1805-1874. Chief of the Chiricahua band of Apache and key war leader.

S ister Mary Joseph marched out of the building with Karl, her fingers pinching tightly on his left ear. He felt her short, unadorned nails biting into his flesh. She breathed in huffs like a mother elk giving birth. Her gait uneven for his long legs outstepped her as she continued across the parking lot of the church.

Where was she going? He thought she was taking him to the principal's office, but she seemed to aim at a different target. He could have outmaneuvered her, but he didn't resist because of the promise he had made to Father Lucian. They approached the porch of a rambler-style house. This was the rectory, the private residence of the pastor. Why was she taking him there? Sister Mary Joseph entered the rectory without a knock, dragging Karl beside her. He had to dodge a little to avoid banging his shoulder into the doorjamb, which twisted his aching ear in the nun's claw-like grip. The startled looks of the men inside told Karl this was an unusual entrance.

"This is the last straw, Father. He has desecrated the Holy Species. Something needs to be done. This Indian stuff will stop. Your softheartedness has allowed this. If you ignore me, I'll call your abbot and have you removed."

"Thank you, Sister," Father Lucian said as he rose from his desk, taking in the situation and staring down the sputtering woman.

Finally, Sister Mary Joseph let go of Karl's ear, but not without a good tug.

Karl winced and rubbed his ear, checking to make sure it was still attached to his head. He examined his fingers to see if he was bleeding and then held the palm tight against his throbbing ear.

The nun stared for a moment. Then she turned and wagged her finger at Karl.

He dodged to the left, hoping to avoid her direct touch. She would not get coup on him.

Father Lucian moved to her side.

"Come, Sister, let me walk you back." He grabbed her elbow.

As she turned to leave, Karl leaned forward and tapped her lightly on the shoulder, and then stepped out of her reach. If she were going to threaten him, he would at least take his coup and count it. That was his warrior right to claim the honor. Any blow struck against an enemy counted as a coup, and she was that.

"You," Lucian said, waving a finger. "Stay put. Brother Mellitus, behave."

Karl wasn't planning on leaving. He had avoided Sister Mary Joseph for over a year, which was hard when she taught in the school.

Karl turned, recognizing the golden ginger-haired monk in a black robe as Father Lucian's friend.

"Counting coup. You must be Crow," Brother Mellitus said, sounding as if they had forced him to utter a dirty word. "Kind of humiliating being hauled in like a child at your age."

Karl smirked. His age was fourteen, but his height fooled people. He had worked all summer bucking hay, and his frame showed it. This man knew nothing about counting coup. It wasn't to kill the enemy, it was to wound their pride, to risk injury. Karl rubbed his ear, yes it was still tender.

"Apsáalooke," Karl said, using his people's name for themselves.

"Different word, same meaning."

"If you say so, pale face," Karl said, glancing around the room. He had never been in the rectory. It was smaller than the farmhouse. This living space reminded Karl of a library with a desk, a few chairs, two tables, and bookshelves that lined an entire wall. So many titles, ones he had not read.

"White man," Mellitus quipped.

"Same word, different meaning," Karl said, examining the rows of books closer, wondering if Lucian would lend them to him.

"Apsáalooke, betrayer of the Nation."

That was uncalled for. Many tribes had scouted. Apsáalooke had the unfortunate luck of being such for Custer—a shame they had to live with.

Karl turned to face the man. "Not any more truthful than Jesus betraying the Jews by not becoming their warrior savior."

"Touché," Brother Mellitus said, as his eyes widened. "Shit, oh dear, a blue-eyed Crow."

Karl narrowed his eyes to make them look intimidating. He liked when people noticed his blue eyes, especially white people when they reacted with either fear or awe.

Brother Mellitus stroked his handlebar mustache and then crossed his arms. Karl felt a chill. Long nose, high cheekbones, and a reddish-golden tendril curled menacingly around his right ear. Images of a man from his history book filled his mind. They said he was blond, but Karl had seen a lock of his hair. It was the color of a fox.

Son of the Morning Star, George A. Custer, the one who attacked at dawn. "Watch him, warrior," whispered the voice of Rebecca in Karl's mind. Custer didn't listen to his Apsáalooke scouts. His *ilaaxkoolasaak*, his spirit, had gone on before him, and he had no choice but to follow it into the afterlife. The Jesus had the same misfortune. Both stories made Karl sad, for different reasons.

Karl sniffed the air. The scent of cinnamon filled his nose. He grabbed his braid and pulled until it hurt. He wasn't dreamwalking. A buzzer rang.

Brother Mellitus rose and walked to another room.

Karl stepped in that direction but saw a book opened on the table, so he leaned forward to read. The clang of a baking tin alerted Karl to the smell of fresh cookies. He breathed in the sweet aroma of snickerdoodles. His stomach growled, reminding him he was missing lunch.

"So, what did you do to wrinkle Sister's wimple?" Mellitus asked as he carried a tray heavy with three mugs and condiments.

"She saw us with the bread. We were testing it. I said the words and did the dance. But nothing happened," Karl said, stepping back to the desk where the tray sat.

Brother Mellitus chuckled as he walked back to the kitchen.

This time, Karl followed him. The man took the baking tin of cookies and spilled them onto a plate. The scent of sweetness, like incense, was intoxicating.

"What dance did you do?" Mellitus asked. His eyes sparkled with mischief.

Karl demonstrated by grabbing a snickerdoodle as if it were a host. He raised his hands above his head and then genuflected and bowed.

"Did you wear the robes?" Mellitus asked.

Karl gasped. "Oh no, that would be disrespectful. One never wears another's regalia."

"Costume for the powwow," Mellitus said.

This man wanted to play word games. Karl was good at word twister. Judith liked to play that game, turning mundane events into dramatic moments.

"Black dress," Karl said, pointing to the monk's cassock and scapular, with a toss of his head in the man's direction. An Apsáalooke never used his hands when pointing.

"Habit, not a dress, buttons in the front, not back."

"Ceremonial clothing, not a costume. Each piece of our regalia is unique and has a special meaning. Our clothing makes us different, and yours makes you all the same."

Brother Mellitus placed the cookie tray on the desk with a bang.

"Were you using consecrated hosts?" Mellitus asked, his eyebrow raised.

"No," Karl said, hanging his head. He had said the words, he had rung the bells and washed his hands. Still, the ritual didn't work. Perhaps the robes had to be worn. He bit the cookie letting the sweetness explode.

"I did everything Father Lucian does. The little bird did not come down. There was no transference."

"It's called transubstantiation," Mellitus said, taking a mug. "It's not for your kind."

My kind. Karl bristled. *Watch yourself*, warned Rebecca in his mind.

"The Jesus was more my kind than he was white," Karl said, hearing Rebecca groan. "I am just as Catholic as you."

"Looks aren't everything, blue eyes," Mellitus quipped. "You need the bishop's blessing to be a priest, to do the dance."

Rebecca and Marie had gone through the Sacrament of Confirmation with the Bishop. Did that mean that they could perform the ritual? There were seven sacraments of the church. He had three and now he wanted the fourth sacrament, confirmation. There were three more after this one, Extreme Unction, Marriage, and Holy Orders.

Karl's stomach groaned loudly.

"Your wheels are squawking or maybe your drums are beating," Mellitus said, chuckling at his own humor. He poured himself a mug of coffee and then sat.

The aroma of fresh brew, like tobacco before it is lit, tickled Karl's nose.

"I will have all seven sacraments. The next one is Confirmation. I want that," Karl said, pouring himself a cup and sitting.

"Be Catholic."

"I am Catholic."

"No, you're Crow."

"I am both. The Jesus was Apsáalooke. He taught like we teach, in stories, and took care of the people. He gave away what he had. Those are all Apsáalooke ways."

"You're a very confused boy," Mellitus said, anger creeping into his voice. "And you are not paying attention because nobody has all seven. Marriage cancels Holy Orders."

Karl slowly spooned sugar into his cup. One, two, three, four teaspoons of sugar plopped into the dark water. So Holy Orders wasn't an assignment from God. He would have to do more research. How could one sacrament cancel another?

"Nowhere in the Bible does it say Jesus was a Crow." Mellitus paused and blew over his mug and the steam danced.

"But he was."

"No, he wasn't."

"He was. Just because it is unwritten does not mean it did not happen. There are other books." Karl stirred the syrupy liquid. The spoon tinkled like bells.

"One book, boy."

Karl sipped the hot coffee, glancing around the room filled with volumes.

"Heathen," Mellitus hissed.

"Zealot," Karl said.

"Do you know what that word means?"

"I think Catholic is Apsáalooke. Our ceremonies are similar," Karl said as he made the sign of the cross, touching his forehead, his heart, left and then right shoulders. "That movement is similar to this." Karl turned and bowed in four directions, west, north, east, and south.

"You have lost your mind. Get off the fence. Stick with Crow and don't take what isn't yours."

"Excuse me," Karl said, face flushed. This man was a nettle. He stung at first and then caused a lingering itch. He would not make him lose his temper. "But your kind took what they wanted." Brother Mellitus raised his mug as if toasting. "You're right. It's our land now."

"The earth belongs to no one and everyone. Everything has a spirit. The Great Spirit gave the world to all."

Brother Mellitus crossed his legs, and his skirt snaked around. "God is the Creator, boy. His message is written in the Bible. I can read it. I know what you believe, spirit animals, Mother Earth, Father Sky."

"Creator, God, Great Spirit, they are words for the same being. What I accept is not much different from your three-in-one God. Nobody seems to explain that."

"Mystery, boy. Not a puzzle to be solved." The mug clunked down on the desk.

"Ah, so you are Apsáalooke, you understand the message of the Great Spirit."

Mellitus sprang from his chair and hovered over Karl. The vein on his forehead pulsed, and his pasty face became ruddy.

Karl reached out and touched the monk's chest.

Mellitus growled. Coffee breath.

He had gone too far. The man raised his hand. Karl closed his eyes. He knew what would happen next.

"Brother Mellitus," Father Lucian shouted.

Karl opened one eye.

"His fault," Mellitus chirped, lowering his arm, and clenching and unclenching his fist.

"He's a child," Lucian hissed.

"No," Karl and Mellitus said together.

Mellitus stepped away and stumbled to his seat. Karl reached out and tapped him. Mellitus whipped around, missing Karl's hand. Today was a counting coup day.

"See what I mean. He won't stop touching me."

"What, are you fourteen too?" Lucian asked as he stepped between Karl and Mellitus.

"He's only fourteen?" Mellitus grabbed his mug, his hand

shaking slightly as if Karl had hidden the truth from him. "Fine, but I see what vexes Sister Mary Joseph. I'm sure you'll receive Extreme Unction sooner than you think."

Father Lucian shook his head and groaned. "Sister riles easy. Brother Mellitus, everyone needs healing in their lives."

"So, it is a healing ceremony," Karl said. "We have that too, only we call it a Sundance."

"Karl, that is enough," Lucian said, his voice firm but gentle.

Karl pursed his lips, but a burning question jumped out. "Why does Marriage cancel Holy Orders?"

"Hold up, Marriage and Holy Orders are two different life paths," Lucian said, shooting a look of disdain at Brother Mellitus, who nibbled on a cookie.

"I will apologize to Sister, so I can make Confirmation and have your Holy Spirit guide. Then I will make a vision quest and receive an animal guide."

"Confirmation is not a vision quest," Mellitus growled. The man looked at Lucian. "You can't be seriously considering this. He just told me he doesn't believe."

"I did not say that," Karl said.

"Our ceremony is a little different. One picks a saint to guide them on their journey. Like you pick an animal guide," Lucian said, taking a seat behind his desk.

Karl picked up his mug and sipped the blackness, savoring the heavy sweetness. Both of his sisters had gone through the ceremony. Marie became more prayerful. The ritual had no effect on Rebecca. She was a warrior to the Crow Nation, not a warrior of the church. Marie selected Saint Bernadette Soubirous because they were always teasing her about her rosary prayers to the Blessed Virgin Mary. Rebecca took Saint Monica because she was the mother of a troublesome man.

Karl shrugged his shoulders. He would rather use an animal

guide. There were four types of animal guides. They come at different times, messages, journeys, life, and shadows. He desired the eagle guide, but he knew that was not how it worked.

"We do not pick the animal, they pick us. Does it have to be a saint? All the ones I researched are creepy."

Father Lucian chuckled. "Yes, a saint. Not all of them carry their eyeballs in their hands."

Karl shuddered. He never liked the statue of Saint Lucy that stood in the nuns' chapel. Every saint he read about was tortured or died young. Karl wasn't sure he wanted that kind of guidance.

"You're not seriously going to allow his early confirmation?" Mellitus asked.

"He shows more understanding than those we confirmed last year. He has more interest. Why postpone when the longing is there?" Lucian asked.

"He's a savage. You can't convert them," Mellitus said. Crumbs of white cookies dotted his black habit.

"Don't be cruel, Brother Mellitus," Lucian said. "Faith comes in stages."

Karl frowned. How could this nettle-man be friends with Father Lucian? Lucian listened when Karl asked questions. He discussed and explained concepts and theories. Mellitus had mud in his ears, and like Sister Mary Joseph, thought Karl wanted to disprove all of Christianity.

"I believe in your Catholic ways, but I also know that everything has a lesson to teach us. Everything possesses a spirit."

"Next, you'll tell me this room talks," Mellitus said, grabbing a second cookie.

"It does."

"Fine, what does the desk say?"

"Stop," Father Lucian said, his voice sounding weary.

Karl stood up and rubbed his fingers on the shiny wood. Spots

184

were cool, and where the coffee mugs sat held a faint warmth. He could make out his reflection on the smooth surface.

"There is no learning, no marks of hard study, no indentations. This desk is for reflection and thinking." Karl turned and moved to an overstuffed chair. "This chair is for relaxing. It calls to me and says come sit and read a book. The church pews say, sit up straight, pay attention. Something important is happening here."

"That is all drivel. It's a piece of lumber," Mellitus said, smacking the desk and then pointing to the chair. "A chair is a frame full of stuffing."

"Brother Mellitus, don't play the devil's advocate. Just admit the boy is right," Father Lucian said, pouring himself a cup of coffee.

"He's not right, pews having spirits, wood asking you to relax, Native nonsense."

Karl picked up a cookie, and his mouth watered.

"I suppose the cookie talked you into eating it."

"Yes, it says eat me, for I am delicious and will nourish you. Just like the bread becoming flesh," Karl murmured as he took a bit of the snickerdoodle, letting the cinnamon sugar tingle his tongue.

"Brother, remember Luke 19: 40, 'Jesus answered, I tell you, if they become silent, the stones will cry out,'" Lucian said.

"You've gone Native, Lucian," Brother Mellitus said, licking his fingers and dotting the plate for crumbs. "I would expect that talk with the Abbot soon."

Lucian was Apsáalooke, even if he didn't know it. Jesus was Apsáalooke, they wrote it in the Bible. Catholic was just another word for Crow. Karl grinned. Catholicism was finally making sense to him.

CHAPTER 17
WEARING WHITE

The worst enemies are ourselves.

Joseph Medicine Crow. 1913-2016. War Chief, author, and historian of the Crow Nation.

Rebecca drove her sky-blue VW down the highway, envisioning herself in white. Today was the day.

Mary, Mother of Perpetual Help Hospital came into sight. The large red brick building looked the same as she remembered it. Rebecca parked, got out of her car, slamming her one yellow door, and stood in front of the entrance. Today, she would make a step toward destiny.

The time had come; she would answer the call of her tribe. Her days of watching her siblings were over. She had graduated with honors from Saint George, a year later than she had hoped, but that was Sister Mary Joseph's fault. The nun added requirements—tests that nobody else had to take—before she allowed Rebecca to graduate.

Rebecca had mapped out how to pay for nursing school. She would begin working as a candy striper and then become an aide while taking classes to become a nurse.

Judith's angry face peered at her in her mind. She could hear her mother complaining that someone needed to help with the younger children. Marie was there. She would help with the little ones. Rebecca pushed Judith's wrath from her head.

Rebecca walked into the business office, pulled out the application, and flattened it before handing the papers to the lady. The woman paused, mesmerized. Rebecca assessed her appearance. Nothing appeared out of place, nobody was behind her. Rebecca's right hand trembled, and her left fist clenched as she shoved both hands into her jeans.

"Is there a problem?" Rebecca asked, trying to keep the anger out of her voice.

"No. Just a second. I have to make a phone call."

Rebecca sat. She had only come to turn in her application, which was due at the end of business today. The woman picked up the phone and squealed into the receiver, "She's here."

Three faces peered from the doorway.

"Is that her?"

Rebecca crossed her arms. Crap, now what? She paid the hospital bill in full a year ago. She should have brought the proof. Was it her name, Knows the Song, or Mackenzie?

Had someone not paid a bill? Momma was a Mackenzie now and had four children at this hospital. Surely Terence paid his bills. Justifications raced through her mind.

A man entered the waiting room. He was clean-shaven, graying, and dressed in a suit. His tag said, 'Dr. Whitmire.' He looked familiar. Is he that administrator, the one who accepted her money back then?

"Miss Knows the Song? Rebecca?" Dr. Whitmire asked, his face bright with excitement.

"Yes, that's me."

The woman handed Whitmire her crumpled application as the other whispering women retreated into the hallway.

Rebecca stood, wishing she had pressed the sheets back into shape before handing them over. She had spent two days laboring, erasing, and picking the right words to go into those papers.

"So, you want to be a nurse?"

Rebecca took a step back.

Why was he acting stupid? Why didn't he look at her papers? Why else would she be here?

Don't sting him yet, cautioned the voice of Grandma Tiama in Rebecca's mind.

She didn't trust her own voice, so she nodded.

"I'm thrilled. I'd hoped this day would come—that you'd choose to enter the medical field. Doctor, nurse, or anything like that. Please follow me. There is so much to show you."

Rebecca shook her head. She had told no one, not even Karl, of her vision in white. Once, when she was younger, she had put on Elanna's nursing uniform. Seeing herself in white had cemented her desire, and every move from that moment forward was to that goal.

"Hold on. I don't need a tour. Are you saying you are letting me into the program?"

"Yes, yes. But you haven't been to the maternity ward."

That was true. When Judith had her babies, she didn't go to the hospital to visit.

"Wait a minute, you didn't even look at what I wrote. Is this a joke? Am I your token Indian? I don't want any handouts." Rebecca crossed her arms and stood defiant.

The gasps from behind the desk told her she had crossed a line.

"No joke. I know who you are. You have nothing to prove. I want you in my program."

Dr. Whitmire headed out of the room. Rebecca scurried to catch up with him as he entered the elevator.

"You have a full ride. Lodging, books, tuition, and a stipend for expenses. It isn't much and you'll live and breathe the program, but you're capable of such dedication because you've done it before."

Rebecca gripped the bar in the elevator, not believing what she was hearing.

The doors to the maternity ward opened. Dr. Whitmire stepped out, and Rebecca followed. She remembered the nurses' station and Orange, the redheaded nurse. The space seemed smaller. The counter no longer towered over her. There were brightly colored walls and decorations making the nurses' station appear more like a nursery school. She turned to follow Whitmire, looking for the glass window with the bassinets of blue and pink blankets. There were none. Where were the babies?

"I don't want labor and delivery or pediatrics," Rebecca said. The application had not specified what kind of nursing. Would he take back the scholarship?

The man chuckled. "I guess I can understand that. You did it right the first time. Why jinx it?"

Did what?

Whitmire paused and pushed his glasses up his angular nose. "The babies are with their mothers. I get complaints saying this isn't the way other hospitals do it. Sometimes the mom is disappointed to start motherhood so soon. Infants thrive when they are with their moms. Come, come."

The elevator dinged and a sea of white-clothed people spilled into the hallway. They moved like a swarm toward her, and they buzzed with excitement. "Is that her? She is so young? How did he know?"

Rebecca noticed a windowed room and froze, recognizing the incubators. This was not the closet space that Karl, Boney, and Daisy had lived in. She wondered how they were doing. Were they as strong and healthy as Karl?

Behind the glass were rocking chairs and cots. The lighting was low, the chairs comfortable, the incubators decorated. Tiny infants were being cuddled and cooed over in their mother's arms.

Rebecca shivered. "I know you. You're that grumpy doctor who sat and stared and told me to fill out forms."

Dr. Whitmire's shoulders slumped for a moment, then he stood tall. "Yes, yes, that was me. Those newborns would not have survived if it weren't for you. You were amazing. No training, no expert advice, and those children survived. This is what you inspired me to accomplish, a unit dedicated to giving these and all infants a fighting chance. So, whatever I can do to help you achieve your dream, it would be my honor."

Dr. Whitmire stepped aside and pointed to the shiny brass plaque that read, 'This Neonatal unit is dedicated to Rebecca Knows the Song.' She ran her hand over the raised letters, so cold to the touch but real. Cheers and clapping erupted around her.

"My dear, you look shaken, pale."

Her knees buckled and someone slid her into a chair. A water glass cooled Rebecca's hand.

"Are you all right?" Dr. Whitmire asked, an expression of great concern creasing his forehead as he held her other hand.

Rebecca let the shock wash through her as she sipped the

water. She pushed the fogginess from her mind as if emerging from a good sweat, from the heat and dimness of the teepee to the freshness of outside. She looked again at the brass plaque. She had a unit named after her, and she wasn't even a nurse. She grinned. "I'm great, just forgot to eat."

Dr. Whitmire continued to talk, and Rebecca listened. Half listened, for her spirit was soaring higher than she ever dreamed possible. She felt the dizzy rush that an eagle must feel when she dives to the earth.

"This is because of the care you gave your brother. How is your brother?"

REBECCA WHOOPED and drummed on her steering wheel as she drove home. Nursing school. Freedom. Her dreams were coming true. She was on the right path. Guilt tried to slip into the passenger's seat, making her worry about leaving Karl. She had worked hard to keep the peace. Would it last without her? Maybe. Karl had a job, and Terence sometimes took Karl with him on accounting trips. He was safer with Terence than alone with Judith.

"I can take care of myself," he had told her. He was fifteen. Yet she knew that taking care of himself meant he could turn on the washing machine and make a peanut butter sandwich. Bills, housing, and expenses were not even in his thoughts.

How would Judith and Terence react to the news? She shook the demons away and rolled down her window.

"I'm going to be a nurse," she shouted to the herd of elk. "He named a ward after me and I'm not even a registered nurse."

She pulled up to the farmhouse and sat in the car. The windows glowed onto the porch. She wondered if she would miss this place like she missed the Rez.

The front door opened, sending a flood of light down the front steps.

"Becca's home," the twins Vicki and Vincent screamed from the doorway, and then they slammed the door shut. Such an opposite pair, she full of spice and he of sweetness.

She entered the foyer to the sound of Judith's voice coming from the kitchen.

"Karl, wait until your father gets home. Stop picking on your brother," came Judith's high-pitched voice from the kitchen in Apsáalooke.

She turned to see Karl with his arm stretched out, pushing on Tommy's head, holding him back as the boy swung wildly, hitting nothing but air. Davy was wailing, although nobody was near him. The twins were running in circles. Vincent paused as Vicki crashed into him. She yowled and Rebecca picked her up as Judith flew out of the kitchen brandishing a handled cutting board. Judith stopped short when she saw Rebecca. Karl and Tommy abandoned the mock fight and plopped to the floor into a cuddle. Davy continued to howl.

She would not miss the noise.

Judith glanced at the children.

"What is your problem, Davy? Stop that noise. Rebecca, where have you been? It's almost dinnertime." She turned, marching back to the kitchen. Rebecca patted Vicki's back while Vincent hugged her leg. The aroma of dinner made her stomach growl.

"Where were you?" Karl asked, dangling his brother over his shoulder.

"Later," she said, grinning like a fox in winter.

Karl followed her as she headed upstairs. "What have you done?"

"I'll be wearing white," she whispered as the rest of the children trailed behind Karl.

He stopped and grabbed her arm. "You are going to nursing school?"

"*Shhh*, I'm going to announce it after dinner."

Karl hugged her tightly. Not wanting to miss out, the younger children ran to her and wanted hugs.

She would miss that.

Although the food smelled delicious, Rebecca ate little. The ham was savory, and the roasted root vegetables' aroma lingered on her plate as she moved them from one side to the other. Karl sat grinning and toeing her under the table as he leaned back after cleaning his plate of seconds. The joy in his eyes mirrored the excitement she felt.

"I've some news," Rebecca said as the dinner plates vanished. "I've a full scholarship for nursing school through the hospital, Mary, Mother of Perpetual Help, and Dr. Whitmire."

"Way to go, Becca," Karl said.

"How did that happen?" TK asked.

"I applied and got accepted. They want me."

"A full scholarship. That's wonderful," Terence said. "Congratulations, I'm proud of you."

Terence approved, and she didn't even have to argue her desire.

"It means living in the nursing complex," Rebecca said, glancing from Karl to Marie. Could they survive without her?

"You mean moving out?" Marie asked, setting the dessert bowls on the table with a loud clunk.

Rebecca nodded as Vincent climbed into her lap. Marie's face tightened as if in pain. Everyone was silent. Rebecca held her breath.

Support me, Marie. Say something.

"You cannot," Judith said, and Rebecca's stomach knotted.

"I agree with Mom," Karl said, grabbing bowls and handing them out.

Judith glared and pursed her lips.

"Who will read us bedtime stories?" Davy and Tommy asked.

"This is Rebecca's life. She gets to choose," Terence said. "We'll miss her, but I'm sure she'll visit."

"No, I need her at home," Judith said.

"I agree with Mom," Karl said again, winking at Rebecca with a grin. He was playing a dangerous game, shaming Judith.

"Stop that. This is your fault. You put those ideas into your sister's head."

"Dear, children grow up and leave home. This is natural, normal," Terence said, patting her arm.

Judith crossed her arms. A battle was brewing. Vincent snuggled close.

"She's not going," Judith said, standing up.

Rebecca recoiled. She hadn't expected a protest from Judith.

"I agree with you. Who will help with the little ones?" Karl said, slumping back in his chair as if defeated by the news.

"I can do that," Marie whispered as she folded and unfolded her napkin.

Ouch, *Basooke*. She wanted her sister's blessing, but she would go with or without it. Guilt washed over Rebecca had she just sentenced Marie to ten years of child-rearing. Judith's hand smacked the table.

"I'm the mother. I can take care of my children."

Rebecca, Marie, TK, and Karl all exchanged quick glances. They realized that was nowhere near the truth. The tension rose.

"But all the laundry, meals, baths, bedtime stories, not to mention cooking and shopping," Karl continued, his voice smooth like a babbling brook. "I think you are right. She needs to stay."

"Son," came the warning from Terence.

Rebecca agreed with Terence. *Karl, stop baiting her.*

Judith stood, her face red and body trembling. "How dare you? I'm capable. I don't need her help. If anyone leaves, it should be you."

"Where would I go, *Ihkaa*? I would not abandon you," Karl said, his words coated with sarcasm.

Rebecca grimaced. He called her Momma. Here we go, down the badger hole.

"Karl, enough," Terence said, his words clipped.

"I don't need your help. I don't need her help."

"Well, if you insist. I guess Rebecca can go to nursing school since you are so proficient," Karl said, pushing the pie toward TK for cutting. Marie twisted her napkin into a rope and rocked. Tommy banged his spoon in a rapid rhythm that echoed in her heart. Davy sniffled. They all knew what was coming. Terence slapped Karl's face for his disrespectful tone.

Judith stood trembling and swaying, gripping the chair for support.

"You should never have survived," Judith said, her voice ragged.

"Yeah, well, live with it," Karl said, rubbing his reddening cheek.

Rebecca was sure a beating was coming. Judith let out a moan, and Terence hurried to her side.

Rebecca frowned at Karl. She didn't know which stung more, the slap or the cutting words.

"Judith, are you all right?" Terence asked.

"I've got a headache. Rebecca, see to the twins," Judith said as she teetered away from the table. Rebecca placed her hand on her mother's arm.

"Of course, Mother," Rebecca said as Karl rubbed his cheek. As much as she liked what he did, it was a dangerous risk.

"Nurse Becca, Nurse Becca," the twins chanted.

Terence helped his wife down the hall. Once they were out of sight, TK cut the pie.

"You get no pie," Rebecca hissed at Karl.

"No pie, no pie," the twins continued.

"Hush or no pie for you two," Rebecca said.

The twins giggled at her threat as she stroked Davy's head to calm his whimpers.

"You're a jerk," Rebecca said to Karl.

"Most people say 'thank you' when you help them. I got you out of the insane asylum. You owe me."

He was right. She owed him for her nursing career. If he hadn't been born early, she'd never have gone to the hospital and taken care of him. Dr. Whitmire would never have seen her.

"They named the ward after me," Rebecca said, grinning. Karl beamed back at her.

"Yep, you owe me big time."

CHAPTER 18
PASQUE FLOWERS

May the stars carry your sadness away,
May the flowers fill your heart with beauty,
May hope forever wipe away your tears,
And, above all, may silence make you strong.

Geswanouth Slahoot (Chief Dan George). 1899-1981. Chief of the
Tsleil-Waututh Nation, an actor, musician, poet, and author.

Karl hoped the gift of the medicinal plants would appease his sister when she saw them. He needed her nursing touch. The cut on his cheek kept pulling open every time he ate.

His fingers burned from the oil of the pasque flowers and he regretted not grabbing gloves. The plant blanketed the prairie this time of year. The dazzling, caustic, solitary, bell-shaped lavender flower returned every spring. If left to seed, the prairie would turn into a foggy carpet of white. "Prairie smoke" is what folks called it when it went to seed. Karl loved that name. The legend stated the plant grew in places that were soaked by the blood of Romans or Danes. The medicine women had used this flower for medicine long before Romans or Danes had invaded the land. It was purple and Karl wondered if the blood of Romans and Danes was purple rather than red.

He carefully placed the flowers in the brown paper sack, which was now overflowing.

He hadn't seen Rebecca in a while. Their time together had become sporadic in the last year since she had moved out. He didn't run to her every time things got violent at home. Bruises and welts healed fine on their own. Today was a Karl holiday—the day after a beating. All had entered the circle of silence. Secrets.

He made his way to Rebecca's apartment. Her blue VW bug with the one yellow door was in the parking lot.

He was aware of real secrets, like the one he carried with him today. He had been thinking of staying permanently with her. She had a spare room, and he knew he was welcome to stay.

Rebecca looked over her shoulder as he entered and nodded. He showed her the bag of flowers before placing them on the counter that separated the kitchen from the small living room and washed his hands.

"Frost tonight, it was today or next year," Karl said, thinking that Mother Nature was being cruel to wipe out the first food for the bees. He would miss the smoky seed pods that followed the lavender blooms.

"Gloves would prevent blisters," Rebecca scolded as she made her way to the counter. "Why aren't you in school?"

"Karl holiday. Or, as we used to say, Karl is sick today," he said, turning to face her.

Rebecca grimaced when she saw his face. Karl grabbed a cola. He sat in one of the two chairs at the counter. Rebecca took down the first aid kit.

"Hey, be gentle," Karl said as she dabbed antiseptic on his face. The black eye was coming. He could feel it.

Rebecca reached for his shirt, as she had done when he was a boy. He pushed her hand away. The closeness between them had faded, and he saw the embarrassment on her face.

"Sorry," she mumbled as she straightened her shoulders. She was like the cat that slept on the porch rail. He occasionally would fall into the bushes and saunter out undaunted tail high saying, "That was planned."

"I miss you," Karl said, rising and going back into the kitchen. He took the tin of sweet potato pie from the stovetop and placed it on the island counter. Rebeca's roommate, Faith Dawson, was an excellent cook. Every time he visited, there were homemade treats.

"Why this time?" Rebecca asked as she took his cola. "You're fifteen now. This should not be happening. You're stronger than him."

"I will not hit him. He is not the problem. Judith is the problem. She sets him up. She frightens me. Yes, I know I could squash her. What would I tell the *Bakuupe*? They are still young and don't understand her anger. Hell, I do not understand her anger."

The faces of the *Bakuupe*, his siblings peeking around the corner with large, frightened eyes, loomed in his memory.

They looked at each other. Terence was not a bad man; he had a sickness. Once he reached a critical point, he got violent, and all Karl could do was wait it out. Terence cared, and Judith dared. Terence hugged and hit. Judith hated. Karl understood that.

"You were born. That's your crime. At least in Judith's eyes. Terence, I can't explain."

"Hardly my fault being born. I should work harder at not

pissing Judith off. But sometimes I suspect she spends the whole day dreaming up something to blame me for. *Axee* does not see or hear her little barbs. I do not bait easily anymore, but I tire of watching my every word," Karl said, licking his fork of the spicy goodness.

Rebecca got two plates from the cupboard and a fork.

"I wish you wouldn't call him *Axee*."

Karl frowned as they stood side by side, leaning on the counter. He knew it irritated her. His fondness for Terence.

"He is my dad. He is the man who says he loves me, holds me accountable, and encourages me. He takes me with him, camping, hunting, fishing, accounting. He read me stories, tucked me in, and held me when I cried."

Rebecca stabbed the pie like a drunk surgeon.

"What do you remember about our real *Basaake*, Endow?"

Karl tried to picture the man Endow, his biological father. He was tall and wore fancy boots with a peacock on them. Karl had only been six when he had found Endow dead in the field. They fished and hunted together, and he had spun many tales.

"I remember a poodle lamp and my friends, Juniper and Tiny. The End of the Road Tavern, and Dan. What do you remember?"

The bartender let him, Juniper, and Tiny hang there on weekends and play pool when the weather was too cold to play basketball.

Rebecca snorted. "Poison. Brown bottle poison. Judith and Endow were like the pasque flower. Once planted, it takes over. Endow would beat Judith. That's why you came early. Maybe that is why she hates you. Her spirit is damaged."

A tightness gripped Karl's chest as if someone were hugging him hard. He closed his eyes. That quickening in his gut when voices rose an octave higher. The inner tension when alcohol-coated breath came his way. Is that how it would be for his siblings, free-floating anxiety?

"That does not make sense. You would think she would be happy her baby lived. Did he drink a lot?"

"Yes. His drinking and violence were like the seasons. One followed the other. You are his son. You resemble him, except you have blue eyes."

Rebecca placed slices of pie on plates.

"I am not violent," Karl said, taking a swallow from the bottle of cola. The memories of the past were tainted with a child's perception of normalcy. "It is what it is," rang in his mind.

They stood in silence. The faucet dripped. The atmosphere was akin to sitting in a field during a thunderstorm, excitement, and fear. Their eyes met.

"Why do you think Jimmy drinks?"

"Not sure. The medical books say it's in the genes."

"We seem to draw the luck on recessive," Karl said, pointing to his blue eyes.

"We make our own luck. Why aren't you leaving?"

"That's our *ashishkawuuhawate*," Karl said, thinking how much he would miss the younger ones and Terence, the chaos of joy that sometimes rang through the house.

"Make your own family. I'm *ashishkawuuhawate*, too," Rebecca said as she shoved a piece of pie into her mouth.

Was that an invitation to live with her? Was that a possibility, even if temporarily? The sad face of Terence loomed in Karl's mind.

He couldn't leave the farmhouse, not yet. She would not like the truth. He needed Terence's love. He wanted Judith's too but knew that would probably never happen. Even if she didn't love him, the yearning for her affection didn't go away. He couldn't please her, but he could please Terence. The man called him son said, "I love you, I'm proud of you." Claimed him as his own, with no hesitation or angst.

Rebecca wouldn't understand that need, so he said, "Jimmy left us. I do not know him. I want Tommy, Davy, and the twins to remember me. And I worry Judith will turn on them." He was reaching for stars. Judith was the doting model mother to her four younger children and gave TK the affection Karl yearned for.

"That's bullshit. You know Judith would never harm those kids. They are her real children. We are her other children, excluding Marie. If you would embrace the white ways, she would have less to complain about. That is how Marie does it."

Karl grinned. That had backfired.

"If Endow was so bad, why did Judith stay?" Karl asked, poking at his pie. "We are supposed to take care of our own. I am all the *bakuupe* have. They are my siblings."

"I don't think your staying will help them," Rebecca said, pointing her fork at him.

When Endow and Jimmy left, Karl felt empty. The birth of his younger siblings had filled that. Now she wanted him to walk away from them. Where were her family connections, her clan, her community? Was she being lured into the white man's world of individuality? He wasn't into basketball or the brown bottle.

"Who do you want me to be?" Karl said, anger rising in his voice. "If I do not finish school, I will be another Rez dropout. The nuns will not take me like they took Marie. I have no intention of joining the monastery, as much as I like Father Lucian. Their ways are strange to me."

Rebecca's bottle of cola clunked on the counter. Was she angry? No, that was a look of surprise. Crap.

"Marie did not tell you. Good news, our sister is a nun. Last September, she dumped her clothes into a bag and carried them to school. I thought she was on one of her 'clothes-for-the-poor' kicks. But, that day, she gave me a note and walked into the convent." Karl grinned. Marie had guts. She just walked out. Karl admired her bravery. Even when Judith went to bring her home, Marie stayed. Judith blamed him as if he convinced the nuns to kidnap her.

"Why did they take her? She's odd. They realize this, don't they? They have seen her moments."

"Is it not obvious? They could not save you, so they saved her. Marie is happy. She goes around humming hymns. They have her working with the first graders. The little kids adore her. I will miss Marie when she has to live at the motherhouse in Texas."

"You have to leave," Rebecca said. She stood and donned gloves, and then placed the newspaper on the table before laying the pasque flowers out. The silky white hairs lay like fur on the stems. Once dried, the herb could be used as a sedative or pain relief.

He had made it seven months without her or Marie. Maybe he didn't need her protection anymore.

"I am a man. I can manage this."

The bedroom door opened, and Faith stepped into the living room. She stretched and wiggled, wrestling with the grip of sleep.

Faith paused, glancing at the bag of flowers lost in the vision of prairie whiteness.

"Who is having trouble sleeping?"

"Rebecca has boils," Karl said, grinning, knowing that the herb treated both insomnia and skin conditions when dried.

Rebecca sneered at him as she arranged the flowers to dry.

"You are eating my pie," Faith said.

"A man takes what he needs," Karl said.

"A man provides," Faith said.

"How many pumpkins would you like?" Karl asked, leaning closer to her, and taking in her almond and lavender scent. She was pretty with her hair all tussled from sleep in her tee shirt that read "Exclusively Rez," and red gym shorts. Karl glanced at her long legs as she moved past him into the kitchen to get herself coffee. She stood next to him and pulled the pie tin toward her. He offered her his used fork.

"Ouch," Faith said, dabbing his bruising cheek.

Karl shivered.

"Just a minor bump, roughhousing with the *bakuupe*. They outnumber me." Time to change the subject. "Becca, Tiny is finally going on a vision quest."

"How old is Tiny?" Faith asked.

"He is sixteen. He has been postponing because he wanted to be taller."

Rebecca laughed. "His name is Tiny."

"I think he is afraid he will walk out with the spirit guide of an ant or pygmy rabbit."

"Small guides are good," Faith said. "Sometimes it's hard to live up to your name. I had several sisters—Hope, Charity, Patience, and Grace—and two brothers, Todd and Tad. The Elders named us girls after virtues."

"The Elders can be mischievous," Karl said. "So, do they live up to their names?"

"Mostly, all except Patience. She was not that. They are all gone now."

"All of them?" Karl asked, wanting to embrace her for so many losses.

"It's just me and Todd," Faith said. Her face softened with sadness.

"I am sorry," Karl said. That explained why Todd was always in a grim mood and protective.

Karl had met Todd several times when he had come looking for Rebecca. The man was older than Becca. Karl felt he should show him respect, but he was not sure how. Todd was serious and solemn. Life had worn away his skin and left him with bare bones. Losing your family would be unbearable. He would be kinder to him in the future.

"But Todd has you," Karl said. "He has faith."

She laughed at his lame joke as Rebecca groaned from the living room.

"Todd is going to bring Carrie Little Owl over. Odin and Sleeps in the River are her parents, Crashes in the Night and Jean, her grandparents. She's in nursing school. I thought since we had the space," Faith said.

Karl waved a fork at Faith. "You are giving away my room? It's okay. Carrie is Lakota. I like Lakota. And she is cute. Okay, I will share with her."

Rebecca shook her head. "We have a sofa, and she's going to be a nurse. Besides, she's too old for you."

"I could be a nurse. If girls can be nurses, why not boys?" Karl said, knowing he had zero interest in dealing with sick and crabby people. "I like older women. You can have a boyfriend and study nursing."

Karl was sure Rebecca enjoyed sticking needles into the opposite gender. She never dated and frightened most men away with her determination and bluntness. Her single-mindedness was a virtue, but he wondered if she was ever lonely.

"You can't even remember to cover your hands when picking pasque flowers. A Lakota woman has standards, requirements," Faith said. "You need to be as smart as your mate, have a home, a job, and a car."

There was the proof that Faith was smarter than him. Karl smiled, thinking he had a job and a car. Two out of four.

"Marriage is sacred to us. The couple balances each other. He brings courage, generosity, wisdom, and bravery and she, fruitful-ness, faith, industriousness, and hospitality."

"I know those virtues. They are very Benedictine," Karl said.

Rebecca groaned, finished layering the flowers, and headed to the kitchen to wash the tongs.

"What is Benedictine?" Faith asked, sipping her hot coffee.

The door to the apartment opened, and Todd entered with Carrie Little Owl.

"The black robes' way," Todd said, a scowl on his face.

"I will teach you," Karl whispered to Faith. "When he is not around."

Todd turned and looked at Rebecca. His harsh tone changed to gentle kindness as he said, "Carrie, this is Rebecca."

Carrie blushed and said, "I've heard so much about you."

Todd squeezed between Rebecca and the wall, moving toward the kitchen, but he lingered a moment, his towering body pressed behind her.

Rebecca took in a deep breath and stood a little stiffer. She didn't move to give him more room or easier passage.

Todd glanced and then studied Karl's face before pouring himself a cup of coffee. They crowded the narrow kitchen. Karl could smell the lingering aroma of cedar and sage from Todd.

"You should learn to duck. Or curb your attitude," Todd said, his voice once again hard.

Karl narrowed his eyes into a glare. He knew the man was teasing him, but the remark still stung.

"Stop picking on him," Rebecca said, stepping out of the kitchen to the living room where Carrie stood wide-eyed in Rebec-ca's adoration.

That stung too, having his big sister still sticking up for him like that. She needs to stop that. *Move on, my warrior sister, move on.*

Todd glanced at the layers of pasque and newspaper. "Planning on murdering someone?"

If they ate the flower in its current state, it would be toxic, causing severe kidney damage and paralysis. Rebecca turned and smiled at Todd before addressing Carrie.

"Welcome, Carrie. Let me show you the space. We have one rule: no overnight visitors unless they are family, and I mean the white man's definition of family."

"Got it," Carrie said with a grin as wide as the Little Big Horn River.

Todd laughed. Rebecca and Carrie left the room.

"You didn't touch that plant, did you?" Todd asked.

Karl moved his blistered hand out of sight.

"Be kind," Faith said. "She is drying these. The herb dried and crushed will convert the enzyme to a non-toxic substance and then she can use it to treat many things, like insomnia."

"Do you feel like taking a nap?" Karl asked Todd.

Todd raised an eyebrow, glanced at his coffee cup, and set it on the counter.

"You are a wise man," Karl said.

"Don't be silly. I'm drinking the coffee," Faith said as she yawned and then laid her head on Karl's shoulder.

"You two are not funny," Todd said.

Karl suppressed a grin and relished the warmth of her breath on his neck.

Todd raised the mug but sniffed it before setting it down without drinking. Faith rose and chuckled at her brother as she headed to her room. Karl fought the desire to follow her, resolving to be in the apartment more often. Perhaps Rebecca was right. It was time to leave Terence and the siblings to form a new clan, a new *ashishkawuuhawate*.

CHAPTER 19
MISTER MOOSE

In our every deliberation, we must consider the impact of our decisions on the next seven generations.

Iroquois Confederacy Maxim (*ca* 1705). The Iroquois are a historically powerful northeast Native American confederacy. Known in colonial times as the Iroquois League and the Five Nations. Today they are the Six Nations. They absorbed many displaced peoples.

R ebecca walked out of the hospital from her graveyard shift. The parking lot was quiet, nearly empty. The streetlights flickered off and then on. The sun was still sleeping. She pulled her jacket tight around her as the morning air kissed her cheeks. With each step closer to home, her body relaxed. Her apartment building came into view. At the entrance, she stopped because a moose blocked the doorway.

The Creator had leftover parts when she put you together. Your small, long head doesn't fit well on your body. Your antlers look like carved bowls. What is that hanging from your neck? You are a horse gone wrong.

The beast raised his monstrous head, blocking out the overhead lighting.

"What do you want Mister Moose?"

He pawed the concrete and the sound was thunderous.

"Twig eater, there are no branches here. Just mortar and brick."

He was a wild beast. She dared not pass him. She waited, remembering the myth of Creation. A woman of the Potawatomi Nation was to populate the world. She invited all kinds of beasts and birds to come to her, yet none proved worthy to father her offspring, and she rejected them all until she met the moose. Rebecca smiled. She understood that. No male of her own species interested her. She thought of the Potawatomi woman selecting a moose. He looked clumsy and yet graceful. This bull was a symbol of strength and protection. She knew one didn't challenge a mother moose.

"No females need mating, Mr. Moose. And I'm not interested. Move along now."

The moose wagged his heavy head and snorted.

"Don't disagree with me," she said. "I'm not a HEA girl." She watched women look for Mister Perfect so they could live HEA— *happily ever after.*

Mr. Moose swung his head and turned to amble down the walk, a slow clopping of his hooves, a beat of four. The sound reminded Rebecca of an irregular heartbeat. She watched him saunter through the parking lot, past her VW bug.

Why was he here? His visit signified to her that she needed to reflect and connect with her inner wisdom. She avoided interference with her nursing goals. Dating was a distraction. People were an interruption. Recently, an orderly had been lingering after her shift. Once she realized his intent, she had avoided him. She wasn't against romance. She didn't have the time.

She unlocked the door to the apartment and was greeted with quiet darkness. The sofa was empty. Karl was usually on the sofa. His bag of chips and empty cola bottle told her he had been there. She looked for his jacket and shoes. They were gone.

Was Karl all right? He said he could manage, but he always said that. Even with his frequent visits, things were different. They were both busy. She missed the closeness they had.

Rebecca opened her bedroom door, slipped out of her scrubs, and got into a long tee shirt and torn jeans. She grabbed her soft robe from the pile of laundry that lay on her bed.

"He's a man," Tiama's voice scolded. "Everyone grows up."

In the kitchen, she grabbed a cola and sat in the predawn light. Growing up Mackenzie wasn't always good. Her empty bed called to her.

The bedroom door opened with a squeak, and Faith rushed out. Rebecca sipped her cola and listened to Faith vomiting in the bathroom.

Was she sick or stressed? In a few weeks, Faith would graduate. She couldn't be that worried about a job. Her tribe would snatch her up in a second. If the stomach flu was lingering, she would have heard.

Rebecca reflected over the last few weeks. Faith had been sick in the morning. Mister Moose's visit made sense now. Faith was pregnant.

Pregnant. Rebecca shook her head to dispel the reality. Faith was smarter than that. Who was the father? Faith rarely went out partying. Todd kept close tabs on her, always hovering nearby. He really needed to give her space.

Faith crept to her room.

Rebecca took a long drink of her cola. *But if she is, Todd won't be happy.*

A door opened with a squeak. Karl, dressed in a tee shirt and jeans, wandered into the living room.

"Where did you come from?" she asked, wondering if he had been sleeping in her room.

"Judith's womb, but my sister might have just picked me out of the pumpkin patch," Karl said.

"Not funny. You better not be sleeping with Carrie," Rebecca said.

Karl paused as he grabbed the chip bag next to the sofa and made his way to the kitchen.

"I am not playing with Carrie," Karl said, shaking the bag of chip crumbs into his hand.

Chips for breakfast. He should eat better—he was so skinny.

"You best be using condoms, or she'll end up like Faith."

"I am not doing anything with Carrie. What do you mean, 'end up like Faith'?" Karl asked, getting a cola bottle out of the refrigerator.

"There's a moose downstairs, visiting."

"A moose? Real or a dream?" Karl asked, opening the cola bottle.

"Flesh and blood. He told me Faith is pregnant," Rebecca said as the bottle in Karl's hand came crashing to the floor.

Rebecca jumped and moved to help Karl clean up the mess. He was grinning. That impish grin.

Crap. She didn't believe it. He had to be joking with her.

She detected the aroma of almonds and lavender on him. He smelled like Faith.

"It's yours, isn't it?" Rebecca said, stepping back, reading the look of surprise, fear, and delight racing across her brother's face.

Karl's grin grew wider.

The glass pieces clunked in the trash can.

"No, no, no." Rebecca threw a towel at him, but wanted to throttle him.

He looked up at her, beaming like the dawn.

"You don't get it, do you? You're only sixteen. She's older than you. There are laws. You aren't even out of high school. What were you thinking?"

Faith's door opened.

Rebecca shoved Karl's head down behind the counter.

"Morning," Faith said. "I need saltines."

Rebecca placed the box of ordinary soda crackers on the counter for Faith.

Faith grabbed for the package, glanced nervously around, and then joined Rebecca at the counter. She unwrapped the stack, pulled one out, and nibbled.

They stared at each other.

"Yes," Faith said.

"But we are nurses. We know how to prevent..."

Karl pinched Rebecca's hand, and she yanked at his hair.

"Yea, well love, passion, what can I say? I'm pregnant," Faith said.

The door to the apartment opened and Todd walked in. The odor of burned wood lingered around him. He had obviously come directly from work or the fire line. It wasn't an unpleasant odor. It reminded Rebecca of teepees and powwows. She was aware that when smoke lingered, it usually meant terrible things had happened to someone. His presence always remained long after he left. In his firefighter gear or out, he was warrior built, tall, muscular, dark, and brooding. A model for those romance novels Carrie was always reading. She shook her head to dispel the Gothic thought.

"What the hell is going on?" Todd said, ignoring Rebecca and standing over Faith.

Rebecca was surprised. He was usually polite and calm. She glanced down at crouching Karl and slashed her hand in the air, signaling him to lie low.

"Todd, not today," Faith said through tight lips.

He crossed his arms. "If not today, then when? Six months from now?"

Faith's jaw tightened, and she drew in a sharp breath.

"This doesn't concern you. I have it taken care of."

Rebecca wondered how he knew. Did Mr. Moose tell him, too?

"You promised to finish school. How is that possible now?" He shook his head, and his long thick hair swayed. Faith stood, and her face soured. She pushed him aside and dashed to the bathroom.

The sound of retching filled the silence.

Todd turned to Rebecca, his breath warm and smoky. His eyes narrowed in disdain.

"How did this happen? Don't you enforce the rules?"

Rebecca flared. How dare he taunt her?

"People need to follow rules."

"Do you know who the father is?"

"No, don't have a clue," Rebecca said, pushing harder to keep Karl down.

Todd stared at her, through her.

His face hardened, the vein on his neck swelled, pulsed.

"Tell me." His voice low, enticing.

Rebecca stiffened. Scenes of Terence and Karl flashed in her mind.

Duck. He wouldn't dare, would he?

Faith came out of the restroom with a ghostly pallor. Todd turned. Karl's head rose over the counter. Rebecca shoved it down.

"I need to lie down," Faith said, using the wall for support. Todd moved toward her, escorting her to the bedroom. Their voices rose from murmurs to shouts.

"Leave now," Rebecca said to Karl.

"No, I am not leaving her. She is having my baby."

Rebecca smacked the back of Karl's head.

"And Todd is acting like a mother moose. He will," Rebecca said as the door to the bedroom flew open. Todd rushed out with Karl's desert boots in his hand.

"Where in the nation is he?" Todd shouted, anger and disbelief fighting for control of his face.

Too late for a quick escape now.

Faith grabbed her brother's arm. "Stop, Todd, please. This isn't our way."

He turned so quickly that she stumbled. Karl pushed Rebecca aside to catch Faith. They both ended up at the feet of the Lakota warrior.

Karl sat with his arms wrapped around Faith.

"Are you alright?"

Todd shook with rage.

"Faith, we are leaving. Come," Todd said, in a parental tone.

Rebecca almost laughed. Did he think a command would sway her? This man had sisters, and yet he was clueless to their ways.

Faith didn't move. Todd stood over them, arms crossed.

"We adhere to the old ways. He does not. What were you thinking? He's a kid," Todd said, his voice now pleading.

"I'm having this child. We'll raise her in the old ways and the new," Faith said from Karl's arms.

Anger filled Rebecca. He was Indian; he too lived in both worlds. Living on the Rez did not protect you from the outside world. The balance between the old and the new ways caused tension.

Rebecca placed a hand on Todd's arm.

He shook her off.

Karl stood. The gangly, blue-eyed Crow challenged the Lakota warrior.

Todd's arm flexed.

"We are going to have a baby. We are going to be family," Karl said as he extended his hand. "My daughter will need her uncle."

Seconds passed. Breaths labored.

"I love him," Faith said into the silence.

Todd stalked out, slamming the door behind him.

Faith embraced Karl with a sob. Rebecca's stomach twisted. She stared at them. She looked at Karl.

She loves him.

Karl was a kid. Impulsive, smart-mouthed, impetuous, kind, irreverent, and compassionate but a kid. What wasn't there to love? Who was this brother? When did he become a man?

She raced out of the apartment to the parking lot and crashed into Todd. He grunted from the impact. Mister Moose stood like an oak in front of them, one eye focused on the sound as he munched on the last of the twigs in the planter box. Drool dripped on Todd's boot. The animal dwarfed the warrior. Rebecca attempted to step to the right, but Todd tugged her to the left.

"*Aho*, message delivered. This one has her calf and bull. Move on," Rebecca said, bowing her head slightly and wondering why he pulled her left.

The moose snorted, his ear twitched, he raised his head with a jerk and one antler thudded to the ground. Rebecca heard Todd swallow.

"Thank you," he said in a husky, unsure voice.

The moose ambled past them as if they were statues. They watched him until he was barely visible in the tree line.

"Good morning world," Rebecca said.

The gift of the antler lay next to Todd's feet on the walkway. Moose drool dripped from his boot.

"He has been here, waiting. I didn't get his message until now. He informed me that Faith was pregnant."

"Who are you? Dr. Dolittle?"

He was angry, and in his anger, he was speaking with disrespect. She placed her hands on her hips. "You know better. The spirit world speaks all the time. You just must listen. A moose visiting has meaning."

"What did he say this time?"

"I need to stand up for what I believe in. He told me not to stand silent about something I'm not comfortable with. And I'm not pleased with you walking out on your sister."

They stood in the long silence of the new morning.

"I need a drink. You coming?" Todd said, reaching down and lifting the thirty-pound antler with ease.

Todd put the antler in his truck bed and climbed in, opening the passenger door for Rebecca.

She needed to convince him to be there for this. They had to help them.

They arrived at The End of the Road Tavern. Todd glanced at Rebecca and handed her a green plaid Pendleton to replace the bathrobe she was wearing. As she slipped out of the truck, the jacket wrapped her in his smoky scent.

Even though it was barely nine in the morning, the tavern was not empty. The smell of bacon floated in the air.

They sat at a table, looking out the dirty window. Dark beer foamed and dripped down the side of Rebecca's glass. Todd wiped the ceramic ashtray out with a napkin. He took out an elk-skin pouch.

She didn't know he smoked.

Instead, he took a pinch of tobacco and placed it in the ashtray and lit it, setting the pouch and lighter to the left.

There was that left thing again.

Smoke rose and sweetness filled the stale air. Todd bowed his head and whispered, "Todd Dawson, Todd Dawson," four times.

"What are you doing?" Rebecca asked.

"We are meeting about something important, are we not? So, for lack of a better term, I am praying," Todd said. "Calling upon family, and the spirit, reminding them of who I am."

Who are you? The angry warrior, the disappointed parent, the protective brother?

Rebecca bowed her head. This wasn't how she prayed.

"What are we going to do?" The tobacco turned to ash.

"She loves him," Rebecca said, raising her beer glass to her lips.

"Why?" Todd's mug clunked on the table, half-empty.

Rebecca had no logical answer to that question. Did love have logic? Terence loves Judith, and she had loved Endow.

"They are in love. We both know that feeling. The protectiveness toward another, the silly pride when they accomplish something. There's no why."

Todd's eyes narrowed. "I recognize why he would love my sister. She has courage, she's alert in mind and spirit and she's strong-hearted."

Rebecca drank deeply of the beer in her stein. Yeah, all women are that. We are the poles of the teepee, holding the family together.

"They made a child. They formed a union. He's a kid. He knows nothing about raising a child. This is not the time. We had a plan, the Nation depends on them."

He was quoting from the women's song. "A nation depends on you, a generation comes from you." She had always liked that song. Grandma Tiama and the women would sing it at the gathering where the young girls were.

"He will learn. I was six when I became a mother. We have four younger siblings. He has experience."

Todd drained his beer and raised his mug, signaling for another of the bartender.

"Six?"

"Yes, my mother was too broken to raise Karl. So, I did it."

He stared at her. Was that admiration in his eyes? She didn't want his awe. She desired his support, his promise that he wouldn't kill Karl in his sleep.

You know nothing. One does what must be done. We do it for the tribe, for family.

"They are too young for this path."

Rebecca knew she had to enlighten him.

"We need to help them. A new generation is coming. We're the Elders. We love them. Let's put aside our differences, our hopes, and help them with theirs."

That was a tall order. Karl still needed to finish high school, get a job, a place to live.

No, this wasn't what she had planned, either. Rebecca slid her silver bracelet off. It was adorned with round circles and animal faces. She opened one and pinched sage powder and sprinkled it on the tobacco embers in the ashtray. She could match ritual for ritual by smudging the negativity, calling for a new beginning between them.

"Powerful medicine you're brewing here. Don't burn down the joint," the bartender said, inhaling the green-scented smoke. He set down two mugs of beer, condensation dripping, forming little puddles of water on the table.

Todd leaned back in his chair. "Do you do that at work?"

"What do you think?" Rebecca retorted. She worked in a

hospital full of *baaishtashfile*, the Crow word for white, and never opened her bracelet there. Yet many times she blessed, and called the ancestors and spirits to help a person in need.

"What else is in that bracelet?"

Rebecca smiled ruefully. "A woman never gives up her secrets. Besides, I'm out when the window to the next life is open. I carry my protection with me."

"What are you talking about? Is someone stalking you?"

She smiled inwardly at his need to protect.

"The window between worlds happens around two in the morning. I carry herbs, powders. I'm not ready to be called away. Spirits can be helpful or troublesome."

Todd leaned back in his chair.

"This brother of yours is doing manly things, but his body tells me he's a boy. I don't know how to treat him."

Rebecca sipped her beer. She wasn't sure how to behave around this new Karl, either. She thought of what made a man. Four virtues came to mind: courage, generosity, wisdom, and bravery. Karl had all that. His wisdom wasn't quite where it should be, but he was young.

"He's a man. He will rise to the challenge." She hoped he would.

"We must raise our children in the ways of our culture. Karl is so *Wasicu*."

Rebecca's fingers gripped her icy mug. This man didn't understand Karl. He shouldn't judge. The Lakota word *Wasicu* was a judgment of Karl's character. It meant he was seeking only what served him, like the white man.

"Calm yourself," Grandma whispered. "Don't shoot your ally."

"We lived on the Rez. Our Grandmother helped raise us. We are damaged. But we've found our path."

More broken than you know.

She shivered, fearing what Terence and Judith would say to this news.

"The next generation depends on them. What gifts does he have? We all have gifts. Do you recognize what your gifts are? Does he?"

Rebecca wrinkled her nose as the sage continued to permeate the air. What was he talking about? Gifts. Did he mean strengths that made them Native?

"The Creator gives us one gift that's stronger than the others. When one goes and looks for their gift, it's revealed to them," Todd explained.

"Are you kidding me?" tumbled out a quick response. "You saw me and Mister Moose. That happens all the time. Karl has been on his vision quest. He hasn't told me about it, but if he has a gift, it will appear. He will use it for the community."

Rebecca started her second beer. Her body relaxed.

Todd grunted and nodded. Rebecca pitched a toothpick pyre and lit it with Todd's lighter. The bartender scowled, and the server clicked her tongue as she brought a glass of water to the table.

"A child is coming. There's no time. We don't need another lost spirit."

"This child won't be lost. His father stands in both worlds," Rebecca said.

Todd crossed his arms. Why was he being so disagreeable? It rankled her that she saw his point.

"Now who sounds *Wasicu*? Warrior, watch and wait." Rebecca wished to find a balance between old and new. Those were the words Karl had preached to her so many times.

Todd sighed, shifting on the bar stool. Gentleness filled his eyes. He had decided.

"We are family." The words stuck in her throat.

Todd placed his hand over hers. The warmth of it spread through her icy fingers, it caused her to shiver.

"I'll try. Lakota and Apsáalooke. I'll learn your ways, respect them, treat them as sacred as my own."

That was too easy. What if he was two-faced?

She didn't understand his spirit, not really. She pulled her hand from his. There was so much at stake. She reached for his tobacco pouch and took a pinch, sprinkling it on the glowing ash of toothpicks. The smoke hovered and rose slowly. This was a sacred moment sealed in smoke and sent to the ancestors.

She needed a promise from him, his word. One day, she would need him to help her. When that day arrived, she wanted him to be warrior Todd. She would need him to rescue Karl and his family.

"I can't explain now. I can't tell you when, but when it arrives, I'll ask for your help. You will come and ask no question, give no judgement. Can you promise me that?" Rebecca asked.

The fire burned. The silence lingered as the beer swam in the veins of her tired body.

"I give you my promise."

Rebecca breathed. Another member of the circle of silence.

CHAPTER 20
AND IT CAME TO BE

How smooth must be the language of the whites,
when they can make right look like wrong, and wrong
like right.

Ma-ka-tai-me-she-kia-kiak (Black Sparrow Hawk). 1767-1838. Sauk, band leader, and warrior.

K arl sat outside of Father Lucian's office door, biting a hangnail, and holding Faith's hand.

"Are you sure?" Faith asked.

"I want to ask, no harm in a request," Karl said. "We can raise the child in all the teachings—Lakota, Apsáalooke, and Catholic."

"That might confuse them."

"Or give them options," Karl said, thinking that understanding the fundamental beliefs had given him compassion for those different from himself.

Faith moved his hand to her belly. He could feel the movement of his child.

"I guess she agrees with you. Outvoted this time," Faith said.

Sister Mary Agnes, flanked by Sister Marie, moved down the hallway toward them. His sister, Sister Marie, was now a novice, and her white veil accented her dark skin and hair. Her black habit appeared newly pressed, and she stood wringing her scapular until Sister Mary Agnes gently took her hands. She stared at him. She hadn't seen his bruises in a while.

He caused her distress, and he was sorry. Once wed, life would become normal. He smiled, and his sore cheek and eye ached.

Marie dabbed her eyes with the end of her scapular. "Does it hurt?" Marie asked.

"Nah," Karl said. "Just a little leftover war paint. It will wear away."

Faith squeezed his hand. He had told her about his past, the abuse. Still, he was aware the results took some getting used to.

"You run too close to the edge," Marie said.

"Come with us, dear," Sister Mary Agnes said, holding out her hand to help Faith and her swollen belly rise. "Let the men talk."

Faith rose, their fingers still interlaced. She reluctantly let go, and followed the nuns down the hall, glancing over her shoulder twice until they turned the corner.

He believed that—all would be fine. Everyone had a worry. Rebecca was sure that Todd and the Lakota Nation would spirit Karl away, turning him into a split soul, neither Lakota nor Apsáalooke. Karl realized that would not happen. He had balanced Crow and Catholic, and he moved easily from Indian to white and back.

This was what he needed. He wanted the world balanced for his child.

The door to the office opened, and Father Lucian beckoned Karl in.

"Thanks for seeing me."

"Did I have a choice? If I didn't see you, you would corner me in the confessional. So, let's talk," Lucian said as he sat down behind his desk. He looked tired, the creases around his eyes deep, and his skin sagged. "I've talked to your father."

Karl's heart sank. Terence didn't approve or agree. They had argued.

Karl touched his bruise and closed his eyes. He wasn't giving up.

"I need to be married. I am aware of the rules. Faith will allow the children to be baptized."

Lucian's lips pursed into a thin line. He inhaled deeply. Karl turned the damaged side away from the priest as he sat. This small room was familiar to him, as familiar as his bedroom at home. He had spent hours in this space hiding from Sister Mary Joseph and reading volumes of theological works.

"Father, will you marry us? That is all I need."

"No."

Karl's gut clenched as if the man had punched him. *That was quick.*

"Why not?" Karl rubbed his hands on his worn jeans.

"Is Faith even Christian?" Lucian asked, folding his hands.

"No, she is Lakota. They have their own beliefs."

"Will she convert?"

Karl shook his head, glancing at the crucifix, large, looming, hanging on the wall over Lucian's right shoulder.

Faith didn't care for the church and how the so-called Christians treated the Native children in their care. There was nothing Christian about abusing children.

"Marriage is a sacrament. Something one doesn't rush into, no matter the circumstances. If you want a sacramental Marriage, she must convert."

What a hypocrite. "That is silly. I am Catholic. That should be enough," Karl said. "I have the other sacraments. Why deny me now? I will raise the children Catholic."

"The requirements are clear. Baptism isn't the only issue."

Karl realized it was because he wasn't eighteen. He stared at the prayer plant on the table next to the window, its red-veined leaves opened wide to the light.

"You sometimes overlook rules. Like for Marie."

In his mind, Grandma Tiama clicked her tongue. Marie deserved the quiet that the convent offered. After years of violence, the orderly life of a nun brought her peace.

"Sorry," Karl said. "That was unfair to Marie."

The smell of coffee tickled Karl's nose. He could use a cup—or a pot—about now.

"Your father and I spoke…"

Karl jumped up and paced the room. Terence was influential. Did Terence threaten to take away his financial support? He tithed and persuaded others to do the same. Was this about money?

"Terence is upset with me, not with the church. He will not withhold his financial support," Karl said, pausing at the prayer plant and turning the little pot.

Terence was a big benefactor for the church and the school. They named the parish hall after him—Mackenzie Hall. They presented this honor to him for his relentless pursuit to improve the parish, through fundraisers and donations from patrons in town. His stepfather was not rich, but no one could raise money for the church like Terence Mackenzie.

Lucian's chair creaked as he shifted. "No, Terence said nothing about money. He's concerned about your future. This is not a wise choice."

Karl paused at the bookshelves, his fingers running over the titles, spotting ones he had yet to read.

"You cannot predict the future. I plan to graduate and get a job."

"You're not old enough to recognize what's good for you," Lucian said, picking up his mug of coffee.

"Old enough. I can father a baby. I love who I love. I have endured hardships and adversity."

"Enduring is not living," Lucian said as the steam from his mug fogged his glasses.

Karl turned and faced Lucian. The man looked tired. The room stood silent. A bright yellow-and-black insect thumped against the window, trying to find the exit.

"Do I not get a choice?" Karl asked, stepping closer to the light and window. The wasp buzzed and bumped, dancing up and down in its striped regalia.

"You do, but someone has to keep you from making a mistake. I have prayed about this."

Karl had prayed the Catholic way and the Apsáalooke way. This was not a mistake.

Karl turned his bruises to the man.

"What is really going on here?"

"It's not that I don't want to help. I agree with Terence. This is about your future," Lucian said as he glanced away. "I need to do the right thing."

"Why is doing this the right thing? Look at my face. Getting married and leaving is the right choice."

Karl moved to unlatch the window and raised the sash. The wasp hung stubbornly against the glass.

"Think this through. What will happen to the other children when you leave?" Lucian asked, his mug's contents sloshing as his hand trembled.

"They are not the chosen ones."

"The chosen one? Don't blaspheme. It doesn't become you," Father Lucian said, rising to grab a napkin to clean the spill.

"They are not in danger," Karl retorted, regretting the petulance in his voice. He took a breath. "Judith is their mother. She will continue in that role. It will, in fact, be easier on my siblings with me gone."

Judith hated only him. Terence's punishments were reserved for Karl. With his absence, the shadow of violence retreated. A trickle of fear rose. What if that was not true?

"Liar," taunted the wasp as he buzzed louder. Karl reflected on the wasp. His presence was a reminder that merely thinking about his dreams would not make them a reality. Resistance to change was self-sabotage. Was the wasp here for him, or Father Lucian?

"I did not make this problem of Terence and Judith. But right now, I can change it. My brothers and sister will not need to live in fear and lies. You can help me break the circle of silence." Karl watched the priest grimace.

"I pray you are right."

"If I am wrong, will you step in and stop it?" The remark was cruel, but the man needed to see his part.

With a paper cup in hand, Karl placed it over the wasp. The protesting buzz echoed in the cup. Then he grabbed a sheet of paper off the desk, sliding it under the cup until the wasp was trapped.

"When did you make your lifelong commitment? You were young, eighteen, I am almost that. I am aware of what I am doing. Age does not dictate love."

Karl placed the cup outside the window and removed the

paper. The stubborn wasp crawled out onto his hand instead of flying away. He was about to be stung for freeing the insect.

"You don't know what love is," Lucian said, sitting at his desk.

His patience was dripping both for the wasp and the conversation.

"I know what it is not. This is not about love or me. This is about your church and rules." Karl wiggled his finger, and the wasp flew off. "I want to embrace your beliefs."

"Then don't argue with me about this," Lucian said.

"Why the hell not? You preach so many good things, and you called me like an eagle's call. I came and I listened. I want more."

"You can have more," Lucian said.

"At what price? My life? Eventually, I will break. Terence will get mad, and one day I will hit back. My staying teaches my siblings that this violence is love. I do not want to teach that. I must walk out."

"You have so much potential. Don't throw it all away."

Then it hit Karl. This man's kindness had a price. Lucian had plans for him. Karl gripped the door handle and let his head fall to his chest. He heaved a sigh, and looked up at the priest in his black robe.

"You were hoping I would become a monk," Karl said.

Lucian's hands were folded tightly.

"God does the calling, not me."

"You are disappointed, I understand, but a preacher does not need to be ordained. I can be a lay minister or a deacon."

Karl realized that was not good enough.

"Will you at least attend the ceremony?"

"I cannot." Lucian's hands unclasped, and he smoothed the papers on his desk. The words stung, and Karl turned the knob.

"I am disappointed that you put the church above a person. This is not the Jesus you taught me about. You are making a mistake. You will live to regret this. I hope you can live with that," Karl said.

Karl walked out of Father Lucian's office. Head down, and shoulders slumped. He leaned against the brick of the building and sank to his knees. He would miss the music, the rituals, and the feeling of community. Tears escaped. He would miss Father Lucian, his sermons, and his confessional advice. He wondered if he would ever set foot in the church again. If he did, would the priest deny him communion? Confession?

A shadow cooled the space where he squatted.

Karl looked up to see Rebecca.

He wiped his eyes with the back of his hand. Why did it matter? He wasn't totally into Catholicism. He still had his Apsáalooke beliefs. Why couldn't he embrace both?

"I'm sorry."

"What? No 'I told you so'?" Karl quipped as he stood up.

"No. I know you wanted this. I'm sorry it won't happen."

"I am not sorry. I finally understand. I am done with these people."

Rebecca pinched off a spent flower.

Life as an adult is full of disappointments and heartbreak. The sooner he learned, the stronger he would be.

"You are hurting, and you don't mean it. They have given you a lot. Don't write them off."

"He—they are always talking about my soul. Yet he is letting me dwell with sin. He will not allow me the next sacrament. I am forced to marry outside the church, and no longer get to have their sacraments. That is all buffalo dung. He will not come to the ceremony. He really wanted me to skip this one and go to Holy Orders. Be a monk." Karl shook his head, and his braids swayed from side to side.

Rebecca placed her hands on her hips. "You're smart enough,

and you know more than most about Catholicism. You could have it if you wanted it."

"Be serious. I would drive them crazy, and many would leave."

"You would at least test their conviction," Rebecca said, looking around. "Where is your faith?"

Karl smiled at the joke. "She went with Marie to the convent."

He watched her face open in surprise. Then she punched his arm. He grinned.

"You're right. You would cause them to reconsider their vocations."

Karl laughed. At least he knew his gift.

CHAPTER 21
BETTER ALL THE TIME

Let us put our minds together and see what kind of life we can make for our children.

Tatanka Iyotanka (Sitting Bull). 1831-1890. Hunkpapa Lakota, holy man, and leader.

S pring was coming. Life would get better.

Karl looked at the Pendleton blanket, the one they stood wrapped in the day they married. Fours stripes of black, red, yellow, and green were on a white blanket made of wool. Simple yet warm. He had envisioned the blanket on a four-post bed, he and Faith snuggled together during the icy Montana winters. Today, nestled deep in the folds was Katie. Her dark eyelashes rested on her chubby cheeks, and her mouth worked on the invisible nipple. His stomach growled. He rose, making his way across the rectangular room to the kitchen. He opened the cabinet and took out the dried milk and mashed potatoes, filled the bottle with water, and placed it in a pot on the stove to warm. Then he refilled the coffeepot with water to brew a second pot of coffee using this morning's grounds.

Spring was coming. Life would get better.

The diapers, soaking in the sink, shouted he had once again been daydreaming. *You have wasted the sun's gift.* He squeezed the water out and hung the damp cloths on the rope in front of the window. He laid sheets of newspaper on the floor beneath the white flags of defeat.

His life was dipped in white, from diapers and formula to snowy days.

Spring was coming. Life would get better.

He fished the bottle out of the pot and set it on the counter to cool, making the water turn white with the powdered milk. He mixed the dried mashed potatoes and used up the last of the cheese to add flavor. While Faith had worked, he had finished high school, thanks to the nuns who watched Katie while he took his exams. That was almost six months ago. Now, he spent his days counting bottles, charting ounces, and examining the contents of diapers.

Karl thought things would get better. He could get a part-time job, but who would watch Katie?

The joy of his daughter and his wife sustained him most days. The growl in his stomach reminded him he needed more than hope to live on. An infant was labor intensive. The constant holding, burping, and feeding. He remembered holding Katie and his textbook, pacing the hall outside so Faith could sleep, his toes frozen, but Katie bundled warm.

Karl sliced the cheese into thin strips.

Katie is a wonderful baby. That is what Rebecca had told him when he'd asked her how she'd survived his infancy.

His siblings weren't like Katie. She rarely cried. He recalled holding her in his trembling hands, breathing her exhale. He was in love.

He stirred the mashed potatoes, poured himself a cup of coffee, and tested Katie's bottle. He turned around. Katie sat in the middle of the room, patiently waiting for him.

"Did you have a good nap? What did you dream?" Karl asked as he moved to the table and chairs. She crawled to him, grabbing his pant leg to stand. He scooped her up, kissed her cheeks, and placed her on the stack of schoolbooks, tying her with the arms of a sweatshirt to the chair. He scooted her to the table, placing a bowl in front of her. Chubby fingers scooped the potatoes. Her fine motor skills were impressive. Karl nibbled a slice of cheese as Katie licked her fingers.

"Tomorrow is Mommy's day off, and we can go shopping for some food. What would you like to buy? I am leaning toward steak, fresh green anything, and chocolate cake." They would really have fried bologna, carrots with tops, and half a chocolate bar.

The diapers dripped randomly on the paper.

"My dear, it is now time to do the clean-up dance," Karl said, wiping Katie's face and fingers. He cleaned. Katie tried to crawl after him. A fifteen-minute activity, but he made it into a thirty-minute workout with dance and chatter. Katie giggled and waved as he ironed Faith's uniforms and the damp diapers dry. Not much cleaning was needed in a studio apartment with a single bathroom and a kitchen on one wall.

After a game of chase and fetch, where Katie rolled a paper ball and Karl ran after it, he picked her up and wrapped her snugly with two blankets, leaving her arms free to move before placing her into a cradleboard. At bedtime, he would have tucked her arms inside. He wove the straps left to right because she was a girl. The willow cradleboard had been Faith's. The shade from Faith's cradleboard had a series of X's on the front. Katie's had beadwork of a Prairie Rose for the new shade designed by Faith and Rebecca. Each child gets a shade for their own dreams and thoughts. As she got older, they would hang something from it to keep her entertained. They bundled up and walked the parking lot, counting cars and looking for the last acorns and walnuts. Katie fussed, so Karl came back to the apartment. The air felt colder inside than out. He opened the drapes on the one window to let the sun in, hoping to heat the space.

He changed her diaper and rubbed her damp hair dry as they waited for the bottle to heat. They then snuggled on the mattress in the corner. Since she was now mobile—he had to lie down with her. That wasn't bad. It just meant he had to wait until she fell asleep to do anything else.

Sometimes he felt like he was living his life through Katie, her sleepy, playful, cranky, feeding times. She drank from her bottle, her warm body across his chest, and her eyes slowly closed. He sighed and eased her onto the mattress. Her eye fluttered open, and he hummed softly, hoping she would not wake and fuss.

Faith was working hard. He had nothing to complain about.

In a month, his classmates would be graduating. He should have waited, as he was missing the parties and bittersweet good-byes. He knew many had plans for college or jobs in a family business. He could have a job. If he wanted to be an accountant, Terence would welcome him and the help. He knew the business and recalled how well they worked together.

This was not working for him. Lucian had been right. He wished he could call and tell him.

Saint Alberic's Abbey had put a different monk in charge of

Saint George's parish, and the nuns were moving back to Texas, being replaced by the laity. He had heard that Father Lucian was ill.

He wondered if Marie would miss them. He had not attended Christmas or Easter dinner. His world had become tiny.

He picked up a novel to reread. Perhaps he'd make a trip to the library tomorrow if the weather held. Lying back on the mattress, he stared at the cracks in the ceiling.

He was a prisoner. Who would watch Katie with the nuns gone? Rebecca? Todd? Not likely.

The door to the apartment opened, and Karl jumped.

"Ah ha, I caught you sleeping with another woman," Faith said. She flipped the one light in the apartment.

"Yes, guilty as charged, but do not worry, this one is the silent kind. She will not speak," Karl said as Katie stretched and grunted next to him. "Your turn to cuddle. I will get dinner started."

"Nope, Rebecca sent me home with food. She claims she cooked too much, and is tired of eating cheese and canned meat."

"Rebecca is a horrible liar, but lucky us," Karl said, peering into the sack which contained fresh fruit, fried chicken, and fry bread.

"Your sister's very kind and generous."

"She does too much for us."

"She's doing what she believes is necessary."

"You always see the good in people."

"I would rather be surrounded by friends than enemies," Faith said, snuggling Katie.

They placed a few candles on the table and ate, relishing the fresh apples for dessert. As night fell, the room became colder, and they cuddled on the mattress, snuggled in the blankets, with Katie between them.

"We should move to a teepee. A teepee would be warmer," Karl said. "If we moved to the Rez, we would have commodities."

Faith frowned and shook her head. "Canned meat, lard, cheese, corn syrup for flavor. Not a healthy diet. Rebecca is sure the government is trying to kill us with those fatty and sugar-filled commodities."

"I bet she thinks we will all have the sugars," Karl said. Rebecca is right, but he yearned to feel full after eating. He would take food over hunger.

"We're lucky. Things will get better," Faith said.

"That is what Katie said."

"Really? She spoke?"

"She laughed when I told her I needed to get a life," Karl said.

"She's your life. For a while longer. I'm worried she's so quiet," Faith said, kissing the girl's cheeks and placing the sleeping child into her cradleboard.

"I sometimes think she is an old woman and one day she will open her mouth and demand an explanation."

"You're a good father," Faith said, kissing him.

"But what should I do next? I cannot do this all our lives."

Faith giggled as she leaned the cradleboard in the corner beside the mattress.

"What is so funny?"

"You. Clan mothers believe that raising the next generation is the highest calling."

"I am not complaining," Karl said, noticing the exhaustion that lingered about his wife.

"Yes, you are. I don't blame you. It is arduous work and dull. Things will get better."

"We need money. I need to get a job. I really want to go to college. Maybe when Katie is in school."

A loud knock on the door caused them to jump. They

exchanged glances in the dim light. Karl rose and walked the ten steps to the door. Faith reached for Katie, who squeaked a protest at being moved.

As he opened the door, he gasped. Before him was Terence. He had not seen his stepfather in over a year.

"I would like to see my granddaughter since you have neglected to bring her to me."

Karl grimaced. Guilty. He had been remiss.

"I figured you wanted nothing to do with us. You did not attend the wedding or acknowledge her birth," Karl said, knowing his words were blunt and harsh.

"The church did not sanction your marriage. Perhaps you'll fix that someday, but the birth of this child is not her sin. She's our first grandchild. It deeply saddened your mother when she wasn't present for the ceremonies. You could've invited her to one ritual."

Rebecca had been there for the placenta, umbilical, and birthing ceremonies. She and Tiama were there for the transfer and naming of character. Karl wondered if Father Lucian would baptize Katie, even if they weren't married in the church. That might appease Terence. Judith wasn't invited because they feared her spirit would taint the child. A prick of guilt needled Karl, even though shunning had been the right choice.

"Was not for me to decide. Lakota ceremonies. Mother is Crow," Karl mumbled. Poor excuse. Faith cleared her throat. Karl pushed his anger and anxiety away. Now was the time for hospitality.

"Welcome. Come in and meet Katie," Karl said, stepping aside. He glanced into the hallway before closing the door. It was empty. Judith had not come. The naked bulb shone in the center of the space as he switched on the light. Terence ducked under the rope that held drying diapers.

Faith unlaced Katie, who was struggling to see the new sound.

Terence smiled as Katie reached for her grandfather. Karl watched in amazement. If Katie said *basaaksaake*, grandfather in Apsáalooke, it would convince Karl that his daughter walked between the worlds and carried messages from the ancestors.

Faith moved to the kitchen and put the kettle on, elbowing Karl to the action of hospitality, food, and drink. Karl opened the cupboard and took out a box of crackers. Faith gathered the last of the peanut butter and apple.

"Did you see that?" Karl whispered to Faith.

"Yes. She is seeking something," Faith said.

A shiver ran through him. He had never understood his stepfather. Was he loved, or was he hated? Judith was so much easier to know. She reviled him from birth, and that had never changed.

Katie sat contently in the arms of Terence. Karl stood next to the window and nibbled on a cracker as Faith poured steaming tea into the glass jars. Terence and Faith sat at the little table.

"You didn't come for Christmas," Terence said.

"I was not invited," Karl said.

"Since when do you need an invitation to come home?"

Karl looked at Faith. Family and home were the foundations of life. Katie pulled off the woolen cap she was wearing, and the static sparked in the air as her black hair stood up.

"She's beautiful," Terence said with a chuckle.

Katie begged for a cracker, and Terence looked to Faith for permission.

"She's small for six months, but healthy," Terence said, looking at Karl.

Was that a question or a statement?

"We're both fine," Faith said. Her breath floated like fog in the harsh light.

Terence handed Katie to Faith and turned to Karl. "Son, this baby can't sleep in this frozen apartment. I could keep ice cream in here and it wouldn't melt. Bring what you need and come home."

That was a command, not a suggestion.

"We will be fine," Karl said, neglecting to tell him they kept the heat low because of the cost. Karl looked at Terence. He had a soft sadness around his eyes and a tightness in his jaw. The man appeared conflicted. A slap should have followed.

"Give me a few minutes to warm the car," Terence said as he turned, dodging the diapers and leaving the apartment.

Faith held Katie close.

"That is not a promising idea."

"He is not the problem. Judith is," Karl said, remembering how nice a warm house was.

Karl looked out the window. No, he had not forgotten the abuse at the hands of his stepfather, nor the constant head games Judith played to ensure the abuse reoccurred.

Katie squirmed. Faith set her down.

"Things will get better here," Faith said as Katie stood holding her leg.

"The other children will be there. Katie needs other children. Already she seems like an observing elder. My siblings are not mean."

"They are both a problem. We leave if it happens," Faith said, putting her hands on her hips.

"It will not happen. I am a father now. I can handle this. The farmhouse is enormous. We can keep to ourselves."

Katie whimpered at the door. Faith went to pick her up and gasped.

"What is wrong?"

She handed Katie to him. The little girl was trembling. Katie's frozen fingers touched Karl's face. A slap was less painful. Katie was mobile, but usually, she was tucked in between them, warm and safe. But what if she woke and crawled away from them? Could they take that chance? The thought of finding his child dead caused him to shudder.

"This is not good. She could freeze in the night. We only just set her down. What if we did not wake up?" Karl said.

Faith cupped her hands over Katie's, blowing warm air over them.

"We could save our money and get a bigger place in a few months. I could work for my father."

"No, you will not leave our daughter with that woman. I don't trust her. She may look like a sweet skunk, but she doesn't tap her feet in warning. I don't want to be marked as foolish."

Karl gathered the diapers and baby items.

"Promise me you'll not leave her alone with either of them," Faith said.

"I will allow no one to harm her, I swear," Karl said, stopping and looking at her and the child. Her lips pursed. She wanted to say more. One promise at a time. The bigger fear loomed in the corner. Could he live there with no bruises? Would it be different now? He hoped it would. He would make it so.

The little family entered the farmhouse. Vicky and Vincent clamored around Faith to see Katie.

"Why is she here?" Vicky asked. "Why are these boxes here?"

"Are you coming to stay?" Vincent asked.

"Your father invited us for a visit," Faith said.

"But I'm the baby," Vicky said with a stomp of her foot as she crossed her arms and pouted.

"That won't change," Karl said.

CHAPTER 22

WHAT KIND OF A FATHER ARE YOU?

A very great vision is needed and the man who has it must
follow it as the eagle seeks the deepest blue of the sky.

Tȟašúŋke Witkó (Crazy Horse). 1840-1877. Tenacious Lakota war
leader of the Oglala band and preserver of the traditional way of
life of the Lakota people.

The farmhouse was large, and Karl relished the energy of
his siblings. The six bedrooms were occupied, but the
nursery stood empty. Faith was determined to raise
Katie steeped in Lakota tradition, so Katie ate and slept with them.

Spring had arrived and old patterns appeared. Karl sat in the
kitchen with Katie, watching the clock. TK had come and gone.
His siblings should be getting up, but no sound came from their
rooms. Terence was out doing taxes for his many clients.

"This will not end well. I got a bad feeling," Karl said to Katie, who mashed her banana into the highchair tray.

Karl scooped sugar into his coffee. The clock on the wall ticked. He decided since it was getting late that he should wake them up. He handed Katie a piece of toast, ran upstairs to the boy's room, and turned on the light. The smell of dirty socks met his nose.

"Rise and shine, guys, hurry. We are running late."

He darted across the hall to Vicky's room. He opened the door and stuck his head in. The room had been transformed. Gone were the two beds, replaced by a canopy bed with pink and purple gauze floating from the posts. Her writing desk was a carriage, complete with wooden wheels and a floral sun hood. Her closet looked like an entrance to a castle. Karl stood, mesmerized.

Vicky yelled, shattering the spell. "I'm telling Momma you were in here."

Karl smirked. "Good. It is time for school. Hurry, or you will be late."

He ran down the steps, skidding to a halt at the sound of Judith's voice.

"This is not a nutritious breakfast. Let Grandma fix you something good."

Heart pounding, he took a step into the kitchen. Katie rolled her banana and toast into balls.

"Morning," Karl said.

"Mom, what's for breakfast?" Davy shouted, darting into the kitchen.

"Nothing, now. He got us up too late," Vicky said.

"There is cereal," Karl said, getting bowls down.

"I don't want stinking cereal. I want eggs," Vicky said.

A chaos of orders filled the kitchen.

242

"I will fix you pancakes. Sit," Judith said, getting out the griddle.

"We missed the bus," Tommy said, looking at the clock.

"Karl will drive you," Judith said, turning on the stove and placing a bowl on the counter.

"You should have gotten us up earlier," Vicky said. "You're mean."

Karl opened his mouth and swallowed his words and refilled his coffee cup. Katie was fine. Faith's words, "Don't leave her alone with your mother," echoed in his mind. He looked at his coffee cup. Was it safe to drink? He didn't know.

Pancakes filled plates. Eggs and sausage were added to the mix. This was a far cry from what he and his sisters ate for breakfast. Karl watched the clock; they would be late for school now.

It wasn't his responsibility to get these kids up and moving. He wondered if Rebecca had felt that way. Her life was on hold because of him and Judith.

The days became familiar. Judith did the bare minimum, as Karl did more. He was waiting for her to turn his efforts into drama. He could hear her saying to Terence, "I only asked that he help since he is living here for free."

No matter which job he didn't do, that would be the breaking point. He would argue he was doing other jobs, but it would never be enough. The danger dance had begun.

The door to the office opened, and Karl jumped. He had forgotten to lock it. This was his father's workspace, which held two desks and a large wooden filing cabinet. Terence had hired Karl to help with his accounting business. Terence would be home in a week from visiting the big ranches north of Elan.

Judith stood in the entryway, her hands on her hips. Her dark eyes narrowed as she looked from Karl to Katie. Karl surveyed the exits, calculating the time and distance to scoop up his daughter and run.

"What are you doing?" Judith asked.

"Working," Karl answered, shifting in his wooden chair.

"Why is she in here? You know we do not permit children in the office," Judith said. "I'll take her."

"No."

"What do you mean, 'no'? Am I not allowed?"

"Correct," Karl said, his mind whirling for a reason that didn't blame Faith.

"Is she not mine?"

Karl looked at Katie, who sat on the floor, making a line with wooden blocks. There was no mistaking who Katie's parents were. Her hair was black, straight, her eyes dark, and her skin brown. Judith was trying to say Faith had lied. Karl knew that was not true.

"If she had blue eyes, would you say she was yours?"

"You would curse your own child? What kind of father are you?"

"It is not my eyes that condemn me."

"I'm not the one who would harm her."

That stung. "I would not hurt my child."

Karl stood up, muscles tense like a bowstring.

"She should talk," Judith stated. "Has God cursed you because of your harsh words to Father Lucian? Are you not worried? She might be deaf or worse, mute. What kind of father are you?"

Karl was concerned, but he knew Katie was not deaf. She just hadn't spoken. The medicine man they visited said she was speaking. They had both forgotten the language she spoke.

"She will say something when it matters."

Katie crawled away from the line of toys she had made on the floor.

"She should walk by now. She's almost one. If you and Faith would stop carrying her everywhere in a cradleboard, she would learn to walk. You suffocate her. Making her cling to your side like woodruff seeds. Children need to run and explore."

Karl's fingers curled around the sharpened pencil he was holding.

"What kind of father are you?" Judith said. "A *squaw* father."

The tip pressed firmly to the paper snapped. He stood there, amazed. Would she stop at nothing? Go so low as to call him an offensive slur for a Native woman?

"What is wrong with you? Why would you say that? We share the same blood. We are Apsáalooke. What made you hate yourself so much?"

"I lived on the Rez. I saved you from that life. And what have you done? You want to bring those ways here. Run back there."

She didn't love the white world, the Catholic religion. She just donned it like a ceremonial cloak.

"This world is not ideal. You hate the white world and yet here you are. I do not understand you."

"And the Rez is better? Poverty, drunkenness, you are just like your father," Judith said, her face turning a ruddy brown before she moved into the room, kicking the toys as she advanced.

Katie frowned and scooted out of Judith's reach.

"No, it is a balance. I pick what is good and balance my life. I look to the future. We need to look before we run and embrace. Endow died, and you ran away. You left us."

Karl thought he had little, no money, no house. Yet he was rich in love and tribe. They had come to his wedding, to the birth of his daughter. They would welcome him on the Rez.

She ran her hand over the back of the leather chair. "There's nothing for anyone at your precious Rez. Look where Endow died, drunk, under a tree, alone."

She never explained why that was true. A man's not born a drunk. What pain and hurt led him down that path? Was she a victim or part of it?

"You are just like your father."

"Which one?" Karl hissed. "I do not beat my wife or children."

Karl glanced at the clock. Noon had not yet arrived. He hoped to finish his work before the chaos of siblings. Not today.

Judith fussed with the spider plant, picking off the dead leaves. "Oh, you will. You can barely handle one. What will happen when there are two?"

He scooped up his daughter and walked out.

KARL AND KATIE took a long drive.

"Good job. She was just trying to bait you," Rebecca's voice in his mind crowed.

His brain pounded with Judith's toxic words, "What kind of father are you?" He glanced at Katie in the back seat. Beads of sweat on her forehead. Karl rolled down the window. Katie wasn't walking, and she wasn't talking. Had he damaged her with this move to the farmhouse?

Should he take her to a doctor? But what would they say? And was it true that Faith was pregnant? Judith's voice roared loud in his mind. Was it a lie to get him to react? The wind blew warm air through the car.

"Is Momma going to have a baby?" he asked Katie. She giggled and clapped her hands. A thrill ran through him.

He would ask Faith tonight. Two little ones? Fear tickled his conscience. He looked at Katie again, deciding she looked normal. What if he was the reason she didn't talk?

He could hear Faith scolding him. "There's nothing wrong with Katie. We will talk to her in our native tongues. She's Lakota and Apsáalooke, perhaps she doesn't want to speak English." Had their efforts confused her?

His joy and fear pulled him in both directions. They might never leave the farmhouse. But they could leave before winter. Karl sighed. Two small children in that hallway apartment, all winter long. He cringed, feeling the walls of his world getting tighter.

If we leave the farmhouse, he would miss his brothers but not his sister. Vicky was constantly telling tall tales that nobody responded to. She blamed Katie for things that the child was not capable of doing. But would Katie? He watched her in the rearview mirror as she played with a rag doll, making it dance as she hummed.

The fields of dusty grain turned to scrub grass and hills. He turned off the highway onto a dirt road. The End of The Road Tavern neon sign caught his eye. It wasn't on the Rez, but it was damn close. It stood as he imagined the gates of hell did. He was on the Rez, so he drove to Grandma Tiama's.

He entered the kitchen and was met with the familiar smells of herbs and bread. Katie squirmed to be freed from his arms. Once he placed her down, she crawled to Grandma Tiama, who was in the living room.

"What is troubling you?" Tiama asked, putting down her weaving and letting Katie fuss with the reeds.

"Nothing and everything," Karl said, picking at the reeds. *I want answers to questions not asked.*

Tiama laughed.

"I think Faith is pregnant. Why has she not told me? And how come Judith knows? Faith did not confide in her."

"Faith is worried you'll not be happy," Tiama said. "Judith knows because all women know."

Karl looked at Tiama. He could not say he wanted more. The

clan came first, then his needs. He wasn't interested in being an accountant.

"I am not unhappy. It is that things will be delayed."

"My goodness. Don't be in such a rush. What you want will come. This is how it happens."

Karl scowled. Not the answer he was looking for. He was ready now. Tiama sounded like Father Lucian, telling him to wait and see. How long did he have to wait? How long before he was free to pursue his life or his interests? Would he ever have the time? He sounded like a white man wrapped around the clock.

It was time to go. He didn't want Faith to worry about where he was, so he kissed Grandma Tiama and took the protesting Katie to the car.

Karl drove, and Katie slept.

He pushed open the front door, and the smell of baked bread and cookies tickled his nose. Book bags and coats stood piled at the entrance. Karl stacked the discarded outerwear into the closet, cleaning up the entryway.

With Katie in his arms, he entered the kitchen. Terence must be coming home, for the fragrance of a pot roast filled the kitchen. TK gestured to the top of the fridge and the plate of cookies.

Karl was grateful for TK's silent presence and quiet, looking out for them. If he had to leave Katie with someone, it would be TK.

"Thanks for saving us a treat," Karl said as he placed Katie on the porch bench with a cookie.

TK shrugged his shoulders. They rarely acknowledged Judith's actions against Karl. What was there to say? Judith liked TK and not Karl. They were no longer in competition for adult approval.

"You are about to graduate. I kind of wish I had waited."

"You'd looked funny carrying a baby and a diploma," TK said.

"Sister Mary Joseph handed me this. She wants all boys to be priests."

Karl looked at the scholarship application to Saint Alberic's College. It was a specific application to the theology department.

"I thought they left for Texas," Karl said, wondering if he could apply for a scholarship.

"Not her. She wanted to see that we all graduated," TK said, crumpling the application. "Not interested in a theology degree. I would rather go to law school."

"Have you told Dad? He would allow it."

"Do you think so?" TK pulled another folded application out of his pocket. "Dad wants an accountant." He unfolded the filled-out application and then refolded it.

Karl wasn't interested in looking at numbers for the rest of his life.

"There is always Tommy, Davy, or even Vincent," Karl said. "I am helping Dad for now. If you apply and get your basic courses out of the way, you can always change to pre-law in your second year. He will not figure it out until it is too late."

"You are devious sometimes. And let's encourage our brothers to be accountants," TK said with a grin.

"We could groom Vicky, as a backup."

"The only money sense Vicky has is how much she gets to spend."

Karl laughed. Vicky must have gotten the white man's character at birth.

TK shrugged his shoulders and headed inside. Karl sat wondering how he could go to college. Not a chance if he was having a second child. Maybe he could get a monthly stipend as Rebecca did. Perhaps he could work around Faith's schedule.

Katie and Karl went inside. Both applications were in the

trash. He fished them out and folded the blank application for the theology program into his pocket.

He was not rushing things, just making them happen as he headed to the office for an envelope and stamp.

CHAPTER 23
UNSPOKEN TRUTH

Everything an Indian does is in a circle because the power of the world always works in circles.

Hehaka Sapa (Black Elk). 1863-1950. Wichasha Wakan medicine man and Heyoka of the Oglala Lakota people.

S ummer was ending and the chaos of restless children was in full swing. Katie pulled the petals off the daisies she had picked. A scattering of white dotted the brown boards.

It should be different. He was a father now.

Karl sighed. Terence and he once again fell into the rabbit hole of tension, words, and violence.

This should have been different. He was an adult, a father, and a husband. But it wasn't different. Why was he even here?

He was lying to himself. The kids were fine, the farmhouse

peaceful in his absence. Now, a year later, the past was shadowing the future. He should have turned in that application. Next year, a baby would be born—a son. A surge of pride filled him.

He heard a car coming up the driveway. Faith was home. He grimaced, and his cheek hurt. He had to convince her to stay just a while longer. We need the money. This misunderstanding would blow over. Life would settle, it always did. They could leave a little later. They could move into a one-bedroom apartment. Just a few more months.

Faith walked up the steps onto the porch. Karl turned, and she gasped.

"I can explain—" Karl started, turning his swollen eye away from her.

She cut him off.

"No. Where was Katie when you met his fist?"

Karl winced. A trickle of shame blushed his cheek, and he smashed the emotion like a pesky fly.

"No. Our children need something else. Our son will not learn this." Faith marched into the house. She grabbed an empty box that was part of a fort. Karl followed her to the bedroom. She tossed in the pile of clean diapers. "I don't want an excuse. I know what goes on. I'm not blind. Your mother doesn't want us here. We need to go. Temporary, you promised."

"Judith," Karl corrected, for he rarely called her mother.

"I can't live like this. It's like ice fishing on a lake in spring, one faulty step, and we're plunged into the silent freeze. I don't know how you can stand the tension," Faith said.

Katie stirred in Karl's arms. She wanted down.

Faith would not enter the circle of silence. That was clear.

"He's not your actual father. You owe them nothing. You have paid your pound of flesh."

"My biological father beat my mother. He drank the white

man's poison. It killed him. This is not the same. Terence is the only father I have. This is his house. Please do not add to the problems. All is good," Karl said, rubbing Katie's back. "I made a mistake. This will not happen again." He knew in his heart that the words were a lie. Things were not different, only delayed. Old habits, feelings, and ways slowly crept back into his life. Judith's angst toward him for being Indian, for being Endow's son.

The echo of doubt laughed in his mind.

Faith tossed her clothing into a box. "That's right, sweep it away. Pretend I don't see what I see. Sometimes you act like a white man, creating the problem and then ignoring it. How can I possibly add to the problem?" She threw her hands into the air. "Nothing will change if we stay here. I know you don't want to speak the truth. It's ugly, but I'll not stand by and say all is fine."

"He wants to help. I have a job. Here I can work and watch Katie. We have been saving. We are nearly there."

"We don't need him. You're not a kid anymore… what am I saying? It wasn't okay then either. You need to let go. We need to leave here before it's fatal."

"Is that how you see me? As a kid?" Karl asked. "Am I just another burden?"

"That's not what I said. Living here's not good."

Faith shoved Katie's clothing into a pillowcase.

"Faith, you do not understand. I am doing this for Katie. We need money to move. Staying here is the only way. I wish I had turned in that college application."

"You're not an accountant. Stop saying that," Faith's voice sharpened in pitch. Katie pushed against him, her feet kicking wildly. "This is not how I will live."

Karl stepped back as if punched. They were a "we", not an "I".

"You would rather live in a freezing apartment and eat commodities from the government? How is that better for Katie?"

Faith straightened. Her round belly protruded.

"I'm thinking of Katie. All white men are the same. There is always a bigger price to pay and usually with our lives. Is this how you want Katie to remember you when he kills you? Are you trying to be like Endow?"

Karl relented and set Katie down.

"I am not Endow. I am not Terence," he shouted.

Faith stopped packing. Katie crawled to the open boxes and pulled out clothing.

"Katie, stop," Faith said, trying to repack. Katie climbed into the box. Faith opened the door, taking the pillowcases of clothing.

Vicky jumped back, brown eyes blinking rapidly.

"What are you doing?" Vicky asked. "Are you leaving?"

Karl held his breath. Faith glanced back at Karl.

"Yes."

"Yippee."

"Quick, run and tell your mother the good news. She can bake a celebration cake."

Vicky stopped her happy dance and raced to find Judith.

Faith pushed the boxes of their meager belongings onto the porch. Katie giggled from the cozy ride. Karl grabbed the sacks she had stuffed and set them next to the boxes. Faith left Katie on the porch and made a quick phone call. Karl stood sentry.

Faith marched past Karl and took a seat among the boxes. Karl did not stop her. The conversation was over. He reentered the disheveled room that reflected his life.

She is leaving. Did she want him? She didn't say. She has an income. He had nothing. He was a man with hopes, a boy with dreams.

Slowly, he packed and then sat on the edge of the bed, waiting.

Karl opened the front door and stepped out onto the porch. Katie hung their clothes on the rail as if it were laundry day.

"What?" Faith asked. Her eyes were red and puffy.

"Are you eating dinner with us?"

The glare he received was dark and cold.

Karl returned to the dining room, taking his usual spot, running his fingers underneath the table, feeling his initials that he had carved there.

Karl stirred the gravy into his mashed potatoes. His appetite waned. The normal chatter of the dinner hour stood muted. Even Terence appeared subdued. Terence had a temper, and Karl could push the man to his limit. If we leave, he won't be able to say sorry; it was another reason to stay.

Terence always soothed the violence with words of love and approval later. Perhaps Faith was right, that he was like an alcoholic. Drawn in for one more moment of approval from the guy who hit him. One more Indian lulled by white men's lies.

Headlights beamed in the foyer, lighting up the stairs. Voices rose from the porch. A knock came on the door. Terence left the table to answer it. The Mackenzie clan pushed into the hall.

Karl recognized the deep voice of Todd and hung his head.

"Karl," came the command from Todd.

Karl shuffled past his audience. His one blue eye focused on Todd, the other eye still swollen shut as his cheeks warm.

What would Todd think of him now? A boy trying to be a man.

Todd's muscular body turned to face Terence. Judith pulled Vicky and Vincent closer to her.

"My sister is on the porch," Todd said, his voice strong but gentle.

"She will not come in," Karl said. "I have tried to explain."

Todd shook his head. His long hair swayed. "Things have changed. I know you're not Lakota, so I'll explain. In Lakota society, a woman divorces her husband by placing his belongings outside the home. This is not her home, but the implications are the same."

No beating ever felt as painful as the words Todd spoke. *Divorce.* She was leaving him. His chest constricted.

"Smart woman," Judith said, stepping into the foyer, her children following, forming a half circle around Karl and Todd.

Karl inhaled the lingering aroma of dinner. Would she ever stop?

"Ignore her," came Tiama's voice as the wisdom of the Elders. Karl moved to the door, but Todd blocked his way. He stood to the left of the Mackenzie family. Terence stood to the right.

"That's my sister and niece. Soon to add one more. Stop counting coup. What happened here is not bravery. Be Lakota."

Karl saw Terence wince, drawing in a sharp breath as if an arrow pierced him. He heard Judith snorting like a buffalo behind him. Todd should not have insulted their kindness. They didn't have to open their home to them, yet they did.

Be Lakota, with their four cardinal virtues: bravery, fortitude, integrity, and generosity. Who was he? Karl Mackenzie or Karl Knows the Song? He had the courage to endure pain, but not the willingness to confront it. What if he said no more... what if Terence withdrew his love? Was a white man capable of loving an Indian?

Karl stood in the middle of the circle of people he loved, respected, feared, and detested. His clan, his family, his life, his world. A circle. Everything of importance occurs in a circle. He wasn't in the circle.

The front door opened, and Faith stood holding Katie.

"Brother, I'm waiting," Faith said.

Todd turned to Karl.

"What are you doing here?" Faith asked. "Why aren't you coming?"

Karl was not sure who she was addressing but decided he would answer.

The words tumbled out of his mouth. "I want to be with you. But I need education and work. Nobody will hire an uneducated Indian. Plenty Coups said, 'Education makes you equal.' I cannot be a homemaker. I need more."

Judith growled, disapproving of the wisdom of the last Crow Chief.

Faith hoisted Katie to her other hip. "Plenty Coups's words are prudent. I need a husband, and our children need a father. These children are the future. Don't dismiss the honors given you as their father."

"I am not scoffing or discarding my duties," Karl said as he scraped the floor with his foot. "I want to be the provider."

Faith turned toward the open door. "Couples share the burden of living. Our roles are fluid, not fixed. We do what we must do. Money isn't what we live for. We can do without. It is time to go."

"Don't rush into the river, sister. I understand your self-determination. But even Plenty Coups listened to the chickadee," Todd said.

Karl's forehead furrowed at Todd's attempt to marry Apsáalooke with Lakota. Plenty Coups wore the legs and feet of the chickadee braided in his hair behind his ear. A chickadee appeared during a vision. The Elders told him to listen.

"I'll listen, but not to false promises or lies."

Faith turned to face them all as she stood near the door. Davy and Tommy inched their way toward the living room.

Karl knew the chickadee had over fifteen vocalizations. He wondered which song of the chickadee Faith would listen to, Todd, Karl, or herself.

Todd stepped aside and stood silently. The clock down the hall ticked. No one moved or spoke. TK turned and left the group.

Katie struggled in Faith's arms, throwing her head back. Todd reached for the fussing child, who pushed him away. She wanted down, not her uncle.

"I love you," Karl said, stepping toward the tall woman in front of him, her round belly between them. "I want to be with you."

"Don't tell me. Show me. Leave now."

Karl heaved a breath. "Faith, this is not the Rez. Things come at a price. We almost have enough."

Faith set Katie down on the floor. Her eyes stayed focused on her daughter.

"No. I'll not pay that price. My daughter will not be a witness to the mistreatment of her father. My son will not confuse love with violence. I will not be a widow. This is familiar to you. This is not good for us." Her hands folded over her abdomen.

Karl glanced over his shoulder at his family. Tommy and Davy were stepping toward the TV. Terence stood silently observing.

He wished he had Marie's conviction or Rebecca's strength. Then he could walk away.

Judith smiled. Karl clenched his fist. Was this Judith's plan all along, to break them up, forcing him to stay at the farmhouse? It made no sense. She didn't love him. She loathed every ounce of Indian in him.

The gravel outside crunched, and a car door slammed. All eyes turned to the open door.

"What are you doing here?" Todd asked as Rebecca entered the foyer, studying the circle of silence, Karl in the center.

"I didn't think you would come," Rebecca said, her uniform stained and wrinkled from work.

"I gave my word," Todd said, and his face darkened. Rebecca took a step toward Karl, examining the bruised on his face.

"Let's go."

Todd reached for Rebecca's arm as the theme song of *Mr. Ed* filtered in from the living room. The circle was breaking.

"Stop. You cannot rescue him, or else the cycle continues," Todd said, tugging Rebecca to him.

"He's misguided," Rebecca said, her hands forming fists. "You don't understand."

"I see what is before me. You would too if you stepped out of the circle. This is for them to fix."

Rebecca bristled, shifting her weight like a bobcat ready to pounce. Her right eyebrow rose, and her jaw tensed. The two stood exchanging breaths. Then her arm shot forward, and she pushed Todd aside as she turned toward Faith, avoiding a direct step over Katie.

"What do you want to do? Do you love him?" Rebecca asked.

"Do you have to ask?" Faith said, caressing her unborn child. "Why did you send my brother?"

"He gave me his word," Rebecca said, clearing nothing up.

Karl realized Faith had called Rebecca, and she had called Todd. He wondered what pact they had entered.

"What do you want?" Rebecca asked again.

"I want to leave with Karl."

Faith looked over Rebecca's left shoulder at Karl. "If you can't be Lakota, at least be Apsáalooke. Stop being white—wanting, taking, lying to me, lying to yourself. This is a cycle, a circle. What will our children see when they see you?"

Rebecca turned. Both women now faced him. "Be Apsáalooke. Stubbornness has no place in a marriage."

Karl opened his mouth to object. He wasn't being stubborn. Besides, what did Rebecca know about marriage? Karl crossed his arms, but his chest ached. He wished his feet would just move toward the open door.

"Fine. What do you want me to do?"

Todd shifted, and the floorboards creaked. "Take a leap of faith. Leave the security of what you know. Do what is right."

Rebecca made a soft snort at his choice of words.

"He wants to stay," Vincent said, causing the focus to be on him. "I want you to stay."

Karl's heart ached for Vincent. Conflicted feelings crashed like an eagle, flying with food as the crows chased him.

"If it happens to them. You and I will make it stop," Todd said, his voice calm, clear, and determined, staring defiantly into Terence's eyes.

Todd's promise left Karl feeling suddenly lighter.

Rebecca beckoned Vincent to her. He came at her with a rush, almost knocking her over. She hugged him tightly. Vicky refused to move as she crossed her arms in defiance.

Faith moved to the door.

"Do you love her?" Terence asked, speaking for the first time.

Karl straightened his shoulders. "Yes, with all my heart."

"Then what are you waiting for?" Terence said. "You have a daughter together. She needs a daddy. Don't let your children grow up without a father."

Karl stared at Terence. He needed to hear those words. Needed to know he was loved.

"This is ridiculous," Judith said. "He doesn't know what he wants. Go run to the Rez, live in a teepee, and eat the government handouts. Be like your father."

Judith turned and exited the room.

Vicky stomped her foot and then trailed down the hall after Judith.

He was not his stepfather or Endow. He would be more. Karl's heart pounded in his chest. Cries and thuds of the past threatened to crush his conviction. He remembered the nights clinging to his sisters while Endow beat Judith and the exhausted silence afterward.

Karl rubbed his sore cheek. He reflected on the circle of witnesses held in silence, never speaking of the violence that repeated itself like the seasons. Memories of violence. A hidden trigger, a spike of adrenalin, for no obvious reason. Not for them or his children.

Karl looked at Faith, who was focused on Katie. The little girl was standing on wobbly legs. Arms waving for balance, then she stumbled forward. One, two, three, four steps as she moved toward him. Karl bent down, scooped her up, and soared her above his head.

"*Até*," Katie said, "*Basaake*."

"Yes, I am *Até*," Karl said, his sight becoming blurred as he held Katie above his head.

Katie had called him "Daddy" in Lakota and Apsáalooke. It was time to leave.

CHAPTER 24
EDUCATED

We also have a religion which was given to our fore-
    fathers
and has been handed down to us, their children.
It teaches us to be thankful, to be united, and to love one
    another.
We never quarrel about religion.

Sogoyewapha (Red Jacket). 1750-1830. Great Seneca, Orator for the
rights of his people and their religious beliefs.

K arl carried the sleeping Elias on his back as he and
Katie made their way up the stairs of Saint Alberic's
College. Their footsteps clunked on the wide wooden
risers to the third floor as they headed down a hallway to the office
of the dean of theology.

Two years had passed since he had the idea of attending college.

We should leave. *This is a mistake*, thought Karl. He had waited too long.

The floorboards creaked and groaned as they walked down the empty hall.

Katie stopped and paused every few steps.

"The wise ones are talking," Katie said, cocking her head from side to side. "Can you hear them, *Até*?"

Karl smiled. At five, Katie's beliefs about the world sometimes frightened him. Three years ago, she spoke her first word and since then she was a constant buzz in his ear. He wondered if her guide was a fly.

"Can you sense the wisdom?"

Katie drew in a deep breath. She wrinkled her nose. "Smells like old leather, like in Grandma Tiama's teepee."

Karl laughed. "After this, I will take you to the church where you can smell holiness. Maybe we should go there now."

Katie put her hands on her hips. She looked like a miniature Faith. "*Iná* said we go, and the hall is telling us to come. After that, you can show me." *Iná* was the Lakota word for mother. Katie used Lakota words for her parents. Elias mixed the languages to suit his moods.

Several students lugging backpacks heavy with texts passed them. Their excited chatter faded as they went down the staircase.

Karl approached an office door that loomed tall and was open slightly. He stopped.

Katie tugged his sleeve. Her thick black hair had fallen out of the tight braids. He adjusted Elias, still asleep, drool slipping out of his open mouth, leaving a big wet spot on Karl's right shoulder.

"Katie, this is a mistake," Karl said.

Katie stomped her foot, grabbed his hand, and with an enormous step, headed through the door. Karl shook her hand off, but she marched forward. She pushed the door open, and three heads turned in her direction. Karl followed his brave warrior and adjusted the diaper bag onto his left shoulder. He could not leave his daughter to the wolves.

"Hello. Who are you?" the man asked.

"I'm Katie, that is *Até* and Elias," Katie said. "We come to..." She paused. "To treaty."

The men wore black Benedictine robes. One of them snorted. Ginger-blond hair turning snow white, blue eyes. Karl's stomach clenched. He recognized this monk, Brother Mellitus, the curmudgeon who almost decked him years ago. This was now a doomed mission. He needed to get out as quickly as possible.

"I'm Father Hilary and that's Father Gordon and Brother Mellitus," Hilary said, grinning widely.

Katie had already charmed one.

One of them was the head of the theology department. Hopefully, it wasn't Brother Mellitus.

The cuckoo clock on the wall swirled, and the door opened. The tiny bird peeped and then sang a tinny song. Katie stopped and stared at the little box.

One o'clock. Karl fished out the paperwork and handed the application and essay to Hilary.

"*Até* wants to go to school. He likes school. This school smells funny, but it will do. The halls talked to me," Katie said, climbing into the empty chair next to Gordon.

"But he is late," Mellitus said, leaning back as if Katie's presence demanded more space.

Katie looked at the clock again. "By your time, not our time."

She crossed her arms and looked at Hilary. Her dark eyes waited with anticipation.

The steam radiator in the corner hissed.

"Yes, I agree," Katie said to the radiator.

Father Gordon gave her a strange look.

"Well, what do you think? Does he get to come? So far all have agreed, it's fine."

"Are you asking about a scholarship?" Gordon asked, looking at the crumpled application.

"It's not based solely on need, and it's given to a man who's interested in the priesthood," Father Gordon said. "You're not single."

Hilary continued in silence, reading the papers before him. Karl took a step backward toward the exit.

Katie had grown roots, sitting still and seeing. Karl glanced around the organized office. He spied a book by C. S. Lewis he wanted to read on the bookshelf.

"What would your major be?" Hilary asked.

"Breeding," Mellitus mumbled under his breath. Gordon and Hilary drew in a gasp.

Karl shook his head. *So, this is how it is going to be, spiritless one.*

"I was planning on a double major in theology and philosophy," Karl said, sending a scathing sneer to Mellitus.

"That won't open many career choices," Gordon said, smoothing his scapular on his lap.

Did it matter what he said? Clearly, only one monk was considering his application.

"You got me," Karl said, leaning against the door frame. "I was hoping to open a lemonade stand at the entrance to the college. Offer prophetic wisdom, healing, and palm readings as an alternative to the guilt on the hill."

Father Hilary laughed. Gordon's mouth hung open for a moment, and then he folded his arms and harrumphed. "That's not what we do here."

Mellitus snickered. "I see you haven't changed, Crow."

"You either, Paleface." Karl stepped in closer to Mellitus, a pointed index finger in his direction. Mellitus slapped his hand away. Temptation taunted him to ask about Lucian, but he decided he didn't want a scholarship because of favoritism.

Hilary looked up from the papers.

"You two know each other?"

"No," Karl said.

"Yes. He's the thorn in Lucian's side. He caused Lucian to come home. Now that addled brain Alcuin is pastor, and the parish has gone to hell."

"Brother, a person didn't cause Lucian's blindness," Gordon said. "You're just mad because you have no place to hide when one of your practical jokes goes haywire."

"Perhaps. One can't live his entire life behind the walls of a monastery," Mellitus quipped.

A sprinkling of guilt touched Karl as he reflected on this news of Lucian. He should stop in and talk to him.

Hilary turned over the pages of Karl's essay.

"Oh, that isn't part of *Até's* work," Katie said, springing up from her seat and coming to stand by Hilary. "I was drawing, sorry."

"*Até*? Is that Crow?" Hilary asked.

"No, it's 'Father' in Lakota. If I were to call him Papa, I would be calling him dried buffalo meat. That is what papa means in Lakota."

Mellitus laughed. Katie smiled at him.

"What were you drawing?" Hilary asked.

"I was drawing the great flood. The Creator made land for *Kangi*, the only survivor of the flood. He sent four animals, a dove, *ptan*, *capa*, and *keya*."

"A dove, otter, beaver, and a turtle," Karl said.

"Turtle brought the mud, and the Creator made us all," Katie explained.

266

"What are you teaching these children? That's not biblical," Gordon said. "Creation after the great flood."

"All nations have a creation story. We all come from earth. That is the Lakota version," Karl said. "All creation has the same elements, earth, and breath. Maybe the Creator made us at various times and in separate places. I am certain he was into experimenting. Hence, possibly another Eden."

Hilary shoved papers toward Gordon, whose face was rapidly changing to a ruddy hue. This was not going well.

"Father Gordon, all the papers are in order. He has references from the nuns who worked at Saint George's parish. Also, an impressive GPA."

Gordon moved the papers closer but did not read them. The hall groaned. Katie cocked her head, looking at the doorway where a shadow appeared, but nobody entered.

Elias whimpered, and Karl shifted the backpack off his shoulders. The boy's hair was damp from drool and sleep. Karl lifted him out of the carrier and held him over his dry shoulder.

Gordon rubbed his chin. "I don't see how this will help you. You need a solid career, in something like accounting, or a trade perhaps."

Karl breathed deeply. "I think I know what I want."

"Son, you have a family and you're Indian," Gordon said. "This program is for men seeking priesthood."

"And you are white. I have an interest in theology, God Creator, praise, ritual, and belief. These men will be more than priests." *Church puppets,* thought Karl.

Gordon bristled. "They will be pastors and teachers."

"We are all teachers and leaders of our people. I believe I can use the knowledge I gain in this program to understand humankind better. A person's religion is the deepest thing in him."

"Still trying to have both sacraments—Marriage and Holy Orders," Mellitus said.

Brother Mellitus was nothing like Lucian, and yet he was Lucian's friend. Karl recalled that day in Lucian's office when they argued about religion. They were both wiser now.

"Are you considering him?" Gordon turned to Mellitus.

The man leaned forward and narrowed his eyes, assessing Karl. It felt like he could see into his soul, grab his spirit, like a medicine man. Katie moved to stand next to Karl. She felt it, too. The man was dangerous, like a hidden wasp's nest in a decaying log.

"Do you believe in God?" Mellitus asked, his voice smooth and oily.

Elias moved away from the men toward Katie, who grabbed Karl's hand and squeezed.

"Could you define that for me?"

Hilary grinned. Gordon shifted in his chair.

"I am not being rude. God has many names, many faces."

"We call our God Wakan Tanka," Katie said. "Great Spirit."

"Not Old Man Coyote?" Mellitus chirped.

"Old Man is the Apsáalooke Creator," Katie said. "I'm part Apsáalooke and part Lakota."

"Why are you encouraging this discussion? There is one God," Gordon said, gripping the arms of the chair.

Karl stood tall and raised his chin as pride surged within him. His children knew their origins. He felt Gordon judging all but his desire. He didn't look the part of a college student, for he was Indian and married.

Karl glanced at the clock on the wall. He needed to feed his kids. This had been a pointless trip.

"We want candidates with questions, ones who want to learn and explore," Hilary said, tapping the stack of papers on his desk.

"How's your spirit, Buffalo Meat? Still split?" Mellitus asked.

"Blended. How is your soul? Still lingering above the flames?" Karl asked.

Mellitus grinned. "I'm old. It is cold in Montana in the winter. Virtuous living is boring."

Gordon stood. "This is a Catholic Benedictine school. You're applying for a theology scholarship. Yet you can't define God."

"I figured that is what theology was all about, defining the faces of God. Appearances are not clear sometimes," Karl said, smoothing his braid with his hand.

"They are to me," Father Gordon said, trembling slightly. "I'm a Benedictine monk and a priest."

"Your name is Gordon. I have not heard of a Benedictine saint named Gordon," Karl said, thinking he could judge too.

The vein on Gordon's forehead pulsed.

"Touché," Mellitus said, eyes twinkling with mirth. "You best parry, Gordon."

"I will not," Gordon said, his voice reverberating to the high ceiling. "We had narrowed our choice to two men."

"Now we have an additional consideration," Hilary said, placing three applications on the desk.

"You can't be serious. You know my vote," Gordon said, shoving his hands into the pockets of his black habit. "This doesn't change my mind. Besides, he was late."

"Depends on your definition of late," Mellitus said. "Be culturally sensitive. He's on Indian time."

"We should all agree," Hilary said.

"The dean has the final say," Gordon hissed, shaking out his scapular before marching by Karl. The air chilled at his passing.

"Temper, temper, temper. One-meter penalty for the saint-less one," Mellitus said with glee.

Hilary shook his head. "Honestly, Brother Mellitus, do you ever stop with the pokes at a man's soul?"

Karl stood riveted.

"Growth doesn't come unless the soil is tilled." Mellitus turned to Karl. "Don't mind him. He wanted Boniface, the Abbot didn't want to waste a good Benedictine name on him."

"Do you have any objections to preaching at Mass?" Hilary asked.

"No, but I cannot guarantee they will return after I speak," Karl said with a slight grin.

Hilary laughed, turning to Mellitus, giving him an anticipatory look.

Mellitus placed a finger to his lips.

Karl knew what that meant. The interview was over. Karl motioned for Katie to come with him.

"Thank you for your consideration," Karl said.

"Don't be so hasty," Mellitus croaked.

He wasn't counting coup today and he didn't want them to choose him and regret it later.

Karl wondered what Lucian had told Mellitus. How much did he know? Mellitus leaned forward, and Katie pulled Elias to her. Karl put a calming hand on Katie's shoulder, hoping to reassure her that Mellitus was not a dangerous enemy.

"I have made my decision. I agree with Father Hilary. The scholarship is yours."

Karl stooped to pick up Elias. He blinked. Had he heard right? White men gave nothing for free, religion did not color their whiteness. The history of church and Natives proved that, just ask any Elder. What was the catch?

Two monks seemed content, only Gordon was unhappy. That was not his problem. The scholarship was his. Education, he would take it.

Katie gave a yip and danced a circle around Karl and Elias.

"Why?" Karl asked, sounding like Elias, as his blue eyes focused on Mellitus.

"I like a challenge," the monk said. "And so do you."

A person appeared at the open door.

"*Iná*," Katie shouted.

Karl turned and saw his wife, Faith. Elias squealed and squirmed his way out of Karl's arms and waddled on his chubby legs to her.

"*Até* is going to school," Katie announced.

Faith stepped into the office and held out her hand as an introduction to Hilary and Mellitus.

"I'm Faith, Karl's wife. Thank you for giving him a chance. He won't disappoint."

"Oh, you have got to be kidding me. This day gets better and better. You married Faith. Gordon didn't think you had faith, and I was worried about what you would do with faith."

"Mellitus, enough," Hilary said, his voice apologetic.

"Are you sure you aren't Standing Holy?" Mellitus said, turning to Faith.

Foolish monk testing the pride of this woman. She was not of Sitting Bull's lineage.

The games had begun. He smiled ruefully at Mellitus. He was ready.

They headed out the door. Katie pushed her way back in and ran up to Mellitus, touching his sleeve before darting back to Karl. If Karl wasn't counting coup, Katie was.

The curmudgeon monk's laughter filled the room and followed them down the hall.

CHAPTER 25
THE RULE OF ST. BENEDICT

Brother, you say there is but one way to worship and
serve the Great Spirit.
If there is but one religion, why do you white people
differ so much about it?
Why not all agreed, as you can all read the Book?

Sogoyewapha (Red Jacket). 1750-1830. Great Seneca Orator
speaking for the rights of his people, and a negotiator.

K arl was grateful that winter was over, and the season
was marching into spring. All winter long, Faith and the
kids drove him to school because a motorcycle didn't
drive well on the icy roads. Now, it was spring, and he could ride
his banged-up Harley to college and back. At least some of the

family was now getting sleep. He figured he was averaging four hours a night, between school, commuting, homework, and parental duties, which started the second he walked in as Faith headed out to work. He finished his studies in the early morning hours to the songs of frogs and calls of owls and felt like the moon chasing the sun.

He stuffed his papers and books into his backpack and stepped out into the morning air, which was still chilly, for the sun had not kissed the horizon.

"*Até*," Katie called, as she ran outside barefooted and in her nightgown. "Hugs."

Karl wrapped her in his arms and kissed her forehead.

"Excellent way to start the day. Go back to sleep now."

She smiled and darted back inside.

Karl rode his motorcycle to St. Alberic's. He stopped at the farm, checking for lights. If on, it meant the farmer was busy inside. He didn't need to be caught stealing from the hand that fed him. He worried about nibbling off the monks. Still, he pulled a few carrots.

Karl hummed to himself as he parked his motorcycle and climbed the moaning steps to the bathroom on the second floor and washed the carrots. They had reminded him of Susan, a girl from a lit class with orangey hair. She had two classes with him, and he enjoyed her cheerful outlook on life. Through the bleak, sleep-deprived months she was a ray of sunshine and he looked forward to seeing her and sitting next to her in class. She always saved him a seat.

He had not seen her in these last few days. They often reviewed material in the same study group. Perhaps he would see her there.

The morning progressed as every morning did. Classes filled

with dorm dwellers, where the men in black stood out in a sea of jeans and tie-dyed tee shirts. Then his theology and philosophy classes, where he and a few others were outcasts. The men who attended those classes believed in their vocation to the priesthood. He and the women sat apart from the sea of men, some in black robes. The curly-haired monk often arrived a few seconds late. Curly Hair sat next to the door, far away from Karl and the women. Sometimes a monk would move to sit next to him as if the lone monk were a danger to himself or others. If the professor noticed the divide, he never commented on it, but it rankled Karl that some felt superior. Classes were for all.

His next class was Study of the Rule of St. Benedict. Since the beginning of the term, he was the only one in the classroom. After spending a couple of days alone, he checked to see if they had canceled the class. The student worker in the registrar's office handed Karl a syllabus and assured him the class was still active. They didn't want him in this class. He was determined to pass this ghost class. Dutifully, he showed up in room 305 and studied on his own, reading a chapter and trying to guess what sort of discussion and insights Father Gordon might share on what he'd read.

Karl climbed the stairs and detoured to Father Gordon's office. The door was closed. It was always closed. He shrugged and fished out his paper from his backpack, and carefully slipped it under the door. Just because they weren't teaching him didn't mean he couldn't learn the material.

Karl pulled out the carrot and stuck it like a cigar in his mouth before opening the door to 305. He entered. Four black-robed monks stared at him.

He recognized them from other classes. The curly-haired, with the funny name, *Jo nick use*. Denis and Cyrus—one was loud and the other quiet. They were always together like thunder and lightning. The fourth man stood rigid in his pressed and starched black habit. He walked toward Karl. The handshake was soft and limp.

"I'm Brother Pius. Brothers Joannicus, Denis, and Cyrus. And you are?"

Karl took the carrot out of his mouth. His heart pounded. Would they know it was from their farm?

"Don't be ridiculous and don't say your actual name," Rebecca whispered in his mind.

"Karl Mackenzie." Knows the Song.

"Where is Father Gordon?" Brother Joannicus asked, his brown eyes peering over the wall of books on the desk where he sat. There were so many books. Karl scanned the titles—St. Augustine... something written in Latin. This man was scholarly.

"Were we supposed to listen to Father Hilary or Gordon?" Denis asked, pacing the aisle. "Father Hilary said meet here, but we've been gathering in the monastery since the beginning."

"Wish I had known," Karl said, as they all looked away.

"The class is intended for those becoming priests," Pius said. "Not for your kind."

"My kind?" Was it because he was Apsáalooke or because he wasn't dressed in black?

"Laity," Joannicus said, stacking the books on his desk.

"It is our home. Cloistered, private. You wouldn't let just anyone wander into your home, would you?" Pius asked.

He would. But before he could answer, Cyrus headed to the door, followed by Denis.

"I will find Father Gordon and tell him we are here and ask him where he wants us."

They didn't want him in the class. The term was almost over. What difference would it make now? The meaningful discussion and debates, the sharing of understanding and knowledge, was useless now. They had both lost.

"We don't want to be here either," Pius said.

"Then leave," Karl said, sitting on the desktop, so he towered over Brother Pius.

"We can't. We have to obey," Joannicus said, stacking the books into three piles.

"Obey? Did the Abbot order you here?"

"We're here. That's all that matters," Joannicus said.

"No. You have not been here all term. I think that matters too," Karl said, rubbing his hands on his jeans, feeling his face getting hot.

"I don't see your point. You're not here to become a priest or monk. You don't have a vocation," Pius said. "Shouldn't you be on a court playing basketball?"

Karl leaned forward. This man was mean. Just because he was an Indian did not mean he played basketball.

"How do you know? Who decides, me or you? Do you have a calling? Besides, my brother plays basketball and we have decided to diversify."

Joannicus separated his books by size into two piles.

"I'm a junior monk, pretty sure hanging around this long speaks to my desire," Pius said, cracking the knuckles on his right hand. How arrogant of this man. Soon he will quote Bible verses and doctrine. His name suits him. Pius was pious.

"If it is all about desire, then I think I have you beat. I have been here all term, reading the Rule and learning without you."

"You obviously don't get it," Pius said. "Are you even Catholic?"

"From what I have seen, you are lacking in some qualities suggested for monks. Humility and hospitality, for example. Yes, I am Catholic." *Don't say it*, screamed Rebecca in his mind. "And Apsáalooke."

"You can't be both," Pius said as he attempted to rise from his seat, but his habit caught on the desk, pulling him back.

"I am both."

"You have to choose."

"I have."

Joannicus pursed his lips against a forming smile, but his dimples betrayed him as he matched his books to the edge of his desk.

There were no rules to say that a layperson couldn't study theology.

Pius glared. "Arrogant fool."

"I am not the one who wants to be a saint, nor the one telling me I have to choose," Karl said.

Pius untangled himself from the desk and stood. Karl moved from his desktop perch.

"I'm not the one who can't be a priest," Pius said.

"I would rather not be a priest. I have no call to celibacy. I like sex."

St. Augustine slid and thumped to the floor.

"I'm sure you do," Pius said with a sneer. "Glad to see that you take heed of 1 Corinthians 7: 9, he who cannot control themselves, they should marry."

"Thank you, St. Paul. I sometimes wonder why call it the Catholic Church and not the Church of St. Paul. I could become a deacon." This was a lie. Karl wasn't interested in becoming a deacon.

"Seriously, I would rather talk about the Rule," Joannicus said, sandwiching St. Augustine between St. Therese of Lisieux and Thomas Merton. "What aspect of the Rule did you choose to write on?"

A scholar and a peacemaker, Karl thought as he moved closer to

Joannicus. He liked this monk. This man could look outside the cloister.

"Well, Joe, I selected the qualities of an abbot," Karl said.

"Brother Joannicus is the proper way to address a monk," Brother Pius said, moving to the chalkboard.

"It is a dumb name," Karl said, knowing that novice monks submitted three names, and the abbot selected one for them. "I would have picked Bernard."

"I submitted three names: Benedict, Gregory, and Dunstan."

"Yet you are called Joannicus. I do not think Abbot Sebastian likes you," Karl said.

Pius cracked the knuckles on his left hand.

"This abbot has issues. He left Father Gordon with his Christian name," Karl said.

"What did you discover about the role of an abbot?" Joannicus asked, steering the conversation away from judgments.

"The burden is not something I want," Karl said, thinking parenting was hard enough.

Joannicus tilted his head. "Perhaps it's not a burden."

Karl ran his hand over his braid.

Joannicus turned to face Karl, parting the two stacks of books. "The job is demanding. The Abbot is human. He'll make mistakes. The first thing you learn is how to live together. The Rule is for beginners."

"I would take the job," Pius said. "The honor is humbling."

Mister Ambitious could use some humility.

"Somehow that does not surprise me," Karl said.

"This is a waste of time. I'm going to the monastery," Pius said, turning to leave and bumping into Joe's desk. The books cascaded to the floor with a loud thud. Karl caught a few and set them gently on the desktop, and helped the young monk retrieve the rest from the floor as his brothers retreated down the hall.

"We are not all that way," Joannicus said as he gathered his books. "Be patient with us."

KARL WALKED toward the back gate of the monastery. They had instructed him to use that door to enter. Who cared which door he entered? He marched past a small grotto with a statue of St. Francis of Assisi and his woodland friends.

So, Frankie, we are the hidden ones? Karl thought.

He approached the ornate iron gate, with an angry angel warrior welded onto the slats. He put his hand on the gate and pushed. The gate groaned but did not open. He followed a small path, hoping to find another entrance but he found classmate Susan sitting on a bench next to a statue of the Virgin Mary in a well-tended garden with several rose bushes. Karl glanced back at St. Francis, who stood among the weeds against a wall. He had noticed she was absent from class, and he had hoped she had gone to the clinic for help.

She turned, and her expectant face dropped to a frown.

"Mary had a hard life," Susan said rubbing her already showing belly.

"I will stick with Francis and his menagerie for comfort and solace," Karl said. "Animals were more thankful and forgiving than most humans."

"That kind of Native attitude will keep you out of there," Susan said.

Karl sat on the bench next to her.

"I would rather not be a monk. Too much condemnation for me."

Susan placed her head on his shoulder. "Do you think I am a slut?"

Karl snorted. "No. And God is not punishing you. A child is

not retribution." Unless you are Judith. "Do you think I am a noble Indian?"

Susan turned and looked at him. "A warrior, rebel, and if you weren't married..." She hesitated, and her cheeks flushed. "I'd marry you."

Karl laughed. "We are friends. That is community, but I love you, too."

She rose, and Karl rose with her.

"I best be getting to class if I want to finish early. As you said, this is challenging."

"You will succeed with a little determination," Karl said. He eyed the statue of St. Francis and the wall.

She embraced him, and he hugged her back, and she headed down the hill.

Karl went back to the gate. The hinges screeched and yielded a narrow passage. Brothers Pius and Joannicus darted behind a bush.

"You realize I can see you," Karl said. "Habits are not invisibility cloaks, although having seen some of you out of habit, they hide the sin of gluttony well."

Joannicus moved to the gate.

"Why did you say to that girl you loved her?" Joannicus asked, tugging on the gate.

"Does your wife know you talk like that?" Pius asked, standing idly by.

"Susan is a friend," Karl said, amused that Pius was concerned about his marriage.

"A girl who is unmarried and pregnant," Pius said, his face soured.

"I did not cause that," Karl said, peering through the angel's eyes.

"She needed a priest and confession. This happens when we allow females on campus."

Joannicus and Karl stopped struggling with the gate.

"You are right. Once we let them vote and wear pants, we opened the door to all kinds of evil. Get over yourself," Karl said, finding Pius old fashioned.

Pius narrowed his eyes as the vein on his forehead bulged.

"Women are not the issue," Joannicus said, his face the color of pink roses. "Morality is. The body is a temple."

Enough with the stubborn gate. Karl walked to St. Francis and placed his foot on the head of the statue, hoisting himself over the wall. He landed gracefully on the other side. This looked like anyone's backyard, with a manicured lawn, a covered patio with benches, picnic tables, a fire pit, and a brick BBQ.

Pius wagged a finger in Karl's face, standing too close.

"You don't belong here. You have no respect for the church or us."

"Respect for the church. It doesn't have a stellar history with my kind, so how can you expect me to see them? They were supposed to be our protectors and yet they turned on us. Truth is not in the history books. You do not know me, and you certainly do not know Susan. You do not know how she became pregnant and where is your compassion? At least pretend to care about your fellow humans."

"Why you arrogant sava—" Pius hissed, his minty breath filling the space between them.

"Brother Pius," Joannicus said, stepping closer to them.

"—sack of garbage," Pius finished.

"At least I care about what happens," Karl said, stepping half a step back.

"We care," Joannicus said, picking a dead blossom from a rosebush. "We just do it differently."

"You should read that Rule of yours more. The path is clearly marked with love, compassion, and understanding. We are all connected. At least I see the connection between man and earth. My ancestors did not waste time sacrificing to please the Almighty. We praised and thanked the Great Spirit for all that we have," Karl said.

"Why don't you just leave and take your mythical thinking with you," Pius said, his tone mocking.

"Myths are not just made-up stories; they hold the truth." Karl's hand formed a fist. This monk needed to be taken down a notch.

The air filled with cigar smoke. Joannicus waved his hand and coughed.

A large man dressed in coveralls pushed his way between Pius and Karl, forcing Pius to move away. He reeked of the barn with his chest pressed against Karl. Ripe and sweet at the same time.

Could he count this as coup? Who was this man, the monastic bouncer?

"You sit," he said to Karl, gently pushing him back. He turned to the monks. "You two are late for class. Shoo."

Joannicus and Pius scurried like bunnies saved from the claws of a hawk.

Karl relaxed his fist and glanced longingly at the sliding patio door. He would be late. Father Gordon was more than happy to fail him for tardiness, and if he failed his classes, they would take his scholarship away.

"Don't argue nonsense with them," the man said, pointing a calloused finger.

"I was not arguing. They were wrong."

The man laughed and puffed on his cigar. "I see truth on both sides. Even if it is right doesn't mean you should do it."

Karl stepped around the man, who was wide as he was tall. "I am late for class. Can I go in?"

The man's bushy eyebrows bounced up and down. "Ah, so you're the one."

Karl turned to the sliding glass doors, seeing his reflection. Skinny Indian dressed in jeans and a thin tee shirt. He had a right to be here.

"What does that mean?"

"The heretic among saints. Your reputation precedes you."

A flash of teeth amidst the straggly beard and mustache. Was that a smirk?

"Wait, what do you mean by that?" Karl asked, curiosity ensnaring him.

The monks were worse than a group of high school girls. He wondered how much truth had been absent in the tales of Karl Mackenzie. How much had Lucian told them?

"I am aware these classes are intended to make them priests, but it is not working."

"What don't they get?" Puffs of smoke lingered in the air.

Karl pulled on the door. It did not budge. Had they locked him out?

"They quote rules but no action," Karl said, knowing that laws, rules, and protocols were never the answer when dealing with people. One had to listen.

The man headed to the gate with his oil can.

"Do you realize they are Catholic? Are you aware the Church has rules? They will be priests someday, teachers of the faith, handpicked servants of Christ."

"They are just men. The Church is not always right. Religion is not a one size fits all. That is not faith."

"Oh, there it is, the heretical ideas. I was concerned you were holding out on me. So, have they saved you? Have you found Jesus?"

Oil dripped on the rusty hinges. Was the man serious? His eyes twinkled. Was that a grin buried in the haystack of hair?

"Is Jesus lost?"

The large man's body shook with laughter.

Karl glanced at the unyielding gate and the locked slider. He sighed, stuck in the yard with the gardener.

"Do you have a personal relationship with Jesus?" Karl asked, peering into the window. The room was large. A stone fireplace stood at one end and a kitchenette at the other. Books and games were on a wooden shelf and a puzzle was on a table. Karl could not imagine spending any time in this place, let alone calling it home. He smiled to himself. It was more like a hotel for lost souls. Check in today and check out on judgment day. The gate groaned but didn't move as the man pushed to loosen the stubborn hinges.

"Yes, I do. What do you think these men do?

"Hide."

The man rolled up the sleeve of his red plaid flannel shirt. Karl took a step back and grimaced. Had he gone too far? He lumbered toward Karl.

"And pray."

The meaty hand banged on the window. A black-robed figure appeared from behind the curtains like a child playing hide and seek.

"You, my friend, have a lot to learn about monks. God is a relentless caller, the hounds of heaven," the farmer said, chuckling.

Did he mean the hounds of hell?

"I know the Creator and arguing nonsense with you will not get me inside," Karl said.

"Enter at your own risk," the man said, stepping aside.

The lock clicked, and Karl opened the door, the smell of coffee called, tempting him. One cup. Would it be stealing? He only had four hours of sleep. He hesitated, closing the slider.

"Thank you," Karl said, turning and seeing the monk who let him in was Brother Mellitus.

"I heard the gate rattling and moaning. I feared perhaps the devil was trying to get in," Mellitus said. "What do you want?"

"Coffee," Karl said, surprised at his words. "And to follow Pius and Brother Joannicus."

Mellitus's face lit up, and his eyes danced to a hidden delight. "Portentous Pius and his holiness went to the novitiate. Are you sure you want to follow them?"

Karl hesitated. He was already late for class. This was Mellitus, the trickster.

"A place or state of being?"

"Should be the latter, alas, it's a place," Mellitus said, pouring black liquid from the urn into a large mug. Then he ladled sugar into the cup. Karl stopped him at five scoops, amazed that the man remembered that Karl liked his coffee sweet.

"That guy outside, who was he?" Karl asked, hearing the screech of the gate protesting the oil on its hinges.

Brother Mellitus snorted, handing Karl the mug of hot liquid. Karl looked at the inscription that read, "World's best dad." There were no dads, just fathers. Mellitus grinned at the ironic mug.

"The farmer, Rose. An oaf if ever there was one. So, you are still here. You can't convert us. If I were you, I'd run back to my happy hunting ground and play Indian."

"Are you sure you want to play this game?" Karl asked before sipping the hot coffee, feeling revived. He recalled the man's idle threats, which amounted to nothing. Karl had made confirmation.

"I'm curious. Do you still think Holy Orders is an invitation from God, Extreme Unction, a form of Sun Dance?"

285

"No. I have learned a thing or two since our last debate. I figured I would become your abbot after I got my degree."

Mellitus laughed and plopped himself into an overstuffed chair. "Over my dead body, boy. Don't you have class or something?"

"Where is the novitiate?"

"Third floor, end of the hall on the right. Don't get lost. We don't send out search parties for lost men. That is how we get new monks."

Karl walked out the door into the dimly lit hallway, looking for signs. Those stairs had to be somewhere.

CHAPTER 26

CONFESSION

I cannot think that we are useless, or God would not
have created us.
One God is looking-down on us all. We are all children of
one God.
The sun, the darkness, the winds are all listening to
what we have to say.

Goyahkla (Geronimo). 1829-1909. Leader, warrior, and medicine man from the Bedonkohe band of the Apache Nation.

September and another term. One down, three to go. Karl had time before his next class. So, he wandered the hilltop, stopping in the courtyard next to the bell tower in front of the church. He stood by the large wooden doors, studying the story carved there. This would be his first visit to the church since his self-imposed exile. He had avoided attending Mass since his wedding. If they wouldn't bless his marriage, he wouldn't grace them with his presence. He missed the ritual, the stories, the ceremony, and the seasonal changes.

He hesitated a moment and then pulled on the iron handle and stepped inside. The door thudded behind him, making him jump. He glanced out the window at the clear blue sky. There was no chance of a lightning bolt. Breathing deeply, he listened.

The holy water font bubbled like a creek. Even though Mass was yesterday, the air was heavy with frankincense. The atrium held a carved bench that faced a picture window with the orchards in the distance. Greenery leaned toward the light like an eager child listening to a captivating story. The aggregated stone floor and the rough wooden planked walls allowed the outside world to invade the inside structure.

Karl thought the sunrises must be spectacular from this vantage point.

A great way to greet the morning instead of sweaty feet kicking him in the face or a wet diaper seeping into his pillow. He smiled. The warm snuggles with "Tell me a story" before breakfast had their appeal, too.

Karl rubbed the apple he had picked up in the orchard against his sleeve. His lunch comprised whatever he could scoop up on his way to the hilltop. It wasn't stealing if it was on the ground. He would be hungry once the harvest was done.

Karl moved through the atrium, this time dipping his fingers into the font and blessing himself.

He stopped and looked at the child-size statue of Saint Alberic of Cîteaux. Alberic was a hermit and became the abbot of a group of lax monks. He researched this saint since the monks seemed to put so much stock in the choice of a saint to guide them on their monastic journey. Karl wondered if the saint drew those kinds of

men to the monastery. The irony was that Saint Alberic was cred-
ited with founding a stricter order of Benedictines, the Cistercians.
The men Karl had met in this monastery swung from rule
followers to rule breakers.

Were there any moderates?

The wooden figure held a crook and a parchment. Squinting,
he tried to see what they wrote on the scroll as he bit into his
apple. The crunch echoed in the silent church.

Probably that beloved Rule of Saint Benedict that the monks
were always quoting to him.

He noticed this church wasn't like any he'd been in. There
were no pews, no formal aisle to the altar, just an open octagonal
room. A stone walkway ran along the outside like a racetrack. He
strolled around the walkway. The shape reminded him of the
inside of a teepee. A circle was a suitable space for prayer.

He touched the rough-cut wooden walls. Were they coated
with pleas? Perhaps the incense was the lingering scent of prayers.

Karl moved to the middle of the space. He turned to the west,
to where the organ with its golden pipes filled the area. To the
south, the opening from which he entered and above a ceiling of
stained-glass squares that poured colored sunlight onto the
golden-tan carpet. The north wall, formed of stained and plain
windows, looked out onto a meditative garden, complete with a
birdbath and lanterns. Facing east, he found he stood in front of
the altar, which was draped in a soft green woven cloth.

Whoa, this is big enough to sacrifice an elk on.

Behind the lectern was an etched glass panel with side open-
ings. He guessed it was the space where the tabernacle was. He
looked down. This is where the fire should be. He looked up into
the rafters. There was no smoke hole for the prayers to rise to the
Great Spirit. They trapped their pleas within the walls of this
building.

He licked his sticky fingers, then wiped them on his jeans as he contemplated where to dispose of the core.

Karl stepped to the doorway by the etched panel and peered inside. A large wooden box, the tabernacle, sat on a plain mahogany table. The house of Jesus. This one was not as ornate as the one at Saint George's church, which was solid gold.

On the floor lay a monk, face down, and hooded. His shoes were off. Karl watched to see if the man breathed or snored. From under the black sleeve, he could make out a plaid shirt.

"Joe?" Karl whispered. "Are you alright?"

The body moved. The hood flopped to the side. Joannicus glanced up and then struggled as he righted himself. Karl reached out a hand to help.

"Sorry, were you praying?" Karl asked, as his stomach rumbled in protest for more food.

"No," Joannicus said, looking around sheepishly. "Basking."

"Looks more like sleeping."

"I have come from my weekly confession. I did my penance and then I let his love fill me."

Weekly? How many sins could a monk commit in a week? Was it sipping too much beer at the abbey's small brewery? Absolution Ale was the name of the beer, and he thought it was clever and somehow appropriate for a monastic brewery.

"We usually dance and shout when we are joyous," Karl said while holding the apple core behind his back.

Brother Joannicus brushed his hands and shook out his scapular. "I get your point, and I felt like I could burst with joy. I understand that's my Southern Baptist upbringing. We—they are more evangelical. I have to work hard at toning it down."

Karl suppressed a smile. Joannicus was not demonstrative. What was there to tone down?

"Damn, that is too bad. I suspect Catholics are asleep in their faith. They never shout, 'He has risen, hallelujah.' If he paid my debt, I would see things differently."

Joannicus laughed, sat, and put his shoes on.

"I became Catholic when I was fifteen on Easter. My father is a Southern Baptist preacher. He felt betrayed because he wanted me to follow in his footsteps. My father and I have an understanding since we're both doing the work of the Lord."

A sadness tinged Joe's eyes. Karl thought the look of sadness didn't match the words. It was probably what he hopes for rather than reality.

Karl recalled his baptism. Nothing happened that day, just water and words, a lot of words. He didn't feel the elation that Joe described, only the warring of two ideologies.

"We have something in common. I am Apsáalooke then when I was eight, they introduced me to Catholicism. Your beliefs are confusing, but the spirit of the religion is sound."

"When I turned eighteen, I packed up and came here. I'm called to testify, witness about the wonders of God." Joe's eyes glowed with excitement as he spoke and walked out of the church toward the atrium. "I'm to share the word, the breath, the story, the prayer. That's the key. Jesus taught in parables. Catching and telling the story is the secret to life."

Now he understood why they called him the holy one. Karl's spirit lifted. The wonder of this man was contagious.

Joe stopped and blessed himself at the bubbling font. Karl followed, doing the same.

"That takes guts. I cannot take the Apsáalooke out of me. It is part of my DNA, but I try to embrace the Catholic."

"Faith is not genetic. It wasn't like I chose to be Jewish because I see Christians as fake."

"I like the narratives. All religions have a lesson to teach. We teach in stories and after each tale, we ask our listeners a series of questions. What did you hear? What did you learn? How did it make you feel?" Karl said. "Stories are a gift."

"Yes. The sacred moments of the ordinary," Joannicus said in almost a whisper.

They headed down a hallway, past the slots and books. On the wall were fourteen brass panels depicting the Stations of the Cross. The journey of a condemned man. To the left were little rooms used for private Mass.

Joannicus paused at the second station, where Jesus takes up the cross.

"I like that these are here. Every day it's a gentle reminder of why I am here. My life is a gift, a sacrifice to God."

Only this route leads to the monastery, not eternal life. Karl had studied the Rule of St. Benedict and knew of the twelve steps of humility. He wondered how many monks paused and reflected as they made this daily walk to the monastery. The Rule was like a written vision quest.

"This life, this vocation, is a journey. So, do you have an animal guide?" Joannicus asked.

Karl glanced around. He didn't want anyone to overhear. The experience was personal, not a secret, and he wasn't enamored with his guide.

"I'm sorry. I shouldn't have asked. It's just that I heard about animal guides," Joannicus said, touching the next tile.

"When I went on my search. I fasted and waited. Nothing happened. I returned, ashamed that I was not worthy, that maybe my blue eyes had offended the ancestors. I was covered in mosquito bites and developed a fever. That was when I had my vision. I wanted an eagle or something majestic. But my guide is a mosquito."

Joannicus stared at him and bit his lower lip. The apple core dripped into Karl's left hand.

"You can laugh."

"I see how it suits you."

"Because I am annoying?"

Dimples graced Joe's face. He nodded as his cheeks burned red. Karl turned and shoved the core into his pocket, wiping the wetness on his jeans.

"The Elders told me the lowly mosquito seeks high ideals and sees life for what it is."

"Thankfully, it wasn't an invitation to ruin people's lives. We already have a monk that does that," Joannicus said, thumping his fist on his chest in a mea culpa gesture. "I'll be going to confession now. That was uncharitable of me."

Brother Mellitus and his caustic tongue came to mind.

"Sorry, I interrupted your penance," Karl said as he studied the last tile, Jesus in the tomb, at the entrance to the silent mausoleum-like building. *Ironic*, thought Karl.

"You didn't interrupt. I was being selfish. I enjoy my alone time with the Lord." Joannicus sighed. "Confession is such a cleansing experience, don't you think?"

"Do we sin that much? Why do we need a third party? God knows what is in the heart."

The silence was thunderous. Joannicus stepped away. Karl touched the top of his head. Had he grown horns and a tail?

"Confession isn't for God's benefit. It's for us. Temptation is all around. To capture the light, you must seek it. Seriously, hearing and seeing the reaction of another can shake you to the core. Compassion and forgiveness are experiences that transform your life."

Karl stood in the secular world and Joe in the monastery.

"I prefer to face the person I hurt and say the words to them directly."

Which he would do when he saw Father Lucian.

Joannicus ran his fingers through his curly hair.

"You're missing the point. Forgiveness is not something handed out like penny candy. It comes from here. Me to you. You to me." He placed his open palm on his chest.

"Brother Joannicus, not all sins can be forgiven."

"All sin can be absolved. It must or else there's no point," Joannicus said as he leaned his back against the wall. "What can't you forgive?"

Karl stepped back and thought about his father, Endow, his stepfather, Terence, and his mother, Judith. Their actions, despite their intention for good or evil, spoke louder than a confessional whispering. He pursed his lips to remain in silence, but the words bunched up inside of him. God was not a label to fix all wrongs. Some acts were unforgivable. An act of goodness does not negate an act of evil. Saving a life doesn't make up for taking one. Sure, he had sins, or what they called sins, like taking those apples.

"I'm sorry. I've no right to press you for answers or grievances against your soul. I'm not a priest yet. I can't hear your confession. I can find a priest," Joannicus said. "Seriously, you must unburden your soul. You don't know when death arrives. The roof could cave in on us or you could have a heart attack."

Karl laughed. "I am only twenty-one. If death grabs me, it will be in an accident. I am not dying, so my spirit is fine. I do not need a priest. When you become a priest, I will confess to you."

They stood at the entrance to the monastery. Joannicus stepped back into the hall.

Karl could sense the wetness of the apple core in his pocket, turning his jeans a dark blue. He leaned forward. Joe's eyes appeared watery. Was he crying? He doesn't even know my pain, and yet he cries for me. Karl shifted his weight, fighting the urge to run from this man who had wisdom beyond his age or experience.

Joannicus turned to the hallway in the monastery, paused, then twisted to face Karl.

"Life is all about love. Only the grace of God can heal you. Let it go. If you don't, nothing changes. I can't explain the mystery of forgiveness, but the healing is real. Please consider what I said. We must forgive each other." Joe's voice cracked, and his lips trembled. "I'm late. The story is about love. I need to go. I'll pray for you. Will you pray for me?"

"Sure," Karl said, uncertain why Joe asked for his prayers. It was a hasty exit. Karl stood in the hallway, listening to the rapid footfalls, confused by what had just happened.

Brother Mellitus popped out of one of the little rooms in the hall.

"Oh, look what you have done. You're so hell-bent on getting knowledge, quick to see what you want to see. Shut up and listen to a wise monk and the howling bellies of your kids. Step into my booth and I'll absolve you."

Karl shook his head. This man was a brother. He could not give church absolution, only priests could do that. Guilt pushed on him as an ache simmered inside of him.

"A braver man would own up to his faults, especially when they leak through your pocket. Are you afraid, Chief?"

Karl's hand twitched. Is taking what fell to the ground a sin? God knew his sins. He no longer whispered his troubles to a stranger.

Mellitus reached into the room and snatched a book. Karl read the title: *The Last Temptation of Christ,* by Nikos Kazantzakis.

"That is a banned book," Karl said.

"Banned? It's enlightening. Isn't that what you're trying to do? Enlighten the self-possessed?" Mellitus said as he thumped Karl's shoulder with the paperback. "It's fiction. You can't possibly believe that Satan was Jesus's guardian angel. Maybe you're Holy

Joe's guardian angel. What do you think, Karl Knows Too Much? Perhaps I'm yours?"

"It is Knows the Song."

Brother Mellitus tucked the offending novel into his cassock pocket and then chuckled as he walked away. "Be careful, little bug, or you will get squashed."

Karl wandered from the hilltop. The conversations left him disturbed. Was Joannicus his friend? He had forgiven Lucian and the others.

You have not talked to him, accused the Elder's voice within him.

When his parents went to confession, did they say sorry, and recommit? He was the one they should ask forgiveness from. Anger licked at his heels as he marched on the path to the farm. He had forgiven them. He no longer lived in the House of Mackenzie horrors. Yet the words rattled around like marbles in a pouch, and he wasn't sure he believed them.

At the farm, two Australian Shepherds came running up to him, wagging their tails. Karl bent down and rubbed the soft, woolly ears. Would they let him partake in confession since he wasn't married in the church? Was there forgiveness in the church? Or was it just à la carte Catholicism? He shook his head.

Karl's stomach growled at him. The orchard was a few steps away. He turned and saw the farmer in his flannel and coveralls sitting on a low stool. The man looked over his shoulder.

Karl stepped into the barn and watched. The ewe paced and bleated in the stall, clearly pregnant and in distress.

"There you are, the man of the minute," the farmer said.

The man of the hour, Karl thought.

"You're welcome to as many apples as you need. I suggest the ones on the trees are better than the fallen ones. I picked a sack of them. Take them home. Make an apple pie for the kids."

"Who says I need apples?" Karl said. Guilt squirmed inside him, making him defensive. Who told him he had children?

The farmer raised an eyebrow as if waiting for him to admit to theft.

"Scholastica and Benedict told me. They can't keep a secret," the farmer said, tossing his head toward the two dogs curled up on the loose hay. "Every week, the monastery gives away extra produce to anyone in need."

"Are you bragging?" Karl asked. He didn't need charity.

"Don't be so testy. Do I look like a snake tempting you with apples?"

"Sorry. When?" Karl asked, recognizing he was being rude.

"Sunday after Mass," the farmer said, as he rubbed the ewe's flanks. "It's not for you. But if you're hungry, then your kids are. It's for them. Don't make me drive to your home to deliver a gift of love."

The large man rose and ran his hand over his crewcut. His beard grew wide with his smile. Karl knew the man would do it.

"Is there a wind whispering about me?"

"No, but you're the most excitement I've had in a while since the raccoon moved into the goat shed. Don't be a prick. I'll leave you a box of goodies on Friday, for the little ones. And mind your story. I believe you're writing it, make the ending worth the living."

CHAPTER 27
CUSTER'S LAST STAND

Our land is everything to us.
I will tell you one of the things we remember on our land.
We remember that our grandfathers paid for it - with
   their lives.

John Woodenlegs. 1909-1981. Cheyenne, author, educator, and tribal president.

R ebecca sat in the courtyard between the monastery and the guesthouse, waiting for Karl. He was late again. She stared down the path that led to the school and dorms. The hoppy aroma wafted from the brewery, robbing her of the scent of the springtime blossoms. From her bench, the serene beauty beckoned her to relax.

She didn't have time for this. It seemed Karl was getting later and later.

Katie and Elias ran in circles around her, giggling and shouting. Men in black robes walked in odd directions, making larger-than-needed paths, as if contact with the children could contaminate them.

She understood the attraction; it reminded her of their lunches in the church at St. George. She was sure Father Lucian was aware they ate in the third pew, but he never shooed them out. She missed those moments. Karl had replaced her with a wife and children.

"One, two, three, forty," Elias counted as he held his hands to his face and spun in place.

Katie ducked behind a tree trunk, barely visible from where Rebecca sat.

Rebecca knew Karl felt an affection for the priest and nuns who attempted to teach the Catholic ways. Like woodruff burrs, some of the practices stuck to Karl. Walking between two worlds was dangerous. You could get lost. His foundation was Apsáalooke. She would remind him. The tribe needed him.

Brothers Pius and Joannicus strolled past.

"We are being invaded," Pius said, loud enough for her to overhear him.

"That is not kind," Joannicus said, his voice faint. "Why are you so negative? Not all are the same. There is holiness in each person."

Pius snorted. "I grew up here, in Montana. Every Indian I know reeked of poverty and beer."

"But the Crow reservation is a dry reservation."

Pius stopped in his tracks and gave Joannicus a hard look. "Just because it is dry doesn't mean they don't drink."

"Karl isn't like that. I've never seen him drunk," Joannicus said. Rebecca agreed, her brother had not fallen into the brown bottle.

"He's Indian. They feel no remorse about taking from others, the government, the school, and the stores. Hand-to-mouth living. I don't mean to be critical but witness how they live. They say that Indians don't understand ownership. I disagree. They think everything is theirs."

"Blessed are the poor. It's not their fault they are poor or alcoholic. We took everything from them. We must take care of each other."

Good, someone recognizes the wrongs of the past, Rebecca thought.

"We aren't pouring the drink down their throats and the poor will always be with us."

"We aren't doing anything to help either," Joannicus said.

"If you talk a little louder, I could hear you better," Rebecca said, jumping up and facing them.

Joannicus looked at his feet. Pius's eyes roamed her, from her shoulders to her knees. He cracked the knuckles on his left hand. Rebecca took in a sharp breath.

The bastard. What was he looking at?

She wore the traditional clothing of her clan, a long plain dress cinched with a four-inch floral leather belt, a scarf, and high-top moccasins.

"Can we help you?" Joannicus said, his voice tight and his face turning pink.

Rebecca smirked. Like you have in the past?

"I'm waiting for my brother Karl."

"Up here?" Pius said.

"What is wrong with here?" Rebecca said, leaning against the bench back.

"Nothing, but we value our solitude and silence," Pius said.

The bells rang and Rebecca wondered how the loud clanking

translated into silence. As for solitude? Why were they always in pairs?

"Karl's children are not quiet. They are always running around like wild Indians." Pius stopped as Joannicus elbowed him.

Rebecca bristled. Wild Indians indeed. Children exhibited the joy of life. They had too much silence. He probably thinks the birds are too noisy. What did Karl see in them?

Joannicus glanced around and then raised an eyebrow.

Rebecca suddenly realized that the sounds of giggles and laughter were missing.

"Shit. Well, don't just stand there. Help me find them," Rebecca said, scanning for some sign of her niece and nephew.

"What do they look like?" Joannicus asked. "I mean, what are they wearing?"

This man was ridiculous. He knew these kids. Karl was toting them around campus, or else how could they claim the kids were noisy?

"Like you and me, only shorter. Katie is six and Elias is four. Just call their names."

"Perhaps they went to find their father," Pius offered, his voice sounding bored.

Rebecca looked at the path that led to the college. A panic rose inside her. Katie might have met Karl. Karl had been as independent as his daughter. She had tried to teach him impulse control, but so often he defied her. She should have been harsher. She had indulged him. That is why she was searching for his missing kids. A vision of two frightened children lost and alone filled her mind.

"Good luck." Pius pulled Joannicus toward the monastery.

"Seriously? Shouldn't we help?" Joannicus stepped away from Pius.

Rebecca called the children's names. No response but the birds singing.

"Which way did they go?" The flock flitted away without a peep.

She tried the brewery door. It was locked, thank goodness. The brown bottle frightened her, and she worried every time Karl indulged. He doesn't drink that much; he can't afford it. The Elder inside her mind scoffed. None can. But somehow, they seem to get inside the bottle. She recalled Endow. She lived with oppression and poverty, being stripped of everything Indian led many to drink. A deep sadness rose, and she pushed it aside. Karl wasn't going down that path.

She straightened her shoulders and inhaled. Mixed in with the odor of hops was the aroma of freshly baked bread. They would be there. What child couldn't resist food and those smells? She opened the doors in front of her and headed down the hall. She stood in the refectory, a room with several wooden tables set for six.

Rebecca turned to see a monk. The contrast between his black habit and white apron made him look like a penguin.

"Have you seen two little kids—a boy and a girl?"

The monk smiled and nodded.

"Katie and Elias haven't visited today. If they do, I'll feed them and keep them here."

Rebecca raced down the hall to the outside. How did he know their names? Had he heard her yelling and breaking their holy silence?

As she opened the gift shop door, a bell jingled. She glanced around the displays of sweaters, hats, and gloves, noticing the bins of rosaries and medals. She listened to the thud and whoosh of the shuttle and pedals of the looms upstairs.

The monk at the counter assessed her attire and went back to his book.

"The strings are on the counter."

Rebecca noticed a plastic bag with colorful bits of yarn. The tag read, 'Elias.' How much time were the children spending? Taking the sack, she exited the building.

She stood at the top of the walkway, dreading the possibility of looking for them among the students. Then she heard Elias shouting and running toward her with a cloth sack. Her breath caught. He stopped and dug his hand into the bag and tossed feathers into the air. The white fluff floated and bobbed on the breeze like snow around him.

"Hay-ay Hay-ay," Elias shouted. "*Hakahey*, the white man is coming."

Rebecca's spine fused, and horror instantly replaced her fear.

"Elias, stop."

The little boy froze a few feet from his aunt. Downy feathers clung to him.

"What are you doing?" Rebecca asked in a controlled voice.

"Playing Big Horn. I'm the caller. Son of the Morning Star is coming," he said, his voice growing weaker.

Pretending to be a scout for Custer was not a game.

"That is not a game to play. Where did you get breath feathers?" Rebecca knew the meaning of the soft white feathers; they were used to help the warrior float to the next world. She was sure Elias did not understand what he was doing.

"The man with blue eyes gave them to me. He said he was the Great White Father to us." Tears welled up in his eyes. "Why are you upset, *isbaaxia*?"

Someone was using this innocent child. Evil, that is what these men were. They were bodies without spirit, attempting to misguide her niece and nephew. Where was Karl? He needed to see this.

"Where's Katie?" Rebecca took the pillowcase from the boy.

Elias pointed to the monastery.

Rebecca and Elias approached the monastery doors. She did not hesitate or knock. On the iron gate stood two metal angels. They whined as she pushed them aside and walked into the cloister with Elias in tow. In the silence, she heard Katie's strong teaching voice. Rebecca hastened to the sound.

"Whoa there, Nellie," came a booming voice from behind her, causing her to jump.

Nellie? Now she was an animal and a mule, no less?

She spun around and faced the broad man in black, short-haired but fully bearded.

"The name is Rebecca, and you can't stop me." Wishing she were a mule so she could kick him to drive her point clearer.

"Missy, this is a cloistered area. You shall go no farther." The wide man blocked the doorway to the community room.

Cloistered, that meant off limits. Rebecca wondered why they hadn't sent Katie out. Hadn't they allowed Karl in? Inconsistent, selective, yep, Catholic. She knew it was because she was female.

"I'm here now, so let me get Katie. I can hear her inside," Rebecca said.

The monk shook his head. Rebecca wondered if she could push the boulder of a man aside. This was like arguing with a toddler.

Rebecca pushed Elias toward the opening, and in Apsáalooke commanded, "Go, get your sister." He darted past the monk, who turned to chase after him. Rebecca saw Pius and Joannicus lingering in the hall, the light from a doorway silhouetted them.

"Hey, you knew she was in here. Why didn't you send her out? Are you the idiot who sent my nephew out with breath feathers?" Rebecca asked, advancing toward them.

"You mean death feathers?" Pius said.

Joannicus pressed himself tighter into the wall.

"What is wrong with you? Pretending to be the Great White

Father. Haven't you done enough? We trusted you, and what has that gotten us? Alcoholism, our land stolen, and our ancestors raped. And now you are trying to whiten my brother and his children."

"What are you talking about? You're a conquered people. Live with it. Don't go blaming us for your inability to keep an eye on your children," Brother Pius said. "You need to leave."

His minty breath wafted in front of her.

"You going to make me? I'm not leaving, we are not leaving. Ever." Rebecca snarled.

"You need to leave now. You have allowed your children to enter our sacred space," Brother Pius said, cracking his knuckles. Brother Joannicus tugged on his arm.

"And you have given my children a warning. Will you give them diseased blankets, too?" Rebecca tossed the sack of feathers at Pius.

"Angel feathers. Protection. They could be that?" Joannicus said as the white tuffs floated around them.

"Are you crazy? Angels? Why do I bother to talk to you?" Rebecca said as Katie appeared in the doorway.

"Oh, hello, *Iná*," Katie said, using the tribal term for an older woman. "We won the fight. We have defeated Yellow Hair. The mud in his ears has kept him from hearing the truth. Is *Até* here?"

Yellow Hair was the name of General Armstrong Custer. Rebecca felt her face getting hot. Battle facts were not taught by monks.

"We won, we won," Elias chanted as he followed Katie.

"Enough," Rebecca said, her voice shriller than she had intended. She shifted away from Pius and Joannicus. "You two come with me. We have some history to talk about. Elias, never use breath feathers unless you are prepared to die. And you..." She turned to Katie. "You have violated a sacred ground, and now you have to fix it."

Katie's eyes were as round as Elias's mouth. Both children hung their heads.

"But we won," Elias mumbled. "Why can't we celebrate? The man said we can eat custard."

"He said Custer, not custard," Katie said. "I made a treaty with the blue-eyed one."

Treaty—code for lies. Hadn't Karl taught them anything about dealing with these people? She herded the kids past the large monk.

"Hi, Bear," Katie said as she patted the monk's belly. "Spring has been good to you."

The monk laughed and pulled out two oranges from his cassock pockets and handed them to her.

"*Aho*," Katie said, giving one to her brother.

Outside, they walked to the bench in the courtyard. Rebecca took several deep breaths. She needed to be calm to teach a lesson. She was the aunt. This was her honor and duty to teach the tribal ways.

"Who is he?"

"He's the Bear. We give him gifts and he gives us food. *Até* doesn't want us taking. But we are not. It's an exchange," Katie said, sitting next to Rebecca.

Rebecca knew that Karl brought home fresh produce. Now she knew where it came from. Bear. The name fit for the man was large, and his beard was massive.

"Why is *Até* so mean?" Elias asked. "Bear is nice. It's a fair exchange. He's the one who gives *Até* the Friday box."

"*Até* didn't say it was him," Katie said.

"It is," Elias said. "Bear is Crow."

"*Até* isn't mean," Rebecca snapped. Or was he? Did his temper flare like Terence's? Had she allowed the violence of childhood to take root in him? We should have left on that New Year's Eve.

"How will I fix the sacred place when we can't enter it?" Katie asked, peeling the orange and releasing the scent of citrus.

The girl was bright, like her father.

"We can send Bear with smudging sticks. He can cleanse. He is Crow," Elias said, handing Katie his orange for her peel.

A shadow blocked the sun, and Rebecca glanced up to see Bear. He held out a basket.

"No thank you, we take care of our own," Rebecca said.

"Why only our own? What about Bear?" Elias asked, fingering the ridge of the basket.

"It's food, not poison. It's past lunchtime. The little ones are hungry. You don't have to eat but do not punish them," Bear said.

"I'll bring our thank-you tomorrow. The Bear is good," Katie said in Crow, placing the basket on the bench.

Too much Karl in that one.

"Yahoo," Elias shouted, digging inside to see what treasures he could find.

"*Aho*, Bear," Katie said.

"No problem, Little Chickadee."

The children squealed with delight, sorting through the food.

"Sorry about the invasion," Rebecca said, realizing she was scolding the wrong monk. "Who is the man with blue eyes? He's confusing the children," Rebecca said. "Don't you know they hold blue eyes in high esteem? Karl, their father, has blue eyes and that is unusual for an Apsáalooke man. It has power."

Bear nodded, a frown on his face. "Our blue-eyed one is not so special. He's Brother Mellitus. I'll tell him to stop with the tall tales. He likes to pick at scabs. He knows better than to call himself a great anything. Don't think you're being mistreated. He's that way with everyone."

"Good. I hope he isn't filling their heads with virgin births and rising Christs." Rebecca crossed her legs and leaned back on the bench.

Bear grunted.

"Jesus was a good man. And Mary is not much different from White Buffalo Woman."

"I'm Apsáalooke, not Lakota. You should learn to tell the difference."

Katie cast a look of disapproval and Rebecca saw Grandma Tiama reflected in the gesture, with her head lowered and gaze upward.

The large man sat down, and the bench bowed. He smelled faintly of hay, earth, and tobacco. Why hadn't she noticed that before?

"I thought you were the wife, but I think you are the sister. Many tribes share the same values. I think Jesus and White Buffalo Woman speak the same message."

Rebecca nodded as she remembered the nuns teaching about Jesus and his message of love.

"I don't think your kind is listening," Rebecca said, trying to curb her tongue and role model tolerance for these ignorant people.

"White Buffalo Woman loved children," Elias said, abandoning his orange for a carrot. "*Iná* told us the story."

"She told us about the pipe and what it means to receive it," Katie added, handing a cookie to Bear.

"Like a peace pipe?" Bear took the chocolate chip cookie.

Katie patted the man's arm. "No, silly Bear. A pipe of truth. If you accept it, then you must listen to the truth and speak only the truth."

"Why?" Elias asked. "*Até* said sometimes the truth hurts."

Rebecca recalled the truth Karl spoke of that caused pain. She and Karl had not talked about the holiday drama or veiled threats made by Judith.

"The message is about love, not truth. We must learn to love all races as our children. Then we can dream together knowing the real meaning of family," Rebecca said. Even though she was Apsáalooke, she was familiar with White Buffalo Woman's words.

"Don't forget the peace part," Elias said through a mouthful of peanut butter sandwich.

"Tell Bear about the medicine wheel. I like that part, only I can't remember it all," Katie said, orange juice dripping from her hand.

Rebecca breathed a sigh of relief. The children repeated the stories of their clans. So, Karl wasn't neglecting their culture while he dabbled in Christian dogma. The bells in the tower bellowed, stopping the conversation. After they rang, Bear rose.

"Another time, Little Ones. I must go pray."

Katie and Elias let out a cry of disappointment.

"Can we come with you?" Katie asked.

Bear looked at Rebecca, who shook her head.

"Tell you what. You learn that story about the medicine wheel and next time you can teach it to me."

"Agreed," Katie said, holding out her orange-soaked hand. Bear engulfed it in his calloused ones. With a bow to Rebecca, Bear lumbered to the church.

"*Até*," Elias shouted, seeing Karl appear from between the brewery and tailor shop. "We got a picnic. Come join us."

CHAPTER 28
NOT MY MOTHER

I am going to venture that the man who sat on the ground in his tipi meditating on life and its meaning, accepting the kinship of all creatures, and acknowledging unity with the universe of things, was infusing into his being the true essence of civilization.

Óta Kté (Plenty Kill or Luther Standing Bear). 1868-1939. Sicangu-Oglala Lakota, author, educator, philosopher, and actor.

Rebecca watched Karl approach in long strides, his loose hair billowing behind him, so carefree. Was he humming?

"We got a picnic. I put chips in," Elias said, jelly dripping down his arm as he squished the sandwich.

"Thanks for bringing them and feeding them." Karl bent down to kiss the top of Rebecca's head.

"A monk called Bear brought this," Rebecca said.

"There is no monk called Bear," Karl said.

"Yes, there is," Katie said. "He brings us things and we bring him things."

"Why?" Karl asked, his brow furrowing.

"Everyone shares what they have, *Até*. You taught me that," Katie said.

Damn, the girl was good. She wisely soothed Karl's concerns.

Rebecca shook her head. "Why are you letting these guys associate with the kids?"

"Nobody seems to mind. They are not being converted. Besides, it is convenient. I already feel like I am not spending enough time with them."

"They are not our kind."

"Our kind? Human? The animals are not our kind, and you listen to them. You should give them a chance. Brother Joannicus is a good man, despite some monks being obnoxious," Karl said, snatching a cookie from the trove of food. He offered Rebecca a bite of his cookie.

"I did that when we were kids—trusted them. They are not saints," Rebecca said, reaching for the cookie as Karl moved it away.

"What is a saint?" Elias asked.

"Someone who dies for what they believe," Rebecca said, scowling at Karl.

"Oh, a warrior," Elias said.

Karl grinned.

"I learned saints have animals to guide them," Katie said. "Just like us."

"That's right, St. Benedict had a raven," Karl said, nibbling the cookie.

"Yes, and St. Ambrose had *akihchilakkaashe*, bees, and St. Daria and Jerome had a lion, and St. Giles had a doe, and Saint Brigid has an *iaxuhke*, fox," Katie said.

"Saints must be Crow," Elias concluded as he fished out more cookies. "We should be saints and I want an *iaxuhke* pet, too."

This was not good. They knew too much about Catholic things and were confusing spirit guides with pets.

Rebecca shook her head, and her long braid slithered to and fro.

"Catholics are sheep, they play follow the leader, we are Apsáalooke. We think before we follow," Rebecca said.

"Bear says we are *iisaxpuatahcheewishke*, butting heads, moving shoulder to shoulder, resisting to be shorn," Katie said.

"What is shorn?" Elias asked.

Katie shrugged her shoulders.

"Bear said sheep put up a fight until you hold 'em then they calm down." She squeezed herself as if holding a wooly lamb.

Elias laughed. "Bear wrestling sheep. I'll draw him a picture of that."

"I do not understand the fuss. Yes, the monks are odd but mostly harmless and they have delightful stories," Karl said.

Rebecca snatched the cookie from Karl.

"I don't call tales of Son of the Morning Star innocuous. And one of them is calling himself the Great White Father?"

Karl's face darkened.

Katie and Elias made mad faces at each other and then broke into giggles.

"I will deal with it."

Rebecca flapped her arms. She didn't trust him. He was too

kind to his enemies. Plus, he still allowed the kids to see Judith and Terence.

A chickadee landed on the other bench and scolded in a high tweet, hopping and bobbing. The little bird lectured Rebecca. *You're inconsistent in your values and ideals, taking the children to family gatherings and then telling our brother Vincent to cut ties and with who? You or Judith and Terence?*

While they watched and listened to the annoyed chickadee, two others hopped in and picked at a bread crust, attempting to fly away with the heavy load.

Katie tossed a chip in the direction of the scolding bird, and it snatched the salty delight, ending the lesson of family and working together.

Rebecca sighed. It was another broken circle. She wanted a different life for Karl and his children. This wasn't supposed to happen. What had she done wrong? Why was he still listening to black robes and their stories?

Anger burned in her belly. She stared at the six birds that had gathered around the picnic.

"You need a breather," Karl said.

"I'm not the one snatching bits of this and that."

Karl bristled. "Stop sounding so white. Some things are important even if we don't understand them. We do them anyway."

Rebecca jumped to her feet as if stung. Why was he being so Catholic? He needed to do something with his life. She knew he didn't want to be an accountant, but unless he was going to teach, this pursuit was useless.

"Stop being so Catholic," Rebecca said, turning away to hide her anger. "What are you doing with that one important life you have?"

"Becca, I am sorry I cannot be what you want," Karl murmured.

Rebecca shook herself. "What *I* want? You don't have a clue what I want," she said, gathering her stuff.

Karl's shoulders sagged.

"Why is *Thunwin* mad?" Katie asked.

"She wants me to be an accountant," Karl said, gathering the picnic.

"You can't be an aunt, you're a boy," Elias said, licking his fingers.

"Accountant is a numbers guy. *Basaaksaake* Terence is an accountant," Katie explained, stuffing the rest of the cookie in her mouth.

"*Biilapxisaahke* lives in a big house," Elias pointed out.

"Houses are not that great," Karl said.

"Why?" Elias asked.

The monks filed out of the church, heading to the refectory.

"It is not the house, but who lives there that is important," Karl said.

CHAPTER 29
BARNYARD BIRTH

If you talk to the animals, they will talk with you, and
you will know each other.
If you do not talk with them, you will not know them.
And what you do not know, you will fear.
What one fears one destroys.

Geswanouth Slahoot (Chief Dan George). 1899-1981. Chief of the
Tsleil-Waututh Nation, actor, musician, poet, and author.

August blasted the plains of Montana. Rebecca pulled the
station wagon off the highway onto Abbey Road. They
headed past the orchard to the hilltop monastery. A
loud pop caused Rebecca to wrestle with the steering wheel.

"Great Thunder Beings," Faith said. "Now what?"

"Flat," Rebecca said as she detoured her way to the barns with a *thud, thud, thud.*

"I hope we have a spare," Rebecca said as she slipped out of the driver's seat.

Rebecca watched as her sister-in-law, Faith, struggled to pull herself from the car. Her round belly stretched the buttons of her blouse. Faith appeared to be miserable. Damn you, Karl, and your summer classes.

Faith waddled past the storage sheds toward the open barn door. At least inside, there would be shade and water.

Rebecca looked for the spare.

A scream punctuated the day.

"What the hell?" Rebecca yelled as she ran to the barn, tire iron in hand. The two Australian Shepherds barked as they circled her.

"Sorry, she startled me." Joannicus stood in a puddle, half a bucket of spilled water pooling at his feet. "Scholastica, Benedict, away."

The dogs didn't listen.

Rebecca rolled her eyes. Of course, the dogs had the names of saints. It figured those monks would give holy names to animals. She turned to the dogs and stared them down. They slunk back.

"Do you realize it's hotter than hell? Why are you still wearing that insufferable dress?" Rebecca asked.

Faith lowered herself to a bale of hay.

"What are you doing here? Karl isn't here."

"I'm aware of that. Why are you here?"

"I was helping."

"Good. Don't just stand there. Come help me change the tire," Rebecca said.

"Seriously, being male doesn't give me instant knowledge of

tires," Joannicus said, his voice sounding irritable. "I should get Karl."

"He knows nothing about cars either," Faith said as she groaned and rocked from side to side, rubbing her belly. Rebecca watched, counting silently how long the contraction lasted.

Faith opened her eyes, smiled, and waved. Scholastica came over and sat next to her.

Rebecca paused, debating if she should leave Faith's side. Second and third babies came quicker than the first.

"Go," Faith said. "Fix the car. I'm fine."

Marching out of the barn, she halted, realizing Joannicus was not following her. She stomped back in and grabbed his arm, which was soft, not muscular, as if his day's work consisted of picking up a rosary. She pulled him out with her.

Joannicus stood next to the station wagon as Rebecca placed the jack under the car and cranked. She yanked the flat off and it clunked to the ground.

A loud grunt came from the barn, and the cow bellowed a response. Benedict approached Rebecca and nudged her leg. Rebecca let the dog sniff her before patting his head. The dog turned and raced into the building.

"Is Faith in labor?" Joannicus asked, glancing at the barn. "I should get Karl."

"You have got to be kidding me. You should help me with this tire."

Rebecca leaned on the tire iron, fighting the urge to whack this man's shins.

Joannicus took a few steps away from her and hesitated.

"Don't you dare run off," Rebecca snapped, getting the feeling the man was deciding when to flee. "If we don't get this tire fixed, then you'll be helping me deliver the baby."

She had never seen a whiter face on a living person.

Benedict raced to Rebecca and yipped.

"Coming," Rebecca said to the dog.

Benedict turned in circles three times as if saying, hurry.

"Come on. Childbirth is beautiful. It's the beginning of life," Rebecca said, enjoying the monk growing paler.

"No. Seriously, you need someone who knows what they are doing. That's not me."

Rebecca set the bald replacement tire on. Beads of sweat dripped down her back. She was sure that her blouse was now two-toned in color.

As she lowered the jack, she noticed the tire was only just barely rounder than the flat one. She wondered if they had a pump but knew not to ask.

Joannicus wiped his brow and shifted from side to side. He looked like a jackrabbit before it darts across the highway.

Scholastica waited at the barn entrance and barked to Benedict, who raced back inside at her insistence. Rebecca stood up, tire iron slick in her right hand. Turning to face Joannicus, seeing him for what he was. A handsome, young man, curls damp and hanging low. What a waste of genetic material. He was Karl's age, twenty-one. She heard his story. He left home at eighteen to go to the monastery.

Karl seemed more adult than this dimple-faced boy. Rebecca licked the salty sweat from her lips. Todd. He was all male, tall and defined. If he were here, she wouldn't be changing a tire. The heat was getting to her. She could change a flat. She didn't need a man.

"Rebecca?" Faith called, her voice a little high and piercing.

"Crap," Rebecca said as the tire iron thudded to the ground and she ran to the barn to see Faith bent over the bale of hay.

A gust of wind whooshed through the barn. Loose hay swirled and danced upward in a twisting column. Joannicus ran to close the door, sneezing as he went. Rebecca looked out and surveyed the steely-blue, clouded sky.

"This is not good," Faith said. "A storm is coming."

As if to confirm the statement, a low rumble of thunder answered, causing the dogs to yip and the sheep to bleat.

"Come on. Help me get a stall ready," Rebecca said as she repositioned Faith.

"Why?"

"A baby is on the way, idiot."

"Seriously? That can't happen. Not here."

Rebecca snorted.

"Take it as a Mary moment—a reenactment of your precious savior's birth. You can pretend to be Joseph. I'll be an angel, encouraging you along."

"I'll go get help."

"Joseph did not flee for help. I need your help."

Joannicus scurried about, filling a feeding trough with hay. Faith and Rebecca exchanged looks and giggled at his efforts.

"Should I boil some water?" he asked, moving to the barn door. Large raindrops pelted the ground, turning to hail stones. "Seriously, Lord? Now?"

Rebecca chuckled to herself, remembering the story of Saint Benedict and his twin sister, Scholastica. She desired to be with him, and he wanted to go to his monastery. So, Scholastica asked God, and he sent a storm to keep Benedict with her.

"Start spreading hay, Brother," Rebecca said. "What are you so freaked out about? Babies are born every day."

"Not here."

"What, no room in the inn?"

The monk's face reddened.

"Be kind, Becca," Faith said.

Rebecca hummed "Away in a Manger" as she searched for a

horse blanket to make the bed of hay softer. The freshly fluffed hay tickled her nose.

"Becca, I need to walk," Faith said. Rebecca rushed to her side.

They paced the barn, with Scholastica and Benedict following them as thunder roared overhead.

"Ready to be the Virgin Mary?" Rebecca asked.

"That is your myth, not mine. Those poor sheep," Faith said as they paused and looked out at the hail-encrusted ewes.

"Not a myth," Joannicus said, brushing off the bits of hay from his habit.

"Oh please, virgins don't give birth. There is one way to reach the egg. What fantasy land do you live in?"

"It was a miracle. You believe in miracles. Karl has told me stories," Joannicus said. "Why must you explain every event?"

"Makes life easier," Rebecca said as Faith bent over with a contraction.

"Where are the wonder, mystery, and joy?" He sounded like Karl as he backed away from them. "Can you explain your connection to the dogs?"

"The dogs sense that birth is imminent. They're smart. That's all."

He wanted her to admit something. She couldn't explain how the animals knew, but they knew.

"A miracle or mystery, perhaps? Seriously, the point isn't how Mary got pregnant. The story is about what she did."

Rebecca didn't want to admit the monk was right. The story was about action and following the path in front of you. Today's path included a birth.

Rebecca walked Faith to the stall. Faith gripped the post and exhaled as if blowing a candle.

The bells from the hilltop rang, the melody floating on the humid air. Joannicus glanced in the sound's direction.

"I don't like how the baby is pushing." Faith lifted her shirt and placed Rebecca's hand on her distended belly. Rebecca frowned. The feet were visible like imprints on the sand.

Joannicus backed out of the stall. Rebecca eased Faith onto the blanket covering the straw pile. Scholastica crawled over to lie next to Faith.

"Oh no," Faith said.

"What?" Panic rose in Rebecca.

"There he goes," Faith said, pointing to the open barn door.

Rebecca ran to the door, watching Joannicus running up the hill to the monastery as large raindrops plopped, disappearing into the parched ground.

"You better be going to get help. And not running away to pray because that is useless," Rebecca shouted.

"He'll send someone," Faith said.

"You're too kind. He has gone to pray. Every time those bells ring, they go, dropping everything, running to the church, like Pavlov's dog."

"Prayer can't hurt. I would prefer help, but it is what it is. We got this."

They were both nurses. This wasn't Faith's first child. They could handle this. The heavy odor of wet wool drifted into the barn. The storm had moved away as quickly as it had appeared. Rebecca looked at the station wagon. Could she get to the hospital on the spare tire? Benedict stood with her. The eaves of the buildings dripped from the downpour. No. Her only prospect was a childish monk. Rebecca unbraided and re-braided her hair. She hoped he would call an ambulance.

Rebecca patted the dog's head. The chickens clucked, resettling for the night.

"He will send someone," Faith said again, making Rebecca wonder if she was sending a message for backup.

She hoped it wasn't another worthless monk. Did any of them have medical training other than hope in miracles?

Rebecca remembered the large man who smelled like this barn—the Bear. She wondered if he worked down here or just supervised the others. Maybe he was the abbot. An abbot who toiled with his monks. That would never happen—the powerful with the lowly.

"Don't underestimate them. They are idealists who believe in love. They are seeds that only open when placed in the fire," Faith said. A fierce pride and affection filled her face. She was talking about Karl more than the monk.

Rebecca listened as the sheep bleated to their young, mothering up for the night. The sound was soothing and melodic as she smudged, careful not to burn down the barn. But thinking that would bring them here in an instant. She watched Faith settle and relax, resigning herself to a barnyard birth.

CHAPTER 30
AMBER ROSE

We shall be known by the tracks we leave behind.

Hehaka Sapa (Black Elk). 1863-1950. Wichasha Wakan medicine man, educator, and Heyoka of the Oglala Lakota people.

The large bronze crucifix stood like a beacon in the monastic cemetery. The life-size statue hung in a watchful gaze over the dead. Karl hoisted himself to the ledge and shimmed up the cross, checking for a nest in the crown of thorns. He had heard that one year a sparrow couple had chosen this site to make their home. Jesus cried white bird droppings that year. He positioned himself between the crossbeam and the drooping head. The bronze arms were warm from the sun as Karl rode on the shoulders of Jesus, hoping he wasn't a burden.

From this height, he watched Katie and Elias searching for

him. This activity honed their skills as hunters and observers. He invented many games to keep them happy when he had to bring them with him to school.

"Why does he hide too good?" Elias asked, following Katie up the stone walk past the headstones.

"We need to look for clues. He came this way. See, the grass is bent," Katie said, pointing to the exact path he had taken.

Pride filled Karl's heart. She was an excellent tracker.

Elias stopped and pointed. A rabbit sat frozen on her hind legs, nose twitching.

"Sister Rabbit, which way did *Até* go?" Katie asked. She turned to Elias. "Give her something so she will tell us."

"I ate it. I was hungry." Elias hung his head. His shoulder-length hair covered his face. "Sorry, sisters."

The rabbit dropped and scratched. Karl stared at the rabbit, willing the fluff ball not to betray him. The whitetail leaped toward the crucifix and scampered to the underbrush at the foot of the statue. The children followed, never once looking up. They were following the rabbit and that was the wrong clue.

A rumble of thunder and a chill filled the air. Karl looked up as a heavy drop of rain fell on his face.

He was not getting down. Father Sky would have to try harder.

The rain turned to hail and stung as it pummeled his body. Not fair. The melting ice dripped off his nose and soaked through his tee shirt.

The children raced back to the brick path. Mrs. Rabbit had led them astray. They squealed with delight and formed ice balls, tossing them as they dodged each other between headstones.

The sun reappeared, making steam rise from the dampened children. Their joy rose to the heavens.

The bells rang, calling the monks to evening prayers. How many strolling monks had been caught in the sudden storm?

Would they change or pray wet? Karl wondered, was the call from the heart or head? The bells tugged at Joannicus. A yearning appeared on his face whenever the ringing called the community to prayer. The sound of heavy breathing caused Karl to look down and see Frater Joannicus huffing and puffing. He was a few months away from the priesthood.

"Where is he?" Joannicus asked, bending over, his hood flopping to one side.

"*Até*?" Katie asked.

"Your father," Joannicus wheezed, his chest still heaving.

Katie shrugged her shoulders.

"We are playing scout and find. We are looking for him," Elias said. "Only he's cheating again."

"It's time to pray." Joannicus started toward the church.

"*Até*," shouted Katie. "Come out, *Iná* is having the baby."

"We give up," Elias called.

Karl grinned from his perch, thinking that Joannicus took praying far too earnestly. She used those words before, but he wouldn't be fooled this time. Faith had at least a week to go and was typically late. He waited until he heard the voices of his children fading as they followed Joannicus to the courtyard, wondering what Joannicus wanted. Then he slid off the cross. Was it that easy to change your direction in life? Jesus slid off the cross in the novel, *The Last Temptation of Christ*. Brother Mellitus hinted at moments that changed the world. Karl shook his head. Mellitus was dangerous, and not your typical monk devoted to the Church and God. And he had loaned him that novel. The man could lead a saint astray. Lately, guilt nagged Karl. His thirst for learning seemed at times all-consuming. And he would never earn a living studying Catholic theology. In his heart, he knew he needed a job, probably as an accountant, or something else just as soul-killing. Karl headed to the monastery, wondering what cross he would choose, and how he could ever slide off of it.

As he approached the church, the melodious voices of the monks in chant filled his ears. Karl glanced around the courtyard. There were no giggles or rustling of bushes.

"Elias, Katie," Karl called. Only the twittering birds answered him, saying we took shelter from the storm.

Shit, shit, shit.

"Children, this is not funny. It is time to go. Game over."

He thought for a moment. Nothing would keep Joannicus from praying when the bells rang. The kids had gone with Joannicus. Had he taken the children into the church? Faith would not be pleased with that. Would his children sit quietly for the half an hour it took for the monks to pray? He imagined Elias asking for drums and Katie being disappointed that there was no dancing.

Karl slipped into the church, hearing voices drift to the atrium. He recognized the psalms—the songs of David. They were slow and metered. There was a soothing pace of call and echo, each side speaking a stanza. Karl paused, taken in by the silence after the psalm, allowing the words to sink and take root.

He shivered and then shook himself. He didn't need deeper roots.

The holy water fountain bubbled loudly as the monks sat in silence. Karl tiptoed in and peeked around the corner. Random patterns of baldness greeted him. Rows of men in black robes with their heads bent. Elias sat wide-eyed among them. Karl knew guests didn't sit with the monks—another kindness they had granted his children. He glanced around, noticing that Katie was missing.

Prayers ended, and the monks, in pairs, approached the altar and bowed before exiting the church. Elias followed, mimicking what they did. Karl smiled at his bold politeness.

The monks passed him in silence, as was the custom after the evening prayer. Silence until morning.

Frater Pius looked at Karl. "What are you doing here?"

Pius breaking the norm. That was a surprise.

"We are under attack," Brother Mellitus shouted, startling a few of the older monks. "Circle the wagon. Gather the women."

"What women?" a wobbly head monk asked, confusion on his face.

"Mellitus, enough," Father Hilary said, taking the old one away.

"What is going on?" Karl asked as Elias hugged his leg.

"Didn't Joannicus find you?" Pius asked.

Mellitus cackled. "We are reenacting the virgin birth. You should witness that. Only I don't think *virgin* is quite the right word."

Pius snickered. Karl wondered if just punching the man would end the word game. Why had they allowed him to stay? He did not promote Benedictine values.

"Where is Katie?"

"She went to see Momma," Elias said. "Momma is having a baby. Katie took the Bear to help."

Karl hadn't seen Faith or the station wagon when he made the walk from the cemetery to the monastery. He glanced at his watch. Where was she? Fear hooked him. Something was wrong.

"The Holy One arrived and Brother Ambrose left with that little elder of yours," Mellitus said.

Karl heard others refer to Joannicus as the Holy One because of his inclination to pray first. The thought of Katie as an elder both amused and worried him.

"Faith is at the barn, giving birth? Who is Brother Ambrose? Is he a doctor?"

"No, he's a veterinarian," Mellitus said.

Karl didn't wait to discover the rest as he raced out of the church, Elias in tow.

SCHOLASTICA AND BENEDICT rose and ran to the barn entrance and barked.

Rebecca looked up. Now what?

Brother Ambrose burst into the barn. The sheep bleated and stirred, expecting food.

"Not now, it's not breakfast. I'm here. No need to panic," the monk panted.

Rebecca stood. What made Ambrose think she was panicked?

"*Iná*, I brought Bear," Katie shouted, rushing to Faith's side.

"Where's your father?" Faith asked with a grunt.

"He is hiding. We couldn't find him," Katie said, kneeling next to her mother, rubbing her arm.

"We have a flat tire," Rebecca said, wondering why Katie was with Bear. Where were Joannicus and Karl? She should have driven the car on the rim to the hilltop.

"Do I look like a grease monkey?" Ambrose barked.

"Did anyone call for an ambulance?" Rebecca inquired.

Katie shrugged her shoulders.

Ambrose ignored her, unzipped his cassock, and stepped out of the black material. His robust belly fell over his belt. He rolled up his sleeves, went to the water pump, and washed his hands.

Katie ran over to the pump and pulled up her sleeves to wash, too.

"Are you listening?" Rebecca asked, her voice edged. "We have a situation here." She glanced at Faith, who was breathing hard, preparing for another contraction.

Soap bubbles floated and popped between them as Ambrose and Katie washed.

"What's the problem?"

"The baby is in the wrong position. We need to call an ambulance. Where's your phone?"

"There isn't a phone down here."

"Why the hell not?"

"The sheep don't need to call me."

Faith laughed.

"What if there's an accident? How would you get help?" Rebecca said, practically shouting at him.

Ambrose shook his hands in the air. Droplets of water fell to the ground. Katie waved her hands in the air. Rebecca stared at the shovel in the corner. One conk that would end this, but he was the only help she had.

"Don't stare at me like that. Do you have a phone in your teepee?"

Katie giggled. "Silly Bear."

Faith laughed again and then she said, "People, this baby is coming. We need to do something. I'm not having a caesarian in this barn."

Ambrose frowned. "Where's the head?"

Faith pointed to her right side.

"I think we have time to move this one. Alright little troublemaker, let's see where you are."

Rebecca watched. Ambrose stepped forward and placed his meaty hands on Faith's protruding belly. His fingers roamed, squeezing with a gentleness she had not expected.

Perhaps he wasn't useless.

Faith's face grew dark with worry. Ambrose gave a grim smile as he patted Faith's knee.

A trickle of worry nagged at Rebecca. She had seen midwives try to turn a breech baby, but she had not done so herself. Confidence, she needed to show confidence.

"Don't fret. I have experience. We can coax this baby to the entrance." He turned to Rebecca. "Are you helping me or just standing around watching?"

Who did this Neanderthal think he was, barking orders?

"I'm ready," Katie said, standing next to Ambrose.

"Excellent. We need the bottles from behind the wall boards." Ambrose pointed to a spot next to the door. "Turn the loose nail and bring them to me."

Katie ran off, moments later returning with two amber-filled flasks.

Ambrose uncorked the vial and handed it to Faith. The sweet smell of brandy filled the stall. Faith gave him a questioning stare.

"You will need this, so sip away."

"But..." Rebecca started as a stern stare peered through the wooly face.

"A relaxed uterus will make this easier. This is all I got. I have a bottle of Merlot if you would, rather. The champagne is for after the birth."

The man was right. Why did he have to be right?

Faith brought the bottle to her lips and swallowed.

"Not bad, kind of sweet and... oh, burns nicely."

We got this. Rebecca looked at Ambrose for cues that she was mistaken as Faith gulped more brandy.

"What next?" Katie asked Ambrose.

"Get me the tall, clear bottles in the kennel," Ambrose said.

"The fortification," Katie shouted with a nod as she crawled inside the doghouse and appeared with two gin bottles.

Rebecca scanned the walls. Was this a bar or a barn?

"Don't give me that face. We have monks who are alcoholics. If I want a drink. I have to hide the temptation from them." Ambrose uncorked and took a long swallow, offering the bottle to Rebecca.

"You sure it is them that have the problem?" Rebecca

murmured, shaking her head. *Not the time for a culture lesson on alcohol and Indians, or hiding booze*, she scolded herself.

"Then I get the birthing box, right?" Katie asked. Not waiting for an answer from Ambrose, Katie ran to the office. She grunted, pulling a wooden box toward them. The box was full of lambing equipment. Gloves, nasal syringes, bottles of disinfectant, and even a sling scale.

Rebecca marveled. Lambing came with everything for a comfortable human birth. This was a good sign unless the baby wouldn't turn. Positive thinking, confidence. She had smudged. Don't let negative energy in.

"This is for sucking the snot out," Katie said, squeezing a bulbous syringe.

How much time had Katie spent with Ambrose, the Bear?

Ambrose doused his hands with gin antiseptic, and a sterile odor filled the air.

"Shall we try?" he asked Faith before placing his large, calloused hands on her belly.

"Listen to the Bear, Sister," Faith chirped. "He has birthed many a lamb. Katie told me."

Katie nodded. "I seen him do it. Elias threw up. But not me."

"I have found the head and feet. Let's go ahead as if we are bakers. Knead in a rhythm of three."

Faith advised them to push left to right. Rebecca knew it was a Lakota belief all things moved left to right.

Faith took several deep breaths and stared up into the rafters as her shoulders and arms drained of tension.

Ambrose's large hands pressed and kneaded. Rebecca pushed, grateful that the baby was not breech.

"What are you doing?" Katie asked, holding a box of navel clamps.

"Helping the baby," Rebecca said, hoping not to frighten her niece.

"This one is being stubborn. We need the head here. And the feet here," Ambrose said, pointing to Faith's belly.

Faith moaned and Rebecca winced, worried at how much pain her sister-in-law could endure. Faith raised the bottle and took a long sip of brandy.

"You should tickle her feet. I'll sing to her. And shine a light. It's dark in there," Katie said.

"Good idea. Fetch a flashlight," Ambrose said, nodding to Rebecca to give the pushing and kneading a second try. The sheep bleated, and the birds in the rafters chirped, adding to the chaos.

"Come on, little one. Move," Ambrose said. "Sweet Mary, help us out here."

Rebecca rolled her eyes. Prayer would not fix a medical problem. But she let a prayer escape to all the deities, even the one Ambrose called upon. Together, they would make this work.

Katie wiggled her way into the crowd of hands and arms. She placed the flashlight's bright beam between Faith's legs and sang a Lakota welcoming song.

There was so much noise. How could Faith meditate in this space? Yet she did. Faith should be a midwife since her calmness would comfort first-time mothers.

They pushed again.

"Twisted tornados," Faith shouted, her eyes wide and her teeth gritted together.

They all watched with amazement the movement of the unborn child. An elbow or knee. The print of a foot. Katie reached up to the foot impression.

"Tickle, tickle," Katie said, wiggling her tiny fingers on the taut belly.

Head down, begged Rebecca as she watched the movement.

Faith released a breath, and Ambrose wiped her brow.

Ambrose cleared his throat and turned to Katie. "Katie love, Scholastica and Benedict need some exercise."

Katie jumped up and started yipping like a puppy. The two Shepherds rose and followed her as she took off running.

"Don't worry. They play this game all the time. The dogs won't let her get lost."

"Can we send them to find Karl?" Faith asked with a giggle.

"You're drunk," Rebecca said, trying to take the bottle away from Faith.

Clearly, she had brandied too much. The centimeter check caused the hay to become wet with birthing fluid. This baby was coming. Rebecca realized a few weeks early was safe, and this wasn't the first child, so she prepared for a short and swift delivery. Pulling a rough blanket to cover the wetness, she and Ambrose got into position. Rebecca locked hands with Faith, marveling at the silent concentration on the woman's face. Where was the screaming and yelling that she had seen so often at Mary, Mother of Perpetual Help maternity ward? Birthing was uncomfortable if not painful, and yet Faith appeared composed. Was it the alcohol or the Lakota calm? Rebecca was sure she would not be so meditative if she were giving birth.

Rebecca breathed a sigh of relief as she handed the wailing infant into the rough hands of the monk.

"Now, now, that's no way to celebrate your birthday," Ambrose cooed, his furry face close to the infant. Rebecca watched the imparting of one spirit into another. He was robbing them of a sacred ceremony.

Rebecca made to pull the two apart, but Faith grabbed her arm.

"Let it go."

"But his breath, we don't know what kind of man he is."

"Oh, I think we do," Faith said, grinning, her words slightly slurred.

KARL RACED DOWN THE HILL. Elias struggled to keep up. After two pauses, Karl grabbed the boy and hauled him like a sack of grain to the farm. Gasping for breath, Karl leaned on the barn door. Elias squirmed to be released. Rebecca banged a bottle with the farmer. Where was the monk? Where was Faith?

"What the hell is going on here?" Karl said, anger bubbling like groundwater.

"We're celebrating the birth of your daughter," Rebecca said, raising her bottle.

"Are you drunk?"

"No, she is not, but I am," Faith called from one stall.

Karl moved to his wife's side. She smiled as her glassy black eyes blinked. He winced at the pungent smell of her breath.

Scholastica and Benedict barked and Katie raced in after them.

Disappointment filled Karl's face. "I missed it all."

"Karl, honey, joyful time, not pissy time," Faith said, handing him his daughter wrapped in a black cloth. A monk's scapular, a thousand times too large, smelling of tobacco and grain. The Bear.

"Where's the vet?"

"We don't have a vet. I am Brother Ambrose."

"He is Bear," Katie said.

"Mellitus said..." Karl's voice dropped. He knew Bear was the farmer, but not a monk. How had he missed that?

Ambrose laughed. "That wasn't nice of Mellitus. But I'm not surprised."

The sheep bleated from their sleeping quarters as if everyone knew Ambrose was a monk.

334

"What is it?" Elias asked, sitting next to Karl, and poking at the infant in his arms.

"A girl," Katie said. "My sister."

"Darn it," Elias said, arms dropping to his side. "You can have her, but I get to name her."

"No, I'm the elder. I get to choose." Katie's voice came loud and sharp.

"I already named her," Elias said, arms crossed as he looked around the barn. "Ewe, that's her name."

"No, it is not," Karl said, handing the baby back to Faith.

That was a terrible name, and it was too soon to name her. They would have that ceremony and the spirit ritual where breath was exchanged later.

The sound of sirens became louder. An ambulance was coming.

"Blessed be the saints," Ambrose said. "Good job, Joannicus."

Karl stood amidst the chaos. Sheep bleating, Faith humming, dogs yapping, Rebecca calling the children from the barnyard so the ambulance could enter.

"Daddy, do we get to ride the noisy station wagon?" Elias asked.

A meaty hand landed on Karl's shoulder. "You go with them. The kids can come with me."

"Yippee," Katie said. "We get to go with Bear."

Elias danced, filled with Katie's joy. Flashing lights filled the barn and Karl felt his head spin. The cow mooed long and low as if encouraging them to leave.

"Karl, the kids will be fine. Let's go for a ride. Don't forget the baby."

Karl stooped to take the infant and deposit it into the arms of the ambulance attendant.

Rebecca started talking medical jargon. Karl caught the words. Hard delivery, sanitizing, and booze.

They placed Faith on a stretcher.

Karl watched the farmer, who was a monk, and maybe a bear, allow Katie and Elias to tug on his arms.

"Karl, come on," Faith called from inside the ambulance.

He climbed in and held her hand.

"I'm wasted. Make sure you tell Katie's Bear thank you. Tell him Amber Rose thanks him, too. She is part bear. They exchanged breath. It happened without pretense or ceremony," Faith said, her face softened into a blissful smile.

Not only had he missed the birth, but the naming ceremony, too. The attendant handed Amber Rose to him. Her dark eyes focused on him. He had a daughter—a healthy little girl.

One moment. One change. A new goal to be present in their lives.

CHAPTER 31
LUCIAN

I have seen that in any great undertaking; it is not enough for a man to depend simply upon himself.

Chief Isna-la-wica Red Cloud, Maȟpíya Lúta (Lone Man). 1760-1826. Teton Sioux. A statesman and strategic genius, and the most capable warrior and tribesman to face the US military and defeat them.

Classes resumed after the holiday break. Karl opened the window in the empty classroom and scooped the snow into a ball, placing it on his cheek. He winced. Rebecca had given him a poultice of camphor, and he wished he had another—holidays at the Mackenzie house. Seeing TK and learning about his new job at Thatcher and Miller's law firm was good. Karl loved them being all together, but as always, it ended badly.

He needed to finish the assignment, so he sat at the desk, letting the ball melt and drip, like his concentration.

He watched the snow falling in big, sloppy flakes outside the window. Before the holiday, Ambrose questioned the time he was spending with Joannicus. The term he used, "particular friendship," poked him like prairie grass in his moccasins.

Words of caution echoed in his mind. *You're both young, and you're not on equal footing. He finds you exotic and exciting, an attraction or a distraction. Don't allow that.*

The conversation rattled him. Was he a disruption? Joannicus was a distraction to him, making him yearn for the structure of a day that didn't involve tears and demands. He tried to imagine the children going to bed on their own, playing quietly while he worked. Yes, without the interruptions, he could do more, but he loved their joyful discoveries.

Karl would soon graduate and move on. What was the big deal? Why couldn't he be friends with Joannicus? He had avoided Joannicus as best he could. It wasn't hard now that they didn't have classes together. He would do it for Joannicus. Knowing that living within a group required fellowship and camaraderie; he didn't want to be in trouble with the community. Had he made Joe's life difficult? He recalled how the nuns scolded Father Lucian for taking him under his wing as a boy and scowled when he and Lucian would go for walks or have lunch together. Karl frowned. He would miss the theological discussions, the more profound insights, and the compromises.

Karl pointed at the crucifix on the wall above the chalkboard. "Really? Have they read about the twelve friends you had?"

"You're a distraction," a voice said from the doorway.

Karl looked over his shoulder, and there he stood, the one he was told to leave alone. Joannicus.

Snow rested on his head and shoulders as he entered the classroom, closed the door, and set his briefcase and coat down. The snow fell in clumps, forming puddles at his feet as he pulled out a red tin and approached Karl.

"What happened to your face?"

"I argued with the wrong person," Karl said. Terence.

"Pius said you were in a bar fight."

Leave it to Pius to have a tale.

"Is it Thanksgiving? I found out Indians don't celebrate it," Joannicus said.

That was a good enough excuse. The back of Karl's head prickled, and he twisted his braid around his wrist like a bracelet.

"Sure. We are not thankful for genocide. Nor do we enjoy Christopher Columbus Day. Was Pius at the bar too?"

"Good question. What is he doing in a tavern?" Joannicus approached the professor's table, setting the tin down on the smooth flat wooden top before leaning on it. A moment of tension, like a trapped rabbit, passed through Karl.

"You can tell me what happened if you want to."

Karl wavered. He hadn't shared with anyone his troubles with his family. Most assumed he drank and got into fights when he showed up with a bruise or black eye. Only Father Lucian knew the truth. Karl remembered his weekly confessions with the priest, revealing too often that his stepfather had beaten him. Lucian always said, "Child, don't speak so brazenly." Later he'd added, "That is not your sin to confess." The seal of confession. The priest had carried that burden and would go to his grave with it. Karl decided he would not ask Joannicus to enter the circle of silence.

"I dislike Father Pius," Karl said. The man wore his priesthood like a crown and expected a bow for his efforts. Becoming a priest didn't make him a better man.

"I don't like Mellitus," Joannicus said. "He stretches the truth and is mean to everyone. Funny, he seems to like you. He tells stories about you."

Lucian's stories, Karl thought.

"He likes to spar with me. And we do not live together. Those are secondhand tales, and Father Lucian is the monk I associated with, not Mellitus."

Karl stood and walked to the opposite side of the table.

"Father Lucian is ill. I assumed he would be the one to leave us over the break, but it was Abbot Sebastian."

"The Abbot died? Now what?"

"We have a new abbot." Joannicus pushed the red tin in Karl's direction.

That was fast. He had never known change to be fast in the realm of the Church. Yet it made sense that everyone came together for the holiday. He wondered who the abbot was now.

Karl opened the tin. The sweetness of chocolate permeated the room. Brownies with sprinkles, his stomach rejoiced with a growl.

"Abbot Gordon Mace is our new abbot. His mother, Mrs. Van Horn, has been sending gifts since the election. She's very generous and kind. We're all going to become very fat."

Karl laughed. That was ironic. The monk without a Benedictine saint's name had become an abbot. God had a sense of humor.

Karl took a brownie and nibbled on the edge since it hurt to open his mouth. Joannicus stared at Karl's cheek. Karl turned his face away, for the compassion was overwhelming as he sensed the struggle within his friend. Would the truth change that? Karl broke the sweet treat in half, offering it to Joannicus.

"My stepfather and I do not get along," Karl said with a half-hearted laugh. "He and my mother have control issues." He could not bring himself to say the word abusive. Karl shook his head slightly before continuing. "But it is important for my children to honor their ancestry. I only visit on holidays. I need to learn to leave sooner than I do."

Joannicus leaned forward and accepted the gooey piece, bits of pink and red sprinkle falling to the tabletop.

"I find it strange that we give the people we love so much power over us even when the relationship is toxic. I'm sorry someone has hurt you. Perhaps it would be safer for you to have someone call you away. When visiting my aunt Venessa, I'd have a friend call an hour into my visit and then excuse myself."

They stood silently, a table separating them, a brownie shared, and sprinkles connecting them.

"Should we be doing this?" Karl asked, changing the subject for fear his entire childhood would come spilling out.

"Doing what?"

"Brother Ambrose made it clear to me you belonged to them. He feels we spend too much time together. He thinks I am a trou-blemaker."

Joannicus chewed and swallowed. "He's wrong. I belong to God. I devote more time to God than I do to you. You are a trouble-maker but no more of one than Brother Mellitus. He has driven potential monks away. I'm here to save souls. You will not change that."

Karl glanced at the door behind Joannicus. Should he open it?

Joannicus moved past Karl to the windows. "Seriously, we're just talking. There's nothing wrong with talking."

"I do not wish to cause a problem. I do not want to be the reason you lose your vocation."

"You are not that powerful," Joannicus said, drawing a line on the window, letting the condensation drops pool and run a race to the bottom. "Stop avoiding me. That's not helpful to me or you. We're friends. I value that, and it feeds me. It disturbs me, but good soil has a few rocks."

Karl smirked. "I am your rock?"

Joannicus smiled back and wiped the window clean with his elbow. "Christ built his church on his rock."

"I wonder what you will build?" Karl asked. A builder needed a foundation.

Joannicus stepped away from the window and stood next to Karl.

"Does your soul need to be saved?"

Karl shivered.

"My spirit is fine."

"Is it?" Joannicus placed a hand on Karl's shoulder.

The door opened with a bang. Panting, Father Pius stood staring at them.

The cavalry had arrived.

Joannicus let his hand drop from Karl's shoulder.

"What are you doing? You shouldn't be..." Pius stumbled over his words.

"Thank you for your concern. Karl's not a threat."

"It's not wise to be tempted by the shiny apple. You're jeopardizing your future."

Karl bristled. Was Pius mocking him with the reference to an apple, red on the outside, white on the inside? He continued to dislike this man. If this was a mistake, Joannicus was choosing to balance vocation and friendship. The least Pius could do was pray for him.

Pius opened his mouth as his face turned red.

Joannicus strolled past him to the door, picking up his briefcase and coat.

Like a lost cub, Karl rose, scrunched his paper, grabbed the red tin of brownies, and followed Joe out of the room. Together they forged a path through the snow, Karl stepping in the knee-deep footprints of Joannicus.

"Are you thinking of leaving?" Karl asked in the near silence of their ascent to the hilltop.

"Don't worry. I'm not leaving here. I have picked out my grave, right side, under Brother Gilbert's row," Joannicus said, stopping and catching his breath. The snow blanketed the campus and obscured the path to the monastery. Even the path that Pius had taken was mostly indistinguishable.

Was he serious? At twenty-three, death was the furthest thing from Karl's mind. Admiration filled Karl. He wondered if his life would ever be so planned.

They walked up the hill to the building with the kitchen and refectory. The freshly baked bread scented the air. Karl hugged the tin closer to himself. Joannicus stopped in a boot-and-cover-all-filled room, stomped his feet, and brushed the snow from himself and Karl. Then he waved for Karl to follow up the back staircase.

"Where are we going?" Karl asked, reluctant to leave the tin and smells of dinner.

"You said you knew Father Lucian. He's dying." Joannicus stopped and turned left. "You can say goodbye before he passes."

Water dripped off Karl's head, down his face. Karl froze. No. Shame swirled. Was he ready? Had he forgiven the man? He wasn't prepared, even if things had worked out for him. They had left so much unsaid.

He had walked away when the man refused to marry him in the church. Could he go back? Was it that easy to return to Catholicism? Would Lucian forgive him for his youthful pride?

"You never really left," the voice of Grandma Tiama whispered.

"We are here at the infirmary. He's inside. His spirit's troubled. I'll wait for you."

Karl stood in the hallway next to a window that reminded him of an ICU unit. Inside lay a man in a bed and a monk sitting beside him. The door opened, and another monk beckoned him in. A soft light lit the place, and antiseptic and musty oil assaulted his nose. A vision of Endow under the tree and the buzz of flies clouded Karl's senses. He shook his head to dispel the images.

"About time," Mellitus croaked. "A man here wants to go home."

Karl stepped into the space, inching his way to the bed. An emaciated monk stared blankly at him. Lucian. His skin, like porcelain leather, dipped and stretched over his bones.

"I'm sorry," Lucian rasped, waving his hand at invisible flies.

"Hush, old friend, salvation has arrived," Mellitus said, grasping the shaky hand. "Get in here, Chief. Lay your hands on him, absolve or exorcise him."

Karl moved to the bed. Lucian continued to mumble his apologies.

"Father Lucian?"

"He can't hear you anymore. He can't see you either. The emptiness of his soul has consumed him because he won't let go of the past."

Karl grasped his wet braid, pulling the moisture to the end, his hand now wet. This wasn't the man he knew. Now Karl understood why Lucian had left St. George. The rumor that Lucian had lost his eyesight and was going deaf was true.

"Forgive him. It's your history that keeps him earthbound."

Lucian had told Mellitus. So much for the confessional privilege. Didn't anyone here follow the rules? Karl winced. No, he didn't cause this blindness or deafness. He was not that powerful.

"I forgave him for not letting me marry in the church."

"It's more than that, and you know it. Just say the words."

Karl stepped away. He was not the mentor, his confidant. He didn't recognize this man. Did the circle of silence cause this? The man's suffering was hard to witness. Was this his fault? Had he confessed once too often to the priest who was obligated to carry his burden?

Mellitus locked eyes with Karl, causing him to inhale sharply. Silent screams echoed in the room.

"What are you waiting for? He suffers for your sins," Mellitus prodded.

"This is not my sin that holds him," Karl whispered. "He needs to forgive himself."

Mellitus grabbed Karl's wrist. He was stronger than he appeared. He pulled Karl's hand to Lucian's. Lucian's icy fingers seized his arm.

"Now forgive him," Mellitus said. "He'll not die until you absolve him, rid him of his demons."

"I'm sorry. I should have done better," Lucian said as he pulled Karl to him. Lucian's hand roamed up Karl's arm and touched his braid. Then he gripped Karl's face in his bony hands. His stale breath lingered between them. The bruise on Karl's cheek throbbed at the touch.

Lucian's eyes opened wide. "It's you. Forgive me. I should have done more. I should have done the right thing."

Karl nodded and placed his hands on the thin hands, trying to release his face.

"It is okay. I forgive you," Karl croaked as his composure crumbled. The right thing, what was that? Turn Terence in and be hated by his family for making them fatherless? Was that the right thing?

"I'm sorry," Lucian muttered, water pooling in his hollow eye sockets.

Droplets escaped Karl's eyes and ran down his cheeks, changing the pristine white linen to gray.

"I forgive you," Karl whispered, resting his head on the man's chest as the hand resting on his cheek fell away. Gone were the breath, heartbeat, and the rise and fall.

He listened to the shuffling. The smell of sulfur filled the air. Karl opened his eyes to see two burning candles on the stand beside the bed. He could see the large pectoral cross against the black habit. Abbot Gordon was standing next to the bed. A black cuff reached over Karl's head and anointed Lucian's forehead with oil.

"Through this holy anointing, may the Lord, in his love and mercy, help you with the grace of the Holy Spirit. May the Lord who frees you from sin save you and raise you up," Abbot Gordon said, his voice breaking with emotion.

Karl lifted his head from the body of Lucian to see Mellitus mopping his face. The man was crying. Mellitus placed a hand on Karl's shoulder and whispered in Karl's ear, "*Gratias tibi, aho.*"

Karl wanted to escape, but a sea of black robes filled the space. The murmuring of prayers rang in his ears.

"Holy Mary, Mother of God, pray for him. Holy angels of God, pray for him. Abraham, our father in faith, pray for him..."

The litany of the saints coated Karl with its ebb and flow.

As the monks filed out, Karl went with them. Outside the building, he leaned against the wall. Lucian was dead. He wondered if he should tell Rebecca. Would she feel sorrow? She never held him in high esteem.

As the church bells tolled, a shadow appeared, announcing a man's year with each *clang*.

"What you did was miraculous," Joannicus said. "You caught the shards of his bruised and blessed life and helped him get from the darkness to the light."

Guilt washed over Karl. "I should have done it two or four years ago."

"Seriously, the time was now," Joannicus said.

CHAPTER 32
XMAS

These (sacred) ceremonies do not belong to Indians alone. They can be done by all who have the right attitude... who are honest and sincere about their beliefs in Wakan Tanka (Great Spirit) and follow the rules.

Frank Fools Crow. 1890-1989. Author, Oglala Lakota civic and religious leader, and preserver of Lakota traditions and ceremonies.

Rebecca brushed the snow off her parka and stomped her boots.

The scent of pine made her feel as if she had stepped into the forest rather than the community center on the Rez. Today, they gathered for the annual winter celebration, otherwise known as Christmas. She spotted not one but two fir trees. The children were noisily darting between the table and the timbers. The decorations were yellow, white, black, and red ribbons, feathers on leather strings, beads, and handmade ornaments—no tinsel or shiny red and green balls. The adornment reached only the height of the tallest child. Excitement buzzed with a soft overtone of wariness.

Rebecca saw Ambrose and Pius—they stood out like a white buffalo. What were they doing here? This wasn't *Feed-the-Poor Sunday*.

She approached the kitchen area. Faith waved at her.

"Before you get crazy, Katie invited Ambrose. You know they come in pairs. That's why Joannicus is here. I don't know why Father Pius is here," Faith said, chuckling.

Rebecca glanced around and saw him.

Joannicus sat like a statue, arms outstretched, supporting a toddler whose dark eyes and somber face followed the activity in the room. *Someone should rescue that child*, she thought. But she appeared to be content.

Rebecca jumped as four-year-old Rosie darted by. She slipped between tables and chairs. Elias tried to block her path, but with the grace and ease of a mountain goat, she scooted past him. Ambrose scooped her up into his arms, where she squealed with delight.

Faith sighed. "That's what happens when you are born in a barn."

Both women laughed. Why couldn't Ambrose be an elder? Since the little girl's birth, she and the monk had come to a territorial truce. Both realized each other's talents and love for Karl and his family. But occasionally, like elk in rutting season, they faced off. Today it felt that way. They were invading her space. She was confident they were responsible for the trees.

Karl came up to her.

"It was not me," he said. "Katie and Rosie did this. I changed it to *Tie It to a Pine Tree* celebration, not to offend anyone."

"You don't think the Elders know it is decorating a Christmas tree?"

Karl shrugged. "Sure, they do, but the kids are having fun. Do not freak out—there are gifts for the children. I squeezed the adult packages, and they are soft. I suspect mufflers, gloves, and hats from the weave shop."

Rebecca's face burned. If only her nieces hadn't invited them.

Katie inserted herself between the adults.

"Bear told us about everyone being together for the big birthday he celebrates. It sounded like a big giveaway—people giving to each other. Rosie and Elias and I wanted to teach him our ways."

Ambrose was instructing the children. Rebecca looked to Faith and Karl for an objection to this indoctrination.

"Being inclusive. That is one of our beliefs," Faith said, beaming with pride.

"Christmas, not a big birthday party. It's about the birth of Christ," Father Pius said, holding a coffee carafe as all around him stiffened.

"So why are you here?" Rebecca asked as Karl drew in a sharp breath.

"Someone had to be with Father Joannicus," Father Pius said, his eyes lingering on Rebecca.

Faith raised her mug. "Coffee?"

Pius turned and poured, the potent brew permeated the air, and the steam rose between them.

"*Philamayaye*," Faith said, using the Lakota word for thank you.

"We have trees, and Santa is coming. Not my idea," Karl said, putting his hands up in self-defense.

"Guess we both agree. Ambrose has some bad ideas," Pius

said. His gray eyes narrowed to a corner where young men were playing drums. A scowl appeared on the monk's face.

What is wrong with drums? Did he think they would sing Christmas carols? This was their winter celebration, not his. At least nobody had set up a nativity scene.

"I'll rescue Joannicus," Karl said, moving away from Pius. He towed Katie along.

Karl scooped the child off of Joe's lap and carried the girl to her mother.

Joannicus stood, shaking his scapular and examining the cloth with its now-darker spot.

Pius tsked and shook his head as Ambrose came over to the group.

"It'll dry," Ambrose said, looking at the damp material.

"What are we doing here?" Pius asked.

"Comingling," Ambrose said. "If nothing else, clean up. I'm playing with the children. Those trees need toppers. Where is Rosie?" The large man scanned the room and lumbered after his namesake.

Faith giggled with a motherly grin.

"Seriously, I don't play with children," Joannicus said.

Pius turned, shook his head, and cracked his knuckles before picking up the plates.

Rebecca picked up the carafe and thrust it into Joe's hands. "Pour coffee then."

The drumming started, slow and steady, the pulse synchronized, heads, hearts, and breath.

"Come on," Katie said, grabbing Joe's scapular. She pulled him to where the adults gathered like a shepherd leading a lamb.

"What is your family? I'm Tiama's great-granddaughter, Spring Flower's granddaughter, Faith Dawson and Karl Knows the Song's daughter, Katie. Who are you?"

"Father Joannicus of St. Alberic's Abbey, order of St. Benedict."

"No, no. That is your job. Who are you?" Katie asked again. Her head wagged like an old woman.

"Joannicus, son of Malcolm Brookes of New York and Marian Tournior of Louisiana."

"Better," Katie said.

Rebecca grinned with pride at what the child knew of her heritage.

"Coffee," Joannicus asked a leathery man wrapped in a worn wool blanket.

The old man squinted up at Joannicus. Karl stood frozen as he watched Joe and Katie.

"I don't like your God," the old one said, smiling a toothless grin. "No preach, just pour." The man held out his mug.

Rebecca held her breath as a room of wolf-wary eyes followed warrior Katie and the white man.

Joannicus smiled sheepishly, filled the raised mugs, then followed Katie to the next table.

Rosie squealed when Todd Dawson, Faith's brother, walked in from outside.

Todd reminded Rebecca of a buffalo stomping his feet and shaking the snow from his broad shoulders. The atmosphere in the place changed. The women sat up straighter and smiled in his direction. Several giggled and scurried around to bring him coffee and food.

Todd was still single and considered a good catch. He hugged his niece and leaned down to kiss his sister. Rebecca wondered why nobody had caught him. Had the council kept him busy, so he had no time for a relationship?

Rebecca leaned against the wall and observed Karl escaping through a side door. *Coward.* He was running away from the potential explosion. Would the old ones not accept the gift offered to them? Would someone sing about Jesus? Which tradition would prevail, Apsáalooke or Catholic?

"Does the wall need your support?" Todd asked, leaning close, scanning her sweatshirt and jeans.

She felt naked, and her cheeks flushed as she shifted, taking in the faint odor of a campfire.

"Yes, the spirits are restless. The black robes are here."

Todd scanned the room. Katie was still towing Joannicus around, introducing him to every Elder. Pius had sequestered himself to a corner near the exit and ate a plateful of food. Ambrose was sitting on the floor in front of Elder Marigold, surrounded by children.

Amusement filled Todd's eyes. "They look contained. And the big one seems to enjoy the stories."

"He's the one who stole the birthing ceremony and imparted his character to Rosie." Rebecca shook her head. The breath of life, the imparting of character, was theirs to give.

"Yes, I can see the resemblance," Todd said as they both watched Ambrose leaning forward with six children hanging off him, drinking in every slow word Marigold uttered.

"He might have earned the right since he assisted with the birth. What is done is done."

He was right. Why did he have to be right?

"Why are they here?" Todd asked as he leaned over her. She could feel his heat.

"Katie invited them to teach them." That happens when one mingles. Karl had stepped into their lives, questioned their beliefs, and challenged them. Now they were curious and intrusive.

"They will not remain long. The tribe isn't leaving, at least not until the coffee pot is empty."

Rebecca laughed.

The kitchen door swung open. A blast of warm air with

cinnamon and cocoa whooshed into the room. An unhappy Elias stomped in, followed by Karl.

"Dad, it's not time, and it's not fair. Rosie's getting presents. It's not time, because the fat white man hasn't shown up. How come she gets presents before the rest of us?"

Rebeca smiled. Elias was so much like Karl—questioning and demanding. She searched the room for Rosie.

Rosie was showing off her gift. The beads sparkled. Rebecca admired the ten glistening pink stones separated by silver roses. Then she saw the crucifix.

Oh, shit. That's not a necklace. It's a rosary.

Rebecca glanced at Karl. They both grimaced.

"Rosie, love," Karl called. "Let me see those."

Rosie scowled. "Mine. Bear gave them to me. This is the big giveaway."

"Bear gave them to her," Faith said.

"But that is a sacred object. We would not let her play with a pipe, would we?" Karl asked.

Faith paused, looked at the sparkling beads and crucifix hanging around her daughter's neck, and frowned.

Rebecca watched Faith look at Karl, touching the leather band around her neck.

Karl touched his chest, where underneath his shirt hung his pouch—one of two eagle feathers.

The two feathers together enabled the eagle to fly smoothly. Faith once owned both feathers and gave Karl her twin feather—a pledge. *I need you. I'm unable to fly without you.* The bond was spiritual beyond the words of a modern "I do."

"Bear said these are Rosie's beads," Rosie shouted, clutching the beads tighter.

"Problem?" Ambrose asked.

"That's a rosary, dear, not Rosie's beads," Rebecca corrected.

"Looks like Rosie's beads to me," Ambrose said. "Besides, it was a fair exchange. I got this cool feather thing and tobacco in a beaded leather pouch."

Faith gasped, putting her fingers to her lips. For in Ambrose's meaty hands was a feather fan with an antler handle used for smudging.

Oh, Rosie, what had she done?

Why hadn't Karl taught her about sacred objects? What was he waiting for?

"Blue-winged teal, right?" Ambrose asked as he examined the leather pouch with the circle of beads on it. "These are the four colors of a medicine wheel—red, yellow, white, and black."

The man knew his birds and was learning Native ways.

"Nice beadwork," Todd said with a grin as he winked at Rebecca. Her heart fluttered. He recognized her art on the leather.

"The circle has many interpretations," Todd said to Ambrose, who nodded with genuine interest.

What was he doing? She fought the urge to grab the items. He was doing it again, innocently taking from them their rites. Those were sacred objects. She turned away.

"The beads are sacred to them," Todd said, placing a firm hand on her arm, drawing her to him. "Don't cut her off from them. She needs to understand their world, too."

"We can't take it back," Faith said to Karl. "He's enjoying it so much."

Rebecca looked at Ambrose, who had rolled the tobacco between his fingers. The sweet smell mixed with the pine, cinnamon, and chocolate. The feather fan placed in his hood poked out over his short hair.

"I could explain the use of the tobacco," Karl said, running his hand through his long-unbraided hair.

"And?" Faith prompted, handing Karl a sage ball and a shell smudging bowl.

"Fine, I will teach Rosie, too." Karl pursed his lips and squinted his blue eyes.

Rebecca could see the thoughts forming.

"The prayers are meditative. She will enjoy the stories. They are called mysteries, joyful, luminous, sorrowful, and glorious. The lessons are in humility, openness, obedience, and faith. We can use the drum to say the Hail Marys. This could work," Karl said, his voice becoming excited.

"Thanks for letting us crash your party," Ambrose said as he approached them. "Pius is pouting, so I think it is time to head home."

"Not so fast," Karl said. "You have the blessing to give. Since you have tobacco and a cool feather, you need to perform the rite."

"You mean I can't smoke this?" Ambrose said, his face falling in disappointment. "It smells so good."

"You'll smoke it," Karl laughed as Ambrose trailed after him.

"Where's he going?" Pius asked, his coat on and his scarf tucked around his neck.

"He has sacred duties to perform," Rebecca said.

"I'm going to the car," Pius said, rolling his eyes and pulling Joannicus along.

Joannicus stepped away. "Seriously, I think I want to watch." His head turned to the table where Ambrose was lighting the tobacco.

Rebecca laughed at the strange joining of Apsáalooke and Catholic, wondering what would emerge from this unlikely union.

CHAPTER 33
DEATH

Dreams are wiser than waking.

Hehaka Sapa (Black Elk). 1863-1950. Wichasha, cultural educator, Wakan medicine man, and Heyoka of the Oglala Lakota.

O n a chilly day in April, Karl sat in the refectory eating the rich, thick corn chowder and homemade bread. The monks ate silently while listening to *The Life of Christ*.

He sat content. Everything was falling into place. Faith was working steadily, and he was graduating this summer. They had another child on the way. Life was good.

Father Joannicus stumbled in late. He lingered, confused. A piece of paper in his hand waved like a flag. Heads turned as he dove for Brother Ambrose. The large man growled.

Katie is right, thought Karl, part bear. He would miss Bear. They could come on Sundays and have dinner with Ambrose.

Bear's dark eyes focused on him. Karl's heart leaped. What had he done wrong? As he stood, the furry head jerked to one side, a clear sign he wanted Karl to follow him. His chair scraped on the floor. Ambrose headed to the exit, grabbing Joannicus by the shoulder and dragging him along.

Brother Mellitus cleared his throat and scowled, obviously disgruntled at not knowing what was transpiring. Karl felt his cheeks burn as he rose, shrugging his shoulders at Brother Mellitus. The man would question him later.

The outside door stood open, and the cold April wind blew in as Karl approached the two men.

"Get a set of car keys and meet us in the parking lot," Brother Ambrose told Joe.

"Shouldn't we..." Father Joannicus stammered, seemingly unable to finish the sentence, his arms flapping as if trying to fly away.

"Go." Ambrose's voice reverberated in the hall. Joannicus jumped and took off running toward the monastery. Ambrose turned to Karl.

"Come with me." Ambrose's tone softened.

Karl's lunch balled in his stomach. Ambrose only barked orders when things were out of control. Something was wrong, but what?

"Where are we going?" Karl asked, walking fast to keep up with Ambrose, who moved as if the devil were pursuing him. They reached the parking lot just as Joannicus came out of the monastery.

"Get in," Ambrose barked, opening the passenger door for Karl. "You, too."

"Me?" Joannicus croaked, his eyes wide with uncertainty.

Ambrose leveled a glance at Joannicus, who ducked into the back seat, his face paling.

"Where are we going?" Karl asked again as Ambrose climbed into the driver's seat.

"To the Mother of Perpetual Help Hospital," Ambrose intoned over the engine's roar.

"Is Rebecca okay?" Karl asked, getting into the passenger seat, his sense of doom mounting.

"Buckle up. It's not Rebecca. It's your family," Ambrose said as he tore out of the parking lot, stones flying, Karl's door slamming shut with the acceleration.

The hospital loomed so large that it blocked out the April sun. Karl entered the crowded emergency waiting room as doors swished and people rushed by. Karl looked for a familiar face.

Ambrose spoke to a woman. "This is Karl Mackenzie."

Heads turned, staring at the two in black habits and the confused, blue-eyed Indian. The automatic doors opened with a hiss, sucking the oxygen out of the air. The walls wavered. Karl stared blankly as the lady behind the desk handed him a clipboard.

"Where's my wife?" Karl asked, keeping his voice at a normal level.

"Sir, I need you to fill out the—"

Ambrose shook his head and waved the scapular of his habit in front of her like a flag. "Saint Alberic's Monastery. We have an account. Look it up."

Ambrose snatched a pen and scratched the paper before handing her the clipboard. The woman stared at him. Her mouth opened and then closed.

The power of monkhood.

Karl scanned the room. His family was not in this waiting space. The doors—they were behind those doors. He bolted to the entrance as the nurse shouted, "Sir, you can't go back there."

It was not a big hospital. Rebecca worked here. He knew his way around.

Karl's vision blurred as he rushed to the automated doors. They opened with a whoosh. And he stepped out of the silence into the chaos of sounds, squeaking gurneys, cries of pain, and shouts of dismay.

Doctors and nurses in scrubs moved in all directions.

"Faith, where are you?" Karl called, feeling the air being squeezed from his lungs.

A man stepped forward, blocking Karl. "I'm Doctor Thomas."

Karl tried to step around him. The man maneuvered to block him again.

"Where is Faith? Where are my kids? I want to see my family."

Doctor Thomas put his hands on Karl's shoulders. His look was firm and focused. Karl felt drawn into the man's kind eyes.

"Mr. Mackenzie, we need to talk. The accident killed your son. He is gone. I'm sorry," Doctor Thomas said, not hiding behind etiquette.

Gone. Gone where? The words floated like a feather on a gentle breeze. What was this man saying? He had spoken to Elias this morning before he had left. They were planning to go fishing.

Dr. Thomas paused, then continued. "Faith is unconscious. The oldest is in surgery. The younger girl, her internal injuries were severe. I'll take you to her."

"My son. Elias, I want to see him."

Karl turned, seeing Ambrose and Joannicus standing a few steps away, talking to the nurse.

He needed to find Elias.

Through the chaos, he saw Elias in a curtained room on a

large gurney. A nurse was pulling a sheet over him. Karl darted to the space, pulled the curtain, startling the nurse, and yanked the sheet off of Elias's face.

"Sir, you can't do that," the nurse said.

"My son, my boy, my love," Karl said, the words moving from anger to tenderness as he picked up his son's body. Gone were the twinkle and the crooked, mischievous smile.

"Elias, come back to me," he pleaded as Ambrose closed the curtain around them.

"Who are you?" the nurse said. "You can't be in here. I have things to do."

"That is the child's father. The dead can wait," Ambrose said.

The nurse scowled and turned. Her rubber soles squeaked.

Karl sat down on the floor, cradling Elias. He pushed the bloody, matted hair from the soft face and kissed the boy's forehead. He could see Joe's feet and black skirts below the curtain.

"Father Joannicus, get in here," Ambrose said, opening the curtains. "I know you carry a kit in your pocket. Baptize this child."

Puzzlement slid across Joe's face, and he slowly shook his head.

"Brother Ambrose, the boy is dead, it's too late, and he's..."

"He is sleeping. Wake up, son. Ask me why. I will answer all your questions. Just open your eyes and ask me." Karl's voice splintered with emotion.

"This is a moment of action. He told me he wanted baptism," Ambrose said, glaring at Joe.

Karl looked at Elias. He could hear the boy asking for the sacrament. Elias never wanted to be left out. Then he remembered that he and Katie had baptized all the newborns at lambing. He was such a sweet boy. He hugged the broken body to his chest.

"Seriously, there are protocols," Joannicus said.

Protocols? Then Karl remembered. Yet only thirty minutes had passed since the spirit had left the body. The boy was still warm.

Ambrose snarled. "He's a child. Explain exactly what grave sin he has committed that would prevent his baptism?"

Joannicus knelt next to Karl. "Do you want me to do this?"

Karl nodded. If Elias had asked, then why not? What else could he give to his son now?

Karl watched as Joannicus baptized Elias with holy water and then anointed him with oil.

The curtains opened and light from the open hall spilled in, framing Rebecca as she stood still in her white uniform, like an angel before him.

A smoky scent tickled Karl's nose as if they were sitting around a campfire. A dark figure stood next to his sister. Todd.

Becca will fix this.

Karl sniffled and stood. Elias's limp body flopped unnaturally. Karl kissed Elias again. There wouldn't be another question.

A nurse paced behind them; her squeaky soles stomped an unnatural rhythm.

"Our son," Karl said as he handed Elias to Todd. The man was an uncle and father. They had both lost a son.

Rebecca snatched scissors off the medical tray and clipped a wisp of Elias's hair, tucking it into her pocket. Todd stood cradling the body of his nephew, murmuring in Lakota.

"Mr. Mackenzie, come quickly," called a nurse, and all heads turned.

Karl moved swiftly, disappearing into a small room a few steps away.

"Rosie." Karl's anguished shout flooded the hallway.

"Oh no, no, no," Ambrose muttered as he grabbed Joe's sleeve, yanking him down the hall to the room.

"Rosie, my baby, our baby," Karl cooed as he scooped her up from the large table that dwarfed her.

The child's eyelids fluttered. Karl smeared the blood like war paint across her cheeks and kissed her face as he held and rocked his daughter.

"Stop. We need..." the nurse said and then paused as Rebecca appeared. Living legends had power.

Doctor Thomas nodded to Rebecca, escorting the on-duty nurse out of the room. Her protests dwindled as she went. Karl watched Rebecca read the monitor and then disconnect the device.

No. Not our Rosie. Karl listened to the faint breaths. Closing his eyes, he sang her favorite lullaby. The same one he had sung to Katie so long ago.

When he opened his eyes, he saw Ambrose poking Joe's chest.

"Anoint her. She's already baptized. I did it the day she was born. Wasn't taking any chances," Ambrose confessed.

He knew it. Ambrose and this child were spirit-bonded. Both viewed the world in awe. How could life sparkle without Amber Rose? How would Ambrose go on?

"How could you?" Rebecca sputtered, her face turning red.

It's okay, Becca. What is done is done.

He and Faith recognized that Amber Rose was a gift to share with all. Rosie knew no bonds in her love. Like her namesake, she bear-hugged the world.

"We will argue later," Ambrose said, pushing her to one side.

Joannicus reached into the pocket of his habit for the second time and smeared oil on the child's bloody forehead.

The aroma of cinnamon oils and the metallic odor of blood filled Karl's nostrils, mingling with the antiseptic smells that lingered around him.

Rosie opened her eyes and smiled. "*Até*, Bear. Elias."

Ambrose beamed back. The little fingers reached out to Ambrose, and his large hand encompassed hers. Ambrose's face scrunched, and his eyes watered his beard.

Rosie made a soft sigh, and her body went slack. Karl groaned as if crushed by her weight. His tears mingled with the blood and oil.

He and Rebecca glanced at the clock on the wall: 4:10 p.m. He knew she should write it down. Recorded or not, it changed nothing. The winds had blown through his life and scattered the dandelion seeds out of his reach.

Karl stood cradling Rosie and kissed her again. Rebecca put out her arms. His heart ached, but he knew this one belonged to the Bear. He handed the extinguished ball of energy to Ambrose. He watched Rebecca's shoulders slump as if he had punched her in the gut.

"Sorry," Karl whispered to her as he touched her arm. She turned away from him, took out her stethoscope, and listened. She frowned as the stern, giant monk sobbed and blubbered incoherently. Rebecca picked up the chart and penned the time. Then she took the scissors from her pocket and cut a piece of Rosie's braid.

Karl noticed Todd standing inside the doorway, empty of his burden, lips tight and still in his firefighting uniform, hand clutching his helmet.

There was a gentle knock, and heads turned.

"Doctor Thomas needs to speak with Mr. Mackenzie."

"Seriously? Now?" Joannicus asked, his voice creaking.

"I'll be back, Rosie," Karl croaked.

Karl followed the nurse. A man limped by him and latched on to his arm, his breath heavy with alcohol.

"So sorry, so, so sorry," the bandaged man murmured.

Echoes of Lucian's deathbed confession haunted Karl's mind. It was the right thing to do.

"Not now, Mr. Davis," the nurse said.

Karl turned to the handcuffed man, leaning on the uniformed officer. This man changed his life. Anger like a spring creek melting poured into him. A warrior's revenge rose.

He doesn't deserve your empathy. He is bound, one life for another.

"You, you're the one?" Karl's voice echoed in his chest. This man has nothing to give but his contrition. Mr. Davis. He is the one who, for the rest of his life, will wake up knowing he killed my family.

"I'm so sorry," Mr. Davis muttered.

Karl swallowed. He had nothing to give him but his forgiveness. Without that, death blocked their lives. A burden too heavy for anyone to bear. A surge of compassion filled Karl. Forgiveness was all that was left.

"It will be okay," Karl offered.

Mr. Davis sobbed.

The nurse gently pushed the two apart, forcing Karl into a room.

Karl almost didn't recognize her. Faith looked so serene in her coma. Karl pinched himself. Was he asleep in this nightmare? He moved to her side and grasped her fingers. They were icy.

"Elias has gone, and Rosie followed him. What will we do without them?" Karl asked as if she would respond. The words fell haltingly as if from a story he wished not to tell.

"Karl, you need to decide which life to save," Doctor Thomas explained.

Karl stared at the doctor.

"We can work on saving Faith or the baby. She's about five months along..."

"You want me to choose?" Tears cascaded down his cheeks. "What kind of question is that to be asking me?" Karl gripped his braid. He couldn't. He wanted them both.

Karl grabbed the doctor and pleaded. "I want my wife and child. Fix this."

Doctor Thomas stood stiffly, taking all the anger like a blade of grass in the wind.

Karl released his grip on the white jacket, then sat beside Faith, holding her hand and rubbing her slender fingers on his damp cheek.

CHAPTER 34
HOPE DIES SLOWLY

And while I stood there. I saw more than I can tell, and I understood more than I saw.

Hehaka Sapa (Black Elk). 1863-1950. Wichasha, cultural educator, Wakan Medicine man, and Heyoka of the Oglala Lakota.

Rebecca entered the chapel. Colored squares dotted the pristine floor. She found him alone with his precious God in this sterile room, isolated, praying for the impossible. He was nothing like Ambrose, who had sat with Rosie's body for an hour while the nursing staff fretted. Rosie was gone. He was with her when she entered and left. Nothing was right about this day. Rebecca cleared her throat.

"Ambrose needs you. I had to take Amber Rose away," Rebecca said.

Joannicus raised his head. Were his eyes red? Had he been crying?

"He loved that little girl as if she was his own," Joannicus said, rising from kneeling in front of the altar.

"Karl's with Faith, in surgery. They are taking the baby who will not live because it is too soon."

She watched his face. An eyebrow raised. He doesn't approve.

"You don't know that. Karl was a preemie. He lived."

"He was older. And he lived because of the care he got." Rebecca's chest constricted. "Even a baby needs a mother. The child will not survive. We don't have the means to help."

"Faith is in a coma. Why are they taking the child now?" Joannicus shook his head.

"So that Faith has a chance. Didn't your God explain it to you?"

Joannicus gasped. Her words cracked the holiness of the chapel.

"Katie's still alive. So is Faith," Joannicus said. He traced the squares of light on the floor with his foot. "I'm praying for them and Karl."

"What good is a prayer to the dying? The doctors are trying to save lives here," Rebecca's voice thundered. "I fear they won't succeed. And then what? He may be a widower with a child. What is left for him?"

Joannicus shuddered, and his cheeks flamed as he held on to the back of the pew.

"He has us, the living," Joannicus said.

Rebecca gripped the pew's back. "I don't like your God. And I don't hold your faith."

"That's okay. I have faith for us all," Joannicus said, standing straight as if his burden had been lifted.

Rebecca balled her fists. She didn't want his holy beliefs. She wanted them to live.

She had witnessed death creep in. She could do nothing but watch as death paraded around her, snatching heartbeats from everyone she loved.

"Why do you keep cutting their hair?" Joannicus asked.

"Why do you keep baptizing them?" Rebecca snapped.

"I need to do something. Can't they be Catholic and Native? Won't they find their way to the Creator, whether heaven or someplace else?"

"I don't know. I want them with the ancestors. It's what we believe. I can't believe Karl allowed you to baptize Elias. Rosie, well, that was Faith's choice."

Joannicus nodded. "I believe Ambrose when he said Elias wanted it... Um, where are the ancestors, if not in heaven?"

Rebecca assessed his sincerity.

"They are all around us," Rebecca said, marveling at his lack of knowledge of the beliefs of others. "The nuns claimed there were many rooms in heaven."

"Perhaps that is true," Joannicus said, a weariness permeating his words.

The door to the chapel opened a grief-stricken body crept in. Joannicus moved to the exit.

"Haven't you been around death?" Rebecca asked, following him out into the hall.

"Of course I have, but not like this. But all those deaths were peaceful. All the rituals are uplifting with hope and joy for the union with God. This is heartbreaking." Joannicus wiped his eyes with the back of his hand.

Rebecca had to agree as they walked to the elevator. This young, naïve monk should hold Karl up. She wondered if he could.

"All death is heartbreaking for the living."

Rebecca pushed the button, and the doors opened with a ding.

"You must have some hopeful ceremonies," Joannicus said. A nurse rushed into the elevator. Her chest heaved as she punched the third-floor button several times.

"Death follows life, follows death, and so on in a circle. Our ancestors gave us life, and we live for our children and their future."

"Similar to us, just not as concrete," Joannicus said.

They both stared at the campaign poster for seat belts of a family on an outing with their children, which read, 'Bring 'em back alive!'

Would that have helped? Anger surged. Too late for that.

Rebecca watched the nurse bouncing inches from the door.

The elevator opened, and she jumped out, muttering, "Where did he go? Oh damn, they are going to fire me."

Together, Joannicus and Rebecca entered the room where Katie was. A silence enveloped the sound of machines. Rebecca surveyed the lineup, Ambrose, and Todd. Karl stood before them, dressed in surgery scrubs. Todd's eyes held a mixture of horror and grief. Something was wrong. She glanced over at Katie. Katie's beautiful face was bruised and swollen. The sight reminded her of Karl. She wished she had some of Grandma Tiama's salve.

"It is a girl, so tiny, so beautiful. She smiled. She didn't even cry. Do you think she will find Rosie and Elias? Will they know she belongs with them?"

"Not a problem. Your kids have a deep sense of direction," Ambrose said, his voice creased with emotion.

Todd's lips trembled. Rebecca's eyes fell upon Karl and the pink blanket. There in his hands lay a tiny bronze, silent infant. She had seen them before. They looked small and alien. Rebecca took a breath.

Karl turned to Joannicus. "Will you baptize her?"

Rebecca could not believe what she had heard. She watched

Joannicus hesitate and look at her. Was he asking her permission? She wasn't the parent. This ritual was not hers. Yet she and Karl were baptized. Maybe having more than one entrance to the after-life wasn't dreadful.

"Here you go. I have named her Almost Joan. You know, for that saint, Joan of Arc, and for you."

The color in Joe's face drained.

"She is so beautiful," Karl marveled as he handed Joannicus his namesake.

Joe's arms trembled, and he looked at the ceiling. Rebecca could see his eyes swelling with wetness. She moved to his side. As soon as Karl turned, Joannicus handed Rebecca the cold little bundle in a pink blanket.

Joannicus once again pulled out his vials of oil and holy water, this time not wiping the river's moisture from his cheeks.

Rebecca tried not to listen to the words he spoke. Instead, she concentrated on Karl's voice, which was strong as he talked to Ambrose and the sleeping Katie.

He didn't need her comfort yet, but he would. She must be strong for when he needed her.

That was not how she felt holding her niece. So tiny, so perfect. She wanted to scream and pound the earth.

The conversation took on a surreal tone. Karl talked as if Almost Joan and her sisters would play together next week. She was sure Karl was losing his mind. Her brother had forgiven the man who created this day. Never had she seen him act so stoic. He should be wailing. Yet here he stands, talking as if the world hasn't crumbled. She pinched herself. The pain registered. Not a dream, just a nightmare.

She wished she was soaring above, swooping in for sips of pain and then touching the rays of the sun like an eagle.

Her eyes met Joe's wide and frightened stare. His head turned, and she followed his gaze. He was terrified, not of death but of living. She saw and felt his dread. What would become of Karl?

The nurse rushed into the room and grabbed the baby from Rebecca.

"Wait," Rebecca shouted, but the woman darted away.

"She could have waited. I just wanted..." Rebecca leaned against the wall. Tears flooded her eyes.

The future was taken from her. The whole Apsáalooke Nation was gone in a heartbreaking moment—all our hopes and dreams. Never would this child see the eagle soar, never savor vanilla ice cream and cantaloupe on a summer day, never hear the cricket sing, smell the campfire, or touch the soft fur of a rabbit. Everything that is us was taken and gone.

She swayed and allowed Todd to ease her into a chair.

Joannicus appeared before her, his trembling hand stretched out, a wisp of hair pinched between his fingers.

Their watery eyes met.

Todd took the locket of hair and kneeled, placing his head in Rebecca's lap. She let her tears drip, mingling with his sorrow as she stroked his brow.

CHAPTER 35
ORPHANS

There is no death, only a change of worlds.

Chief Si'ahl (Chief Seattle). 1786-1866. Suquamish and Duwamish leader, ecological protector, visionary, and orator.

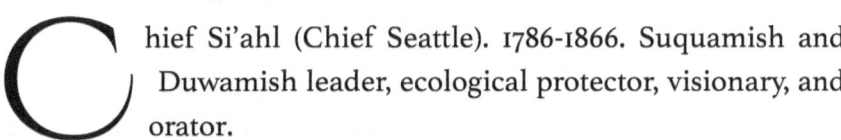

REBECCA WOKE WITH A START. The events of the last forty-eight hours came rushing back. She rubbed her neck to get the soreness out. Brother Ambrose snored loudly next to her in the waiting room.

She needed to find Karl.

She headed to the nurses' station to ask about Faith and Katie. The nurse smiled a weak smile and pointed to a room. Rebecca re-braided her hair and ran her palm over the wrinkles in her uniform. She stood in the doorway. The pumps hissed and the dials clicked. The sun laced through the trees from the window. Karl sat between Faith and Katie's beds. He looked like the crucified Christ, his arms stretched out, holding a hand of each love. His head drooped as if to say, *I am defeated.*

"Karl, let me take over. You need some rest."

Karl glanced up and shook his head. "No. I am not leaving them."

She turned and saw Todd sitting in the corner. He shrugged, stood, and headed to the door, escorting her out of the room. They walked to the end of the hallway. The dark circles under his red-rimmed eyes told her he had not slept.

"Unless you're going to tranquilize him. There's no point," Todd said.

The thought danced by her. She hesitated.

"Where is young black robe?" Rebecca asked.

"In the chapel praying."

What good was prayer now? Death gulped the air they breathed.

She glanced out the window and watched a lone coyote stroll across the parking lot. She nudged Todd and pointed with her lips. A coyote meant chaos. Well, that was happening. Coyotes mated for life. Rebecca scanned the area, looking for the mate.

"Coyote teaches duality. We are all connected," Todd whispered.

A cry of agony echoed down the hall. The nurses looked up from their station. Rebecca leaned against the window and dropped to the floor. She gazed up at Todd. Their eyes met as pain floated between them. She knew. He knew.

Faith had died.

Todd ran to the room. She steadied herself, hands printing the glass. She pulled herself up and marched to the room. A nurse followed.

"I will document this," Rebecca said. The woman did not argue.

Rebecca's hand trembled as she took the stethoscope and placed it on Faith's chest. There was no heartbeat.

She placed her hand on Karl's arm.

"No, no. Faith, do not leave me," Karl moaned.

He gripped her arm, pleading with her to use her power to restore life. Rebecca knew with certainty that she was helpless to ease his agony.

"There was more to say. She did not meet Almost Joan," Karl said. Anger tinged his words.

Rebecca swallowed. She had watched Karl chatter yesterday, telling Faith about the accident and Almost Joan. He talked about the other children as if she heard him.

Rebecca didn't believe that those near death were aware of their surroundings. She was sure their focus was on the next step. Faith had never woken up. She had walked on to be with her babies, trusting that Karl would follow her. Rebecca's heart grieved for her brother. She glanced up at Todd, horror etching his face. What could she do? Nothing. The word echoed in her mind as her fists tightened.

Karl wiped his nose on the bedsheet and kissed Faith a dozen times, smoothing her hair and caressing her cheek.

"*Até*," came a weak voice. Karl rose and turned to Katie's bedside.

"Baby, I am so sorry. It is just us now," Karl said, wiping his face of the tears.

"*Até*, *Iná* had to take care of Almost Joan. Joanie is a good name. She likes it. Joanie Tea, for Uncle Todd. Elias is so silly."

Rebecca heard Todd let out a soft exhale. He paused next to his sister, gripping the bed rail.

"Okay, I understand," Karl murmured. "We are going to miss her."

"*Até, Iná* needs me."

Karl scooped Katie off the bed and into his arms. Buzzers screamed, and Rebecca unplugged them.

"Baby girl, stay with me. I cannot do this without you."

"You're not alone. I called Bear. He'll take care of you," Katie said, focusing on Karl.

"No, no, no. I do not want him. I want you. Stay. Please stay."

"He's here. I have to go, *Até*."

Karl climbed onto the bed with Katie cradled in his arms.

The door opened, and Ambrose and Joannicus entered. One smelled like a bear fresh out of his den, the other like Sunday Mass.

A nurse arrived. Rebecca glared at her, and she backed out of the room. What did "time of death" mean? Nothing—just marks on a piece of paper. Rebecca glanced at the clock. The space was quiet except for Karl's ragged breathing, Ambrose's sniffling, Todd's deep breaths, and the shuffling of Joannicus. The bed groaned as Karl rocked.

A swirling force beyond her control had broken their circle. The cyclone of Old Man Wind shattered her family.

She wanted to smudge and drive the heaviness away, bring back the energy before evil encapsulated them all. She stood frozen, witness to the draining of life.

A commotion in the hall pulled her out of herself as she recognized Judith's voice. She moved, but she was too slow. Judith entered the room. *Who had contacted them?*

Judith glanced at Karl and Katie and then to the bed that held the body of Faith, and she snorted a laugh. Her floral perfume made Rebecca queasy. She might have been white in her soft-green power suit if it weren't for her dark eyes, skin, and short hair.

Todd's face steeled, and his eyes grew hard. Terence, Davy, Tommy, Vincent, and Vicki crowded into the small space.

The darkness loomed. Smudge, Smudge.

Rebecca fingered the bracelet that held powdered herbs as she glanced at her siblings. Tommy towered over both his parents. Davy searched the room for a hiding spot. The twins stood side by side next to Terence. Vincent's face was etched in compassion, and Vicki beamed with annoyance.

Karl swung his feet to the floor, carrying Katie's body to Faith. He placed her in the bed as if she were a newborn. The two monks blended into the background.

"This is a fine mess you have gotten yourself into," Judith said as Karl turned and faced her.

Terence stepped forward and embraced Karl, who seemed riveted to the floor, staring down at Judith.

"We are too late. I'm so sorry, son."

"Thanks," Karl mumbled.

Vicki huffed and crossed her arms before exiting. This show was not about her. The room blackened. Rebecca wished the windows opened so that the evil would escape.

Forgive her. She is only fourteen, a voice inside Rebecca said.

"What can we do? Have you thought about burial arrangements?" Terence asked. "I requested a Mass to be said."

"How will you pay for that? Don't come begging us for money," Judith said.

"Judith, dear, we will help if we can."

"There is nothing we can do. He brought this on himself," Judith said, turning to her husband. "They are not Catholic. Indians do not have funerals. I will not hang around the Rez for days."

So she wouldn't grieve or remember. Rebecca shook her head. An Indian funeral was not like a Catholic service. But there was a gathering, a giveaway, a feast, and family and friends surrounded one. It lasted for days. Her forgiveness had run dry.

"What the hell," Rebecca growled. "What are you doing here? You never liked Faith. Besides grandmother bragging rights, you didn't have time for the children."

"I wasn't welcome. And I don't want to linger around the campfire telling tales," Judith said.

Is that what you call Indian ceremonies--campfire gatherings? Had all her Native heritage been drained? Rebecca recognized the hatred that Karl lived with. And worse for having blue eyes, which spoke of white influence. But Karl looked like Endow. Nobody could accuse her of infidelity.

Judith pointed a finger at Karl. "Why weren't you with them?"

There was a sharp intake of breath from Terence and Todd. Rebecca could not believe the question. Ambrose rumbled low, like a wolf in the corner.

"I would have died too," Karl said. A sardonic smile lit his face.

"Yes, perhaps so. And yet here you are. She wouldn't have been out if you were home. This is your doing."

"Shut up, *Ihkaa*," Rebecca snarled, breaking the rule of speaking Crow.

"Whoa, Rebecca," Terence said. "Your mother isn't blaming anyone."

The mud in his ears must be thick. She just said it was Karl's fault. Mitchell Davis caused the accident. Alcohol was the real culprit. Pinning this to someone was as useless as saying God has a plan. Rebecca gritted her teeth.

Karl moved around his parents and climbed into the vacant bed.

"Here is your chance, *Ihkaa*. Send me away. I want to be with my family, complete my circle."

If Judith had moved one muscle, Rebecca would have tackled the five-foot woman to the ground. Rebecca sighed, glancing at Karl. Would he follow Faith? That would be just like him to do something impulsive. They came so far together that she would be alone.

"You should have died years ago," Judith sneered, shooting a scathing look at Rebecca.

Rebecca felt her skin flush. Was it anger or shame? She glanced at Todd, standing like a cedar absorbing the storm.

The Mackenzie clan stood frozen, watching Judith. Rebecca pushed her way toward the bed. She would be a shield between her mother and brother if nothing else.

"Mother, you do not accept God. I am not sure you believe in anything," Karl said, rising on one elbow. "The wind blows loudly through your soul."

"Neither do you. And this is your punishment."

"My punishment for what? Not dying in the hospital twenty-five years ago?" Karl's voice was loud and harsh.

Rebecca shuddered. He had spoken what they both knew, what they all held in secret.

Ambrose cleared his throat. "Enough of this nonsense. We can't second-guess the mind of God. Prayer would be more proper than finger-pointing. We are all in shock. Grief soaks us like rain. May we anoint them?"

"She does not believe," Karl said.

"But we do," Ambrose said, nodding to Joannicus.

"Then I see no harm. As Katie said, we may as well try all the ways we know to unite them. Almost Joan needs her *Iná*."

Judith clicked her tongue and hissed, "Sacrilege."

The woman was jealous. Karl had successfully balanced both

worlds, and she could not stand the one she was born into and barely fit in the one she desired.

The smell of holy oils filled the room, and silently, Joannicus marked Katie's forehead.

Rebecca noticed Todd had already cut off part of Faith and Katie's braid. There was nothing left to do. Judith needed to leave.

"*Ihkaa*, let's go," Rebecca said, taking the opening in the tension Ambrose had provided. And silently thanking him for once again stepping into the storm of events.

Judith didn't move.

"I don't take orders from you."

"*Ihkaa*, enough. Go home."

Judith glared at Rebecca. Hurt registered.

Why couldn't she be nice?

She had wanted a mother. She had needed a mother. Judith was not that woman. She was toxic. Could she not see the grief that drenched this man, her son?

"I warned you that nothing good would come. You didn't heed my words. Now you see what your interference has created. Sometimes things should be left alone," Judith said, trembling slightly as Terence moved toward her.

"I did the right thing. Can't you be kind for once? He has done nothing to you. Maybe you are right. You should just forget he ever existed. You bring evil. You've been nothing but a shadow at the entrance to our life. The sun is gone. You're no longer needed. When it returns, do not darken our doorstep."

A hand came up and slapped Rebecca's right cheek.

"You ungrateful child."

"You unloving woman," Rebecca said, rubbing her face as her left hand fisted, and she stepped toward Judith. "You are without relatives," Rebecca hissed.

This was the worst possible insult to a Crow.

Karl gasped and swung his legs over the edge of the bed, but Todd was quicker. He wrapped his powerful arms around Rebecca.

She would not have hurt her—she would have just pushed her out of the room.

Terence grabbed his wife and exited the space. The boys followed them out.

The youngest brother, Vincent, paused at the door.

"This is so messed up. I'm sorry. Here," Vincent said as he handed Rebecca a smudging stick of lavender and cedar before turning and walking out. Rebecca's eyes teared up. Vincent was respecting the Native ways. Even though his exposure was limited, he had tried to be helpful. She had disowned Judith and feared that would extend to her half siblings.

A nurse and security guard rushed into the room.

"The only people allowed here are immediate family," the nurse's voice quaked. The security guard looked at the three Indians, Ambrose, and Joannicus.

"This is it. My sister and brother," Karl said, invoking the right of an Apsáalooke with no relatives to ask someone to be his clan. Only Todd was Lakota, not Apsáalooke. Todd had lost everyone, and Karl was adopting him, including him in their circle.

Where did that compassion come from?

The rites and rituals were blending. She needed to smudge. She wished to clear the room of harmful things and prevent Karl from cutting or, even worse, ending his life. They faced death, and gaining a brother did not ease the pain. She was no longer 'auntie mom.' She had no mother or father—only Karl and now Todd. The weight of loss was too heavy, and Rebecca's knees buckled as the muscular arms of Todd held her.

CHAPTER 36
YOU HAVE LOST A SON

You finally learn wisdom comes only when you stop looking for it, and start truly living the life the Creator intended for you.

Leila Penn Fisher. 1912-1986. Hoh, basket weaver, and spiritual Elder. Excerpt from *Wisdom Keepers*, by Steve Wall and Harvey Arden.

Rebecca opened her eyes. Dim light filtered in. The heavy fur weighed her down as the scent of sage tickled her nose. How did she get here? Whose teepee was this? Reality slid in, and the past seventy-two hours washed over her like a bout of flu. She lay back down. Life changed in three days. Not unlike the Jesus in the tomb. What was she thinking? She heard the murmured prayers by the men in black; their haunting chats coated her like hardened tree sap. The worried faces of those monks hovered over her.

The past became clearer. Her grief was crushing her. She was a nurse. She handled stress, lack of sleep, and people dying. Somehow, the world crashed. Control was gone. Todd brought her here, and she drank the grieving tea. Peyote was for healing. She slept and dreamed. Bodies came and went. She stood in the circle that the rain of tears dissolved. Jimmy, Marie, and Karl all washed away. She remembered sending Judith away, cutting her out of the circle. That was real. The younger siblings—did they leave with Judith? She touched her cheek. It was tender. The slap was real. She was alone.

Just a dream. She needed to find Karl. But she knew dreams were windows, and she didn't like this view—open plains with no humans and no family.

She listened. A fire crackled. Was it day or night? She sat up again. The flap to the teepee opened, and the smell of venison rushed in. Her stomach churned.

"You're awake. Eat," a familiar voice said.

Todd.

A protest formed on her lips. But seeing his face marked with paint—or was that blood?—caused her to take the stick of food offered. Had he drunk the tea and entered the spirit world to grieve? Had he seen Faith and his other sisters? She knew they gave the markings to him, and he would wear them until they faded. Were his tears spent? Had he sweated? Anger and envy rose inside of her. He seemed strong, and she felt like a rabbit born out of season.

The warm meat exploded on her tongue, venison sweet and spicy.

"Karl, where is he?"

"Home."

She jumped up. "What the hell? Are you crazy?"

"No."

"He can't go home. Wait. Whose home? Not my folks?" Rebecca asked, falling back to the furs as a wave of dizziness blew through her.

"Bear took him," Todd said, an amused smile on his face.

"His name is Ambrose," Rebecca snapped. "Only Katie calls... called him Bear. Nobody else."

She watched him bristle. Guilt wrapped itself around her. Todd's last sister had walked on. He was alone. She hung her head. She reached to smooth her hair and wondered if Karl had cut his braids. Todd's braid still hung. Rebecca then noticed the bandage on Todd's arm. Alarms rang in her head. He had marked himself with his losses. This time on his right arm. The left still held the marks of his original family. She counted them, seven scars. His parents, four sisters, and a brother. So many lives, so much sorrow. She paused and stared at Todd, seeing his burden for the first time. He sat beside her, looking ragged and worn, like a tree after a storm. That's not Todd. Even after a day of firefighting, he glowed with strength. She pinched herself. It hurt. No, this wasn't a dream.

"How many fingers does Karl have?"

Todd looked at her as if she had gone insane.

"Ten," he said tentatively.

"You have seen him recently?" Rebecca asked, gripping Todd's scarred forearm.

"He was with me yesterday."

Todd placed a hand on top of hers. The touch was soft and warm. Rebecca startled and pulled away.

Todd rose and moved to the cooler to retrieve a quart jar of water.

Rebecca sighed. Why had she pulled away?

She should comfort him.

It was an ancient tradition to chop off fingers when you lost a loved one. She could see Karl respecting that custom. Five fingers were one too many.

"I need to..." she said but paused. What did she need to do? Count his fingers?

Todd handed her the jar of water.

"Karl is safe," the Elder in her head said.

Was he safe? Would the monks convert him completely?

"And what if they do?" the Elder whispered.

Hot tears squeezed out of her eyes. Her hand brushed them away as she drank from the wet, dripping jar.

"I'm sorry. You must hurt," Rebecca said, wanting to help.

His face darkened, and he stiffened. "I'm a warrior. I'll grieve and then heal. The tribe and friends will carry me. I'll be fine. What does Karl have?"

"He has me."

Todd sat down and bit his lower lip. "You cannot help him. This is not your journey."

"I have to support him."

She gulped more water, quenching the fire in her mouth from the cayenne pepper that seasoned the deer.

"You do not understand." How could she explain? "He has never been alone. He needs me."

"Ah, little bee," Todd murmured, tugging on a string in his moccasins.

Don't pull that thread. All the beads will fall out, thought Rebecca.

Why was he calling her a bee? She was not busy all the time. And she certainly did not treasure the sunny days. She preferred the evening, and everyone learned bees flew home once the sun set.

"Your brother is stronger than you think. He must find his own path. You can't lead him."

"What about the bundles for the ceremony?"

"*Wanagi Wicagluha*, the third rite, the keeping of the spirit. It has been taken care of."

"I missed it?"

"It will be tomorrow at the monastery."

"Wait, what?" Rebecca asked as she chewed the meat, grinding it like a ravenous cougar.

"They will bury Faith and the children in the secular cemetery on their grounds. Karl has approved."

"But that isn't Lakota or Apsáalooke."

"Karl has agreed to it." His voice was stern, like a parent's.

"What about the blanket?" She was thinking about the wedding blanket that Faith and Karl had worn on the day they married.

"Karl tore it in half. It's wrapped with Faith and the children for the Catholic funeral. They invited everyone."

She licked her lips, and her tongue burned with the spices.

"What about our traditions? What about the belongings? Has he given them away?"

"Did you not hear me? They invited everyone. The Lakota ways will be honored. Your grandmother has spoken and selected Apsáalooke ways. As we speak, the teepees are being set up."

He respects tradition but in Karl's style. Was there nothing for her to do?

The bill. Another bill was owed to Mary, Mother of Perpetual Help.

"What about the bills? They must be astronomical, even if I can convince them to add my discount?"

"No cost."

"No bill?"

Todd smiled a crooked smile. One side of his lips lifted. "The monastery paid the bill."

"Why?" Rebecca shook her head.

"Because they care."

Normally, the tribe paid for the burial. Fear tickled her. Had they bought her brother with kindness? She didn't trust these monks. Yet Ambrose was family to Katie, and Joannicus had respected her traditions.

Her jaw ached as she chewed and watched Todd rise. His movements were smooth and slow. She saw his burden. He carried his sorrow as if he were bringing home a slaughtered deer.

Todd lifted the flap of the teepee. Grandma Tiama stumbled into the dim light of the teepee. Todd reached out to help her. Grandma Tiama wore a black scarf on her head, a sign that she was mourning. The flap dropped, smacking another woman who tried to enter. Two young women glared at Todd as they followed Grandma. Rebecca swallowed the half-chewed meat.

Tiama settled on the furs with Rebecca, pulling her grand-daughter's head into her lap. Rebecca did not fight the gesture as the two other women snuggled in close.

Todd stood off to the side.

"Shoo, warrior. Rest. Your services will be needed later," Grandma Tiama said to Todd.

Rebecca watched the two women drooling over Todd as he left. She had often wondered why he had never married. He was always the talk among the women at powwows. "Oh, that Todd, the best elm tree in the forest, supple, sleek, yet strong and adaptable."

She understood now. Why marry when things like this happen?

Moisture escaped her eyes. With an arthritic finger, Grandma traced the tears that pooled on her cheeks.

Softly, the women sang a soothing tune. Emotions rose to the sky as they smudged with heavy scents of sage and cedar. They braided and oiled her hair before she allowed them to cut it short.

She drank the herbal tea offered to her. The smell of peppermint filled her nose.

"Grandma, what am I going to do?" Rebecca asked.

"Live," Grandma Tiama said.

"I'm aware, but Karl," Rebecca said. "How does he continue?"

"Karl must decide to endure."

That was not a reassuring answer.

"What if he falls into the brown bottle? What if he seeks to join Faith?"

"You can't guess what he will choose. He is Apsáalooke. Show him a life worth living. You and he must separate. Allow yourself to grieve, daughter of my daughter. He is your brother, but you have been a mother to him. It's like you've lost a son. He has lost a union. Witness to him that life goes on even after loss. This is winter. Spring will come. It always does."

Certainly, life continued, but it echoed hollowly. Everything he loved was just taken from him. How would he find his way? She could barely see the path.

"You are too close. I should have stopped this bond, but you two needed each other. The moment has come to walk different paths," Tiama said. "Your time as mother has ended."

"He still needs me."

Tiama held out a black scarf. To wear it meant grieving, acknowledging the loss, and not attending social gatherings or powwows. Their teepee would stand empty this year at Crow Fair.

"What do you need?"

She could not answer that question. She didn't know what she needed, but she recognized he could not help her, and she could not aid him in his grief.

Rebecca felt herself curl up like a squirrel in winter.

She was alone, abandoned. She covered her head with the black material and pulled the fur over herself. Grieve. She had lost a son. The echo of those words bounced in the hollows of her chest.

CHAPTER 37
LEAD ME TO REST

My home is where my tipi sits.

Awé Kúalawaachish (Chief Sits in The Middle of the Land). 1795-1877. Apsáalooke chief, wise and able negotiator and orator.

K arl stood at the guesthouse window and listened to the drumming, soft and slow, like a heartbeat. He reached for his braid. It was gone. He had cut it off. The sky was heavy with large gray drops of rain plopping down, switching to fluffy flakes and back. The smells of roasting beef and venison filled the hallway and room.

Karl and several monks had spent days digging a hole. He rested his head against the cool window and closed his eyes, recalling the view from the bottom of the hole: blue sky, white clouds, the darting of a few brave birds calling the season to hurry.

It was more like chipping at marble. The spring thaw came and went, slowing their progress. Solid in the morning and mush by afternoon.

Life echoed emptiness.

Today was the funeral, Catholic-style, with a bit of Lakota and Apsáalooke mixed in.

When did he ever follow tradition? What does it matter? It is all meaningless.

Karl turned. It was time. The world continued to run, even without his participation. He was insulated, unable to touch or be touched. Waving his hand as if smudging or swatting an annoying gnat changed nothing. He was trapped.

Was he between worlds?

Then he heard a faint command. Move. He glanced about to see if it came from outside him or inside. No one was nearby.

Just moving took significant effort. He crossed the courtyard as the wind gusted and pushed him forward. Ten more steps and he would be in the church.

Lakota, Apsáalooke, Mackenzie, and monastic crowded into the church, each with their rituals and beliefs. The clans outnumbered the monks. All groups moved as one. Karl sat, rose, kneeled, and sat again with the slow rhythm of the black-robed dance. The words and actions swirled around him like a drug-induced trip. His only anchor was the coffin, which loomed white with his torn wedding blanket draped over it.

None of it gave meaning or comfort. He closed his eyes. The hospital haunted him. A pain, starting in his chest, spread across his body and threatened to choke him. He opened his eyes and grabbed for his braid. His hand slipped through the air.

Three Lakota and three Crow moved to carry the coffin to the atrium. Father Joannicus led Karl past the open coffin. The faces of Faith and the children looked unreal. Their lips were too red, their fingertips blackened, and their skin was an off shade of brown. He kept watching, waiting for their eyes to open, for them to scream, "Fooled you, *Até*." But the feathers in the coffins did not move. No chest rose with breath.

Lakota friends placed cookies for the children, jewelry, and toys in the coffin.

Grandma Tiama stood with Rebecca and Marie. Each carried articles of clothing to place in the grave with the casket. Marie's black scarf contrasted with her order's pastel habit.

The Mackenzie family passed stoically by the coffin. No drama leaked from them.

This might be funny... if he thought they cared.

Respectfully, monk after monk passed by the one coffin. Brother Ambrose placed a small ball of wool next to Elias. Joannicus dropped in the pink rosary.

"Do not judge the gift, grieving one," came the whisper inside his mind.

Three Lakota and three Apsáalooke carried the coffin to the hearse. All followed the slow-moving vehicle to the monastic cemetery. Rows of headstones stood left and right, divided by a path to the large life-size bronze crucifix. They carried the casket through the monastic cemetery to a small secular space. This was where spinster aunts and mothers of monks lay buried. They didn't have to allow his family burial here, but they did.

After they completed the Catholic rite, a Lakota circle formed. Several monks left. Brother Mellitus glowered and clicked his tongue, hushed repeatedly by Ambrose. Father Pius cracked his knuckles. Tension around him threatened the sacred. Too Native for some, Karl didn't care. Katie would want it this way.

A fire sparked, and the smell of sweet grass permeated the air. The Shaman spoke in Lakota and then in English.

"Wakan Tanka, behold us. We keep these souls for Mother Earth so that our children will walk the path of life sacredly."

Rebecca handed five locks of hair to the Lakota Shaman. He passed the locks through the purifying smoke, then secured them in a buckskin bundle.

"This is now a sacred place. May our grandchildren walk the path of life with pure hearts and firm steps."

Karl swallowed hard. What grandchildren? There will be none. Anger fussed within him. Fight the emotion. Safe within his globe. He clenched his jaw, attempting to be strong.

The man turned to the gathered crowd.

"My relatives, we shall gain great knowledge from these purified souls. Be good and love. That is Wakan. May this help us to remember all our gifts come from Wakan Tanka. They are all Wakan. Treat each other as such."

The group murmured in Apsáalooke and Lakota and moved closer together. The old man turned, the bundle in his trembling hands stretching toward Todd. Todd lowered his eyes and shook his head. There were gasps of shock.

The bundle belongs to him. Why is he refusing it?

Todd whispered to the man. The Shaman turned to Karl.

No, no, this is not right. He was not Lakota.

"Behold the future," Grandma Tiama muttered.

The old one stood, offering the leather bundle. Refusal was impossible. The calloused hands cupped around Karl's.

"Will you honor us as keeper of the souls of our tribe?"

Karl swallowed. He nodded, and with quivering hands, he accepted the souls of his family.

The Sacred Pipe was lit, passed sunwise around the circle, and smoked.

The man turned to face Karl.

"I am to instruct you on your duties. The Keeper of Souls

393

should not fight or use a knife. He must constantly pray, being an example to all." He turned to those in the circle. "People love and honor this holy man, bringing him food and gifts." He faced Karl, wrinkled eyes opening wide. "Keeper of the Souls, offer your pipe to Wakan Tanka for the good of the Nation. You have a pipe, don't you?"

Karl nodded, listening to the murmuring of Grandma Tiama, her Crow prayers echoing the words of the spiritual Elder.

Again, the man cupped Karl's hands.

"Keeper of the Souls, your hands are Wakan. Treat them as such."

Karl shivered. He now understood what Joannicus meant when he said his hands were sacred during the rite of Mass.

The man reached up, hesitated as he looked into Karl's blue eyes, and then his palm shaded them.

"Your eyes are Wakan. See all things as sacred."

An arthritic cracked finger touched Karl's lips.

"Your mouth is Wakan, and every word you speak should reflect this sacred state in which you are now living. Raise your head often and look to the sky. By this action, you remember you care for these souls. Today you are Wakan. Teach others as they have taught you. So, it shall be. *Hechetu welo.*"

The shrilling began, and the last of the monks scurried like rats up to the hilltop. The high pitch of the mourners broke their armor-protected curiosity. Karl felt alone as he held the bundle to his chest.

"Let them run," Grandma Tiama said as she tapped Karl's arm. "They will return."

KARL SAT IN THE REFECTORY, surrounded by food and the belongings of the dead. Normally, these items would be given to family and friends, but Karl let them select what they needed instead. The ritual was a mixture of Apsáalooke and white. Tribal members had helped with the cooking. They would be near the monastery for several days. He wondered how long the monks would tolerate their presence.

People moved like ghosts around him. Karl stood, glancing at it all—a great giveaway. Ambrose picked up a wooly sheep and slipped it into his pocket. He had given that to Amber Rose on her first birthday.

Karl fingered a lopsided clay basin, not quite a fruit bowl or cup, Faith's attempt at pottery. He could feel her love and his loneliness.

"Why would anyone want this stuff?" Father Pius asked, standing next to Brother Ambrose. "Personal toothbrushes, combs?" He cracked the knuckles on his right hand. "I can't believe those silly novices gathered that."

"I told them to treat everything as if it were a chalice," Ambrose said.

"They consider all objects as having an essence. A purpose," Father Joannicus said. "What they said in the graveyard makes me think they have much in common with our Benedictine ideals."

Karl took the pottery. *God, earth, breath, Faith, clay, spirit.* He hugged the bowl to his chest.

Insulated in his bubble of grief, he sat, watching the tears, the hugs, and the calls. Their bodies were gone, but not their spirits.

In a year, he would release them—too long.

Karl watched the room divide between monks and tribes. Each side was leery yet united in food and purpose. Judith stood out only because she wasn't wearing black or the traditional black scarf. She refused to honor any tradition. Todd hovered over Grandma Tiama. Terence seemed the only one comfortable enough to move among them all.

What were they doing here? Rebecca had severed the bond. Or had she? He snorted. Bond? What bond?

A three-year-old child approached Karl, smiling. She looked at the bowl in his lap, which now held the sacred bundles. Karl stared at her. They locked eyes, and slowly her face sagged as a frown weighed her chin, and it quivered as tears formed in her eyes.

Rebecca grabbed the child from Karl's vision.

"Stop that," she hissed at him as she stroked the tearful girl's head, returning her to her mother.

Rebecca appeared next to him.

"You can't do that. You can't drink her spirit."

Karl caressed the leather bundle. The deer hide was soft.

A shadow loomed. Judith cleared her throat. She stood before him, flanked by Sister Marie and Terence.

"This has been nice. I hope you thanked the Abbot for his kindness," Judith said. "But we shouldn't overstay our welcome. Let's go. Gather your things."

What was she talking about?

"Go?" Rebecca's voice was pinched.

"Home," Judith quipped, giving her a hard stare.

"No," Rebecca said.

Karl glanced from one to the other. He must be invisible.

"Rebecca, I don't think this is your concern," Terence said. "Your brother needs family, time, and a place to grieve and heal."

"The sacred bundles, he can't leave," Rebecca said. He knew she was grasping for a reason to stop him from returning to the farmhouse.

"That isn't even our tradition." Judith crossed her arms.

He had blended Lakota and Apsáalooke. He accepted the bundles, so he was duty-bound.

Karl covered his ears. Their squawking hurt.

"They can erect a teepee anywhere," Judith said. "Honestly, souls can be kept in cookie jars."

Karl stood. Enough.

"Many will come, disturbing your peace at the farmhouse, But I will consider your kind offer," Karl said, knowing he was lying, for he had dismissed the idea even as it fell from her lips.

"No, you won't consider it," Rebecca said.

"That's the problem. You two are selfish. They were my grandchildren. You kept them from me," Judith said, her voice calm and treacherous.

"This isn't about you, Mother," Rebecca said.

"*Ihkaa*, they are gone. You can have whatever possession they had that brings you comfort. That is what the giveaway is about," Karl said, baffled by Judith's grief. Had he dishonored her by keeping their visits to a minimum?

"Don't be fooled," the Elder in his mind whispered.

Judith looked sincere, hands gripped in each other, standing close to him, peering up.

"Go home. Father, take her home," Rebecca said, her voice hard and gravelly.

"Rebecca, calm yourself," Terence said. "You're overreacting. We've all suffered loss here."

Rebecca turned to Karl and grabbed his arm. "Don't go home."

"*Balakibia*," Judith said to Rebecca in Crow. "Leave him. He's not your son. You're not his wife."

Karl felt the gut punch and knew Rebecca did, too. She had spoken in Apsáalooke. Yes, they were close. That was how they had survived. Judith was right. It was time to walk his own path.

Rebecca trembled as the words spewed forth. "How dare you call yourself *Basahke*, his mother, my mother? You never wanted Karl. Why now? He has nothing for you. Leave him alone."

Karl heard the rosary beads of Sister Marie clicking. Judith was baiting them to react. Did she think in his weakness that she could send his spirit to walk on and join Faith and the children? He needed to stop this.

Karl placed a hand on Rebecca's shoulder. "Do not follow her down this path. It is a trap."

Rebecca turned to him, placing her head on his chest as he held her.

"She should have been your *Basahke*, loved you, and taken care of you like she has others. She left it for me to do. I have always fixed things. I can't this time. I can't bring them back."

As if approaching a feral animal, Todd moved closer to Rebecca. The elk teeth on her dress trembled like wind on the water's surface.

"It hurts more than any beating. I could heal you then. I did. Long ago, you wanted to stay. So, we stayed. And for what? To be standing here with her fake outreach of compassion. If you go, it will kill you. She blames you for their deaths. She blames you for her life," Rebecca sputtered. "You cannot go. Promise. I'm tired of the circle of silence. You know it will happen again. She will make sure of it."

The vein on Terence's forehead pulsed. Rebecca's body stiffened. Someone was going to get hit. Karl closed his eyes.

Todd stepped forward, and Karl pushed Rebecca to him. He encompassed her, crushing her to his chest even as she tried to push him away. Karl saw his exit. He stepped away from them and headed to the hallway, colliding with Joannicus. He shoved the bowl into his arm as he scooped out the sacred bundles.

"Keep this safe for me," Karl said.

"Sure," Joannicus said without hesitation.

Karl scooted past him and out into the daylight. He could hear Rebecca wailing. He headed to the church. The bundles weighed heavily in his hands. A place, a hallowed place. He entered the little chapel inside the church and ran his fingers under the table for the key. He unlocked the tabernacle and removed the chalice that held the extra hosts. The wooden floor of the tabernacle was false. Mellitus had shown him the hidden spot. They had argued about its purpose and who knew about it.

"Sorry," he murmured, just in case there was a relic in there. He knew about the relics. All Catholic churches had at least one somewhere. He hadn't found where the pieces of St. Alberic were hiding. The Latin *relinquo* meant "I leave" or "I abandon."

"These are the relics I leave behind. It is a first-class relic I surrender. Earthly remains," he said to the Jesus on the crucifix.

Guilt nudged him, for he knew he should not relinquish them.

"I am sorry," he said, his voice constricting as he caressed the bundle one last time. "This is a good place. Many will come and pray. You could grant them miracles if you get bored. I will be back. I cannot take you with me, and I fear you will get lost with me."

Moisture darkened the bundle, and Karl wiped his cheeks and slipped the sacred bundles into the hollow. He replaced the wooden board and chalice, locked the tabernacle, and returned the key. He stood gripping the little table. The atrium door opened, and voices echoed like thunder. Karl slipped out the side exit.

CHAPTER 38

TINY

You have to look deeper, way below the anger, the hurt,
*   the hate, the jealousy,*
the self-pity, way down deeper where the dreams
*   lie, son.*
Find your dream. It's the pursuit of the dream that
*   heals you.*

Tamakoce Te'Hila (Billy Mills). 1938- . Oglala Lakota, 1964 Gold medalist. 2012 Presidential Citizens medal, co-founder of Running Strong for American Indian Youth.

In late spring in Montana, the weather is unpredictable but stable enough to live outdoors. Karl built a lean-to, cutting branches for a roof and sides, arguing with the forest that he could use a knife because he abandoned the sacred bundles. The blade glistened, and the echo of the Lakota Elder swirled in the air every time he gutted a rabbit or fish. He wasn't sure if he was winning the argument.

Shame.

He didn't want to be here.

Karl went through the motions of living. Every physical pain, cut, and sore muscle reminded him he lived.

He was a blade of grass, stuck bending to the whims of nature and gods.

Day after day, he questioned—shouting, singing, and screaming.

Why?

"Lakota *winyan*, where are you? I have nothing to follow. Come back," Karl spoke to the huckleberry bush.

"Nobody comes for you?" the mountains asked in response to his questions.

Where was Rebecca?

"So, end it, warrior," buzzed the insects that floated around him.

Shut up.

But you are here in the silence to hear me, echoed the voice in his mind. *Let me in.*

The voices danced with the sun, the rain, and the moon.

Spring welcomed summer. Coolness gave way to boiling. He existed, but why? Exhaustion followed him like a Rez dog.

Every night he sat wondering, watching, weeping. For what? The fire burned and crackled, and sparks rose. At night, visions of the ER dotted his sleep like the stars. Anger bubbled every time he woke from the terror.

"If you are waiting for death, then perhaps you should not eat," the voice boomed. He sat up, looking for the person who spoke. He saw nothing but the dying embers of his fire. Were the little people talking to him? He knew they existed and often aided the Apsáalooke people, but he was not near the Pryor Gap or Castle Rock. He had not left an offering. Why would they visit him?

One hot August morning, Karl hiked out of the forest and sat in an open field, determined to wait for death. Birds sang. Insects buzzed. The day waned. Bats darted. Raccoons waddled by. Twigs snapped. Karl startled awake. Nothing had feasted upon him but mosquitoes. Dawn peaked over the horizon. The sun warmed his cooled skin. The damp grass stood up. Closed buds opened, and a mother *uuxe* with her twin fawns stepped cautiously on spindly legs.

The sun baked his already tan skin. Sweat dripped and thirst cracked his lips. Heat exhaustion threatened to bring visions of the dead. Soon.

Then the sun ran away. Thunder rumbled in the distance. The storm would not make him leave. It would pass.

Perhaps taking the sadness with it, for nothing seemed to fill the emptiness.

Karl rested his head on his knees and folded his arms. The rain flowed freely from the sky.

Water dripped from his nose and short hair. The clouds ran away, and Karl stretched out in the grass. The odor of earth and sweat surrounded him as the sun sucked the moisture from his clothing. Soon.

Karl stayed another day, another night. Soon.

Twilight. Yellow eyes stared at him in the moonlight, a low growl.

Move along, he was not dead yet. Come wolf pack, and he wouldn't resist. Brother *cheete*.

Hunger gnawed. All night the *appaake* buzzed, whispering in his ear, sucking the blood from his veins.

Night gave way to dawn another day. He had waited. Death refused to embrace him. Life filled his lungs.

Not soon enough.

An *iisashpite* jumped into his lap, warm and full of life. Karl grabbed the unsuspecting rabbit and snapped its neck.

Dinner.

FALL COLORS FILLED THE FOREST. Animals began the forage for winter. Rain soaked his lean-to. Coldness nipped at him every evening as the sun went down. Nights took on a frosty grip. The squirrel scolded him for staying so long. Like a Rez dog, he wandered along the border of Indian country. Taverns marked his trail.

The bare trees and hard, cold ground made sheltering outside a challenge. Sleep consisted of a nap on a bench or the public library. Winter leaned closer with each day.

Karl sat in the dark corner of the tavern, peeling his arm off the sticky table.

He raised his near-empty pitcher. The bartender yielded no guilt for causing another Indian to fall into the brown bottle. The bartender continued to serve you until you ran out of money. Karl's week in this bar would soon be over—drinking from opening till closing, living off greasy burgers and fries.

He imagined the headline. Another Indian froze to death. The survivors would be so angry, and Judith would celebrate. He swirled the beer and watched the foam shift like snow drifts.

Glancing up, he saw the shiny black head of a short man standing next to his table.

"Karl," the man said.

"Tiny?"

"What are you doing here?"

"Drinking beer. What do you want?" He hadn't seen Tiny Stones in the River in years, not since they were teens. Karl still had the rock, the flat, plain, ugly one Tiny had given him. It was a good skipping rock, yet he had never thrown it into the water. Tiny wore his name well. His shoulder was even with the high bar table.

"This isn't a place for you. *Disahkaate* is looking for you," Tiny said.

Rebecca could have found him. Everyone knew where the drunks lay. Had she rejected him like she had Jimmy? Silly notion. Rebecca would never abandon him unless death came. He snorted, imagining a bony hand reaching for him from the grave. Not even mortality would stop her. A childhood emotion of independence fussed over him.

He wished she would just let him go, let him out, let him run free.

"Since when do we run when she calls? Have a beer with me," Karl said.

"I think not. You need to come with me."

"I need to finish my beer. One should not be wasteful."

"What do you call drinking the white man's swill?"

That hurt. He was not numb yet.

"Tiny, have you heard? I am alone."

"Not true," the small Indian said. His braid whipped from side to side as he shook his head. "You just want to be left alone."

"They are dead. I have nothing," Karl said. Seeing the hardness on Tiny's face, he added. "Go home."

Tiny wagged his head again. "I'm here."

"Sent."

"Regardless of how I got here, I'm here. Even *bishee* scat has a purpose," Tiny said, climbing onto the stool. He wrinkled his nose.

Karl looked at his dirty fingers. He attempted to wipe them on his stained jeans. There was no use. The earth had encrusted him. Perhaps he was half in the grave already.

"You stink," Tiny said.

"That is downright mean. You are still small," Karl said.

The server came.

"Two coffees and lots of sugar."

Tiny remembered.

"Coffee does not diminish the effects of beer," Karl said, gulping the contents of the mug, fearful that Tiny might send it away before he could numb his brain.

"Beer does not diminish the effects of living."

The coffee arrived, and the beer mugs clinked as they were removed.

"You should just go away," Karl said. He didn't want to live without his family. Gloominess had not washed away with the changing seasons nor drowned in the liquid he consumed.

Tiny looked at his coffee mug. "Tell me a story."

The beer raced in Karl's veins. A story. Which story? His story wasn't a happy one. It didn't even hold hope.

"The man should have died. Instead, he did not live happily ever after."

"That is not your story." Tiny snorted. "You are happy because you aren't living."

His story wasn't the tale of Cold Feet and Sings in the Night. What about them? Ancestor myths. He was not like either of them. He wasn't called from death to be someone's lover. The keeper of knowledge and wisdom was not his path.

The room spun. The alcohol made him feel heavy in mind, limb, and spirit.

"How is Rebecca?" Karl asked.

"The Elders have told her to stop wearing the black."

Karl poured more sugar into his mug. The year wasn't up, and she was told to stop grieving. He was not ready to do that.

Karl squeezed his mug. He had envisioned her in a hut composed of willow sticks wrapped with blankets and canvas. The rug covered the earthen floor with a fire pit glowing white hot. Pitchers of water hissed as the steam rose. The cedar scent filled the air. A sweat lodge—yes, she was praying and purifying herself from the poisons surrounding her. Was he included in that toxicity?

"Good for her. Shake me off like the sweat of a sweltering day."

Tiny clunked his mug down with a thump.

"I'm sorry for your loss." Tiny looked at the table, the dirty dishes, and then around Karl.

He was looking for the sacred bundle.

"They are not with me."

"Why not? It was your responsibility. You gave your word."

"Breath wasted," Karl snapped, thinking of the prayers he had whispered while his family died around him and remembering the shouts to the sky as he sat in the forest asking why? Nobody answered his cries—not the ancestors, not the Jesus, not the living, and not the dead. *Nobody*. A wave of loneliness splashed over him. He grabbed the coffee and drank, scorching his throat.

He was not dead yet. The in-between is too much.

The coffee cup warmed his fingers. Tiny remained perched on the bar stool.

"Is this who you are? How you honor us all, blue-eyed one?"

"Fuck you," Karl spat as Tiny's face moved to compassion. He had the same look when they found Endow dead.

"I am alone."

"You choose to be."

"Then leave me to my choice," Karl growled.

"Don't be your father or Jimmy. Be Karl," Tiny said as he placed a stone on the table between them. The blue stone with gold veins was polished. It was a step up from what Tiny used to collect—lapis lazuli from the Big Horn Mine. Karl wondered if Tiny would say it traveled here from California. But he said nothing, just slid off the stool and walked away.

With no more taverns to visit and winter's inevitable appearance, Karl headed back to St. Alberic, not to the hill. The wind blew fiercely, rattling the barn's walls. The cow bellowed, and the horse neighed back with calm. Karl placed a blanket on the old mare and patted her head.

"You need this more than me," he said to her. The two Australian Shepherds, Benedict and Scholastica, peeked out of their cozy, straw-lined wooden house. They had each other to keep them warm. Karl climbed to the loft and stood at the window, staring at the monastery. They were warm and well-fed. Did Joannicus wonder where he was?

The moon and the stars hung crisp in the darkening sky. What was he waiting for? Dawn did not ease the pain or erase the emptiness. Nothing lay ahead.

He glanced down at the sheep that were a mass of wool. At least they have each other.

A gust of wind filtered through the cracks as he closed the shutters. He thought of the day Amber Rose was born. In this barn, her life started, and maybe his would end here.

He made a deep burrow in the hay pile. The feral gray cat inched his way into the pile. Curious, his yellow eyes watched cautiously as he crept into the hay.

"Come to count coup, have you, brave Lucifer? Cold will do

that. Come in here. You keep the mice out, and I will listen for the gigantic rat."

Usually, he left before Brother Ambrose's arrival. Some mornings he stayed hidden, listening to the man preach to the animals as if they were his children.

Karl curled up, awaiting sleep or death, unsure which would arrive first.

The odor of coffee filled his nose. Don't wake up. This dream is pleasant.

"I could stick a pitchfork in you to see if you are done," Ambrose boomed.

Karl froze. He had overslept. The large rat had arrived.

"You aren't fooling me. I know you are in there. I have hot coffee."

Karl listened to the squeak of the thermos lid. The aroma of the dark brew called, as did his bladder. The ladder groaned as Ambrose left the loft.

"Yes, I agree. I should have stuck him with a pitchfork. He'd be down here by now to help us," Ambrose said.

Karl heard no other voices. Who was he talking to?

Karl crawled out of the hay and brushed himself off. The steamy coffee caused his stomach to gurgle, but it took the chill out of his body. He looked down at the barn floor from the ladder and saw that his escape route was blocked. The sheep were coming in and filling up the space.

Ambrose looked up.

"I was not going to leave. No need to trap me with sheep," Karl said as the herd bleated.

"You can still escape. Jump out of the loft door. The snow will cushion your fall."

Karl climbed down with the thermos as Ambrose brushed

snow off the backs of sheep as they entered the barn. Karl pushed his way through the sea of wool.

"Feed the critters. If you can find your motorcycle, park it in the equipment shed. The key to the guesthouse is in my office. I'm going to prayers."

An objection formed on Karl's lips, but the man was already heading to his truck.

The bleating sheep shuffled and moved through the barn as Karl worked. The key glistened on the nail as the sun peeked over the snowdrifts.

He was not staying.

Karl made his way to the lump that was his motorcycle and worked to move it into the equipment shed. He could leave, for the truck had plowed a trail in the snow.

It only leads to the monastery, The warrior's voice in his mind chuckled.

He was not staying.

Karl entered the guesthouse, exhausted, for the snow was knee-deep, and he had not taken the plowed road.

A monk stood in the hallway. He looked like a Friar Tuck, round in body and face, his hair neatly trimmed.

"I'm Moses. Brother Moses. I think a warm shower would be helpful, don't you? You appear a bit frozen. You shower. It is down the hall. This is your room. I will fix some coffee," Moses said as he opened the door to the room labeled, 'St. Placidus.'

Karl peeked inside the plain space. There was nothing but a bed, a desk, and a colorful wool blanket.

This will do for now.

Karl stood in the shower as the water pelted his body. He soaped up twice, wondering if the layers of grime would wash away.

Once showered, he found a hygiene kit, shoes, jeans, wool

socks, a tee shirt, and a sweater. Karl dressed and headed to his room.

"You can put your dirty clothes in this basket, and they will be washed," Moses said.

Karl looked at his thin socks that had holes in them. Were they worth washing, or would they fall apart? He dropped the wad of clothing into the basket.

This is crazy. What was he doing?

The odor of bread from the kitchen filtered down the hall. Karl's stomach protested.

The bells clanged. He noticed it was noon—prayer time for the monks. The bells rang four times a day, calling the monks to prayer.

Death. Karl pushed the thought away. Where had the morning gone?

"Shall we go to praise?" Moses asked, smiling.

Karl shook his head.

"Oh, well then, coffee," Moses said as he trotted back to the parlor. Karl slowly followed. Exhaustion swept over him. Moving felt like he was dragging a buffalo with him.

They sat. Karl sipped the black liquid, and Moses drank a glass of milk. The monk lacked the hood of the professed.

"You must be new," Karl said.

"Mee-maw and Pops, my grandparents, sent me here to visit. They died, and the next day, they made me a novice. Sometimes things are really sad."

Yes, thought Karl. Salty drops fell into his coffee. A white handkerchief appeared.

"You are missing prayers."

"Yes, but it's okay. Brother Ambrose said I'm going to be with you. Father Joannicus claims you can pray everywhere."

"I don't need a sitter."

"I know," Moses said, smiling brightly.

Life did not ruffle this man—such simplicity.

Moses led Karl to the refectory downstairs. Lunch was in silence, and Karl was grateful for that. He felt eyes upon him as he sat with Moses. Mellitus wandered by and yanked on his short hair. Joannicus gave a gentle smile. Pius shook his head in dismay. Where was Ambrose?

He needed to tell him he wasn't staying.

Although he was hungry, and the food was delicious, his appetite waned. The familiar setting smacked of his former life.

Teardrops fell into his soup. It needed salt, anyway. He wiped them away with his palm.

Karl's shadow of Moses annoyingly followed him. Together, they moved through the day of monastic routine.

The strange circumstance of Brother Moses tickled Karl's curiosity.

"Is Moses your Christian name or your Benedictine name?"

Moses shrugged. "My name is Moses. Probably wasn't my birth name, but it is the name my Mee-maw gave me. Even though I know she wasn't my biological grandma. She said she found me in the garden. Just like the Bible Moses, that's how I got my name."

"My sister named me," Karl said, wishing to see Rebecca. Why hadn't she come to visit him? She always knew where he was. Why was this time different? Had the Elders told her to stay away?

The week progressed into months. Day after day of simple routine. Moses, sunrise, Moses, sunset.

The sun hung low. Half swallowed by the earth. Again. Karl stood outside, facing the west. The night was upon him, and the air was bitterly cold.

"Why do you face west every evening? Is it an Indian ritual?" Moses asked, rubbing his hands for warmth.

"I was trying to stop the sun from setting."

Moses pursed his lips and cocked his head. He didn't laugh. The shadows of twilight reached out.

"And if you succeed, then what?"

"Then the darkness will not come."

"Are you afraid of the dark?" Moses asked.

"Yes. The night brings visions, dark memories," Karl said, the gates of water building up in his eyes.

"They are only nightmares. I have a dream catcher. It will help you," Moses said, pulling out a small willow hoop covered in natural fibers and soft owl feathers under five beads.

Karl wondered if that was true. Could it silence the replay of those days of death?

Moses reached out and patted his arm. "Hang it in the window, and the sunlight will dissolve the bad dreams in the morning."

"Why do you carry it in your pocket?"

"I was waiting for you to ask me for help."

Karl took several deep breaths and blinked back his tears. The water flowed against his will.

They stood in silence as the sky darkened and the stars winked. Moses held out his hand. Karl grasped the warm softness as Moses led him into the guesthouse. Every footstep was heavy as if they anchored him to the earth.

Moses opened the door, and the fresh smell of clean linen and cookies surrounded them. His frozen tears melted, and new ones formed.

"It aches to get up. It hurts to eat. The pain is always before me. I am not sure I am alive living in this glass bottle with everything else on the outside. It is lonely."

"I am here. We are all here. The light is coming," Moses said, taking him to the door labeled, 'St. Placidus.'

But he was not staying that long.

CHAPTER 39
BROTHER JACOB

Let me be a free man, free to travel, free to stop, free to work, free to trade... where I choose my own teachers, free to follow the religion of my fathers, free to think and talk and act for myself, and I will obey every law, or submit to the penalty.

Hin-mah-too-yah-lat-kekt (Chief Joseph). 1840-1904. Wal-lam-wat-kain band of Nez Perce, humanitarian and peacemaker.

Rebecca appeared at the barn. Scholastica and Benedict announced her arrival.

"Traitors," she hissed at them but stroked their fur as she passed.

Karl was staying with the monks but wasn't available when she came to see him. They even went so far as to distract her with theological and cultural arguments. Both Mellitus and Pius left her head spinning and soul fuming.

The grinding stone spun. The pedal squeaked a drum-like rhythm as Ambrose's foot pumped. Sparks flew when the metal touched. They made electric ones. A couple of swipes and your blade was surgically sharp. The monks held a mixture of modern and old fashion. Men were living in this world despite following an ancient rule. Tribal wisdom dipped in modern insight.

"Where is he?" Rebecca asked, not waiting for small talk or proper greetings.

"Who?" Ambrose asked.

"You know who. Karl."

The wheel stopped, and Ambrose rose from the bench. He held the blade up, and it glistened in the light. Was that a horse plow blade? Rebecca followed Ambrose to what she assumed was the office, an opening more enclosed than a stall with a large file cabinet and a makeshift desk. Then she noticed the children's drawings covering the wall. The man kept Elias and Katie's art. He grabbed a log and placed it in the potbelly stove. No phone, but there was a stove. She shook her head, remembering the birth of Amber Rose.

"How is he?" Rebecca asked as Ambrose sat in the old wooden banker's chair that protested his weight. Rebecca lowered herself to a milking stool, which made her feel like a child at the feet of an Elder.

Ambrose smiled a weary smile. Rebecca figured that if anyone cared for Karl, it was this man.

"He's sad. The year is almost up, and he's still sad," Ambrose said.

"But alive."

The Elders stopped her from intervening, cautioning her to allow Karl his grief. So, she threw herself into work, picking up the slack Faith's death caused, serving both tribes. She met resistance because she was Apsáalooke and not Lakota.

If it weren't for Todd, she would have given up. She remembered the day he asked her to see Sally Two Shoes. A rash covered the little girl. Rebecca recognized the illness and feared an outbreak of rubella. The parents resisted the modern ways. Todd's presence calmed them and allowed her to keep the spread to a minimum.

She needed to thank him for his help, and she needed to see Karl. She missed him.

"You cut yourself off from family," the Elders in her mind scolded. *But Judith is toxic*, came the swift justification.

Ambrose rustled a stack of invoices, bringing her back from the base of the mountain of loneliness.

"Can I see him?" Rebecca asked as her heart ached.

"You have seen him."

"Mass doesn't count. He was dressed up as an altar boy and disappeared like smoke."

The monk smiled.

"You are keeping him from me on purpose. That isn't right." Rebecca bit her lower lip. She would not cry.

"I'm sorry, this is hard on you. He is a man finding his way. He'll be fine. You'll be fine. I promise."

"I miss him."

"He misses you, too. But he is learning balance. You would be a distraction."

Rebecca stood. That wasn't true. That wasn't fair.

"I know him better than you do. I know what he needs."

Ambrose ran his calloused hand over his beard.

She would not see him today—that was certain. One more month and the year of Lakota mourning would be over. Karl would be free from all obligations. She could last one more month.

Rebecca turned and walked out of the barn as she swatted the wetness from her cheeks.

THIS APRIL WAS SOFT, not hard and unyielding. The sky-tears had saturated the earth this time, leaving everything soggy.

Today they would release the spirits of her sister-in-law, Faith, and the children. It was the Lakota way. They had done the Catholic funeral Mass mixed in with the Apsáalooke giveaway and days of lingering and remembering. Only Karl had disappeared that day. She knew of his time in the wilderness as well as the bar hopping. When she had tried to find him, tribal members had warned her to stop.

Today, he will be freed.

An inkling of doubt crept in. Who would she find? He hadn't spent the year with the sacred bundle. Would the Elders be upset? Would the ancient ones be angry? Was there a penalty to pay for his brazen ways?

She shook her head. *Everything will be fine.* Karl always had a reason for his actions—focus on the good. She found strength in knowing she would see him today.

She ran her hands over her buckskin dress before entering the church's atrium. Todd stood with the Lakota Elder and four young women. Todd looked serene, and she envied his calmness. The four ladies stared at her as she stood up straighter. Her Apsáalooke regalia was not like theirs.

She had a right to be here. She fasted and wasn't on her moon.

The scent of the dried ceremonial herbs wafted through the air from the basket one girl carried. Rebecca turned when she heard Karl's voice.

He wore the black cassock of a monk, minus the scapular and hood. Joannicus and Ambrose were with him as they greeted the Elder.

She shook her head. Rubbing her eyes, she looked again. It was Karl, his braid now longer, hanging thick and blending with the black material. A fire burned in her belly.

"I'll get the bundle," Karl said, breaking away from the group. The group exchanged looks of confusion. They had expected Karl to be with the bundle. Curiosity propelled them forward, and the group followed Karl into the church.

Karl came out of the blessed sacrament chapel holding the bundle.

"I housed them in the tabernacle," Karl said. A slight smile played on his lips as Joannicus drew a sharp breath.

"All our prayers surrounded them," Karl said, looking sheepish.

He had done it again, mixing the religions so the line was blurred.

Rebecca envisioned Faith having a long talk with the Jesus while she and the children rested in that box. She wondered what they had talked about.

Karl stepped away from them to be next to the Elder. Rebecca grabbed his arm.

"What is going on here? Why are you dressed like that?"

Anger crawled up her spine. She now understood why Ambrose sent her away. If she had known they had spirited her brother, she would have forced the issue like a point of an arrow. She was aware that becoming a monk took at least five years.

"I am a novice. Let it go for now," Karl said, his voice soft and calm as he leaned over and kissed her forehead.

Rebecca stumbled back as if a chasm opened before her, and she might fall.

She watched Karl and the Elder leave. The women and Todd followed. Father Joannicus stood next to her as Todd turned, a concerned look on his face.

"Are you alright?" Father Joannicus asked. "He didn't tell you, did he?"

"No, he didn't. Karl isn't monk material," Rebecca said, steadying herself against the wall. "He doesn't have a calling. He has fooled you." As harsh as it sounded, it was the truth.

"Karl questions everything, but I'm sure Brother Jacob will enrich our community."

"You can't allow this to happen."

A look of sympathy and compassion caressed the monk's face.

"That is between Brother Jacob and God."

"You idiot. He doesn't believe in your God."

She recognized the truth. Karl was fascinated with Catholicism, but he was Apsáalooke. And he was grieving in pain. They had taken advantage of him.

Rebecca followed Joannicus to the atrium.

How could he do this? Why was she even thinking like that? Karl wasn't staying.

"I need to talk to him."

"You can't. He's a novice. I guess you're not familiar with how this works. A novice secludes himself from the world to listen to the call from within."

"He did that already," Rebecca hissed, recalling Karl's time in the wilderness.

"He was not listening then. This is his choice, freely chosen."

"This is wrong. You are not his kind," Rebecca sputtered, not exactly sure what she meant by that and recognizing how white she sounded.

Joannicus held the outside door open. "Come, we need to go. An alternative path awaits us."

Rebecca pushed forward. The sun blinded her as she fought the urge to scream.

She needed to talk to him. She would find a way. He would listen to her.

She and the two monks hurried to the secular cemetery. Lilies and daisies, a blanket of white, covered the grave. Rebecca noted Karl stood with a few monks. Rebecca stood alone, glaring at Karl —now called Jacob—who didn't notice.

Todd stepped in front of her. She stepped to the side to keep her eyes on her brother. Todd grunted, and she realized that he was holding the sacred bundle out to her. This was an honor she didn't expect. She was not Lakota. Her eyes clouded with the kindness of this inclusion. She opened her arms to hold the five spirits taken from them.

The breeze from the east held a nip. Spring had not really arrived.

Todd gripped her elbow as they walked to the tree line and into the ceremonial circle scraped into the ground—the strong and heady smell of sage covered the earth.

The Lakota Elder spoke. "Souls, you are with us, but soon you must leave. Wakan Tanka is bending down to see you. We who have loved you and taken care of you are here. This day is sacred. All the past is still within us."

Todd dug a hole in the earth that Rebecca knew stood for a buffalo wallow. The scooped-up dirt was positioned in a mound. They drew a cross, pointing in the four directions. They placed the Sacred Pipe, the stem to the west, and the bowl to the east. Rebecca bent, placing the bundle on the red road north of the drawn cross.

The Sacred Pipe was lit and passed sunwise to all assembled. Ambrose, Moses, and a reluctant Joannicus smoked. The smoke twirled and rose to the sky. All of them watched it go. The young girls wept, and she saw the tears on Brother Jacob's face while Moses and Ambrose mopped their eyes.

Todd moved slowly to the headstone and embedded a modest post instead of the normal six-footer. Both made a concession. Atop the post hung strips of buckskin. Tied to the skins were small possessions of the deceased: Faith's heart necklace; feathers and stones, which Elias always had in his pockets; Katie's bird foot; Amber Rose's felted lamb; and a knitted set of pink booties for Almost Joan.

Rebecca wiped her cheeks with the back of her hand. Nature and the elements would wither the tokens as memories of Faith and the children faded. Traditionally, there would have been a pyre, with the smoke rising to the sky and the spirits following. She realized that was not acceptable in a Catholic cemetery. These monks had already made many exceptions, from allowing Faith and the children space in this ground to teepees, lingering tribal members, and unfamiliar rituals.

The Lakota Elder spoke. "Before you leave us, we have brought you this food to share with us."

The four young women divided the meal among themselves and ate. Rebecca saw the similarities between this and the Last Supper. One last meal was shared with the loved ones before they moved on.

The weathered Elder spoke again. "Children, you are about to leave on a great journey. All here have loved you."

Todd walked over to the monks and forced the weeping Jacob to stand next to Rebecca. Todd motioned for Rebecca to pick up the sacred bundle. She did, and together they placed their hands on the bundle. This was her smallest circle of family. Despite his weeping, Karl appeared healthy. His angular face was no longer thin and wan.

How could he appear strong, and she felt so worn?

"You loved them and kept them at the center of our people's hoop," the Elder said.

Rebecca stole a glance at Karl, knowing that was not quite true. The Catholic tabernacle was not the center of their people. Maybe for Karl, since he was now Brother Jacob. Is that what happened? The sacred bundle became infused with Catholicism —did Karl have to listen?

Her hands tingled. Or were they just cold?

"You have been kind to your loved ones, so be kind to every-one. The sacred influence of your loved ones shall remain with us," the Elder continued.

Todd led them north to the four young women who each touched the bundle. The last girl produced a sapling—a Japanese maple, small and red. This tree didn't belong among the pines. Rebecca found that ironic as she stared at her brother in his black robe—an Apsáalooke among the Catholics.

Jacob unwrapped the sapling, and Todd placed it in the hole. Rebecca pressed the bundle to her chest and leaned toward Jacob.

"Why?" she whispered.

"I love you," Jacob said.

Rebecca's mind reeled. Was he speaking to her or the bundle? He hadn't answered her question.

"Behold this tree," Todd said, his voice quaking slightly. "This tree will be at the center of our sacred hoop. May it always flourish and bloom in a Wakan manner."

Todd escorted Jacob back to the monks, wiped the dirt from his hands on his jeans, then gripped Rebecca's elbow as she held the bundle.

Together, they walked north.

They stopped four times, raising the bundle and calling out.

"Always look back upon your people, that they may walk the sacred path with firm steps," Todd said, his voice clear.

They stopped at the gates of the monastic cemetery. Rebecca felt drained as if she had been lifting weights for hours.

"Come, it is time to walk on. They are on the Red Road, the path home," Todd said as he pushed open the cemetery gates. The hinges moaned. Faith and the children were heading beyond the land of the living. Rebecca leaned on Todd as she glanced over her shoulder. Jacob, in his black robes, was heading up to the monastery. She would not be speaking with him today.

CHAPTER 40
THE TODD EFFECT

Humankind has not woven the web of life.
We are but one thread within it.
Whatever we do to the web, we do to ourselves.
All things are bound together.
All things connected.

Chief Si'ahl (Chief Seattle). 1786-1866. Suquamish and Duwamish
leader, ecological protector, visionary, and orator.

Rebecca slammed her fist on the grimy counter of Big
Bovine Bar.
"Hit me," she said.
The beer frothed over the glass.
Damn you, Karl. Damn you, monks.
Emotions wobbled like the warning needle on the dashboard.

How could he? Brother Jacob. After all that she had done for him. When would he listen to her wisdom? She had accepted his bonding with Faith. At least she was a part of his life then. Now, he was sequestered behind cloistered walls where women could not enter. She envisioned herself scaling the wall to his window.

He had said he loved her at the ceremony. He looked well. This was his choice. But it came as a betrayal.

Brother Jacob. That wasn't the name she had given him. Her head swirled.

She had tried knocking on the locked monastery door. When had they started that? They did not lock it when she and Elias got Katie. Perhaps that was when.

Had she cursed them and kicked the door? She wiggled her foot. Yes. It hurt.

A peanut bounced past her. What was it with these guys thinking a girl drinking alone needed a man? She turned, ready to fight.

Todd stood next to her. The scent of cedar and sage filled her nostrils.

"What are you doing in this place?"

"I could ask you the same question," Rebecca said.

"You and your brother have the same taste. I figured you for a silver bullet or Seven-and-Seven kind of a girl."

"What does that mean?" Rebecca asked, wondering how he knew about Karl's binge with beer. Everyone seemed to know more about her brother than she did.

Todd smiled.

What was she missing?

"I watched over him."

He watched but did nothing?

"You let him drink? What is the matter with you?" Her temper boiled. "You realize the brown bottle took my father and sucks my brother Jimmy. Yet you let Karl follow that path. What if he hadn't stopped drinking? Endow couldn't, and Jimmy can't. You could have killed him."

"I wouldn't have let that happen. I see what hurts him, harms you. I understand Karl is a part of you. You two are a package deal —breath and soul, hot and cold."

She gulped her beer, letting it drown her anger. She wasn't mad at him. This wasn't his fault.

"Have a beer with me," Rebecca said, trying to be kinder.

"Sure, but not here."

Rebecca looked around the dingy bar, filled with white men of all ages. Nobody approached her, and she was ready with a sarcastic, get lost remark if they did.

"I can take care of myself," Rebecca said as the room wobbled.

"I wasn't worried about you," Todd said as he steadied her, gripping her waist, and she let him. The floor was the alternative, and it looked unsanitary.

They exited the bar to the crisp twilight air. She shivered, perhaps more with rage than cold.

"He didn't even take care of the bundle. He put them in the tabernacle. It's as if he is thumbing his nose at every ritual. I'm surprised that God didn't strike him dead."

"He was probably hoping for that. I see nothing wrong with his choices. Each man grieves alone. Their spirits were inside him, not in the bundle. He kept his word and duties," Todd said.

He put them in a box. That was not right. Maybe their spirit followed him, for he hadn't perished in the wilderness. But he ended up with the black robes, who prayed formally three times a day. She recalled Karl telling her their life was a balancing act. She didn't see him as balanced. Teetering but not balanced.

"He could have told me what he was doing."

"Does he need your permission?"

She turned to strike Todd but missed him completely and spun around, falling into a snow pile.

The cold and wet seeped through her clothing, setting her teeth to chatter. She wanted to wipe the smirk off his face.

Todd held out a hand to assist her. She squirmed deeper into the snowdrift.

"I don't need your help. Who put you in charge, anyway?"

"Faith," Todd said.

Her skin was goose-pimpled. Had Faith asked him to watch her?

"I think you have mistaken me for my brother," Rebecca said.

Faith would have expected Todd to be a brother to Karl. But that was her job.

Coordination was failing as she reached for the extended hand.

Strong arms guided her to a truck. She wobbled like a leaf in the wind, fragile and vulnerable.

The sound of the pickup door banging woke Rebecca up. She wiped the drool from her chin and looked around.

"Where are we?"

"Home," Todd said, getting out of the truck.

"I'm not done drinking. This side trip will not change that. I'm drinking until I forget why I started drinking."

"Well then, get inside before you freeze."

She followed him onto the porch of a small cabin. She cocked her head and blinked. Was that an owl face patterned in the stacked wood?

Once inside, she watched him shed his jacket, move to the stone fireplace, and strike a match. Sulfur filled the air. She liked the odor, for it reminded her of evenings spent with Grandma Tiama. The kindling crackled while the cabin swayed and danced with shadows. Her stomach spun with the room, forcing her to close her eyes and steady herself by leaning against the door. Opening her eyes, she found Todd standing a foot away with a stack of clothing and a towel.

"You are dripping on the floor," Todd said. "Change in the other room."

She removed her moccasins and took the clothing. The wooden floor was cold on her feet. The log-framed bed was large and masculine. Now she understood Amber Rose's comment that Uncle Todd slept in the trees. Tears blurred her eyes as she thought of the children frolicking under the fur blankets. She peeled off her damp jeans, socks, and shirt. She shivered. The soft woolen sweater hung to her knees. She looked around the room. There was not much in the way of decor. This was a bachelor's space—a cedar chest, dresser, and closet. That explained why he smelled of the forest.

She reentered the main room. She noticed the glass embedded between the rocks of the fireplace glowing with color. The aroma of venison stew filled her nose. Was he cooking?

A pot on the wood-fed stove told her she would be invited to dine. Todd turned from the propane refrigerator.

"You need to eat."

"It will only come back up."

"You are planning on drinking that much?"

She nodded. "Why aren't you drinking?" she asked him.

"Tried. It didn't change reality, only numbed it for a while."

Todd clunked a bottle of whiskey on the coffee table.

She stood in front of the fire. All the furniture was handmade from wood, some crooked limbs and some straight, as if the forest had bent itself in thanks for his effort to save them from wildfires. A single moose antler lay on the mantel with several clay bowls filled with Elias feathers and pebbles. He had understood the gift of the moose.

A picture of him and his siblings, five sisters and one brother, sat on the small desk under a window. They looked happy in that photo. Todd was now the sole survivor of the Dawson clan.

She glanced at the photo of Faith and the children, all staring at her accusingly.

We are gone. What are you doing here?

He brought her here. She didn't ask.

She turned away from them and warmed her back.

Todd handed her a bowl of stew, then set the glass jars next to the whiskey bottle.

"Eat."

He placed another dish on the table.

Rebecca sighed.

"Can't you just let me drink to forget? Just once, let me forget, not care, be irresponsible."

"Forget? That's impossible. You've seen life and death you never forget."

"Then let me pretend," Rebecca said as she sat on the couch, tucking her legs under.

He smiled a sympathetic smile, a lovely smile, that grated on her nerves

"Brother Jacob, that's not his name."

"That's okay because I heard it'll be Father Jacob soon," Todd said as he sat on the sofa beside her.

He knew more than she. How could that be? She reached for the jam jar of amber liquid, which rekindled the fire inside her. "They can't do that. There are steps."

"He has apparently taken them. This is his choice. Let him go. It's time to live your life."

"You know nothing about him or me or them. They invent their own rules and revise them whenever they want. He can change his name to Jesus, but that doesn't make him priestly or monkly. Karl believes in *Baaxpee*, not God. He's just playing to learn their secrets. My brother won't be praying to their God. He will pray to *Akbaatatdia*."

"I don't think gods care what he calls them. They are all the same," Todd said. "I have noticed the same tendencies and desires in them all. He's not the problem."

She set down her half-eaten bowl of stew, savoring the richness, the right amount of spices, green and orange vegetables, and tender chunks of meat.

What did he know about her?

She refilled her glass, detesting he was wise and right. His jar was almost empty, so she poured him more.

In her drunken state, she peered at him. She remembered how much Todd had lost. He was so brave, so courageous. How had he mourned? When? Where?

"What is it?" Todd asked, leaning forward.

Her cheeks reddened.

"I'm sorry for your loss," Rebecca said, reaching over and touching his arm, feeling the raised skin of his scars.

"Thank you." His eyes slid over to the photo on the mantle.

Rebecca bit her lower lip as questions about him swirled— stories Faith had told her of his protection and sacrifice and how he had cared for them all when their parents died. He had been both mother and father and brother. She had family and would mend the bridges she burned. She would reach out to Judith and her stepfather. She glanced at the photo of him and his siblings. He had now lost everyone and was truly alone. Yet, even in his pain, he appeared sympathetic and open.

"How come you have never married? You're handsome, responsible, compassionate, and just the guy a mother would approve of."

He stared at her. A crooked smile played on his lips. Had she gone too far?

"I have joined," Todd said, finishing the drink in his jar.

Rebecca caught her breath. That explained the stew and the orderliness of the space. She wondered who the lucky woman could be. The girl from the ritual? No, they were too young. She sighed.

"Congratulations."

"No, you can't congratulate me yet. She isn't aware that I married her."

Rebecca paused as relief rushed in, followed by confusion. "How does that work? You should probably tell her, or she might find someone else."

He laughed. "I doubt that."

"What is wrong with her?"

"Nothing's wrong with her. She's beautiful, intelligent, and strong-willed as a buffalo. A warrior princess."

She didn't believe him. This woman had to be blind. Todd was a worthy man.

"Maybe it is not her, but you?"

"Me? I have the Lakota qualities for a mate, a home, a car, a job, and I'm as smart as the one I desire."

"You are too perfect. What is your flaw?"

Todd winced and studied his empty glass. Rebecca reached for the bottle, shaking the last drops into Todd's jar.

"What is that supposed to mean? Too perfect?"

"You are saintly. You care for others, listen to the Elders, and help the grandmas. Tend to the youth. Save the planet, seems over the top."

"Compared to you? You've rescued your brother, healed the sick, and tended to the children and the old. I think we are the same. Perhaps it's time to be selfish."

Now there was a thought—someone taking care of her.

"You have a warped image of me. I don't need anyone. I'm aware of what men think of me. Becca the bitch. I hear the whispers."

"I suspect you come across as strong and independent. That scares some guys. They think to conquer you."

Rebecca laughed. "So, I'm a mountain. Ice and cold."

"Even mountains melt."

The fire danced on the logs as it warmed the room, and the heat of the whiskey melted her insides. She stretched her legs onto the coffee table, feeling relaxed for the first time all day.

"Why haven't you married?" Todd asked.

"Nobody has proposed to me."

Todd leaned forward. His dark eyes penetrated her.

"Will you marry me?"

A laugh burst forth. He was tipsy. She was drunk.

"Will you marry me?"

Crap, he was serious.

"Maybe," Rebecca murmured.

The first wave hit, and her stomach lurched. His face was so close to hers that she inhaled the heavy aromas of sage and cedar. She bolted for the restroom.

The porcelain was a cool anchor in the spinning room. She heard footsteps outside the door as sweat dripped down her brow.

"A glass of water would be nice," Rebecca called.

"What did you say? You need something?"

"Yes, please," Rebecca said, biting her words. This man was truly annoying.

Rebecca woke. The furs and a heavy arm rested on her. Her eyes snapped open, and she slowly eased Todd's arm off her before slipping out of bed. She held her breath and listened to his

431

rhythmic breathing. Todd turned over. His smooth muscles flexed and then relaxed. She stood in the predawn light, then shivered, stepping on the discarded sweater and socks, grateful that she still had on her bra and panties.

Her head throbbed. *Water.* Her body felt heavy as she stumbled to the kitchen for a drink.

"Stupid, stupid," she muttered under her breath. "I should not have done this."

She frowned as she filled a glass of water.

Damn you, Karl. This is all your fault.

What did you do? The question and Karl's impish grin entered her mind as she gulped the water, turned, and gathered her clothes.

"I did nothing. Shared a bed, we were drunk..." She paused, trying to remember through the fog exactly when the room had stopped spinning. She shivered again, clutching her garments to her chest. She had almost kissed him.

She dressed and realized she didn't even know where this cabin was. How could she have been so stupid? She had a moment of weakness—a lapse in judgment.

Her hair hung long and loose as she ran her fingers through it before braiding it. Todd's truck keys were on the table. Cedar and sage tickled her nose. They had curled under the furs, his warm body touching her. It was time to leave.

A spider swayed on a thread of web in front of her. She understood what that meant.

He was right—she was not in balance.

Rebecca grabbed the keys and headed quietly out the door.

The truck roared as she started it and pulled out. In the rearview mirror, she saw Todd standing on the porch, his chest bare and his boots in hand.

Keep on driving, don't look back. That is what Karl should be

432

doing. Wait—that is what he was doing, only in the wrong direction.

"Who are you to decide? Where are you leading?" the Elder's voice in her head asked.

She found the road.

The morning was frosty, and the truck bumped along. He needs to fix the shocks on this thing. He needed curtains on the cabin windows to keep the morning sun from creeping in and waking one up at dawn.

The Big Bovine Bar and Bakery sign flashed open. She parked the pickup and entered. A young woman looked up.

"Hey, you left your jacket here."

Freshly baked goods wafted in the air.

"Thanks. Coffee to go and some cinnamon rolls."

"Sure, thing, honey. Glad to see you are alright. You had me worried. Leaving with that guy and you being all sad."

What she really meant was drunk. *And if you were so concerned, why didn't you call the police?*

Rebecca held her tongue.

"You seemed to know him. I figured he was your beau or husband?"

"Not my husband," Rebecca said, pulling out a few bills to pay, recalling he had proposed, and they had shared a bed.

"Too bad, you make a fine-looking couple. And he's a handsome fella."

Rebecca gathered her purchases and walked back to the truck.

Good looking. Not all men were eligible for happily ever after.

She shook her head to dispel the image of Todd standing on the porch, waiting for her.

She sipped the hot liquid and glanced in the rearview mirror.

Two Lapland Longspurs chased each other from frozen bush

to frozen bush. It is too early for a spring frolic. They were chirping loudly as if scolding her for ditching Todd.

He had been honorable, and she snuck out like a squirrel raiding the bird feeder. Guilty as charged.

He is waiting.

She turned the engine over, driving to the cabin. She wondered how angry he would be.

The door flew open as she stepped out of the cab.

"What the fuck, Rebecca?" Todd said. He was dressed in a flannel shirt and worn blue jeans. He was apparently not pleased to see her.

"Coffee?" she said, pushing past him into the warm house.

He glared, standing before her with his hands on his hips and his long black hair loose. "I have coffee."

"Do you have cinnamon rolls?"

"What you did was mean, no note, and you took my truck—"

She placed an icy finger on his lips.

"Shut up and kiss me."

CHAPTER 41
MONASTIC LIVING

For a long time, I have been walking and seeing nothing.
Now I find this song, and it cheers me.

Nitinat Song—Ditidaht First Nation. The Ditidaht First Nation is
a First Nations band government on southern Vancouver Island
in British Columbia, Canada.

J acob pressed himself to the brick wall in the dim hallway of
the monastery, close to the exit, eavesdropping on the
monks gathered in the community room.

They were still talking about Rebecca and her kicking
the monastery door. Her behavior reminded him of Judith's. He
understood alone, abandoned. Had he pushed her and disappointed her so much that the little Judith inside of her burst forth?

Would she ever talk to him again? Why did he leave her? He was a terrible brother.

"What the hell is he doing here? Father Pius asked. "His sister is crazy. She came into the monastery once. What will stop her from doing it again? Why didn't Abbot Gordon send Karl out and lock the door?"

"She won't do that again," Brother Moses said. "His name is Jacob. You forget that a lot."

"He doesn't belong with us. Ambrose pressured Abbot Gordon into it. He is fond of the underdog, and Crows are certainly that."

Maybe Apsáalooke were underdogs, but they endured, resilient and fierce.

"Father Pius, stop," Joannicus said. "That's not what happened. We voted."

"Jacob didn't follow the proper procedures. Don't deny it. He has his degree—why is he still here?"

"His life changed. Why don't you give him a break?" Joannicus said. "Show some compassion."

"He has had breaks—free handouts from the government and us. They get away with everything. He doesn't even believe in our God."

"Do you mean Indians? Didn't we take everything away from the Indians?" Moses asked. "Besides, he says this is only temporary."

"He cries all the time. It's tiring. It's been over a year," Pius continued as the sound of cracking knuckles drifted into the hall.

"Seriously, you don't need to be around him when it happens," Joannicus said.

"Right, as if I'm going to walk out during prayers because he's sobbing or give up a meal because he needs a good cry."

Jacob had listened long enough to racist Pius and his misguided perceptions. He turned and bumped into Ambrose.

Ambrose motioned for Jacob to follow him. They entered Jacob's cell on the third floor, which held a desk, a sink, and a closet—the same as any monastic cell. The bed had heavy curtains drawn against the wintry nights. A bookshelf held a Bible and *The Rule of St. Benedict*. Jacob's space was unadorned—different from the cell Joannicus occupied, with its stacks of papers and discarded clothing. Jacob had seen other monks' cells. His neighbor Ambrose had peppers and tomatoes growing on the desk. Jacob swore that once he heard the bleating of a lamb. Of course, the man denied the sound.

"Where are your things?" Ambrose asked. He bent and picked up a bottle of Absolution Ale.

Jacob moved to the closet and pulled out Faith's misshapen clay bowl. He placed it on the empty shelf with a blue rock and a smooth skipping stone. He opened the drapes. The dreamcatcher twirled as the dust motes danced. What else did he own?

Ambrose snorted.

"Why do you insist I belong? I have overheard the whispers," Jacob said, pulling the blankets up on his unmade bed, envisioning the cell of Father Pius, sparkling clean with the books on the shelf in alphabetical order.

"Whispers of narrow-minded men do not decide your fate. Someone will always complain. Stay. Because I understand this is only temporary." The man winked.

"Rebecca is pissed. She will be back."

"How soon? It has been a week. She's not lurking, not that she ever really lurked. No, she would just march in. Perhaps she has come to terms with your choice."

Jacob folded the torn wedding blanket and placed it at the foot of his bed. He ran his hand over the folds, feeling the soft wool. Rebecca didn't leave something unfinished—she would return. He knew she wanted to talk to him, and he had denied her that. He didn't want to argue or defend his choice. She wouldn't let him get away with, "I'm already here, so I may as well stay."

"She can't decide your life, either. The woman is not mad at you. I told her no. Has anyone ever told her no?"

Jacob laughed, wondering if that had ever happened. Rebecca was like the wind—unharnessed. One either endured her gusts or bent to them.

Ambrose scratched his face through his beard. "She makes you laugh. She can hang around but needs something to distract her, like a brawny man."

Jacob laughed again. The idea of Rebecca with a guy was absurd. He'd have to be exceptional. Even though there were eligible men around, he hadn't noticed her dating. She devoted her energy to family and to him. She would have to find another cause.

"I miss her."

Ambrose paused his cleanup, arm full of bottles. "Faith is inside of you, and Miss Ballistic can visit once a month. I realize you're a pair. She will accept the rules. You can't leave the grounds until you are professed."

Ambrose shoved a trash can into Jacob's arms, filling it with empties. The can became heavy as the bottles clinked.

Ambrose didn't understand—this was more than the blues. The day held distractions and a pattern: bells, prayers, food, work, bells, prayers, food, study, bells, prayers, food, and bed. Only bed wasn't restful. The memories haunted him—what he should have done and didn't do. The yearning for his losses had not diminished and crept into his bed. In the silence and darkness, the ache robbed him of peace.

Jacob hugged the trash can. "I do not think you understand that the past haunts me."

"I listen to you at night, pacing and crying. Stop drinking so much—it will not help. You'll never forget. The emptiness and pain will fade, but you'll never forget. Pray, meditate, and quit trying to drown."

Jacob set the can down. "You do not get it."

"I know."

"I lost everyone. There is nothing to fill the hole, the vacuum. None of my rituals soothe the ache. You do not know."

Ambrose paced, his sandals squeaking. He stopped and glared.

"Are you aware of what they call me?"

Jacob overheard the whispers of the new monks as they wondered what the felon's crime was.

"You can say it. *Ex-con.* It's true. I served my time in prison. I paid my debt to society. But do you know the story? I killed my best friend, who was going to be a priest. I was driving." Ambrose stopped. He ran his hand over his face three times—a gesture of a shaman. "He'd have made a great priest. I could blame the ice, the alcohol, or my youth, but in the end, my friend is dead. A day doesn't go by that I don't pray for his soul and wish I had chosen a different path. It's my burden—my cross to bear. I live with the shame. You can move on or bury yourself under the mountain of emptiness. There is a difference between what happens to us and what we make happen."

Ambrose left. His walk was heavier than before. Jacob wished he hadn't opened that wound.

Jacob went to the closet and unpacked a small suitcase, putting his underwear and tee shirts in the drawer. He unfolded his dress shirts and slacks, noting the wrinkles in the sleeves. Then he sat, holding his head in his hands.

The walls to his cell grew confining, so Jacob left and wandered the courtyard, noting the bushes and trees still barren of growth—mere buds hoping for a signal. Life was a lot of waiting: waiting for a birth, for prayers to begin, for someone to die, for night to fall or the sun to rise. And for what?

He sat on the cement bench in the peaceful backyard garden. A flock of nuthatches clung to the leafless tree next to the St. Francis of Assisi shrine. The misplaced saint was outside of a Benedictine monastery. St. Francis and he were misfit souls.

The tears flowed.

The old gate leading into the backyard groaned.

Moses grinned sheepishly as he sat beside Jacob, handing him a handkerchief from his seeming endless supply. Moses looked like the stereotype of a Franciscan monk, round and balding, but dressed in black.

Jacob wiped his face. Behind the wall, the fountain bubbled. Jacob breathed deeply as his throat ached.

"Will I ever stop crying?"

"If you don't cry, you might drown inside. Mee-maw used to say 'Let it out, let it flow. Saltwater cleanses.'" Moses patted Jacob's arm. "Water heals and changes everything."

"Grandmas are wise."

Moses nodded as a flock of nuthatches flew around the statue of St. Francis.

How many times had Moses sat and listened to his weeping? He needed to focus on something else. He folded the handkerchief.

"I cannot stay long," Moses said. "Ambrose is sad. I want to cheer him up."

"That is my fault. I was uncharitable when he was telling me not to listen to the wagging tongues."

"Oh, you mean those who say you don't belong? Brother Mellitus tells me every day to go home. More than once, he has packed my suitcase. Sometimes he calls me Friar Tuck, yet he knows I'm Benedictine." Moses turned to the statue of St. Francis.

The nuthatches paused their pecking to listen. "No offense, Francis, but I wear black, not brown."

Jacob wondered why Mellitus was so bitter as the flock of nuthatches flew over the wall as one. Moses never said a mean word, even when one was warranted.

"He makes me sad for him. We come for different reasons and stay for other reasons. I came because Mee-maw said to. She said I'd be happy here." Moses rubbed his own arms in a hug and frowned. "It's sometimes hard to accept what is. But I'm content."

Guilt slapped Jacob. He had done it again—deflated another soul. Was this his purpose in life?

Jacob knew that Moses came with an inheritance from his grandparents. Was Moses here because of the money? The idea of buying a monk galled him. He didn't even have money to offer.

Moses rose and shook himself and looked at the farm below. "I'll go see Ambrose. He needs me now."

Brother Moses understood life. He was a healer who accepted life. He processed what he saw and reflected it back.

Jacob had known many skilled healers. His Grandmother Tiama and Sings in the Night, the giver of blue eyes. Rebecca was a healer when she wasn't trying to control the surrounding circumstances.

"Yes, heal him. Tell him I am sorry."

Moses paused and cocked his head.

"You can tell him yourself. I like that word—*heal*." A smile filled his face, and his round cheeks lifted. "Jesus was a healer, and the people came to him, and he touched them."

"I thought the power of God healed them, not Jesus," Jacob said, unable to stop himself from playing the devil's advocate.

Moses shook his head as if to say, *you are misguided*. He moved closer to Jacob.

"Jesus came. The wounded reached out." Moses held his hand

above Jacob's. "They touched and were healed. That was all. No big dance, no smoke, whistles, or bells. Just one hand touching another." Moses let his hand rest on top of Jacob's. It was warm, soft, and heavy. Jacob could sense the tears coming to his eyes but blinked them back.

"Remember when Jesus healed the blind man? Moses asked. "I wonder what the blind man saw when he opened his eyes."

"Jesus?" Jacob offered, wondering if he would even know which man healed him.

"I'll be back," Moses said, heading out to heal Ambrose.

Jacob continued to sit on the hard cement bench.

Balance and control—the tears need to stop. Yet, even as he thought this, he knew emotional fortitude was not his talent. He wasn't a healer or a genuine believer like Joannicus, nor could he speak the truth plainly like Ambrose. He wasn't a realist like Pius, either. He didn't have Rebecca's strength, Rosie's stubbornness, or Katie's joy. What did he have?

The gate grated. He didn't look up, because if he didn't look up, nobody would bother him.

Mellitus sat beside Jacob. "If you sit too long on that bench, you'll get piles."

Jacob sighed, turning to avoid the old monk's direct gaze.

"Ah, the tears of a clown. Why are you sucking the life out of my *confrères*? Get your own life."

Jacob sighed again. There was little denying that he was a burden and causing anguish.

"What do you want, Chief?" Mellitus asked as a fawn bolted from the brush.

"I want nothing." *To find a purpose, to find peace.*

"Not true. Everyone here seeks something. Do you want to be abbot?" Mellitus stroked his goatee. "No, too kind. Do you want to convert us?" He narrowed his eyes. "You can't change us, even if you study our ways. We are too different."

"I do not want to change you. I want to be changed," Jacob said. He had discarded his old life and his former name and put on a black robe. Yet when he looked in the mirror, he didn't recognize himself.

"You're broken and confused. You have nothing to give us in return. We can't change you. You do that yourself." Mellitus stuck out his walking stick and poked the bush.

That was true. He was a clean slate, a seed waiting for spring. He wasn't sure what would happen next.

The older man was watching him intensely, with a grin playing on his lips. Jacob elbowed him.

"Broken is good—it means open. Entering this community is a submission to God, giving him all. I have nothing left but my life. I have given him everything else," Jacob said, sensing a shift within himself.

His gray eyes narrowed, and Mellitus huffed. "He took everything from you, and you are still here. You're a stubborn man. Perhaps your name should be Job."

Jacob chuckled. Mellitus was right—he was stubborn, and still here. They would have to live with him and he with them. Could he live with this curmudgeon?

Mellitus poked Jacob's shoulder with his long bony finger. "The difference between you and Job is that I don't hear those hallelujahs coming from your lips."

Not yet, thought Jacob. The wounds of life needed scars.

"Perhaps someday. Today, I want to call a truce," Jacob said. It felt good to want something.

"What, no treaty?"

A rabbit hopped, then paused—frozen and listening.

"If only you could honor that—no treaty—just your word. I need you to stop telling Moses he does not belong."

"Why? Is it working?" Mellitus laughed a cruel cackle. The rabbit dashed to the underbrush. "What a baby. Is he crying himself to sleep at night?"

"No, he is only sad that you are sad. So no, it is not working. He is determined to be your friend."

"That's not good. I don't need a puppy."

"If anyone does not belong here, it is me. When you feel that urge, come tell me to stop playing permanent guest."

Mellitus grinned maliciously. "I can do that. Are you going to cry every time I say it?"

"Wait and see," Jacob said, wondering what brought Mellitus to the monastery and why he stayed.

"Why are you here? I mean, why do you stay?" Jacob asked, not expecting an answer.

"Blue-eyed one with a clever tongue coated in kindness. I'm a catalyst of change."

"No, you are not."

Mellitus picked up a rock and tossed it to the left of the statue of St. Francis. Jacob noticed the small pile where it landed. Mellitus was counting coup with stones.

"Believe what you want, oh ye of little faith. I give you another year before you run away."

Faith. The tender face of his wife appeared before him—the soft dark eyes that drew him in every time she looked at him. Her constant words of encouragement had told him she believed in him, that faith was still with him.

"Is that a challenge? I hear I only need something the size of a mustard seed."

"But you have a grain of sand. You can't get through the pearly gates clinging to the scapular of others."

"I have not decided if that is my eventual destination. The smell of sulfur is nice. I am trying to decide between priest or warrior, Catholic or Apsáalooke."

Jacob recognized he could be both whole and broken. Today there were losses, tomorrow things could change.

"Watch your back. Remember who opened the door for you?" Mellitus said. "Not all are friends."

"I remember," Jacob said, recalling that it was Mellitus who had let him into the theology program. "Thank you."

Mellitus slapped his hands on his knees. "Don't get all sappy on me. I didn't do it out of kindness. There's more to you than blue eyes, Chief."

Jacob snorted. *Chief.* There weren't any more of them. A chief needed a tribe and had criteria to meet. No, that wasn't his path. Maybe Mellitus was a motivator. He certainly enjoyed a challenge and counting coup. This man was not an obstacle.

Jacob rose. A strong warm breeze blew by him, lifting his scapular like a leaf. The black material danced its own powwow. Spring had decided it was time to awaken.

"Come on, Brother, let us go move some mountains," Jacob said.

CHAPTER 42
LIFE WITHOUT REBECCA

They are not dead who live in the hearts they leave behind.

Tuscarora Nation proverb. The Tuscarora ("hemp gatherers") are a Native American people of the Iroquoian language. The Tuscarora settled in the region now known as North Carolina.

Brother Jacob stood in front of the picture window in the church's atrium next to the giant philodendron. The space was open, with a little bench in front of the window inviting one to contemplate the territorial view. The holy water font bubbled merrily behind Jacob as he observed the spider web in the corner of the window. Outside hung its twin, covered in dew. He looked down at the farm and orchards below and saw a light from the barn. Moses and Ambrose were tending to the animals. He was awake and should have joined them, but he was too nervous. The barn calmed him with the smells of earth and hay, and the greetings of the beasts. Physical labor worked the body of its restlessness.

He glanced at the sundial in the garden. It was half an hour before the bells would ring, summoning them to pray. His stomach churned. He had taken the black a year and a day ago. Should he be doing this? Nothing better had come along.

He heard a gentle swish of a robe and looked over his shoulder, even though he knew it was Father Joannicus. He could recognize the gait of each monk. Some walked quickly, and others with a foot that dragged or rosary beads that rattled. One had a knee joint that clicked. He wondered if they knew.

Joannicus stood beside him as the sun broke into a thin line, lighting the horizon with splashes of color and long shadows. Jacob watched the outside spider move and the dewdrops glisten. Was the inside spider jealous of this brilliant display? Two webs, two spiders. He was aware of what spiders asked. Their question resonated in his mind and heart. Is your life in balance? His outer life was balanced by the rhythms of Benedictine living, but his inner life teetered.

"Another glorious day."

"Are you always cheerful in the morning? Jacob asked.

Joannicus glowed. "Doesn't it inspire you to pray?"

"Not this early in the morning."

"I can't help it. I awake and see another day to serve the Lord."

"I usually rise and say, 'Hell no, not again.'"

"Seriously? Every morning you curse the light?" Joannicus placed his hand on Jacob's shoulder.

Today, Jacob would say the words and make simple vows to enter the community. Discernment was not part of this path—he was here by default. It was where he had ended up and saw no reason to leave.

"Is Rebecca here?" Almost a year had passed. She hadn't attempted to scale the walls or break into the cloister. They had seen each other at Mass, and she had waved or nodded in his direction. He missed her.

"Seriously, she has come to terms with your staying with us. That is what Ambrose told me. She is the only member of your family in attendance."

Jacob winced. Had he shared too much with Joannicus about the past and his childhood? Yet, the circle of silence was no longer a vortex that swirled around him. He was grateful to have her here.

Jacob viewed the two spiders. The web vibrated as the outside spider moved, sending out a silent signal. What is out there?

"You should be nervous. That's normal. Be brave, be joyful," Joannicus said.

"I do not know what I am doing here."

Joannicus sighed, and Jacob regretted his gloominess.

"I do, and so do you. You just don't want to admit that God has a plan for you."

Jacob shivered at Joe's words. "A plan. I'm not happy with his plans so far."

Joannicus picked up a shriveled leaf that had fallen on the floor next to the thriving philodendron. He scooped up the spider from her web and walked her outside through the large carved wooden doors. Jacob wondered if this was kindness or a death sentence. She had worked for days on the web and in a second, her life was destroyed, transformed from inside living to outdoor life. Did she have the energy to begin again?

Joannicus carefully placed the dead leaf on the shrubby potentilla to the right of the doors.

"This plan is not well thought out. If you come across the blueprints, can you give me a copy?" Jacob said as he observed the spider exploring her new world.

"That's not how it works. You can stand on the bank or dive into the river."

"Not sure I remember how to swim."

Joannicus held the church door open. "There is always someone on the shore. This life isn't so bad."

"Your life or mine?"

"Our life. You can float, can't you?"

Jacob was tired of standing on the edge. Monastic living was neither awful nor blissful, but there was comfort in it. He was entering the monastery, making a promise. In three years, he might solemnize that promise. They would place a cloth over him as he lay on the floor—a symbolic death to his past. He would arise a new man. Jacob moved to the open door, feeling a chill of dread. He wondered who that man would be.

They entered the church, and the door clunked with a reverberating echo in the atrium's silence.

REBECCA STOOD at the window of the abbey guesthouse, sipping ginger water, hoping it would settle her stomach. She should not have eaten that cookie. But it was a warm snickerdoodle, right out of the oven. She was hungry, so she gave in to temptation. She watched Father Joannicus, Brother Moses, and her brother Jacob walking around the courtyard. Jacob seemed at peace, ready to move forward. If she lost her family and babies, moving forward would be impossible.

Yesterday, she sat in the stairwell of the guesthouse as she heard the voices of monks and her brother. He had laughed, something she hadn't heard since the funeral. Her brother had laughed.

After the bells rang, the men headed to the chapel. Rebecca

grabbed her shawl and marched to the church, following the scurry of monks.

This was the rite of simple vows—a ceremony from novice to junior monk. He was joining the black robe tribe. Did he belong? Would he fit in? She wondered about his happiness.

They were on different paths now. This parting was bittersweet.

She stood in front of the holy water font, dipped her hand in, and blessed herself. She hadn't done that since school years ago, and yet it seemed natural. It's just a ritual—their tradition. Each has a purpose, and all are sacred.

She listened to the running water of the font. It was an artificial trickle mimicking a spring. It was just like them to use fake nature for a ritual. She moved to her seat.

She sat so she could see Jacob, who was in the first row. She watched his leg pump up and down. Was he nervous, excited, or both? They had kept her from seeing him ever since she had kicked their front door—eight long months with only the Bear for company. He wasn't so bad--more teddy than grizzly. Katie and Rosie loved Ambrose, the Bear.

A familiar odor of aftershave wafted by. She looked around and saw Terence. She breathed a sigh of relief when she did not see her mother. Neither she nor Jacob needed Mackenzie drama. Ambrose, who was sitting in the row in front of her, turned and gave her a nod and thumbs-up as he glanced over her shoulder, monitoring Terence. Ambrose, the Bear, would protect Jacob.

Rebecca returned her attention to her brother. She barely listened to the songs and the reading. Thinking about her life moving in another direction, she hoped their paths would run parallel or maybe even cross sometimes. She wanted to share her joy but feared it would cause Jacob pain.

The music stopped. Jacob rose and stood before Abbot Gordon. His face was calm and his blue eyes were bright.

"What do you seek?" Abbot Gordon asked.

"I ask for the mercy of God and for the grace to serve him faithfully in this community," Jacob said in a voice so firm that Rebecca was forced to believe him, especially when the community answered, "We also accept him."

She swallowed hard, placed a hand over her abdomen as her stomach rolled.

Obedience, stability, and *conversatio morum*—conversion— were the three vows a Benedictine makes. She could see Jacob staying in one place. He was changing, but could he be obedient?

When the Abbot asked, Jacob answered, "I am resolved," she knew he had moved on. A sense of relief flooded her.

Jacob knelt in front of the Abbot as the paper he held rattled in his hands. His voice was strong. "In the name of our Lord Jesus Christ, I, Brother Jacob Knows the Song-Mackenzie, promise before God and his saints, in the presence of our Father in Christ, Abbot Gordon, and the monks of St. Alberic's Monastery, stability in this community, conversion through a monastic manner of life, and obedience according to the rule of our holy Father Benedict and the norms of our congregation. I am resolved and will sign this document today."

Jacob's voice called her back from her thoughts as he stood arms outstretched and chanted, three times, each time an octave higher, "Uphold me Lord according to your word, let my hope in you not be in vain."

His voice reverberated around the church, sending shivers through her. She hugged herself, praying that the words would hold true.

The monks came forward to show support and welcoming. One by one, they embraced Jacob. Some were formal, with a bow and a touch on the shoulder. Ambrose, however, smothered him with a chest-crushing embrace—a bear hug.

Jacob again knelt before the Abbot. Jacob was clothed in a scapular. The black cloth hung over his shoulders, covering front and back. It reminded her of a warrior preparing for battle. They gave him a new copy of the *Rule of St. Benedict*. Would it be enough? She knew the Rule was the foundation of a monk's life. She hoped Jacob kept the lessons of Grandma Tiama in his heart as he added this extra layer of life.

The final blessing and incense filled the space. Rebecca found her stomach clenching from the odor as she dashed out of the church. She shouldn't have eaten that cookie.

Sweat poured down her neck as she sat on the bathroom floor. The porcelain felt cool. A door opened. She should have locked it. She breathed heavily and tried to quell her nausea as she glanced under the stall to see the hem of a black habit and moccasins. It was Jacob.

"Go away. I'm fine," Rebecca said, her voice was hoarse and rough.

"No," Jacob said. "What is wrong?"

"Nothing," Rebecca said, trying to sound normal. The incense followed him in—the damn aroma of holiness. Thankfully, there was little left in her stomach.

She stood and flushed. Paper towels, like a flag of surrender, hung over the stall door. She grabbed them and wiped her forehead.

"This is the girl's bathroom, you know. You need to leave. I'll be out in a minute."

The door opened and closed, and Rebecca waited, resting against the wall. Todd had encouraged her to attend, even in her condition. She wished he had come with her. She went to the sink, washed, and splashed water on her flushed face, wanting to brush her teeth.

What story should she tell?

She exited the bathroom and was met with the worried faces of monks.

"Come with me. You need to rest," Ambrose said, grabbing her elbow and moving her out of the church. She leaned on him, grateful for his support and quick intervention.

"Terence?"

"He's gone. I allowed him to watch. He left without Jacob seeing him. Except for you, there was no Mackenzie drama."

She allowed herself to be taken to the guesthouse and fussed over. Ambrose helped her into a chair and propped up her swollen feet.

"You're not a spring chicken, Missy. Rest," he scolded while fixing tea.

He was all growl, that Teddy Bear.

"Thanks for the tea and insults," Rebecca said, thinking she was only thirty-something, not an Elder.

"You're welcome. Drink. You look a quart low."

Rebecca laughed, "So now I'm a car. I hope it is something classic, like a Maserati. I had it under control, but your stinky thurible got the better of me."

"I know, you prefer cedar and sage to frankincense and myrrh," Ambrose chuckled.

"If I had to pick between the three gifts, I'd take gold," Rebecca said, sipping tea and resting the saucer on her swollen abdomen.

Jacob entered the room and stared at her round belly. "You are pregnant," he said.

"Told you he was smart," Ambrose said.

"Are you happy?" Jacob asked.

Rebecca grinned, knowing he had questions and worries. "Yes, I think I am."

"And the father, is he pleased?" Jacob asked, his blue eyes wide with mischief.

"Is that your clever way of inquiring who?" Rebecca quipped.

JACOB SMILED when he saw Rebecca and Todd with the baby after not seeing her for a month. She had attended Mass regularly. The infant began to fuss, and Todd rose and took the baby out of the church. Jacob watched Rebecca as she glanced out the window, watching Todd pacing outside with the baby.

Rebecca looked good for having given birth a month ago. Anxiety and joy competed as he thought of meeting his nephew, Holbrook.

When the final amens arrived, he rushed to the atrium. He found himself trapped. He was forced to smile and nod at people who were leaving after Mass.

"Come on," Moses said. "We're going to the guesthouse to see the baby."

When did this become a monastic event? He thought she was here to visit him, not all his brethren.

They entered the hall, and Holbrook's cries stopped Jacob. Moses put a gentle hand on his arm. Jacob was not sure he could move forward.

"It's okay. I'll go with you," Moses said.

Brother Mellitus pushed by them. "Come on, Chief, you're Apsáalooke."

"Stop being a bully, Mellitus," Ambrose said. "I get to hold him first."

The chaos was overwhelming, and Jacob stumbled for a chair

as the room spun. They never fussed over a child before. They usually avoided them as if they were dangerous vipers.

Jacob opened his eyes. Moses was fanning him with a copy of *Liguorian*. Rebecca sat, shaking her head.

Todd took Holbrook from Ambrose and held the child out to Jacob. The child was so light and, his head was wobbly. His dark eyes stared at Jacob. His shell of gloom cracked. Memories of his children flooded his senses, the smell of life, and the dark lashes on warm cheeks. Jacob struggled to breathe. He couldn't stop his tears from falling on the baby's forehead. His children were gone and a new life squirmed in his arms. There was hope.

Moses handed him a handkerchief.

"You can't baptize him that way," Mellitus said as Ambrose let out a low growl.

"He's going to be a priest. He can do it anyway he wants. They are water and words," Moses said.

"And breath," Jacob said, inhaling close to the child, the smell of milk on the infant's breath. He remembered Ambrose imparting his spirit to Amber Rose, and Faith's approval.

"Not the right ceremony, it won't take. Tears don't count," Mellitus grumbled as he left the room.

"You don't know that. Jesus uses spit to cure. Jacob is Apsáalooke and Catholic. He knows things," Moses said, following Mellitus out of the room.

Rebecca giggled as Ambrose shook his head.

"We were hoping you would baptize him in a more formal ceremony, but I suppose this will do," Todd said, standing proudly beside Rebecca.

As Jacob held his nephew, he felt Faith's approval of this bond, this moving forward toward the land of the living. A bittersweet joy filled him.

Jacob stood in the parking lot as Rebecca left in a truck with Todd and Holbrook.

"Why so sad?" Ambrose asked.

"I think I lost something," Jacob said. "And gained it. They want me to baptize my nephew."

"That is good. She is accepting your choice and wants to be a part of it."

Jacob nodded, still in shock at her request. They were a circle with a different center.

"This is the first time I have held a child since I laid my children to rest. What if I cry while anointing the sick or baptizing babies?"

"Tears are holy. Do you know any priests?"

Jacob shot him a confused look. "Of course—dozens. Why?"

"Then you ask them to do that part. You can help them during the holidays with the long confessional lines."

Ambrose had a point. Not all ceremonies involved infants or death.

"What if there are sins I cannot absolve?" Jacob asked, letting his insecurity show.

"Really? Forgiveness means giving up all hope for a better past. You, of all people, know that. It's essential to do something today and let tomorrow be tomorrow."

The scars on his heart were real. Pain came at unexpected moments, and he suspected that it always would catch him and trip him up. But he couldn't spend the rest of his life waiting to stumble. The past formed the man he was today. He reached with the courage to grasp the positive and turn away from the destructive memories. Embracing the positive, he let the ache of what he had lost wash over him.

"So, what have you decided, priesthood, or should I build that lemonade stand?" Ambrose asked.

"I will tell stories on Sundays."

"I like stories. Will they start with 'once upon a time'? They don't have to end with 'happily ever after.' Some tales are tragic."

"I remember, as a child, my grandmother always asked us for a story. Everyone loves the parables. I will need to gather more stories.

"I can't wait. I'm glad you are staying."

"Ah shucks, I bet you say that to all the new monks," Jacob said, punching Ambrose's arm. He would be here a while.

"Bet I don't," Ambrose said as they turned and walked into the monastery.

CHAPTER 43
EPILOGUE: SARAH WARNER

Children learn from what they see.
We need to set an example of truth and action.

Howard Rainer. Taos Pueblo-Creek, teacher, poet, and photographer.

T he blue Volkswagen Beetle slid to a stop. Sarah Warner was sure she was off the highway somewhere in Montana. The sudden November snowstorm had brought her to this large red barn. At least it was shelter. She looked at her sleeping baby in the seat next to her. They would be warmer inside.

A snow-covered face pressed against her window, causing her to jump. She fumbled to lock the door.

"Jesus Christ!" she shouted.

"Not even close, but thanks for the compliment." The large man's beard was quickly turning white. "I'm Brother Ambrose. You can't stay in there. This storm is getting worse. You best come with me to the monastery."

Her shout woke the infant, who started fussing.

"Come on, Missy," Ambrose said. "The barn's no place for a baby. Boy or girl?"

He was right, yet she didn't know this man.

"Boy," Sarah shouted over the wails of the baby. "Who are you again?"

"Brother Ambrose, but I'm about to become the abominable snowman. Trust me, we need to go while the road is drivable, or else we will have to hike up. The visibility is already terrible."

She had to admit that a blizzard was surrounding them. Snowflakes were piling up quickly on her windshield. A kindness was being offered, and she would have to trust this man.

Sarah grabbed her son, the diaper bag that doubled as her purse, and several baby blankets before stepping out into the fast-falling snow.

"I'm Sarah. This is Paul," she said as she climbed into the old truck. *Would this old beater make up the hill?* she wondered.

They crept up the narrow road, wipers thumping madly and wheels slipping.

"That boy has an excellent set of lungs," Ambrose said, his gloved hands gripping the steering wheel. He squinted, trying to make out the road.

Sarah tried to quiet Paul, but he was hungry and probably in need of a change. She hoped they would make it to the hilltop.

Finally, a brick building appeared through the snow. Two black-hooded figures stood waving their arms as the truck came to a stop, bumping a curb. One was tall and one short. The shorter one opened her door. She looked into the startled face of a young man while Paul wailed in her arms. Ambrose tossed the keys to the tall one and shoved her suitcases toward the short one.

"Park it somewhere. I've got to get our guest settled in."

Sarah followed his large footprints as he forged a path. The startled man followed her. Paul continued to cry, his hot tears melting the snowflakes on his cheeks. A blast of warm air greeted her when she stepped inside the building.

"Here you go. There are hot water and cookies in the kitchenette." Ambrose pointed to his right.

Sarah peeked in. The smell of fresh cookies called to her. She couldn't remember when she had last eaten. Paul's wails turned to whimpers in the warm air.

"Joannicus, don't just stand there. Take this stuff to St. Monica." The man scurried down the hall. She recognized the long robe as belonging to a priest and felt enormous relief. This wasn't a prison—all the rooms were named after saints.

"Which one is my room?"

"St. Monica. She was the mother of St. Augustine, a troublesome child. Not that this one is—he is probably hungry and tired. I will let you get settled and rest. Welcome to St. Alberic's Monastery. Dinner is served downstairs at six p.m. Please join us, both of you."

The young monk who had taken her luggage gasped. Ambrose shot him an annoyed look.

"It's a baby, not a wild animal. Christian up, Father." Ambrose turned and escorted the young monk away.

Sarah woke with a start and noticed that it was after six. She and Paul had fallen into an exhausted sleep. She fed him again and made her way downstairs. The dining room was a sea of men in black robes. Ambrose rose quickly and banged the table, causing the dishes to rattle. He greeted her with a grin.

"We eat in silence. Your spot is over here." He pointed to a table that was man-free. The warm bread and savory stew revitalized her. They were polite, but the quick glances and the swift exits told her they were not used to children or women. Paul slept, but she guessed that if he woke and she whipped her breast out, the room would clear faster than a stampede of elk. She wondered if Snow White felt this out of place with her seven dwarfs as she did with these seventy monks. The snow continued to fall, and she knew that Mother Nature was not listening to her wishes.

After dinner, she returned to her room. She found a soft woolen blanket, booties, and a shawl there. Tears came to her eyes as she tended to her son, making a crib out of a dresser drawer, and then setting it on the desktop. She moved it closer to the bed so night feeding would be easier.

Morning came, and she woke to the sound of bells. Grateful that she had napped when Paul slept, she opened her door to find two baskets—one was tightly woven and lined with sheepskin. It was just the right size to use as a carrier. They filled the second basket with breakfast items: hard-boiled eggs, fruit, and bread. She made her way to the parlor, following the aroma of coffee.

The snow stopped midmorning. The monk named Joannicus darted around the guesthouse, cleaning and hiding.

Sarah bundled herself and Paul up and followed the snow labyrinth, finding her way to the church. She opened the heavy, carved wooden doors. A font of water bubbled as she entered the atrium. Across the space were windows with a pastoral view. She saw the red barn and could barely make out her car. If she had stayed there, they would have been buried. She shivered at the thought.

The church was warm. She unbundled herself, placing her coat and basket on a chair, taking in the space's openness. There was a carpeted octagon with a gravelly walkway and alcoves with stained-glass windows. She walked the octagonal shape, breathing in the incense-laden air. The silence was soothing—chairs in rows, a large table, and artwork adorning the walls. Sunlight splashed colors on the carpet through the stained-glass windows as dust motes danced in the rays. She paused at a red and white ikebana flower arrangement in front of an icon of the Virgin Mary.

"Like me, they gave you no choice." Her plight was not the same. Mary had to deal with the will of God and Sarah with the will of a maiden aunt.

The interior of this church comforted her. She always liked churches, especially Catholic ones, although she was not Catholic herself. The incense lingered, and the candles glowed. It was almost like having a dinner date with God. She had not found her faith, even though she had tried. Most religions were pristine and polished, more like a business interview for a job. Were you going to heaven or hell?

She sat in a chair facing a flickering red candle. She had made a hasty departure with her son from North Carolina two weeks ago until the storm ended her progress. Hot tears dropped on her sleeping infant. But, they didn't wake him from his milk-induced coma. Where should they go? She couldn't stay at a monastery forever.

The voice of her maiden aunt haunted her with the words *honor, protect, and defend. Bloodlines.* Apparently, Mary had the same dilemma. She had to travel to Bethlehem because of blood-lines. Mary had Joseph, but Sarah had nobody. Because she was not married, they would take her child away. Leaving was her only option.

The family code of *honor, protect, and defend* was hers alone to uphold now.

She bent over and gazed at her sleeping boy. Tears rained down, and she wiped them from his face with her thumb.

Her heart raced. What if they came after her? They would not separate them—a mother and her child belonged together. The nine months of her confinement had given her time to plan her escape—only she hadn't foreseen the loneliness.

She sniffed and found a handkerchief dangling in front of her. A tall man dressed in a black cassock and scapular stood near her. She gasped.

He looked Native, yet his eyes were the color of the sky. A long black braid hung down his chest, nearly invisible but for the red beaded clasp and white feather hanging mid-chest. She lowered her eyes.

"Sorry, I did not mean to intrude," he said.

"It's okay. Just hormones."

"Could be," he said. "They can cloud things. Whatever it is, it will get better."

She took the handkerchief and wiped her eyes. She had to find a new home.

"I am Father Jacob. You must be the guest that everyone is whispering about," he said as he sat down.

"I'm Sarah. We aren't guests—they didn't really invite us. We won't be staying long."

"You will be here a while. The cold north wind pushed you our way. It also keeps me from returning to my parish. We are stuck here."

Sarah ran her hand over the soft sheepskin. She would not be a burden.

"It's a good thing that Thanksgiving is coming. Brother Barnabas always makes more than we can eat."

"That's a week away. I can't stay that long. I mean, I don't have a way to pay."

The man stood and waved as if he were brushing her words away.

"They do not expect payment."

"Everyone has been so kind," Sarah said. "I don't know how to thank them."

"Prayers—say tons of them. Stay, but if you linger, you risk becoming permanent." Jacob laughed sardonically.

She would not be staying.

"I'm afraid we are disrupting your life." The heat kicked on, and there was a gentle *tick, tick* of the radiator's metal expanding.

"Disruption can be a good thing. The real problem is they dislike change. I am sure you have noticed the rhythmic balance: pray, eat, work, pray, eat, and sleep. Visitors are good, they shake the balance a bit, and bring a new perspective."

His sarcastic humor amused her. The wind blew hard against the church, causing the boards to groan at the assault. She didn't like change either, but it had come fast and furious with motherhood.

"I've seen that other monk in the guesthouse. He works hard to avoid us."

"That is Father Joannicus. He is an academic—he has zero experience with anything under the age of sixteen. Don't take his behavior personally. He is easily spooked."

His presence was calming. There was no condemnation, just a gentle curiosity.

"You are safe here."

She grabbed the basket with Paul in it, ready to run. How did he know she needed sanctuary? How did he know she was hiding and running?

"I did not mean to frighten you. Nobody has asked for you."

Paul protested at the sudden movement.

"We aren't lost. I just haven't found a place to call home."

"Me either."

Jacob placed a hand on her shoulder and she released her grip on the basket handle. He had to be joking. She knew priests and nuns entered convents and monasteries because they believed they were answering a call from God. She wondered if it was a collect call. The winter rattled the windows.

"Weren't you called to this life?" Sarah asked, the baby wiggling in her protective embrace.

"No, I stumbled here by default. They are very clever, these monks with their kindness and hospitality. One day, I was wearing blue jeans, and the next day *this*." He waved his scapular.

Sarah laughed, even though she was sure this wasn't the complete story. Paul squirmed and let out a cry that echoed in the church. He fussed louder and batted his hands against the air. Sarah tried to calm him.

"Let me try. I have some skill in this department," Jacob said, holding out his arms.

A moment of trepidation passed through her as she handed over the yowling infant.

"How old?" Jacob asked, holding the infant like an expert.

"Three weeks."

She observed him cradle the baby and gently sway, humming over Paul's protests. A sudden wetness cooled her shirt. The child's wails had caused her milk to drop even though she had nursed. Her face flushed hot.

"Oh, damn," she said.

"Go tend to yourself. But come back!" Jacob called after her. "We will be fine."

Sarah rose and paused. Could he be trusted with her child? It's not like he could go anywhere. Snow made a stroll outside more like a climb up Denali.

Jacob sang as Paul wailed. He rose and walked, rocking the infant.

She darted out of the church to the restroom. The words

"Come back" haunted her as she grabbed paper towels. Did he think she was about to abandon the child? She had heard of that happening—leaving children at churches. She would never abandon Paul.

She stopped in the atrium. The singing had stopped, and the font with holy water bubbled. The wind wailed. Sarah hurried back to the church and paused when she heard sniffling. It wasn't Paul crying—it was the priest. She walked up and dangled the white handkerchief in front of him.

"Damn hormones," he muttered, taking the cloth. He dabbed at his eyes.

The baby lay content in his blue blanket.

"Does he have a name?" Jacob asked, his voice cracking with emotion.

"Yes—it's Paul."

"Ah, Paul the Converter. Good name."

He smiled at Paul and handed him back to Sarah. The church bells rang over the howling wind.

"They will come to pray now. You are welcome to stay. It can be quite soothing and healing. Things will get better. A child is a gift from our ancestors."

"I supposed so. The past comes forward." There was truth in that statement. She and Paul came from noble people. Maybe Paul would carry that goodness to future generations.

"The best of the past. To live is to feel some sense of what you have lost," Jacob said.

Jacob sat next to Sarah as the monks came into the church to pray. Voices blended in melodic tones, chanting ancient prayers, and bringing chaos into balance. Her son was a blessing. That was enough.

ACKNOWLEDGMENTS

This work of fiction is a product of my imagination, with support from research and reading. When I wrote Karl and Rebecca's story, I wanted to be authentic. I wanted to address the issues of alcohol abuse and child abuse and neglect by individuals in both Indigenous and Catholic culture. My intent was to look honestly at the issues, but in doing so, I discovered that these are tough issues to deal with. It is very important that one educates themselves and then speaks out, destroys stereotypes, and supports constructive change.

I spent a lot of time listening to tribal members, their trials, hopes, fears, triumphs, and successes. I wish to thank them for their honesty and for allowing me the opportunity to listen and learn.

I was blessed to find Eddie Big Medicine and his wife Laurie. Eddie provided me with resources and insight into the Crow culture, which improved and polished this story. They reminded me that one cannot discuss these subjects in Native American culture without pointing out that these problems are a result of the severe and sustained destruction of an entire people's culture by the invasive people and their government. I hope that I captured that idea in the story's body. Still, it bears calling out again here. Sustained, multi-generational trauma to a culture and the individuals that make it up have a many-generational effect. The survivors and their children and grandchildren for generations to come suffer and struggle. I cannot thank Eddie and his wife enough for all the help and wisdom they have given me.

I went to a Benedictine college and majored in Psychology because at that time theology was not an option for women. I have always been interested in why people do what they do, believe what they believe, and what events influence them. During my time there, I studied and learned about the Rule of Saint Benedict and became an Oblate. In doing so, I learned how to apply the spirit of the Rule of Saint Benedict in my day-to-day living. I discovered that spirituality is connected in so many ways; the similarities intrigued me and the struggle to balance belief and culture inspired me to write about this topic. I was also fortunate to be welcomed into many Benedictine communities. From that I absorbed the rhythms of their lives and listened to their hopes and prayers and dreams. I wish to thank Benedictine Fathers Jude Anderson, Alfred Hulscher, Benedict Auer, and Gerard Garrigan for their patience and kindness in answering my many questions about how a monastery works and how one lives the life of a monk.

This story has taken years to write and would not have even come to this point if I hadn't joined the Puget Sound Writers Guild, who listened tirelessly to my story. Their insight and critiques have proven invaluable. Thank you, present and past members.

Even writers need company sometimes. Over the years, there have been many small group gatherings, much like an office without a building or cubicles. Thanks to the Covid pandemic a small group of dedicated writers was formed online. We called ourselves the Reel Dames (because we started out watching movies virtually together). Thank you, ladies, for encouraging me to read, write and spin a tale. Without our weekly sessions, this work may not have been completed. I hope I have been an inspiration to you as well.

Writing takes hours and hours of time. Thank you to my family, who have allowed me that time and space while encouraging my writing. Special thanks to my husband, who has read and reread this story too many times to count.

Books do not make it to the shelf without publishers and editors. Thank you, Wayzgoose Publishing, particularly Maggie, my editor, who took a chance and has polished this tale with me.

Books do not impact lives unless they are read and talked about. You will note that if it wasn't for my belief in families, this group of an unlikely family of monks raising a child could not have blossomed into the *Benediction of Paul* series. I have been so blessed to have found my first audience. Thank you to the many friends at NCCSD, NCSEA, and all organizations who help children. My husband attended many conferences, and I spent my time in the hotel writing my story. The dedicated folks in these organizations work diligently for children and families. They took an interest in my creative endeavors and their curiosity, enthusiasm and friendship kept me focused. I wouldn't be here today writing if it wasn't for you all.

ABOUT THIS SERIES

Thank you for reading Book 4 of *The Benediction of Paul*. Here is the entire series:

Book 1: *Winds of Life*

Book 2: *Less Thunder, More Lightning*

Book 3: *All for One Child*

Book 4: *Counting Coup: The Making of an Abbot* (prequel to the series)

www.ingramcontent.com/pod-product-compliance
Lightning Source LLC
Chambersburg PA
CBHW022016050726
47499CB00004BA/1023